I0762944

Adventure Is Out There!

A Twisted Tale

For more Twisted adventures, check out:

A Whole New World by Liz Braswell
Once Upon a Dream by Liz Braswell
As Old as Time by Liz Braswell
Reflection by Elizabeth Lim
Part of Your World by Liz Braswell
Mirror, Mirror by Jen Calonita
Conceal, Don't Feel by Jen Calonita
Straight On Till Morning by Liz Braswell
So This Is Love by Elizabeth Lim
Unbirthday by Liz Braswell
Go the Distance by Jen Calonita
What Once Was Mine by Liz Braswell
Almost There by Farrah Rochon
When You Wish Upon a Star by Elizabeth Lim
Fate Be Changed by Farrah Rochon
Sally's Lament by Mari Mancusi
How Far I'll Go by Keala Kendall

ADVENTURE IS OUT THERE!

A TWISTED TALE

LIZ BRASWELL

Random House Books for Young Readers
An imprint of Random House Children's Books
A division of Penguin Random House LLC
1745 Broadway, New York, NY 10019
penguinrandomhouse.com | rhcbooks.com/disney

Jacket illustration by Jim Tierney
Jacket design by Scott Piehl

Library of Congress Cataloging-in-Publication Data is available upon request.
ISBN 978-1-368-10826-3 (trade) — ISBN 978-0-7364-4787-4 (ebook)

The text of this book is set in 12-point Bulmer MT Pro.

Manufactured in the United States of America
1st Printing

For Cleopatra Josephine Miccolis

—L.B.

A NOTE FROM THE AUTHOR

Up holds a special place in many young moviegoers' hearts, perhaps because of its focus on something that's actually the *opposite* of happily-ever-after: the immediate joy of exploration. Its story celebrates the adventures we have out in the world in the here and now—or in our minds when we imagine what wonderful things we might find in faraway lands.

Ellie found the clubhouse through her neighborhood wanderings and had no issue boldly investigating the abandoned (and sometimes dangerous) building. Together, she and Carl explored as much of the natural world around them as they could during their lives—and Ellie dreamed of going even farther. Of course, Carl managed to do what so many of us wished for as children: he found a most unconventional way to his dream destination, bourn aloft by balloons.

When I was young, I explored our backyard and the surrounding few acres of woods like it was an entire unknown world. Our stream was a mighty river, our patch of white pines an endless forest. Our swamp was an intricate maze that had to be crossed very carefully on dead logs and tuffets of grass—or I'd fall in and get *that look* from Mom when I came home with boots full of mud.

(Luckily, I never broke my arm like Carl, however.)

Mom might have given me *those looks* but she also taught me the different calls of a chickadee and how to carefully remove a daddy longlegs from the corner of a room and deposit it safely outside. She knew the names of all the wildflowers and weeds in the yard and how the only difference between those two categories of plants is human chauvinism.

Prepared by these initial gentle lessons, I am now slowly working toward my certification as an urban naturalist. My field of study is the opposite of the lush and gorgeous forests of Venezuela that Ana studies; it is the cement sidewalks and polluted waterways of Brooklyn. Which still support a surprising diversity of life: seaside goldenrod, little brown bats, migrating warblers, dragonflies.

(Nature is out there!)

My mother's respect for living creatures has also been

passed on to the next generation: to my daughter, who has received praise from strangers for her kind and careful spider removal, and to my son, who has spent several summers employed at the Central Park Zoo in New York City.

Many of the Bloomington Zoo details in *Adventure Is Out There!* come directly from his own experience. Every night he would come home and tell stories about working with both the animals and the people there—from the way uniforms, food procedures, and sanitation are all used to prevent the animals from getting sick, to how he had to teach baby penguins to swim, to the unusually intelligent and humanlike behavior from one of the cotton-top tamarins.

(Some of these stories had to be changed a bit for the time and place of the book's story: 1940s America didn't have wide use of surgical gloves or the range of disinfectants we have now.)

Sadly not all of the funniest and best stories could make it into the manuscript (ask me in person about "The Worst Bird"). But the most important takeaway was how much every single person who worked at the zoo loved the wild world and would do almost anything to keep animals happy, healthy—and from going extinct.

I hope those of you who are young or young at heart never lose the Spirit of Adventure or the love of animals you possessed when drawing a picture of a lion or a giraffe—or a frog or a bat—in third-grade art. Even in the grey depths of the tallest corporate tower, you can imagine your way to the tepuis of Venezuela or plan a hike in a state park.

Always remember: adventure is out there!

—Liz Braswell

PART I

Grounded

PROLOGUE

"Carl, this really was the best birthday ever," Ellie whispered. "You know me so well—so much better than *anyone*. I can't believe you did all this for me."

"It wasn't anything," Carl said. "Thinking about you and how you smile, what *makes* you smile . . . it's easy. It makes the whole world brighter for me. Making you happy is really more a gift to me than you. I want to see you smile and laugh every day."

"Every *day*?" she asked, finally turning from the aerodrome's runway to look at him. His eyes looked deeply into hers; they were the color of the skies she had imagined flying through. Airplanes zoomed in her head.

"Every hour. Every minute."

"Carl . . . What are you saying?"

"I don't know, Ellie. I just want—I'm saying—I don't know what I'm saying. . . ."

"Okay, let's stop saying anything, then." She closed her eyes and leaned forward.

Once Upon a Time in Small-Town America

Once upon a time in a small American town, the war was over.

Bloomington, USA, had everything anyone could possibly want: prompt milkmen, friendly postal workers, green trees in clean yards, and an inexpensive bus that could take you to the doctor or to the two main streets to shop or to the big plant right outside of town that made things out of aluminum and lead.

One of the two avenues for shopping had grocers who sold produce, general merchandisers who stocked needful things and notions, a hardware store, and churches of several popular sects. The second had a Woolworth's and boutiques that peddled fine cloth and tailored clothes and cut crystal and gifts and jewelry—and there was also an ice cream shoppe.

The town park had a gazebo and was swept clean and decorated with bunting for parades on holidays. There was a USO hall nearby for the soldiers, all coming home now. There were two movie theaters, one of which showed first-run features only.

All right—maybe it wasn't *that* small a town, but it was a nice place to live and a perfect place to raise kids, which might have been why the McGills decided to raise as many as possible—eight, at last count.

They lived in a slightly too small farmhouse on Chester Street. On weekends and in the summer the place was thunderously loud, a happy cacophony of kids and laughter and singing and smears of grape jelly on the walls. On school days everything was a little calmer, at least after post-breakfast goodbyes. Then the oldest, Reggie, would collect his lunch bucket along with his dad—Big Johnny—and they would set off for the plant together. Little Johnny and the other siblings old enough to go to school would line up for inspection: fingernails attended to, the right pants smoothed down, shirts—in Sean's case, Great-Aunt Betty's favorite housedress, bleached and hemmed and taken in and made mostly plausible as a men's shirt—worn with mostly clean cuffs. Letty was a just a baby who lay and cooed quietly to herself while watching the fuss with her big eyes. Darlene was still a toddler, and "thirteen-month twins" Bobbie and Dorothy wore matching dresses to elementary school and had lesson books tucked under their arms (and never failed inspection).

Oldest of the girls was Eleanor, known to everyone simply as Ellie.

She was the spitting image of Great-Aunt Betty from coal country, or so Mrs. Myrtle McGill said: short and shapely, legs and arms naturally rounded with muscle, sinew, and spitfire. Green eyes and chestnut hair would have made for a real country lass . . . if she ever let herself be described as such. Ellie could beat her brothers in races and rassling, leaving Bobbie and Dorothy to learn the homey arts of cookery and straight stitches from their mother. She spent as little time as possible inside despite the love and laughter there. She liked her family, she really did. But the house was small and the bodies were many and the voices were loud (though sometimes her voice was the loudest of all). There was never any room left over for her own thoughts, which were too big to fit inside the walls—or even her own skin sometimes, which was why her father would occasionally come out with an exasperated "Ellie, can you never stop your wigglin' and squirmin'?"

For as long as she could remember, her thoughts had been huge: vast landscapes, empty of people. Mountains bigger than cities, snowcapped, whose peaks touched space. Valleys like the Grand Canyon but filled with greenery and animals. Wide-open skies in strange shades of blue with rows of foreign birds ranging across them, honking in accents, splitting the heavens in a feathered line. Different trees from home, different creatures from home, different *grass* from home.

None of this fit into the not-quite-big-enough farmhouse. To be fair, no one there made fun of her long monologues on the jungles of South America or devoted recitation of the latest exploits of her favorite explorer, Charles Muntz. The McGills put up with their fidgety, dreamy girl with patience and affection—but none of them truly understood her deep fascination with places outside the most perfect town in America. There were birds in Bloomington too, sparrows and starlings and swallows and even swans occasionally, *and* Flash Gordon movies with newsreels and an extra double feature on Sundays . . . surely they didn't have *those* in her golden deserts?

"If you're feeling restless, go out and explore the neighborhood!" her exhausted parents would declare.

So she did.

And that was how, when Ellie was nine and the radio was full of upsetting news from overseas instead of her favorite shows, she found the house.

Remember: this was at the start of World War II in a perfect American town, and no one worried about kidnappers—just Nazis and maybe now Communists. Children had free rein on their bikes and push-scooters and feet. But even with that liberty did Ellie wander a *little* far from where her parents assumed the imaginary boundary line for wandering girls lay: approximately ten feet past the crumbling brick wall of the old flour mill. The rest of the street was mostly abandoned since developers had paved the spanking new Meadow Avenue straight through the meadow and built their ticky-tacky houses there.

(And as much as the McGills had time to worry about anything, her getting tetanus on a rusty nail or falling through a decaying floorboard was *much* farther up the list of concerns than "encounters with a scoundrel.")

Ellie didn't worry about anything at all, and now she had a magnificent old house to herself. It was *huge* (at least, when only inhabited by one adolescent girl) and shingled with curving slate tiles like the silver scales of a dragon or ancient fish. One tiny gable and a pointy attic gave it an off-kilter, fey look, and the porch was—well, of no interest to

Ellie. A real copper weathervane graced the roof, its twisting and turning reminding her of something more complicated and mechanical . . . It gave her ideas.

Away from two other girls and a toddler squirmily sharing a bedroom with her, Ellie could finally decorate a space of her own. At home she had to keep her maps, pictures, newsletters from Charles Muntz, posters, advertisements of exotic landscapes, and her most prized possession of all, her *adventure journal*, in an overflowing cigar box under her side of the bed. She didn't even have a lock for it.

At Ellie's new Explorers Clubhouse she could post whatever she wanted all over the walls, so she could see them all at once, eyes flitting from one bright, happy thing to the next. There was no fear of Bobbie "accidentally" finding her stash and using the pictures there for some stupid little craft project (usually with scissors and paste, which permanently ruined the image) or Little Johnny's even stupider gang of friends going through the pile and laughing uproariously like it was an embarrassing collection of movie star photos.

At the clubhouse, Ellie could talk as loudly as she wanted as often as she wanted to whomever she wanted. Meaning: the spiders, the squirrels, herself, and of course the invisible crew who followed her orders and helped pilot her *Spirit of Adventure* flying machine (named after Muntz's famous zeppelin). Ellie could run around *inside* as much as she wanted without anyone telling her to calm down, to do something quiet instead, to stop moving because she was giving mommy a headache. There were no teachers telling her to behave, to sit still, to constantly demand why she couldn't work peacefully on her sewing projects like the other girls in home economics or play jump rope nicely, waiting for her turn in line instead of trying to use one of the extra ropes as a "vine" to swing off the jungle gym.

In fact, maybe she would hang a swing from one of the exposed attic floorboards, down to the living room . . . she could slide down it like a fireman, or Tarzan. . . .

She could wear her prized *Spirit of Adventure* helmet and goggles that the McGills all pitched in to get her for her birthday, and she could wear it *all day* on the weekends, even when she was eating, which was absolutely not allowed at home.

(Did wearing it so much do strange things to her hair that made her mother sigh? Perhaps. But Ellie thought she sort of looked like a lion when her ends were all frizzy and stood straight out, or that it was a halo of fire; something impressive and coronal that gave her majesty, unlike her missing front tooth.)

Over the course of several generative months the house transformed into an aerozeppelin, Ellie's brilliant cross of an airplane and a blimp that could go faster and turn more sharply than a normal blimp but also hang noiselessly in the air so she could observe migrating animals below or map out the entire course of a river uninterrupted while her crew brought her hot chocolate and snacks.

And where would she go?

Indistinct visions of jungle and forest coalesced one portentous day into a single clear picture, thanks to a *National Geographic* book at the library about Charles Muntz and the real lands behind Sir Arthur Conan Doyle's *The Lost World*. The bonus centerfold poster was an etching of the world's tallest waterfall, arcing off the top of a flat-topped mountain: Paradise Falls, Venezuela. Ellie had never seen such a spectacular place before—in a book *or* her dreams.

So she ripped the poster out (of the library book! But destiny sometimes called for drastic actions) and pasted it into her adventure journal. She imagined her way south, steering her aerozeppelin to the great adventure that was out there.

And something else transformed in those weeks of inventing, building, and imagining.

Ellie was too busy testing the wind with her finger at recess to care about the jump ropes; sometimes she just sat at the base of the jungle gym, watching the sky and thinking about flying. She sat a little more still in class and actually focused on drawing in art—colorful houses, aerozeppelins, waterfalls, mountains, birds. At home she was bursting to tell everyone about the adventures she'd had but at the same time already thoughtfully planning where she would go the next day. She began to finish her whole dinner, including the beans.

It was like just knowing she had a place and a time where she could do anything she wanted, to be herself, was enough for her body to wait patiently until it could be free.

Her parents wondered: Was Ellie growing up?

Her teachers didn't ask questions; they just sighed in relief and moved on to other Children Who Needed Extra Help Behaving.

And now that she had a place to be the Ellie of her dreams, the clubhouse started showing up in the plans of Future-Ellie. The picture of Paradise Falls that she had carefully pasted into her album soon sported a brightly colored drawing of the clubhouse collaged onto it. She would live there; it would be the base of her operations, and where she would return after each amazing exploration.

The house was also how she met Carl.

Years later, she would still tease him about his strange appearance at the (seemingly) abandoned, rickety old structure. Shy, quiet Carl didn't normally stray far from his own house, which was on the *right* side of Meadow Avenue, closer to the high street shopping district. But he had his helmet and goggles on, and after the one o'clock matinee his father had bought him a *Spirit of Adventure* helium balloon that a representative of Charles Muntz's Society of Young Explorers was selling in the lobby. Between the balloon and his helmet and a truly exciting newsreel about Charles Muntz in China, Carl was buoyant with wonder: Adventure was truly out there. Maybe even at the end of the sidewalk.

If only he had known how prophetic that was!

True, it was her carefully painted *Spirit of Adventure* label on the door that caught his attention—was there ever a more obvious sign in his life?—but, as he only admitted years later, it was the sound of her voice that actually lured him in. Ellie's twangy, loose-voweled shouts that caused her teachers to shiver in dismay and even got on her father's nerves made it sound like she was having *the most fun in the universe* and that there was a whole world inside that house, where kids could be free and wild and do whatever they wanted.

On Ellie's side, his arrival awoke an idea she never had before: Was it possible to want to be all by yourself . . . *with* someone? When Carl appeared it was like all of her secret, unformed prayers had been granted. *He was even wearing the helmet and goggles*, which, to be fair, were pretty common among fans of Muntz—but still.

She greeted him the way she was used to with kids her age at school: aggressively. Playground bravado. But when he shrank back into the shadows Ellie realized she was dealing with a different sort of human. She wished she had something to calm him, like a baby squirrel, to let him know that she was all right, that they were the same: explorers.

With a burst of generosity and genius she remembered her collection of bottle-cap pins, carefully took one off, and pinned it onto his shirt. It was from a grape soda, her favorite flavor, although the background wasn't *all* purple, which was her favorite color, and which it really should have been instead of just a picture of grapes.

So when that terrible accident with the attic board occurred and he broke his arm, she had nothing left to give him except her deepest secrets: her adventure journal, and her plan to live above Paradise Falls. It was unclear if he really believed she was actually going to move her clubhouse to South America—he was shy, not stupid—but he was absolutely willing to go along with whatever schemes she had as long as they involved him.

Ellie fell in love with Carl's room from that first time she snuck in, as much as he loved her clubhouse. Imagine having so much space in your bedroom that you could have a *tent* on your floor! And all of his models, and toys, and books . . . and not having to share them with sticky toddlers and girls with scissors . . .

"You got your own radio in your room?" she asked in awe, leaning over the giant brown box on his desk, with its strange dials and knobs. "Lucky! The only show I get to myself is Muntz's *Adventure Hour* if something isn't happening on the news. Otherwise it's my sisters' dumb music. . . ."

"It's not, um, that kind of radio. . . ." Carl was nervous, obviously torn between being delighted to explain something he loved and terrified that the wonderfully energetic girl would accidentally break something much more important to him than his arm. "It's a transceiver—I can receive *and* broadcast. Send messages, in Morse code, to other amateur radio hobbyists."

"*What?* Like secret codes, and you can talk to people all over the world, like in the movies? Like 'Dot dot dot dash the enemy spy is actually the *mailman*'?" Her eyes grew so wide they took up most of her face.

"Yes. No. Not the whole world, I can't transmit that far. Actually, there's rumors that soon we won't be able to use them at all because of the war, but . . ."

"Aw, phooey, it just ruins *everything,* don't it?" Ellie said disgustedly. "Well, then you'd better show me how it works, quickly. I want to see how you talk to people I haven't even met yet. *And* in code!"

She wasn't paying attention, now on to other things in his room, but Carl's face shone in revelation: *She assumed they would be friends from now on*, until some indeterminate time in the future. More than that, she fully expected a demonstration of his radio (which most other kids found boring).

They were kindred spirits. It was that simple.

And so she kept sneaking in, even if she had spent time with him already earlier in the day. They were inseparable.

Or would have been: Sadly, despite the proximity of their neighborhoods, they did not go to the same school. But the moment the last bell rang Ellie tore out of the classroom like it was on fire and Carl left his own, carefully undoing his Methodist Boys School tie along the way. They met up for adventures in the clubhouse, in the park, in deserted lots, and even in other people's backyards, one of which Ellie was sure had a hidden cave full of treasure (next to their storm cellar).

Neither set of parents was quite sure what to make of it. While Mr. and Mrs. Fredricksen were glad to see their son come out of his shell and make a little friend, perhaps they would have preferred it be someone he met at the YMCA. Ellie was nice enough, and eventually they had her over for dinner, but they worried about the injuries Carl sometimes received under her tutelage and the dead exhaustion he often suffered, falling asleep in front of his radio with a smile on his face.

For their part, the McGills were relieved that they didn't really need to worry about Ellie now that she had someone keeping watch as she ran around on her adventures. Too bad it was a boy . . . Still, Mrs. McGill would pack them brown bread and jelly sandwiches for picnic lunches, which were sometimes enjoyed miles away and sometimes in their own backyard, on different branches of the same small but rangy apple tree that grew there. When Ellie was invited to Carl's house for dinner, Mrs. McGill made her stand perfectly still beforehand while she brushed her hair straight and neat, and Mr. McGill made sure she brushed her shoes until they shone.

Under penalty of severe punishment from both parents, Ellie did her best to behave at these dinners, which were not at all like supper at the McGills'. She had to sit still and make small talk from appetizers and soup *all the way through tea and dessert*, and not try to grab the potatoes before they were all gone or get up to use the bathroom if she could avoid it. Sometimes Carl would give her a smile of encouragement and she felt like a champ—but the only way she could really get through these evenings was by pretending she was an anthropologist there to study the strange ways of the Fredricksen Kindred, observing their rituals and traditions for later notes.

Any suggestion that Ellie and Carl's friendship was a short-lived folly of youth faded as the two kids grew (a little) taller and didn't show any signs of parting ways. When Carl got a shiny new bike for faster, longer adventures, Ellie rode on his handlebars. When neither had any spending money at all and there was nothing to do, they made an adventure of collecting scrap metal around town to sell and used the bits too small to bother with for building whimsical little model airplanes and rockets, which Carl hung from his ceiling as proudly as his kit models.

Finally, almost reluctantly, Carl did make a few other friends at school; he joined the lepidopterist club because it was peaceful and involved just two other (myopic) boys. Ellie found a local stickball crew that didn't mind girls. But none of those were *friend* friends.

In fact, the only hitch in their otherwise very solid relationship was neither financial nor social: it was a basic disparity of energy. Ellie seemed to have a boundless well of it; she could come back from an Outdoor Guides expedition up Mount Pisgah—earning a Humble Helpers badge along the way—and after she rattled off all her adventures to Carl she would *then* drag him into the woods to show him what skills she had learned. She thought nothing of an eight-mile hike to a secret waterfall, and if Carl began to protest she would tell stories about her cousin when he was in the Civilian Conservation Corps and how they would climb a mountain without even a bedroll—for fun!—and ate only what they could forage, trap, or fish. Carl was impressed but *not* a member of the CCC and wouldn't have foraged fresh songbird eggs even if he had been starving. The sort of adventures he imagined having as an adult involved a long trek to a nice snug little cabin, preferably with a provisioned larder and some previously stacked wood or very handy deadfall nearby.

One day when he felt like he couldn't take it anymore, halfway through a tour of the Seven Tiny Hills of Marshfield, the next town over, Carl made an amazing discovery. He had been sweating more than usual because of a present he had brought along in his pack for Ellie that he had intended to give her as a reward after they completed the seventh hill. But when they had stopped under a shady tree for a water and apple break (after only the second hill) and she started to get ready to go again, he quickly dug it out and gave it to her.

"*Advanced Single-Engine Flying Instruction Manual*," she read aloud in wonder. "Subtitle: *Army Air Forces Training Command*."

It was a book written for aviation teachers to make sure they drilled their students properly in everything necessary to pass and get their wings. From preflight checklists to the proper distance to keep when formation flying, how to turn loops, how to train for emergencies, how to navigate by maps and remaining fuel. There were drawings and descriptions of all the gauges and panels and switches and knobs and levers.

"For *me?* Really? To keep?" she asked in wonder.

Carl nodded; he had seen it in the window of a secondhand bookstore and his mother had been excited to assign him extra chores to pay for it.

Then Ellie did the strangest thing—she immediately began to read it.

And *kept* reading it.

After an unusual—but not awkward—five minutes of complete silence while she sat absorbed in the book, Ellie finally looked up.

"I'm such a silly-sally! How about I read aloud so both of us can learn from it at the same time. We can take turns—that way we won't get tired. And you can completely interrupt me and ask questions. I don't mind. Not like Miss Thompson at school. She never explains anything."

So Ellie started all over again, from the front cover, the copyright date, the whole thing, not missing a single letter or period of her wonderful new book. They wound up spending most of the afternoon that way, trading it back and forth under a tree, occasionally getting a drink of water, imagining planes in the silent sky above them, the third through seventh hills forgotten.

Not only was it Carl's most favorite day ever, but it was the beginning of a whole new era for the two of them. From then on he *always* brought a book, magazine, pamphlet—literally anything to read and share—and Ellie did too. It didn't stop her from busting on ahead when they got up again, but it did give Carl a chance to regain his breath and catch up.

As the years passed, flight manuals and Muntz's Club mailings and Outdoor Guides pamphlets and books on the unexplored parts of the world were swapped out for things that they had to read for school; homework was more fun that way. Sometimes it was poetry. And sometimes, when it was a warm, pollen-filled day, Carl would be reading Keats or Cervantes and Ellie would find herself nicely overwhelmed with the afternoon and the words, and her head would slowly collapse onto his shoulder. Carl never stopped reading; his eyes might have flicked toward her closed ones for a moment, but the weight of her against him was all he really needed to know she was "listening."

As for the rest of the world . . . everything that was

happening in a nation now at war was new and exciting, if a little scary. Ellie finally found herself interested in listening to the news. Carl speculated on whether or not he would eventually be drafted (and privately: whether he would start shaving first). There were endless volunteer opportunities, like packing up and distributing comfort kits for soldiers. Ellie joined the USO as soon as she was old enough. Ration coupons for food and gas and luxuries were terrible, but *everyone* had to use them and most were united in going without, for the war effort. At least publicly.

For Ellie and Carl, far from the front, deep in the woods or banging around their little town, life was about as peachy keen as it could get.

ONE

The summer Ellie turned thirteen, Carl found a beat-up old bike that they decided would be hers, and they spent the whole summer fixing it up.

(Of course she named it the *Spirit of Bloomington*, and Carl found an airplane decal in a Cracker Jack box that fit perfectly between the handlebars. They completed the aircraft theme with a couple airplane spotter cards tucked in the spokes to make a flapping noise when she pedaled fast.)

Suddenly Ellie had a freedom to explore even farther than she had ever dreamed—by herself! She could travel *ten times* what she could on foot and still be home when her mom demanded (an hour after sunset). She could ride to the shops if she wanted to people-watch—like an anthropologist—or had a penny for candy. She could swing by Carl's house and throw something through his window for him to find later (a strange nut, a mysterious map, a note in code).

She could *go to the zoo* all by herself.

Life got a lot more exciting when she didn't have to pay bus fare, and the zoo was free Wednesday afternoons and Saturday mornings before noon. Which was great, because Carl had to go to the Young Methodists Association on Wednesdays; she could spend all afternoon there.

Seeing animals from the deserts, mountains, and jungles that Ellie had only read about was a big step forward for her dreams of exploration, and colored her new imaginings dramatically. She watched cloud rats from the Philippines scuttle through the branches of their nocturnal cages, tails much prettier and furrier than a true rat's. She loved the tiny squirrel monkeys with their large eyes and expressive hands; she imagined herself sitting high in a treetop canopy with a pair of binoculars and a notepad, scribbling down her observations on the family units. She always waited around to watch keepers feed the vampire bats and dearly longed to wander the caves where they were originally found.

But by far her favorite place to hang out was the aviary.

The birds were, of course, fascinating and spectacular. There were the Victoria crowned pigeons with spangled feathers on their heads that didn't seem like pigeons at all, and the Waldrapps, which were becoming endangered despite their terrifying naked faces. There was a myriad of pretty little exotic ducks paddling in the artificial river that cut through the exhibit, and teeny tiny warblers that weirdo bird nerds came from long distances to view, worried they would never get a chance to see them in the wild.

Once in a while she got lucky and caught a glimpse of the Head Keeper, Margaret Klein, attending to the birds herself. She was the only actual trained zoologist at the zoo and yet before the war she had been allowed to hold only a secretarial position, albeit one that included care of the aviary because birds had been her focus of study.

She always cut a striking figure, in impossibly chic suits with her work boots and hairnet, and was just as comfortable talking to a septuagenarian birder as a five-year-old who was scared of the peacocks. She could also literally coax birds out of the sky or off a ledge, her nimble hands shooting out to gently grab one for an exam even when her workers couldn't manage.

But besides getting to occasionally watch a real zoologist in action, the main draw of the aviary for Ellie was the exhibit itself. As soon as she went through the second set of doors, its moist, warm air would envelop her with the fruity smell of topical plants, and she was in another world.

Along the railings were neat little signs with pictures of

each bird and colored maps showing where they were from: countries like Bolivia, newly renamed Thailand, and the Congo, bright splotches in red, blue, and green. When Ellie spotted the right bird from the picture she would put her finger on the map and close her eyes.

"I am in Ecuador," she would murmur. And she would smell the air and believe it.

No one who knew Ellie from school or stickball would have believed she could stand so still for so long.

By the time she was fourteen Ellie could recite twenty-six facts about the white-winged wood duck and greet most of the zookeepers by name.

"Heya, Agnes! Hola, Señora Juarez, Miss Jenny, Miz Smith." She would wave like they were old friends. Because of the war, most were women and old men, all able-bodied younger men having been drafted and sent overseas or farther south to train.

(Including the zoo's director, Leroy Reardon, whose wealthy family had financed the zoo's construction as a gift to the city and a way to give the rich playboy something to focus on and maybe get serious about. But the zoo didn't really notice its director's absence.)

By the time Ellie was fifteen—and still dragging her feet when the aviary was supposed to be closing and locked for the night—the Head Keeper had had enough.

"Why don't you just apply to be our intern and be done with it?" she asked in exasperation—but with a smile. "You're here all the time anyway. You probably know more about some of these animals' habits than their own keepers. Might as well get paid for it!"

"You're joshing me," Ellie said, eyes wide.

"It's not as glamorous as it sounds." Which was ironic, really; Ms. Klein was the most glamorous professional woman Ellie had ever seen in real life. "There will be a lot of . . . excrement shoveling, cleaning, and feeding. But I'll take you on as my special Avian Assistant when there's time, and you can help me with my rare birds breeding program. It's a lot, but it's fascinating, I promise."

So just like that, Ellie entered the workforce as a young woman, now with spending cash. Some of which, of course, she gave to her parents to help out, the way Reggie used to before the war.

"I don't even have to work anymore," Mr. McGill said, laughing. "I'll just have my kids go out and do it for me while I stay at home and listen to the radio all day."

And Ellie had money to treat *Carl* to things for once.

Of course the best part of her job was getting to go inside the cages and work with the animals. On the weekends she came in at five thirty a.m. and helped Mr. Hua prepare the food for birds: fancy seed for the pretty singing finches, squiggling mealworms for the hornbills, dead and dried ones for the crested coua, thawed frozen mice for the secretary birds, Flamingo Feed™ for the flamingos, fruit for the golden-headed quetzal, nectar for the hummingbirds and African sunbirds. She wasn't skittish about the bugs and didn't look away from the dead mice—but did avoid touching them with her hands. She also had to clean out the food and water bowls and sweep up any debris or droppings that came too close to their feeding area.

Sometimes she was allowed to hold a non-dangerous snake while the zoo vet examined it, which she loved, and always wished she could get a photo of herself with one to show Carl.

Mostly Ellie did whatever the official zookeepers told her: clean something, sweep something, find the first-aid kit, go yell at the kids throwing peanuts at the monkeys.

She talked to the animals—not expecting them to talk back, of course—and asked them about the places they had been. A few had been born or hatched at the zoo, but before the war most had been captured in the wild. She bet Hernando, the Galápagos giant tortoise of unknown age, had seen a thing or two in his time. Imagine a cold-blooded reptile cavorting in the same place penguins did! Someday she would get to see them in their natural habitat . . . and maybe Hernando would still be around, and she could tell him all about how his old neighborhood had changed.

She spent less time with the Head Keeper than she had hoped or feared; Ms. Klein was kept thoroughly engaged by her duties trying to run the zoo while wartime rationing and shortages were still relevant. Maybe that was all right, though: Ellie still stood in awe of the woman, who didn't seem to be quite real with the way she checked a bird's oviduct with one deft and neatly manicured finger (an invasive maneuver that some keepers couldn't even watch) and then grabbed her matching hat and bag to go meet with city officials about permits.

Of course, all things bad *and* good come to an end . . . In the fall of 1945, Japan surrendered and the war was over. After all the celebrations and parties, in the spring of 1946 it was time for Director Leroy Reardon to come home to his zoo.

Ellie was cleaning the windows of the cloud rat exhibit with old newspaper and vinegar when Margaret came up to her, her shiny pumps clacking against the tiled floor and a tightly rolled telegram clutched in her hand.

"Ms. Klein," Ellie said, immediately jumping up. There was something strangely formal about the situation: The Head Keeper always wore work boots during the day, outside the administrative offices.

"Miss McGill. I thought you should hear it from me, before rumors inevitably start circulating." Then she paused, lips twisting a little. Her lipstick stayed perfectly applied and didn't smudge. "Leroy Reardon has been discharged—he is returning to the zoo, and is once again taking charge of it."

"Jeepers, that's great! About time, isn't it? Seems like everyone else has come home already, huh?"

"Yes, I suppose it has. . . . I just wanted to assure you that despite the change in administration, your job is secure. It is through the city, not the private trust that supports the zoo."

"Why would my job be in trouble?" Ellie asked curiously.

"Because you were, ostensibly, my hire, and . . ." The other woman seemed to suddenly really see Ellie, the sixteen-year-old girl before her, in coveralls that were slightly too big, her hair kept out of the way in a bandana, a crumpled newspaper in her hand. "Oh, forget it. I just wanted to reassure you. There's going to be quite a hubbub on his return. A press conference and a party for everyone at the zoo—everyone will be invited, including our star intern."

"That's amazing. A party at a zoo! That's better than a prom," Ellie said excitedly.

"I agree wholeheartedly. Well, carry on, but keep this

to yourself until the official announcement. Loose lips and all that."

Margaret strode off and Ellie turned back to her work. Her first workplace party—just like an adult! Just like the Christmas party the plant threw for its employees every year. Her father and Reggie always came home cheery and pink cheeked, with little gifts from the bosses—candy or handkerchiefs with the company name on them.

She scrubbed off some particularly greasy fingerprints and thought with a grin about how she was just like Cinderella with the announcement of the ball, down to her chores and friendships with the mice (er, cloud rats) and doves (Victoria crowned pigeons).

The afternoon before the party, Mrs. McGill very kindly invited Carl over for an early dinner—along with Great-Aunt Cleo—and made a festive meal out of it. She cooked up corn fritters, mashed potatoes, and a new recipe she had found in a magazine: jellied chicken salad. Which was questionable, but her pull-apart cheese and onion rolls were definitely not.

When Carl arrived he formally knocked on the front door instead of just coming on in through the kitchen door, as had been routine for the past nearly ten years. Ellie just gaped at her best friend for a moment: He was dressed in a jacket and tie and his hair was parted in the middle and slicked back. His cheeks were pink from being freshly shaved and smelled of cologne. This was far more trouble than he usually went to for their socials or dances; he was so dashing he almost looked like a movie star.

Not, maybe, a lead, but like the handsome and funny best friend who winds up with the comedienne. Which made her the comedienne, she reflected. She wasn't sure she was actually that funny. On purpose, anyway.

Ellie had put on a dress that highlighted the green in her eyes and tied her hair back with a simple bow (no longer as red and frizzy, her locks were still a thick handful to brush through, which her mother still loved doing). She had only a pair of working girls' oxford pumps, but it all must have done the trick, because while she silently admired Carl he was less quiet.

"Ellie," he breathed, "you look *amazing*!"

"Aw, thanks, Carl." Unsure what else to say and feeling herself both glow and blush, she grabbed his hand and dragged him inside. "Aunt Cleo's here."

"Oh, great, that means your mom's cooking something special," Carl said eagerly. "I'll sit across from her and pass her things."

There was no children's table at the McGills'. At no obvious signal all the children (except the baby, in the rocker) ran out of whatever corner of the house they were playing in and threw themselves into seats that were assigned to prevent squabbles. Mr. McGill sat at one end with Reggie on his right, Mrs. McGill at the other, near the rocker. Ellie and Carl sat next to each other, which wasn't entirely etiquette appropriate, but it did give Ellie a break. The geometry of a large table in a large family meant that people in the middle spent most of their time during the meal passing food rather than eating it.

"Say grace for us, Aunt Cleo," Mrs. McGill suggested.

Aunt Cleo bowed her tiny head to the point where the giant bee skep of her piled-up braids nearly touched the bowl of mashed potatoes and her mouth was hidden in the folds of the enormous shawl she had wrapped too many times around her scrawny shoulders.

"Nurken flur mmrsm femresh dshem, fufrrrm menn assre," she intoned quickly and seriously.

The twins giggled and poked each other. Little Johnny snickered. Mrs. McGill gave them an acid stare.

Ellie and Carl smiled at each other and sighed; they had been through this a million times.

". . . murfle flaven, *AMEN*!" she said and looked up, as proud as a schoolgirl after a long recitation.

The McGills dove into the food practically before she was done speaking. Ellie grabbed two rolls and the dish of margarine since they were the closest to her. She split one roll, carefully buttered both sides, and put it on Carl's plate. She just smashed a piece of margarine on top of her own; the rolls were still warm, and it would melt all over the surface like a cracked egg. Ellie loved that.

Carl nodded in thanks at the roll but was too busy attending Aunt Cleo to speak: Mrs. McGill had passed him the jellied chicken to serve her first.

"Where's the chicken?" the diminutive matriarch demanded. She used her fork to tap at the sparkling confectionary tower Mrs. McGill had created: a clear Jell-O masterpiece with tiny bites of meat suspended in the bottom layer; the layers above it dotted with cauliflower; and, at the very top, peas. *"Why is my chicken behind glass?"*

"It's Jell-O, Aunt Cleo," Carl explained patiently. "Here, let me cut you a slice. You can eat the whole thing. It's amazing."

"You've outdone yourself, Myrtle," Mr. McGill said, admiring the swaying, wiggling tower.

"It looks tasty, Ma," Reggie added.

"There's more peas and cauliflower that I couldn't fit in it, in bowls," Ellie's mom said, her cheeks glowing with pride.

After he had served Aunt Cleo, Carl found the peas and carefully counted out ten into the bowl of the serving spoon, then neatly offloaded them onto Ellie's plate. Ten was the maximum she could fit threaded on the tines of a fork, and the most peas she would eat in one sitting.

"How was the wedding?" Aunt Cleo asked conversationally as she gamely nibbled at a forkful of chicken encrusted with clear slimy bits.

"Whose wedding, Auntie?" Mrs. McGill asked as everyone at the table not stuffing their faces looked confused.

"Why, them's, of course," Aunt Cleo said, poking her now empty fork at Carl and Ellie. "My memory's a steel sieve, so I don't recollect how it went this afternoon, but I'm sure it was nice."

The silence was so thick that not even a cricket called.

"Aunt Cleo," Ellie said gently, "we didn't get married this afternoon."

"Well, you're all dressed up for it! Shame on you for confusing an old lady. So you've already been married awhile then, I suppose. What did I get you again?"

Little Johnny guffawed. Straight up laughed until mashed potato atoms flew out of his mouth.

"Aunt Cleo," Ellie said, face flushing hotter than her mother's oven that afternoon, "we're not married."

Aunt Cleo just cackled. Kindly.

Ellie and Carl looked at each other again, but it wasn't with amused tolerance this time. Carl's eyebrows were raised in alarm; Ellie's leg began shaking like she was in English class.

"Well, I mean," Mr. McGill said diplomatically, slicing his jellied terrine with care, "you two *are* together all the time . . . here. . . . And you *are* dressed nice. It *could* be confusing. . . ."

What was her father trying to say?

Was he trying to say anything?

Ellie focused on shoveling her food in as fast as possible. "Gonna be late," she muttered through a full mouth.

Carl, as if he had read her mind, was doing the same.

But the tastes and travails of family dinner were immediately forgotten when they got to the zoo—which was closed to the public for the occasion but lit up like a carnival, with festoon lights, bunting, and a live band.

Ellie grabbed Carl's hand and pulled him through the crowds to the front. Though it was only staff and their plus-ones attending, there were *a lot* of men in the crowd that Ellie didn't recognize or remember seeing before. Strange.

And where was Leroy?

Everyone was whispering the question—except for Carl, who asked it a little too loudly. Ellie looked over where Margaret and the other administrative staff were standing, but they seemed just as perplexed.

Suddenly there was an imperious honk of a car horn and the throaty roar of a large, expensive engine.

Everyone turned to watch as a very fancy, shiny silver car rolled through the deliveries-only gate and growled up the main promenade, stopping just shy of the stage.

"A *Jaguar*!" Carl murmured dreamily.

Someone rushed over to open its door. Leroy Reardon climbed out, resplendent in a long camelhair jacket thrown over his shoulders and a handsome fedora he donned as soon as he was out of the car. Even his moustache seemed golden. He looked like every American Ideal in one perfect package: fit, brassy hair and thick moustache, loud stock-market voice, immediate decisions, commanding presence.

Everyone cheered madly, Ellie and Carl loudest of all.

Leroy strode forward, waving genially at the crowd and grinning with great square white teeth clamped together as though he had a cigar in the corner of his mouth (he didn't). There was a microphone all ready for him, but he swept it aside, not needing technological amplification to make himself heard.

"My fellow zoo enthusiasts, it is *grand* to be back in the United States of America, at my little zoo, where I belong." He had to wait, of course, for the audience to stop cheering and clapping. "I was more than proud to do my part in the war . . . but am heartily relieved that peace has finally been declared. Because we have *won*."

The applause surged for "we have won," because only a dirty traitor wouldn't clap at that.

"And now that I'm back, I have some wonderful changes to announce. I've loved this place ever since my father built it and gave it to me as a boy. But now I'm grown up, and I want the zoo to as well. To be not just a nice place for little boys, but for boys at heart and people of all ages. I aim to make it a diamond-class attraction, internationally renowned and world famous!"

"Did you know anything about this?" Carl whispered.

She shook her head. But it sounded amazing, whatever Leroy had planned.

"Maybe they'll put in a Ferris wheel," Carl said hopefully. He loved carnival rides. Actually, he loved almost everything about carnivals, especially kettle corn and balloons. Even now that he was seventeen.

"We all know and appreciate what a great job Miss Klein here has done with her birds and whatnot, the rare babies everyone was all excited about," Leroy continued. "But that's not *fun*! That doesn't bring in the crowds! Do you know what does?"

He paused for dramatic effect.

"Fantastic animals!"

And with that, two men pushed a cart out from behind the Jaguar. On it was a glittering golden cage. Inside the cage, with barely enough room to turn around, was a ferocious wolf.

The crowd gasped in shock. There was no mistaking it for a domesticated dog. Its eyes were golden and wild; when it panted its giant pink tongue lolled back, revealing canines large and sharp enough to disembowel a cow.

"Oh my," Ellie murmured. "I wonder if it's terrified by all the smells and people. And there's only one? Wolves are social. They need their families."

"That does seem a little strange. Maybe there's more in back?"

Disappointingly for everyone, the wolf did not howl.

"A Russian wolf, caught by my own men at the edge of the snowy steppes," Leroy declared. "He is our new symbol, our ambassador for the newly reinvigorated Bloomington Zoo. And he's just the beginning! I aim to travel the world, bringing back all kinds of incredible creatures, from places men have never set foot. And speaking of men . . ."

He set his jaw with a look of fierce determination.

"It's a new age now. Boys have gone to war and come back men. And while we thank the ladies in our lives for keeping the home fires burning while we were gone—"

"And the factories running," Ellie couldn't help adding quietly. "And the shipyards moving . . ."

"And the farms producing food for everyone," Carl contributed.

"Now we're in the atomic age, where men control the very powers of earth and nature . . . itself. Only the bold, inventive leadership of masculine power will take us further into the future. So with all due gratitude to Miss Klein and those ladies who ran the zoo through the war and its difficulties, it's time to give returning soldiers a chance to retake their rightful place in the workforce. I am particularly pleased to announce the appointment of a Purple Heart veteran and man I am proud to call my comrade in arms, William Hodgson, to the position of *permanent* Head Keeper and Chief Administrative Officer of the Zoo."

Ellie somehow wasn't clapping. Her hands didn't curl into fists forcefully at her sides out of anger, either; they hovered, uselessly, in a nowhere land above her thighs, like those of a robot from one of the Saturday afternoon science fiction serials.

Carl's left eyebrow rose in a question. "Miss Klein? He means *Ms.*, right? Isn't that the woman who gave you your job? The head of the zoo?"

His words sounded far away. There was handsome Leroy, applauding a man who awkwardly got onstage, waving and blushing. This fellow wasn't bad-looking, skinny and blond and flexing his fingers as if he desperately wanted to be holding something, and still wore bits of his army uniform like he couldn't quite let it go, or hadn't fully adapted to civilian life yet. He muttered thanks to Leroy and smiled in embarrassment with a crooked front tooth and a face of endearing self-deprecation. Flashbulbs went off like fireworks; people loved the story of a war hero amply rewarded for his time in saving the world.

Elsewhere in the crowd, someone was handing Margaret a pretty little bouquet of flowers tied in a cone of paper; she was nodding politely. William was talking now, and Leroy was looking serious and clapping, but the new permanent Head Keeper and Chief Administrative Officer of the Zoo didn't have his friend's lung power; in need of the now-absent microphone, his words were lost in the breeze and shuffling crowd. Then there were more bouquets, tiny ones, handed out to various lesser female employees. Still employed? Ex-employees? For a strange moment it seemed like some sort of outdated social ritual, like a centuries-old formal dance, men giving women flowers in a specific order unknown to the casual observer.

Here's your flower, now disappear, Ellie thought. Anemone, heliotrope, all those pretty garden flowers that the Greeks believed were girls caught in the crossfire of the gods and love and therefore discarded, healed, or otherwise disappeared by being turned into flowers.

Ellie didn't understand what was happening, exactly, or what she felt. She looked at Carl. He shrugged helplessly, his mouth turned down in a classic Carl way, his glasses riding up on his cheeks a little, following his thick eyebrows in their upward journey.

When it was all over Ellie immediately rushed up to Margaret.

"Ms. Klein! I'm so sorry! Ms. Klein!"

The older woman looked around with a quick flick of her eyes and long black lashes. Ellie was being a little loud.

"Nothing to be done," she finally said with a rueful smile. "I don't *own* the zoo, after all. I'm just an employee. Besides, this will give me much more time to spend with my wonderful birds. No more administrative duties and bureaucracy for me! Let someone else spend his time filling out forms and requisitions for Flamingo Feed™ and permits for large animal enclosures within city limits."

"But—"

"*And* I will actually get to spend more time with my star intern," she interrupted, fixing a piece of Ellie's hair, an annoying strand, behind her ear. Not like her mother. Like a punctilious aunt, fingers with carefully manicured nails spending as little time as possible actually touching her. "Come to the aviary for lunch on your next day in! I just received the latest copy of *Zoological News BiMonthly*, and it has a fascinating article on the snakes of Bermuda I think you'll enjoy. They're pink, apparently, just like their famous sand."

The idea of lunch with a woman like Margaret Klein normally would have stopped Ellie dead in her tracks and line of thought. Now it would not sway her.

"But your special breeding programs—the sage grouse and Iberian rock sparrow . . . Are they in danger?"

"Don't worry about it. Where there's a budget, there's a way."

Carl was standing back with the rest of the crowd, letting the two women have a private moment. He gave a little wave and had a slug of the punch they were giving out.

Margaret saw him and smiled. "Go," she told Ellie. "Gobble up as many petits fours as you can—let's enjoy the party! I will see you soon for lunch."

Later, when the punch was just pink swirls at the bottom of a glass bowl large enough to wash a pig in, Carl and Ellie wandered off to stand in front of the snow leopard enclosure and watch Spot, the male, sit and bathe his long, long tail with his tongue and blink sleepily.

"I think Ms. Klein *knew* it was going to happen," Ellie

ventured. She was tired and maybe a little bit sick to her stomach, having taken Margaret's suggestion as a directive. Between her and Carl they must have gorged on two dozen tiny cakes. "She seemed unsurprised."

"Well—men coming back from the war need jobs."

But from his tone it was obvious he wasn't presenting it as a belief, merely an objective statement of the facts as he saw them.

"William Hodgson didn't have a job at the zoo *before* the war," she pointed out. "Why can't he just go back to whatever stupid job he *did* have?"

"Actually, during the war he was a pigeoneer, one of the last. Did you know that? It was his duty to take care of and train messenger pigeons sending secret strategic objectives in code back and forth to France. So he's not entirely, you know, ignorant of keeping animals and working with them."

"How do you know all this?" Ellie asked suspiciously. "Have *you* been communicating with the enemy?"

"No, it's all in the souvenir card they were giving out," he said a little sheepishly, handing her a pretty printed announcement of the evening's events, with an etching of Leroy and his moustache at the top, an introduction of William in the middle, and at the bottom a thank-you to all the women "who also served by standing and waiting."

Ellie took and read it; she knew Carl would paste it in

his own scrapbook, which was sort of a reverse of her adventure journal: memories and prizes and newspaper clippings about subjects he liked. The lovingly preserved past, instead of pages filled with ideas for the future.

"And what about the rest of them?" she demanded. "Men? Did they expect the world to stay the same when they came back? To have jobs and take hold of the world again now that they were done?"

"Those that *did* come back probably did," Carl said gently. *"Dulce et decorum est . . ."*

She nodded glumly, chastened but not convinced.

He walked her home, a long quiet stroll. As evening drew on, the sky turned rosy and orange over by the plant and remained streaky milk blue over everything else. People were engaged in all of the end-of-day, rolling-up-the-sidewalk routines of a snug little town: calling in the cats; putting out empty bottles for the milkmen, full garbage pails for the garbage men. Shopkeepers turned their "open" signs around and made sure their doors were locked. There were more young men than there had been a few years ago, fit back into places where Ellie hadn't even realized they were missing: sweeping up for a grocer, walking with girls, laughing with friends on a corner—one was on crutches, with a missing foot. An older woman, kerchief in her hair like Rosie the Riveter, sat on her stoop, keeping a wary eye on them. She could have been a mother or an old maid; it was hard to tell whether work, parenthood, or both had exhausted her.

"But what *about* the women?"

"They don't have to work anymore," Carl said, not really thinking.

"What if they *want* to work?" Ellie demanded. "Margaret always wanted to study and work with birds. She went to *college* for it! My cousin loves being a telephone operator. She likes having her own money—but she also likes having a place to go every day, and the other women who work there all go out together afterward just like men. I know old Greta loves the heirloom barnyard animals. She talks to them like her children; they've been a great comfort since she lost her son in Normandy. And Elspeth stays late every day making sure that everyone in the Mouse House is fed and healthy. For no extra pay!"

"But those women didn't have any expectation of having those jobs forever. It was only supposed to be temporary, a new thing for—"

"Horse-hooey, Carl. And what about *me*? What if they wanted to replace me with a sixteen-year-old boy? As part of this 'men taking back their jobs' or 'ruling the world into the future' nonsense? I took this internship *with the expectation* that it could lead to something else! A forever job at the zoo, if I wanted!"

Carl was quiet for a few moments, thinking. Their footsteps made different sounds in the dust, hers with a smaller heel, and more force.

"It's complicated," he finally said. "Everyone should be able to work if they want . . . and isn't that possible in America? Now? We have so many new and exciting things we're doing, there should be jobs for everyone. It's not like the Depression."

"Sure, Carl. But there aren't that many heads-of-zoos. Seems like the tendency is to give those rare jobs to men so they can go back to being the sole breadwinners. And we go back to being . . . homemakers or whatever."

"Ha, you as a homemaker," Carl said, guffawing before he caught Ellie's look.

"I *can* cook. If I want to," she said frostily.

"But you *don't want* to. And that's fine! And anyone who really knows you knows that. I mean, anyone who *really* knows you . . . anyone you're *with*, I mean . . ."

Ellie was about to impatiently demand what he meant but suddenly found her face flushing—just like his. She forced herself to notice the cracks in the road. One looked like the Orinoco river, dangling like a long earlobe.

"Anyone you chose to *be* with, you know, would know that and respect that."

She looked up at him. He held her look for a

moment—just a moment!—and then also found something interesting on the road to admire.

"Well, thanks for inviting me. It was a lot of fun," he finally said when they got to her porch, adjusting his glasses. "A party at a *zoo.* Even if things got a little . . . off."

"Yeah. It was. Thanks for coming, Carl."

Ellie wondered if something would happen. The air, she was pretty sure, was charged. This was the part in movies where *absolutely nothing* might be happening between a guy and a girl friend, but an overzealous dad came out on the porch anyway, sometimes with a shotgun.

But when the door opened it was her mother. And all she had was an empty bottle to set out for the milkman.

"Oh, hello, Carl. Ellie." Mrs. McGill didn't say anything even *slightly* untruthful, like "Didn't realize you were back already" or "Oh my, didn't hear you out here." As a devout churchgoer, her devotion to the Word was strict and literal, and as the mother of eight, the need to explain herself was nonexistent.

The bottle down, she waited patiently.

"All right, well, g'night, Carl," Ellie said, sighing.

"Good night, Ellie, Mrs. McGill," Carl said, touching a hat he wasn't wearing. He strolled off into the night, whistling, and Ellie grudgingly followed her mother inside.

The twins were in the middle of tying Sean up with

what looked like an old pair of suspenders. Reggie was reading one of his books for night school in the corner. Darlene was petting the cat. Mr. McGill was sitting by the radio with his ear practically up against the speaker, trying hard to listen while his offspring raged around him.

"How was the party, Ellie?" he asked dutifully upon seeing his daughter.

"Swell, Dad," she answered dutifully back.

She slipped into the bedroom she shared and sat down hard on her bed, easing out of the shoes that were already a little too small for her still-growing feet.

She lay back and looked fondly at the things tacked up next to her bed: a photo of the tabletop mountains in Venezuela, a cheap etching of the Alps, and a postcard she'd found delivered dead letter with a jungle print on the front. When she was younger she just took the pictures she liked and stuck them to the wall willy-nilly to fuel her dreams. Getting to these places they depicted was as easy as imagination, like going to Oz or Wonderland. *Carl would take them in his balloon someday.* She smiled at the memory.

She was sixteen now. Not an unheard-of age to be married, out in the country. To be *a homemaker*. She hadn't really thought about going to college or a vocational school. There was no money for it anyway, and the war had thrown even normal things into chaos, made it seem like life would be unconventional, unpredictable, and a little different from here on out.

What did one actually do these days to become an explorer?

Charles Muntz was intelligent, adventurous, fearless . . . and born wealthy. And born a man. Some lucky women, like Amelia Earhart, had mothers who encouraged them to shoot rifles and wear boys' clothing and get educated *like* a man.

Some women, like Margaret, could have their whole unusual career destabilized by outside, completely conventional forces. And she wasn't even married, with babies to take care of.

It wasn't long before Ellie's younger siblings found their big sister and picked at her dress and wanted to know if she'd brought any cakes home. As she indulged them Ellie caught a quick glimpse of her mother. Momentarily freed from her children and done with nighttime chores, she was taking a quick moment to herself, looking at a magazine. Still standing up, as if she didn't dare tempt fate by actually sitting down for a few minutes. She didn't look unhappy—just tired and lost in what was probably an ad for laundry soap with one of her favorite radio stars, or maybe an article on some aspect of home economics.

Ellie had never asked her mother what her dreams were;

she had never thought to. Mrs. McGill was a *mother* and seemed content with that. Had she always just wanted to be married, with children?

Long after Ellie begged off from her siblings' attention with pleas of exhaustion these thoughts continued to circle her head slowly, like koi at the Japanese Dream Pools in the zoo, striking their tails lazily against the walls of their tiny pond.

TWO

Saturday night the Bloomington USO had a social for soldiers called home but not quite *home* yet. Some of those who weren't lived farther off into the deep country; some of them were caught in a holding pattern of getting medical exams, trying to secure their benefits, and figuring out what to do next. As a registered USO junior hostess, Ellie was expected to facilitate at the event. She wore her *other* nice dress to the party, one that was a little more dowdy and old-fashioned than the one she had worn to the zoo: it had ruffles at the shoulders, roses all over, and a long skirt that did little for her figure. Which was absolutely appropriate and positively fine with her; hostesses were there to make the soldiers feel comfortable and merry . . . and that was it. There were strict rules to keep anything beyond that from happening. Dating servicemen was forbidden. If you had a phone, giving them your number was forbidden. Leaving a social without a chaperone or *alone in a private car* was also forbidden. In fact, the official government booklet outlining these rules was the only thing that convinced Mr. and Mrs. McGill that junior hostess-ing was suitable for a teenaged girl at all, much less their Ellie.

Carl was also supportive of America's men in uniform with all his patriotic heart, his piggy bank, and his own volunteering, which was probably why despite there being a dance involved he agreed to come almost before Ellie finished inviting him (though he couldn't chaperone her home, not being over twenty-one).

He planted himself near Ellie but not *too* close, always offering to bring out more chairs or carry heavy boxes if the other hostesses needed it. Ellie manned the door to greet the soldiers coming in. The first vet to arrive had his arm in a sling and thick, oiled-back black hair.

"Buy you a Coke?" Ellie said brightly. This was her standard opening line.

The young man looked her up and down and grinned. "Sure, why not? You remind me of my kid sister, and that girl *owes* me."

(The Cokes, and almost everything else at the USO party, were free for veterans and the volunteers. Ellie tried not to take advantage of this, but it was hard when your family could only afford a treat like that once a week or so.)

She played table tennis against any challenger—or Carl if there wasn't one—and often with such fury that the men laughed and rubbed their wrists theatrically afterward. She served popcorn and peanuts and tried to make pleasant conversation, but not everyone wanted to talk about cleaning up puffin excrement or how the cutest baby snakes had just hatched at the zoo (Carl always listened attentively). She even helped some men write letters—those who had problems spelling, or didn't know the zip code, or were unsure what one should say to a long-distance sweetheart. Sometimes she just sat next to the quiet ones who stared out the windows or into space, seeing bullets and hearing bombs instead of dancing couples and swing music.

"We should bring in animals," she suggested to Mabel, one of the senior hostesses. "They have 'animal ambassadors' at the zoo, like a giant Dutch bunny that everyone loves to pet, even grumpy old men. Maybe we could do the same with puppies? Everyone loves puppies. It might help some of the soldiers who don't talk, don't you think?"

Philomena, another hostess, laughed—but not unkindly. "Ellie and the puppies. That's what the boys come here for." She gave Carl a wink, which Ellie had no idea how to interpret.

"It's not a bad idea, though," Mabel said thoughtfully. "Might relax them, having something they can pet—shut it, girls."

Ellie watched the hostesses cover their mouths, overcome with mirth. They weren't *that* much older than Ellie. But despite the now hundreds of hours she had probably spent with them, they weren't "her" girlfriends—like the ones at school weren't, like the tomboys on the old stickball team weren't. She wondered if she would ever have a gal pal she could share a sly joke or her secret dreams with.

They were all expected to take a turn on the dance floor with the men, though mostly the soldiers didn't ask Ellie. When they did, only once in a while did they press a little too close or look her too intently in the eye. Sometimes she felt something wobble in her chest when one smiled a certain way, or his hand clasped her on the waist . . . and she wondered what it would be like if it were someone else whose arms she was in. Someone she actually cared about.

Carl tried very hard not to watch while she was dancing with these men. She wished he would say something.

Maybe *she* would have to.

"Say, Carl, why don't you and me go for a spin?" she asked brightly. "Show 'em how it's done."

"Oh, I'm just having a conversation with this fellow here," he said politely, pointing to the older man next to him. "He worked the radio during Operation Dragoon in France. . . ."

She made a comic face at the soldier. "Carl *hates* dancing."

"What's the matter with you?" The man whacked Carl on the shoulder avuncularly. "I'm boring, I ain't got nothing interesting to say to a kid. Go take this girl for her dance!"

Carl set his Coke down and put out his arm like a gentleman; she took it proudly. She hoped, sneaking a quick look around, no one would start a fight over this. Really, she was here for the soldiers. But no one gave them so much as a look, or at least a second look, and soon they were spinning around the floor. Carl was graceful enough to not be embarrassing—thanks to Mrs. Sutton's Etiquette School for Young Men—but he didn't look her in the eyes the way movie stars did on the big screen, not even with humor like Ginger Rogers and Fred Astaire. The one time she caught him looking at her he immediately began talking.

"Has this been an all right USO social for you?"

"Carl, what a weird thing to say. It's been fine." She shook her head and laughed. He smiled, also realizing how ridiculous he sounded.

Their dancing was far more relaxed after that—but it

wasn't satisfying, somehow. And that was the only dance he gave her that night.

By eleven p.m. Ellie had feet that burned from playing table tennis and then dancing in pumps, and even *her* seemingly limitless supply of energy was exhausted. Her dad—despite having worked a full day at the plant, and despite his limp—showed up like he always did at exactly 11:15. He gave Carl a friendly handshake and good night but did not ask if he had "taken care of his girl."

During the walk home, the usually chatty Ellie was silent for a while, thinking about things. But when Mr. McGill asked her about the evening a burst of energy showered over her like a spring rain and she told him everything, from the soldier with the tattoo of a bulldog on his shoulder to how Mabel announced that she was leaving at the end of summer to work in the big city at a bank to how stupid Carl was for not wanting to dance more.

"Ellie," her father said after a long and thoughtful pause, "boys just don't . . . *like* dancing as much as girls.

"Even if . . . he *likes* the girl," he added after another long and thoughtful pause, and a sideways glance at his daughter.

"That's dumb," she declared, deciding to only think about the first thing he said. "Dancing is almost as fun as an obstacle course race. More, because you're sharing it *with* someone instead of just trying to beat him."

Mr. McGill laughed at this but stayed quiet for the rest of the walk, enjoying the special time alone with his daughter.

Despite the late night, Ellie showed up at the zoo the next morning extra early in her work coveralls, hair in a bun under a kerchief. Normally she would just report to the sea lion enclosure and wait around with them; the sea lions for their morning fish, Ellie to be given her morning duties, both of which were handed out by the same woman, who—at least during the war—had been in charge of animals in the "danger line," ones considered potentially harmful to visitors. Apparently interns were included in that.

But Ellie decided to go into the main office first and ask the question that had been bothering her. She practiced it in her head: "In light of the announcements at Mr. Reardon's party I just want to make sure there were no further personnel changes that affect *my* position as well." That sounded professional, didn't it?

The guards and zookeepers sleepily touched their hats when she arrived at the grand little brick building. Inside it was mostly an open space jammed with desks, books about animals, photographs of animals, and many, *many* little animal statues in porcelain and bronze. She was not surprised to see William there now, hunched forward in his chair, hidden behind a newspaper; she was, however, completely taken aback by the giant wolf guarding his desk.

It leapt up immediately and lunged at her.

Ellie screamed as the yellow-eyed monster knocked her down and slapped her to the floor, planting its massive paws firmly on her chest. Its mouth cracked apart like it could take her whole head in one gulp. Her vision was filled with ivory fangs, wet with slaver, a gaping maw opening wider and wider . . . and dripping more and more slaver . . . and . . .

Yuck . . .

The wolf wasn't actually tearing her face off.

It was panting and drooling on her . . . and then licking her all over.

That was when Ellie remembered that she hadn't done a perfect job of washing up after breakfast that morning; the only water available was a freezing pitcher her mom kept for emergencies when the bathroom was occupied—which it always was.

The Siberian wolf of the steppes was now helping himself to what egg literally remained on her face, licking her clean with the efficiency of a mama cat.

"Oh, get off her, Sasha." William got up, throwing his newspaper down. "Come on, boy! Rude!"

With a little bit of a whine the wolf stepped back—but

only a little, and he did so expectantly, eyes and ears all aimed at Ellie.

She cautiously picked herself up, not letting him out of her sight for even a blink.

"I don't have anything else," she said. The wolf stared back, also unblinkingly.

She cautiously reached out her hand and was immediately rewarded: he pushed his shaggy head into it, guiding her fingertips to where she could best scratch his itches.

"Sorry about that. Sasha expects everyone to have a treat for him. Spoiled old thing," William said affectionately.

Ellie gave the wolf a good scratch around his thick mane-like neck fur and under his chin, the way she would a cat, wondering at the multicolored pelt and the terrifying eyes.

"*This* is the Russian wolf, from the snowy steppes?"

"Well, he was from the steppes *once*—or maybe his grandparents were," William said politicly. "In truth, Leroy bought him from a tsirk, a Russian traveling circus. No need to be afraid of him at all. He's as friendly as a pup and can balance plates on his nose like a seal. They also trained him to act all growly and fierce like a real wolf."

Sasha whipped his head around at that, his doggy eyebrows frowning as if he could understand.

"Oh no boy, you *are* a real wolf, yes you are," William

said, grabbing him in a hug and nuzzling his face into his fur. "You're the *best* wolf, I mean it. Don't ever call him a *D—O—G*." He lowered his voice for the last bit. "He's very sensitive. We got to know each other very well back at the alpine haus, didn't we, laddie? Leroy treats the two of us so well, doesn't he?"

Ellie watched them thoughtfully. She had been prepared to hate William for kicking out Margaret. But the way he was interacting with Sasha . . . he really did love animals, or at least this one. And there was something strangely akin about the two: each had been picked up by Leroy and dropped someplace both were a little uncomfortable being, to make for a good brochure.

Maybe he wasn't the man to ask about potential changes to the internship position. Not yet.

"I came to see if Ms. Klein was in," Ellie said, trying on her most grown-up voice, the one she used to speak to disapproving matrons at USO dances.

It must have worked; William looked over at her with new interest.

"No, not yet. I'm told that she used to be first in, last out, but, ah, maybe she's . . . enjoying a bit of a . . . break . . . from her old routine. You know?" He looked back at what was presumably his desk, once Margaret's, the largest one, now topped with piles of paperwork. Neat stacks, to be sure, but crushingly tall. "You don't happen to know about which vendor she—uh, the zoo—prefers to order Flamingo Feed™ from, do you? I saw from the logs that sometimes we used to use WildFoodsForYou, but Leroy wants some budget tightening to free up funds for other, um, programs, and CheepBirds—get it, 'cheap'?—is a little, well, cheaper, and . . ."

"I'm afraid I don't know, Mr. Hodgson," Ellie answered honestly. "Mr. Hua just has bags of the stuff that he pours into sealed coal bins to keep the bugs out. That's what I scoop their daily servings from. I don't know where it comes from."

"No, of course not," William said with a sigh.

"What was it like serving with Mr. Reardon overseas?" Ellie asked curiously. "Were you there when he caught the Nazi?"

"Caught? Nazi?" William looked confused.

"In the paper . . . the *Bloomington Eagle*. They published a photo of Mr. Reardon, holding his pistol against a man with his hands tied behind his back . . ."

"Ohhhh, right," he laughed. "Yeah. That wasn't a Nazi, that was a German pacifist who was escaping his own country. Five minutes after that photograph was taken we were having beers with him in the mess hall. I think we got him sent to Canada finally."

"Oh." Ellie thought about the article. It hadn't actually *said* that the person in question was an enemy, just that he was a German prisoner. Still . . . "But it must have been scary, doing border patrol in the Alps?"

William gave her a look she couldn't quite read, like he was gauging her, trying to decide what to reveal. "That post, it was my last one, and I was sent there because I was wounded but still wanted to serve." He pointed at his left leg, which did show a faint wobble when he moved. "I probably shouldn't be saying this, but it was a cakewalk—the place was a Nordic skiing center in peacetime. In the war, it was quiet and snowy and you could still get fondue."

"It was your last post?" Ellie asked, working through his specific words and sifting through them for meaning. "Was it also Leroy's *last post*?"

"It was his only post. Leroy's family wanted to keep him safe—like any parents would. They got him assigned there."

"So he was never at the front?"

But her question would remain forever unanswered.

Margaret burst through the door like a gust of fresh air and bright sunlight, her navy skirt and jacket impossibly crisp, the act of sweeping off her jacket while still holding a sizable briefcase a tour de force of efficiency and glamour.

"Good morning, everyone, good morning, Mr. Hodgson. Sasha," she added, putting out a gloved hand for the wolf.

He happily pushed his nose into it and closed his eyes. She scratched him by the ears. "Oh, and Miss McGill. What a pleasant surprise so early."

"Yes, we were just talking about you, you came in the nick of time," William said eagerly, spinning around to find the paper he had been looking at. "I have a great many questions for you, Miss Klein, and that big brain of yours . . ."

"Oooh, I would love to help," Margaret said, sounding regretful and pleasant, her elegant black eyebrows arching up while her pursed lips curved down in a moue, "I really would, but with the pay cut I've taken I really can't afford to actually start until nine on the dot, you know, but I would be more than happy to help you then. Just need to freshen up a bit first before I start the day. Maybe collect a few fallen bird feathers to sell for hats, you know. The sparkly ones. A clever girl can make a pretty penny that way."

"Uh . . . of course . . . it's just that . . . Leroy is coming in at nine, and, uh . . ."

"Oh, we'll have to make it later then. Can't wait!" She gave him a wink that was somehow friendly but unsexy, like a pal who "got" it. She pulled her gloves off and threw them at her own desk, now a tiny, schoolhouse-sized thing that had a third of its surface taken up by an ugly lamp in the shape of an elephant; somehow when the gloves hit the trunk of the lamp and stayed there with a satisfying *whap* they looked more like a pair of boxer's mitts.

"Walk with me, darling?" she ordered Ellie, striding out of the room again.

Ellie ran after her, almost stumbling over her feet as she double-timed it.

But Margaret didn't head toward the private employees' ladies' room, nor the larger public one. She headed straight to the aviary . . . was she really going to pick up feathers and sell them for money?

But the ex–Head Keeper rapped smartly on the semi-hidden employees-only door; it popped open for her like a cave in a fairy tale. By the time Ellie had followed her, blinking, into the sudden darkness, the other woman already had on a different pair of gloves, as well as a pair of jeweler's glasses with specialized lenses clipped to the ends.

"All right, let me see it."

Helen, also wearing gloves, carefully reached into a tank that was empty of water but full of clean shavings. She handed Margaret a tiny, ugly monster: a bug-eyed, featherless baby bird with an unsteady neck and a mouth that opened randomly, hoping food would somehow find its way in. Margaret carefully took the thing, propped its head up, checked its neck, then pulled out one of its sad little bony wings and gently let it snap back. "Definitely putting on some weight—has it been taking the mealworm soup?"

"Every fifteen minutes. All blessed night," the other woman said with a rueful smile.

"Great. Let's add a bit of blood meal, for the iron, and maybe try a little mouse pâté."

"You got it, boss."

"*Not* your boss. Not anymore," Margaret said, carefully putting the bird back into the tank, in a fake nest made of what looked like sweater lint and old socks.

Helen grunted unpleasantly and waddled off into the shadows, which smelled of bird and grain.

Margaret took off her gloves and glasses and rested for a moment against the lab table.

"*That's* the sage grouse," she eventually explained. "Mom abandoned the nest—it's the only one to survive this clutch. No idea what in the enclosure might have scared her off—maybe she's just a bad mom. They're declining in the West, you know. Migrations along the Mississippi Flyway have become more and more hazardous, and they're letting cattle and corn take over all of the natural prairies."

Ellie tried to listen to what the other woman was saying—she really did. The prairie wasn't super interesting, not being jungles or volcanoes or oceans—though it *could* be conflated with "desert," which was, at least, a little interesting.

Most of her mind was engaged with working out what she was witnessing right now, before her.

"You sneak into work early, to . . . work?"

Margaret blinked, pulled out of her thoughts about conservation and birds. She gave Ellie a wry smile.

"Yes. I do. Speaking of, it's time for me to go and *officially* clock in now. As office manager. Those phones aren't going to answer themselves!"

"But . . ."

"We have a lunch scheduled for today, don't we? We can talk about it then."

"Yes, I was going to ask—there's no eating or drinking allowed in the aviary . . ."

"After ten years at this place, I think I've earned special dispensation. Besides, it's quiet and no one will bother us. William *does* love his birds . . . but he spends his lunch feeding our very own wild, invasive rock doves on a bench in the park nearby."

"Rock doves?" Ellie asked. She knew ring-necked doves and collared doves and even turtledoves from nursery rhymes, but not rock doves.

"Pigeons," Margaret said with a laugh.

***

For lunch Ellie had packed herself an apple, a roll, a slice of liverwurst, and a thermos of milk. She arrived early to make sure there was a free bench and that it was free of bird droppings. She kept re-wiping the seat nervously with her kerchief, reminding herself to remember to not put it back in her hair. Maybe Margaret was only having lunch with her to be kind, or maybe it was because she was now just a glorified secretary with extra time on her hands. Whatever the case, Ellie wanted to make the best impression possible.

The ex–Head Keeper showed up precisely at twelve thirty; the little zoo clock with the monkey banging the bell chimed the half hour as she approached.

"Hello, Miss McGill! May I sit?"

"Yes, of course, Ms. Klein. It's your bench, I mean . . ."

The other woman laughed and sat down. She had a little lunch sack as well, but it was leather with her monogram imprinted in gold. She pulled out a little glass jar that said "Dannon," a fancy European yogurt that had a generous dollop of strawberry jam at the bottom. She must have misinterpreted Ellie's impressed stares as she began to swirl it around with a tiny silver spoon.

"Mom's idea. My stomach's been a mess since the . . . reorganization," she said, so matter-of-factly that Ellie was taken aback. How could someone so . . . chic . . . be so down-to-earth? "Oh, look, there's the Australian duck. I hope he doesn't want a treat, he won't like yogurt."

"The reorganization . . . that's just the way it is now? It's all . . . permanent?" Ellie ventured, curiosity—as always—getting the better of reticence and politeness.

"Well, Leroy's family basically owns the zoo, so what Leroy says, goes. So yes. William is now the permanent head of the zoo, while I was only interim. But technically I am now office manager rather than assistant to the head of the zoo, which I was before the war, when it was old Grimshaw in charge. Poor old boy. He was a delight and had pretty much assured me the position would be mine when he retired."

"What happened to him? Did he retire?"

"Not exactly," Margaret said tonelessly. "He was British. Despite his age, when the war started he went back home and volunteered for yeomanry . . . then went off to France . . .

"According to his beliefs, he is now in Heaven, meeting all the extinct animals he wished he could have saved in his lifetime."

"Oh," Ellie said, taken aback. She thought about everything she had just been told but couldn't come up with anything positive. "None . . . *none* of this seems fair."

"No, it's not," Margaret agreed. "*But.*" She put her

spoon down and looked hard at Ellie. "Nothing in life is fair. William has his job because of nepotism and is utterly unqualified for the position. He *is* trying his hardest to figure it all out, I'll give him that, but he's overwhelmed. If I didn't make sure the sage grouse was being attended to, or that the at-risk lizards in the reptile house were given their regular antifungals, well, it wouldn't get done. The animals would suffer. That wouldn't be fair for *them*, either. They didn't ask to be here. We have a responsibility to them for their very lives."

"That's true," Ellie said thoughtfully, looking at the little brown duck with the curved head that kept dipping down into the water, sticking its tail feathers way up into the air while trying to reach the deepest, tastiest bits at the bottom. She knew all about Australian wood ducks but not whether this one had been hatched in the zoo or hatched free.

"Also, only the unambitious watch the clock and work their assigned hours," Margaret added. "If you want to get anywhere in life—especially if you're a woman—you have to go above and beyond. Work twice as hard."

"But you have, and . . ."

"Oh, this is a temporary setback." Margaret waved her spoon around in the air. "Believe you me, I've already done a *thousand* things poor William never will. Do you know: I was on the expedition that brought back the great-great-great-grandfather of our friend here?" She pointed her spoon at the duck.

"From *Australia*?" Ellie breathed. "You *went* to Australia?"

"Mm-hm," Margaret said with undisguised satisfaction. "For my graduate thesis I was studying the incubating periods of different members of the Anatidae family. And let me be completely honest with you: the reason there was money for a *girl* in the grant is because A, the person who was in charge of it died and left the committee in chaos, and B, I sign all my professional papers M. R. Klein. Not only does everyone just go ahead and assume that anyone in academia is a boy, but if you're reading quickly it looks like 'Mister Klein.' My middle name is Ruth."

"Oh, I never would have thought of . . . any of that," Ellie said, amazed.

"You had better start thinking," the other woman said sharply. "Lest you end up like me and my generation, or worse. But back to the wood ducks. Aren't they sweet? The only members of their genus, by the way—*Chenonetta*, not *Anas*. They're a little like our wood ducks; they nest in hollows near water, tree cavities and the like. Oh, it was awkward but marvelous, wading around those stinking marshes. And the ponds further in . . . I shan't lie; I was truly hoping to see a platypus in the water."

"And did you?"

"Sadly, no—although I saw a water ripple and trail of bubbles and decided that it was one swimming below the surface. No real proof, of course, but it's all I had."

All she had . . . ripples on the surface of the water, no actual evidence or sighting of the impossible animal underneath. A PhD and travels all around the world, and all she had were memories, what was basically a secretarial position, and lunch with a sixteen-year-old intern. Margaret didn't seem as angry as Ellie would have imagined considering her recent demotion, but . . . wait. Demotion. What had she said before to William? Something about a pay cut?

"Did they . . . can I ask . . . did they reduce your salary?"

"They sure did. And may I add, it wasn't even close to the level of actual Head Keeper to begin with. As interim head they gave me fifty percent of my predecessor, because 'my needs were less.' A man needs more because he has to support a family, you know. I need less because I am either an old maid who needs nothing but toast and fish for her cat, or I am a girl soon to marry a man, quit my job, and have him support me. From each according to his ability, to each according to her needs. I rather thought we differed from our Russian friends in that way.

"And anyway, who is in the lofty position of getting to decide what each person's needs are? *I* feel I need a day at the Russian bath house, speaking of Russians. Maybe Comrade Leroy will grant me one."

Ellie's head spun with all of the different names and ideas Margaret chatted on about. The only people who spoke to her like this at all were librarians and teachers, and it was never as equals, sharing lunch on a bench.

Besides, this was all very nice . . . but it still left the question Ellie had to ask.

"Are you going to be all right?"

"Oh yes, I'm sorry, I'll be just fine, dear." Margaret patted her hand. "Except for all my scientific journal subscriptions and my taste in clothes I am quite frugal in my spending habits. I always pack a lunch. And I have savings. I shan't complain about my own funds after what everyone has been through for the past twenty years."

They paused to watch a purple gallinule making its way in the water; a cartoon bird like from the movies with its bright yellow legs and *huge* feet evolved for walking on vegetation growing on the top of water. The birds didn't seem real until you looked one in the eye—which was red, very serious—and saw the avian intelligence in there; feral, hungry, contemplating danger. A real being despite its ridiculous appearance.

"These fellows are quite the fliers, you know, despite their body shape. They're happiest in the tropics, of course, but have been found as far away as Iceland, if you can believe that! Scientists often find vagrant gallinules all over the world . . . traveling to find a better place to live . . . 'Adventure is out there,' as they say."

"Wait—*you're* a fan of Charles Muntz?"

Margaret laughed. "Who isn't? I can tell you Leroy certainly is. He's always talking about the man and his wonderful exploits. Nor do you have to be a *fan* of him to have seen his newsreels or advertisements for his books, or heard his radio show. I know you always admired him. I remember when you used to come into the zoo with your goggles and helmet tucked under your arm."

"You noticed that?"

You noticed me?

"Absolutely. You stand out, Ellie McGill. And us girls who stand out have to stick together."

THREE

From Ellie's perspective, there wasn't much change to work except for having to deal with "the new recruits"—as Margaret called the recently hired men—who were mostly all right if ignorant about their responsibilities. She had to explain multiple times that polar bears and penguins did *not* live together (because they lived on opposite sides of the world), and the difference between a carnivore and an herbivore. Which was important at feeding time . . . both for the animals, and also to not irritate Mr. Hua. She did her best to avoid Gus, who spent all his time avoiding work and played nasty pranks on the younger female employees.

But political and personal agita dissolved like vitamin powder in Gila Monster Mash™ amid the bigger zoo-wide excitement (which was possibly the plan): Leroy had begun to put together his first *collection expedition*. The office buzzed like an early summer hive as lists were made, orders given, and supplies received. Crate after crate came through the building, each containing something more magical and romantic than the last—magical, at least, for someone who dreamed of adventuring. Mosquito nets, camp beds, canteens, tents, spirit stoves and fuel . . . and of course food, which included provisions like fancy tinned fish and meats that the veterans examined with wonder: it was nothing like what they had received in their mess kits overseas.

"Aw, doncha even get a B-Ration with them? You know, bread or cookies or something to go with the meat?" a soldier joked while Ellie waited in the office for Margaret and one of her "lunchtime lectures."

"We have tins of cream crackers, don't you worry, and preserved rum cake," Leroy reassured him.

Ellie thought about the sugar rations her own family was still forced to use. With eight kids it was impossible to have a separate cake for each birthday during the war, so Mrs. McGill made one for each month with birthdays. Of course Leroy was rich, and the rich could always get whatever they wanted whatever the circumstances—wartime, depression, scarcity, or hoarding. . . .

For the first time in her life, Ellie seriously considered something she would normally never, ever do.

Would Leroy even miss a single pilfered tinned rum cake?

To be clear: She didn't want a tinned rum cake. And even if she did, she would never *actually* take one; she had been raised better than that.

But the question remained: Would he even miss it?

She looked away from the crate, feeling guilty for even having such thoughts, and accidentally caught the eye of the soldier. He shook his head disgustedly. Not at *her*—at the cake, at the world they lived in. It was the first time she felt a kinship with one of the new recruits. Strange to share a feeling with someone who had been overseas, trained with a gun, lived in barracks, and experienced combat—someone who'd had a thousand different life experiences she hadn't yet and maybe (hopefully?) never would . . . Yet the two of them still had an invisible thread that connected them together against the world: poverty. Ellie turned this idea over in her head for a while, wondering what it meant while she cleaned the chinchillas' cage in the Mouse House.

But in the end there were more exciting and immediate things to ponder than the connectedness of humanity. Where was the expedition going, for instance, and *who* all was going on it?

The answer to both came the next Saturday, when Ellie was hoping to take off a little early to go on her own,

Ellie-sized adventure with Carl. He had no objections to showing up at the zoo and waiting until she was free. At one time Ellie thought this was because he loved the place and the animals as much as she did. After the fourth time she had to point out the difference between a golden-crowned warbler—from Mexico—and warbling vireo—from the woods nearby!—she began to suspect that maybe it wasn't the birds he was there for.

It was probably the sea lions.

You would *think* Carl would like the aviary and its birds; he loved everything else about things that flew through the air, like she did (when the zoo stopped selling balloons because of tank and rubber shortages Carl was heartbroken).

Strange.

Anyway, it wound up being extremely lucky for Carl that he did come early. While he waited (by the sea lions), Ellie went to the administrative offices, debating exactly how to ask William for the time off without sounding like a typical lazy teenager on a beautiful summer afternoon (she wasn't, but it definitely was). But before she could finish her request the Head Keeper suddenly looked up at the ceiling, distracted by the loud buzzing of an airplane flying overhead.

"Yes fine whatever all right," he said, leaping out of his chair and pushing past her.

Ellie followed, curious, wondering whether she should

feel insulted that her work wasn't considered important enough that requesting an afternoon off got no argument—or even thought, it seemed like. To her surprise William went out the *back* door, the one that led to the elephant enclosure. Carl came trotting around the side of the building, also aware something was up.

The small plane wasn't flying past; it was circling overhead, lowering itself in lazy, menacing spirals down to the zoo.

The elephants were not happy about this. The matriarch, Mrs. Jumbo, trumpeted a challenge, shepherding her baby and the juvenile Fanny as far into the corner of the paddock as they could go. The plane dipped a wing and banked hard in response, almost as if that was what it wanted them to do—like it was a harrier, one of those giant birds that slowly flaps its wings over a meadow or marsh, flushing out prey.

"Look at that," Carl breathed. His eyes were wide and unblinking, and he was in danger of letting his mouth hang open. "It's a P-51 Mustang."

"I can see that, Carl. You can tell by the sound of the engine and the square wingtips. Very nifty, but it's scaring the elephants. Mr. Hodgson, can we do something about this?"

But once again the Head Keeper paid her no mind.

Leroy had come striding up, gleeful and expectant, commanding his attention.

The plane was obviously aiming to land *inside the elephant fence*. From an aerial perspective it made sense: the enclosure was the longest, flattest area near the zoo that wasn't an actual road.

From an animal safety perspective it was madness.

"And the drop tanks for long-range recon are made out of *papier-mâché*, would you believe it," Carl continued blithely.

But Ellie had rushed over to the elephants.

"Mrs. Jumbo, there there," she murmured, trying to calm them. "It's okay. It will be all quiet in a moment. It's almost over." The large matriarch snaked her trunk out and ran it up and down Ellie's arm, looking for comfort.

In a final burst of noise and a horrific cloud of dust the plane was on the ground, taxiing to a halt. Drawn by the sound, a crowd of zoo workers now peeped around the administrative building. But not the actual elephant keeper, who was now a man named Charles.

Mrs. Jumbo trumpeted her anger at the plane—and maybe the world around her.

"Gosh," Carl said, finally noticing. "The elephants are really upset, aren't they?"

The canopy of the plane popped back and the pilot leapt out. It was a woman! A short one. All sorts of crazy thoughts went through Ellie's head, and by the look Carl was giving her, it was obvious he was thinking the same thing: *Amelia Earhart*, back from being missing all these years!

Leroy had run over to give her his hand as she jumped to the ground. She obviously didn't need it, but the grace of the move made them look like dancers. She pulled off her cap and goggles and Ellie was surprised again: she had a short-cropped bob, sharp bangs, and black eyes. The ease with which she tucked her helmet under her arm, the way she slouched on one leg, impressed Ellie so much she could barely stand it.

"William, I'd like you to meet my good friend, Lucy Dinh," Leroy said. Lucy stuck her hand out like a man and, to his credit, William shook it with minimal hesitation.

"Here she is, Leroy," Lucy said, patting the side of the plane like it was the flank of a pony. "Checked her out myself. Flies beautifully. Never used beyond a test flight—not even a scuff to the leather inside. Your ride has arrived in pristine condition."

Leroy actually rubbed his hands together.

"I cannot *wait* to take her up! Oh, she's going to take me there in *style*! Are the others ready as well?"

"All three of them! Even managed to get that TP-51C model, the one converted with the passenger seat in the back, for Chester and Diana."

As if that wasn't excitement enough, a car came purring up the service road. It stopped richly and noiselessly, as if its tires had the same soft relationship with the pavement as the gloved hand touching its leather-covered steering wheel. A short, pale man got out; he wore a slightly old-fashioned, almost costume-like linen jacket and straw boater. From the back seat came a tall, handsome Black man in a long raccoon coat, smiling like he had made this perfect day all by himself. Leroy gestured impatiently to William; the soldier nearly saluted, then ran around to open the passenger door. A flawlessly beautiful woman with chestnut hair and tanned skin and perfect makeup and many diamonds walked carefully on needle-sharp heels over the uneven ground.

"Diana, my darling." Leroy "took" her from William; he put his hand out and she daintily put her fingers on it, like a trained parakeet hopping from one person to the next.

"What is going on?" Ellie asked in wonder. It was like a circus, but of eccentric rich people. But Carl wasn't listening; he was gaping at them.

She smacked him in the ribs.

"What?" Carl yelped. "The Bentley Mark VI doesn't

come with a radio pre-installed . . . but look between the wipers! That's a tiny aerial antenna! Boy, imagine rolling down the street, listening to jazz on an AM station playing through those speakers. . . ."

Ellie thought about apologizing and explaining that she had thought he was looking at the woman, then decided not to.

Diana was wearing what looked like a *leopard fur* draped around her shoulders against the cold (what cold?) and had a matching purse. Her shoes were obviously crocodile. She was a walking taxidermy shop.

"William, these are my other good friends, Diana Von Schlegel, Dan Mattington, and Chester Gadfrey Fieldstone the Third."

"Call me Chet," the lanky man in the raccoon coat said generously. "Everybody does."

"No one does, Chester," the man called Dan said. He suddenly noticed the elephants with delight. "Say, Leroy, is this where you got me my elephant foot ashtray? Is one of them wearing a dummy leg?"

"No no, *I* bought that for you, Danny you dummy, in a little bazaar in the Maghreb," Diana said.

"These are *zoo* animals. They're like family," Leroy said with a laugh.

"'*Bought in a little bazaar in the Maghreb,*'" Ellie growled in a whisper. "What about the *elephant's* family? They're very social and mourn death just like people."

"Oh," Carl said in dismay.

"This is my team, William!" Leroy cried, throwing an arm around the two men's shoulders. Diana posed, pouting with kissy lips; Lucy just crossed her arms and scowled. "These are the people going on the expedition to South America with me!"

"Yes, sir," William said, trying to sound neutral. "A pleasure to meet you all."

"We're going to bring back a polar bear!" Chester promised. "Not this time, of course. No polar bears in Venezuela."

Ellie turned to Carl in shock.

Venezuela? he mouthed, also surprised.

"I'm sure you'll find something interesting. Boy, wish I could go with you," William said wistfully. "I'd be useful, too. I know all about bivouacking and survival. I had a stint in Japan—"

Leroy laughed heartily. "We need you *here*, making everything ready for my return! We'll need new cages and tanks! Or wait, you know what? A *whole new building*!"

"Say, Leroy, let's grab dinner at the Pheasant and Fusty tonight!" Chester said, clapping his hands. "It's a perfect place to celebrate our embarking on this fantabulous adventure! They don't segregate out folks like me—and they have that private dining room with all the animal heads on the wall. It's just like dining at a zoo."

"I'm in," Dan said, polishing his glasses.

"But that's way over in Billings!" Diana objected. "We'd have to drive all night just to get there."

"No, we can *fly*," Lucy said with a grin. "Now that Leroy has his own ride, I can take Diana in my Stinson, and the boys can go in the converted P-51 I sourced."

"Capital!" Chester declared.

"Say, though, isn't that an interesting idea," Leroy said. He put his hands up as if he were marking out a sign. "*Dining . . . at the Zoo!* We could bring in some sort of world-class French chef and serve all sorts of rare and exotic game. Linen and silverware outside the lion cage! What do you think of *that*, William my boy? That'll put us on the map! No other zoo does *that*."

"Well, uh, it does seem a little strange to be eating animals we might have on display . . . I mean, maybe alligator is all right . . . elk . . ."

Leroy cracked up. "*Elk?* I shot an elk over Christmas when we grew bored staying inside. Beautiful cow. Made a nice New Year's dinner. No, elk isn't strange or exotic."

William looked confused. "Elk season ends November 30th, in Oregon where my cousin lives, at least . . . and you shot a *cow*? Isn't that *always* illegal?"

"Wait, Mr. Reardon! Before you go to your fancy dinner . . ." Ellie called out, running over to him, Carl close behind. Leroy turned back and looked at her, with the sort of interest an entomologist might have for an ant that suddenly began talking to him in human speech. "Did you say you all were going to *Venezuela*?"

"Why, yes. It did slip out. Bit of a secret—keep it under your hat until the big farewell party. Don't want to leak it to the press!" Leroy said with a wink.

"Like, Caracas? The Andes? Mochima Bay? *Paradise Falls?!*"

"Why, you've hit it right on the nose, young lady. We're off to Paradise Falls itself, in fact. What a clever girl you are!"

"Oh, I've always wanted to go there all my life, Mr. Reardon!" Ellie gushed.

" 'All your life'? How old are you?" Diana asked dryly. "Fifteen?"

"I'll make sure we bring back a little something for such an enthusiastic zoo employee," Leroy promised with a smile that twisted his moustache askew and made Ellie's heart flutter a little. "*And* her . . . ah . . ."

"Carl." Carl introduced himself, putting his hand out.

"Hey, boss, we should head out," Lucy said, looking at her watch. "It's going to take at least an hour to get a safety check done on the planes even if we radio ahead."

"Right, right, let's go. I've heard their venison Wellington is to die for . . ." He turned, and the glittering group of five—and the Head Keeper—retreated loudly to their cars and plane (and office).

"Wow, Paradise Falls," Ellie said, eyes far away, seemingly having forgotten Leroy as well. "Gee. I would love to go with them."

"Sounds like William would as well," Carl noted archly. "And he seems better qualified for it than that Hollywood starlet type."

"I wonder what they'll bring back—I mean besides animals. Do you think he'll bring back a stone for me from the waterfall? Or maybe a pressed leaf or something?"

"I think you would be extremely lucky if any of those—ah, *busy*—people on their animal collecting expedition remember to grab you a souvenir, since they don't even know your name. But maybe a stone? Who knows. Hey, but can you go this afternoon? Did you ask?"

"Oh yeah, I think it's all right. Old Willy's got a lot keeping him busy right now. Let's grab our rides and get out of here!"

* * *

Carl's bike was a graceful three-speed, a sophisticated dark blue with gold racing stripes and decals he had carefully applied: a white star in a blue circle, his initials "CF" in grey letters next to it in imitation of the squadron codes used on B-17s.

Ellie's bike looked very different from when she and Carl had first remade it; over the years she had slapped on every purple-colored sticker and decal she found. A tiny pinwheel was mounted onto one of her handlebars like a propeller, and she had removed the playing cards from the spokes of her wheels that had made the satisfying *fwapfwapfwap* when she rode. She was no longer a child, and there were times when she wanted to ride silent and fast and not be distracted from her thoughts.

After Ellie carefully got out of her Bloomington Zoo–emblazoned coveralls and tucked them into her bag, the two took off into the late afternoon heat. The tires of their bikes split the dusty roads, kicking up a wake of low-hanging beige clouds that took time to settle. Pollen and related plant and tree bits floated leisurely through the mellowing sunlight, sparkling and making the journey seem even more magical.

(At exactly rider height, gnats unfortunately also floated through the air. Carl and Ellie didn't have fits when one went into an eye or into the nose, but it wasn't pleasant.)

When the road ended and became a country path, they parked and dismounted. Carl took out the compass while Ellie consulted the map they had found in the archives of the town hall. Everything looked about right, although the chestnut tree on the old chart was a good two feet from the stone wall, not as it was now, acting as the endcap for it. The whole place had grown wild since the neat fields of the mapmaker's day; scrub now filled the edges of the giant golden squares of land, and the insides had turned from wheat to meadow.

They had a slug of water each from Carl's canteen and then set off down the path. As Ellie kept an eye on the map (was that rise high enough to warrant a topographic line? Was that ditch once a stream?) she only vaguely noticed the plants she was stepping around and through: grasses, weeds, brambles . . . nothing where they lived was poisonous or itchy except for poison ivy, and nothing was at all deadly. They could tromp around for hours and suffer nothing more than a few mosquito bites and maybe a rash. She wondered about Margaret in Australia, where it was said that everything, even the *dirt* in some places, was poisonous. . . . Had she been nervous all the time? *Aware* all the time? Constantly engaged with her surroundings? What about looking at the map?

"I think this is it," Carl said, pointing to a gigantic

spreading oak tree. Its long limbs reached out to the four points of the compass and every direction in between like human arms inviting travelers in. The trunk must have been four feet across.

"Looks like! This big fellow's even labeled right here." Imagine a tree that was so ancient and eternal it had been used as a landmark by everyone, from native people to European mapmakers! "The boulder is supposed to be south-southwest about a hundred and twenty feet into the middle of the field—there's no other markers. We just have to find it."

Pulling her socks up and setting her jaw, Ellie marched into the hot meadow.

(Not that she specifically avoided long marches in the noonday sun; on the contrary, she was glad when she found herself on one. It was good practice for eventual slogging through jungles in faraway countries that didn't have fans or bottles of Coke kept in iceboxes.)

The giant boulder, the glacial erratic that was their goal and destination, wasn't exactly hard to find.

It was an absolutely enormous grey chunk of rock that stood by itself in the middle of the flat field, over five feet high and twice that across. A few small plants grew on top where stone had been degraded into soil by weather and lichen, but the rest of its surface was obstinately, outrageously bare in an otherwise verdant meadow. It was slanted like it had been pushed to the side by an impatient giant and had an overhang that would have nicely sheltered the two of them had there been rain.

"I'll bet that's where the petroglyphs are!" Carl said, pulling out his flashlight. It was a heavy, handsome thing that looked a little bit like the periscope of a submarine and was painted army green like a real army one. She kind of coveted it.

But its light shining into the niche revealed absolutely nothing.

Well, there *was* a carving that said "1862," which was mildly interesting, and a "Jessame ♥ Tabitha," which also sparked the imagination, but that was all.

"Could be worse," Ellie said thoughtfully. "At least there's no 'Kilroy was here.' No one's been to this rock in a long time."

"And it's still a glacial erratic," Carl said, trying to sound enthusiastic. "That's something. Think of it being left here by itself after all the ice of the glaciers pulled back, and staying here for thousands of years, all by its lonesome."

Ellie smiled. Carl could be whimsical when he tried.

"Well, time for a snack, anyway. I brought some filberts, uh, somewhere. . . ."

The beam from the flashlight bobbed and spun dizzily

as Carl began to dig around in his bag, forgetting it was still in his hand.

"Wait! Look!" Ellie grabbed his arm and directed the light up at the *underside* of the overhang.

There, now black as velvet against the illuminated surface, were deeply cut symbols that had been unnoticeable before.

"I'll be!" Carl said in amazement. "How was anyone ever supposed to see *that*?"

Ellie had an idea how. She plunked herself down and pulled Carl with her so they were both sitting. Then she lay back, head on the dirt, face pointed up to the stone above them. He followed suit a little reluctantly, but the soil under the rock was dry and mossy, and what little grass grew was harmless and clean. Their heads touched, legs pointing east and southeast, and they marveled at the ancient symbols.

They weren't of elk or people or hunting scenes or animals running in packs and herds; they looked like ranges of mountains in upside-down Vs, a hollow sun with bright rays, dots scattered everywhere in the background that could have been rain or snow or dirt or stars. There were circles with circles inside them and wavy lines and upright objects that looked like simple pine trees.

Carl swung the flashlight slowly back and forth over

them and it was almost like an old-fashioned movie, shadows lengthening and shortening and making the images appear animated.

"What do you think that is?" Ellie asked, pointing at a collection of two circles-in-circles. "You think it's the moon? Like a couple phases of the moon shown at once, at the same time?"

"Maybe," Carl said. "Maybe it's the seed or grain of some sort of plant that was important to them. And the circle inside is the germ, or it represents life."

"I wonder who they were," Ellie said. "I wonder what they were like."

"I wonder how old this is. I wonder why there hasn't been a book or something about it."

"We should come back and take a picture of it. Maybe you could borrow your dad's nice camera. We could send it into *Muntz's Monthly*! I'll bet they would print it. Two teenagers rediscovering ancient Native American art? That's news!"

"Gosh, that would be pretty great," Carl said. "Could you imagine our names in a magazine?"

"Too bad we don't know the real artist's name," Ellie said thoughtfully.

There were nuts to eat and a whole world outside to return to, but the symbols were mysterious and the ground fairly comfortable. Carl dug the end of the flashlight into the dirt so he wouldn't have to hold it. The meadow very subtly turned colors, yellows growing more orange, plant shadows getting blacker and bluer. The breeze picked up, bringing the sweet summer smell of milkweed flowers.

Ellie imagined people long ago also passing time under the rock, these images their radio, their entertainment, their news; having nothing more to enjoy than the coming of night and the calls of the birds and foxes.

She found herself drifting and turned to rest her head more comfortably against Carl's. His hair was so thick and shiny, and smelled clean like soap. If every adventure could end this way, no wonder people kept doing it, no matter what they actually found.

She tried to swat away some annoying (but gentle) pokes in her ribs.

"Ellie," Carl whispered. "The sun set. It's going to take us over an hour to get back."

Despite his not showing up on the porch the other night, shotgun in hand, Mr. McGill could be quite terrifying in matters where his oldest daughter was concerned . . . and though he wasn't home *that* night, all of Ellie's siblings were terrible tattlers.

So they hiked quickly back to their bikes and rode home

as the stars began to slowly show themselves in the sea-blue sky—the end of a perfect day.

When they got to the turn for her house, Ellie slowed down.

"Going to see me home?" she ventured casually. "Mom and Dad are at the school talking to the teachers about Little Johnny. Letty and Darlene are with them. Won't be *too* noisy or busy . . ."

"Aw, I can't," Carl said. "I have a date."

She felt herself go tight all over. Tight like a water balloon right before it explodes.

"A fellow from the Bloomington Amateur Radio Club is going to come over and check out my equipment, see if he can tinker with it to make it stronger. And he's going to show me some tricks and shorthand with Morse code. I can't wait to find out if he actually made contact with anyone recently despite the war ban!"

"Aha," Ellie said.

And then: "I see."

Surely . . . surely *she* was more of a draw than some old radio fuddy-duddy?

Carl must have read her mind.

"I *promised* him, Ellie. Explorer's Oath."

"Explorer's Oath," Ellie agreed glumly.

"Another time, I promise."

"You don't know how rare it is for both my parents to be out. . . ."

Carl looked at her appraisingly. But he didn't say anything. *Why would that be important? What are you implying? Gosh, I sure won't overbook next time!*

Oh, why did he never actually say anything?

He got on his bike and pedaled off.

"Adventure is out there!" he called over his shoulder.

FOUR

Apparently Leroy's return from the war to the zoo meant—besides the more severe changes—a lot more parties. This time it was a fabulous black-tie affair arranged in honor of the expedition to Venezuela. Reporters were invited to cover the crème de la crème of Bloomington society as they hobbed and nobbed with one another in their best gowns and suits; even the mayor came in a hat and tailcoat (with his granddaughter, who was eight, and far less interested in standing next to her penguin-looking grandpa than in pulling away to look at the real penguins. Ellie couldn't blame her at all). There was also a nonlocal crowd of *extremely* wealthy-looking types who all knew Leroy and his friends—scuttlebutt had that they helped fund the whole trip.

Everyone was glittering and dressed to the nines:

Chester wore a long jacket and waistcoat from the turn of the century, Dan and Leroy shone in tuxedos. Diana turned heads in a skintight red cheongsam.

"Does it bother you that I'm wearing this?" she asked Lucy while posing for a photo.

"Not a bit," Lucy said dryly. *She* wore silk pants, a man's white silk shirt, and four-inch heels. "Because you're an idiot. Also, and more importantly, I'm an American. I don't care what you wear. Also, my parents are Viet, not Chinese. Also, you're an idiot."

But she grinned and pressed her face close to Diana's when the reporter asked them to pose.

Ellie was tasked to walk around with a tray of champagne, which she did with as much aplomb as anything she did for the USO—and without complaining about the extra work (for no extra pay).

"Hey, where's that little man of yours?" Leroy asked when she came over to offer him drinks. William and Dan stood on either side of him; the Head Keeper slugged the contents of his crystal glass down in one nervous go. "Didn't you invite him?"

"I'm *working*, Mr. Reardon!" she said with a laugh.

"Well, I hope we're not paying you overtime."

"She's not being paid at all for this," William pointed out.

"Smart," Dan said. "That's the way to run a zoo."

"Well, *you're* going to run that boy right into the ground if you're not careful. Leading him on the way you do," Leroy drawled.

Ellie laughed, but nervously this time; her tray wobbled. "Oh, I don't think so, Mr. Reardon. . . ."

"Now, Leroy," William said. "I have never seen Miss McGill behave inappropriately around Carl . . . or any of the many teenage boys who come around to the zoo to make trouble. Why, she's a USO junior hostess! As respectable as they come."

"Believe you me," Leroy said, turning his head as if to begin a speech—but then he saw someone else he wanted to talk to and the rest of his body turned that way too.

"Thank you, Miss McGill," William said apologetically. "You're doing a perfectly swell job."

Ellie nodded politely—then rolled her eyes the moment she turned around. *Leading Carl on.* What a ridiculous idea. He hadn't even wanted to see her home last night.

"Hey, watch it," Diana said as Ellie smashed into her. The remaining drinks on her tray sloshed dangerously but didn't quite tip onto the beautiful red dress. "This is designer, you know."

"Sorry, I'm so sorry, I'm just . . ."

But Diana was already laughing at something someone else had said that she hadn't even heard. It didn't matter; the men who were standing there were charmed. They turned toward her like sunflowers following the sun—or anhingas or cormorants, more accurately, drying their wings in the sun's light. Was *she* leading *them* on? Ellie didn't think any of the men expected a kiss or a date or to go steady or anything. She bet if Leroy had said the same thing about Carl to Diana, the woman would have laughed or had a quick and deadly comeback. Even if Ellie had the nerve to say something (if she had actually thought of something to say) she wasn't really in a position to make a scene. He was her boss.

It wasn't until much, much later in the evening, when everyone was collecting their purses and prizes to go home, that Ellie had another thought. It didn't help, but it made her consider the whole conversation in a new light: How much was Leroy watching her that he actually *noticed* her, and remembered—if incorrectly—how she and Carl interacted?

A week after the last of the confetti and ribbons had been cleaned up, Leroy and his friends were gone, off in their planes, and it was back to work at the zoo as normal—almost. The storerooms were a mess, the administrative office looked like a hurricane had blown through it, and Leroy had left a giant to-do list written in black paint and hung on the wall, regarding the number and type of enclosures that should be prepared in advance of the exotic new species that they would find and bring home.

"But there's no corresponding list of *which* exotic new species they might take," Margaret pointed out to William. "When you go on an even halfway scientific expedition, you have to have a clear idea based on previous findings of what you might see there, what can be reasonably studied *in situ*, and what needs to be brought back to the States. Leroy and his friends are just going in to grab a bunch of random animals out of the wild with no forethought at all. How do we prepare for that?"

"Birds can go in the aviary," William hazarded. "Quarantined in the clinic first, of course. We'll have a new tank in reptiles, which could also work for new bugs—"

"—invertebrates—"

"—if he gets big ones . . ."

South American invertebrates? Ellie imagined giant centipedes, giant cockroaches, and giant leeches that lived in trees and dropped like sticky vampires onto people passing by below.

(Strangely, perhaps, she did not imagine beautiful, iridescent butterflies or furry moths with frightening designs on their wings. But of course they were, objectively, far less interesting than land leeches.)

"Miss McGill, get that mop and clean up the puddle of soda in front of the snow leopards!" William snapped when he saw her eavesdropping and dreaming about what Leroy would bring back.

"Yes, sir!" she yelped, running out.

Despite these moments, things were a little more relaxed without the big boss around. Some of the new hires loosened up maybe *too* much—which was irritating, but it also made work easier. Old zoo employees, those who knew what they were doing, could get on with the important things without being bothered. Margaret still "assisted" William, but it was more that he consulted *her* on business and paperwork. Ellie also saw her giving the permanent Head Keeper a carefully worded tour of the aviary, teaching him about the birds without exactly lecturing. The ex-pigeoneer was very excited about the Victorian crowned pigeon and the Nicobar pigeon. "One of those giant birds could carry a whole encyclopedia of messages!" he marveled.

Sasha the wolf enjoyed spending afternoons lounging on Leroy's large, unused desk; it had no piles of work on it, sported a comfy leather blotter, and commanded a nice view of everyone coming and going. William began to worry about the number of treats people secretly fed him. Between that and not being forced to perform on command or interact with crowds of strangers, Sasha became a gloriously happy wolf—probably the happiest, fluffiest wolf ever to have come from the steppes of Russia.

Outside the zoo, school was almost over for the year and the weather celebrated by switching to full-on summer heat with a fierce blue sky and blazing sun. From nowhere at all—maybe the admen from the radio put it into the air—came the collective idea of *beach*. Despite being far from the ocean, the young adults of Bloomington caught and transmitted the seaside dream like a fever. It was time for an afternoon at the swimming hole.

Lucky teens had friends with cars; Carl and Ellie biked to the river, of course, and parked them up against the chestnut tree where the old sign was nailed: "Private Property! Trespassers Will Be Shot!" (The sign itself was full of buckshot wounds. The tree had escaped relatively unscathed.)

When they got to the river's edge there were already a dozen people at the illicit swimming spot, the best sunbathing rocks staked out with old blankets and tablecloths. A trio of kids no older than nine were fishing farther downstream, and Ellie wondered vaguely if their parents knew their whereabouts. The current wasn't that swift, but the pool was deep directly under the small falls; drowning was a definite possibility if you didn't know how to swim.

An older foursome had quite a picnic set up and lay indecently close to one another.

One of them, a woman behind a pair of glamorous, waspish sunglasses, noticed Ellie and waved—it was Mabel, from the USO. Ellie waved back. The muscled, freckle-pelted young man on the blanket next to her looked at Ellie and Carl over his own dark glasses and then immediately lost interest. Ellie was pretty sure he wasn't any of the soldiers she had met at a USO social, but without his shirt on, it was hard to tell.

And also it was a little distracting.

Ellie had brought their usual picnic blanket. It was a clever thing: a patchwork quilt sewn the way her mother had taught her, but out of leftover parachute silk. Not that different, philosophically, from the imaginary zeppelin younger Ellie had cobbled together from spare parts and dreams. But this invention actually worked in the real world: a cloth light as a feather and tough as nails—if not entirely as soft and comfy to lie on as an actual padded quilt.

Despite the heat of the day, under the shade of the trees it didn't feel warm enough to swim in the icy waters of the river yet—but Carl and Ellie had worn swimsuits under their clothes just in case. Carl unbuttoned his shirt and took his shoes, socks, and long pants off, folding them neatly and setting them where they wouldn't get wet or dirty. Ellie stripped down to her swimsuit, which was a lot more modest than what other girls were allowed to sport (and not at all like what Esther Williams modeled in pinups or Jane Wyman had worn on California beaches a whole *decade* earlier!). It was an old-fashioned two-piece with shorts and a scoop-necked tank top with thick straps that were almost sleeves. The material was dark blue wool and not particularly stretchy.

Still, she noticed Carl noticing her from behind his giant glasses when he thought she wasn't looking. They let their legs dangle over the rocky ledge into the numbing water, not ready to dive in just yet.

"I wonder if Leroy and everyone are camping right now, maybe right near the falls," Ellie murmured. She assumed the water there would be warmer than the gelid current her feet were currently in . . . but maybe not? Paradise Falls began at the top of a very tall mountain. Perhaps it was colder up there . . .

Carl laughed. "Isn't Muntz also supposed to be down there now, too? Looking at dinosaur skeletons or something? Maybe they'll run into each other."

"He went back to keep looking for that bird he's after—some sort of large, flightless bird. Like a cassowary or emu or rhea—though rhea makes the most sense since they're already in South America. In the last *Muntz's Monthly* they said he found part of a skeleton of one and that he planned on returning to find more, or a living specimen."

"I love that you still read that."

"Hey, they have things in it the adult journals sometimes leave out. Like jokes and puzzles," Ellie said in fake defensiveness. "Wouldn't it be amazing if Leroy *did* run into him? Maybe they'll meet, like: 'Dr. Livingstone, I presume?' In the middle of the jungle! Drinking gin and tonics to keep the malaria at bay and being all 'tut tut' and 'jolly full of insects out there, isn't it?' "

"Based on the one time I've met him, I don't think Leroy talks like that."

"Well, he was distracted then. I wish I could *be* him," Ellie said with a sigh. "Imagine deciding you wanted to go out exploring and not only being able to fly planes but being able to just *buy* them—just like that. And getting all your rich friends to pay for everything else and just *go.*

"I mean, I absolutely love Ms. Klein, and being her intern. She does all the right things, the hard things. But while she's being an office manager and working overtime saving birds, Leroy is out there, on an adventure. I'd rather do that than shovel pangolin poop or check sage grouse oviducts for eggs, if you really want to know."

"I wonder if they were rich first, and then all these other

things like explorers and pilots? Or the other way around?" Carl mused.

"Well, Leroy has his family money, of course. They own plantations all over the Caribbean. I think Diana was some sort of society girl before she began acting? I don't know about Lucy or Dan. Chet's father owns a bunch of mills down south—I heard him talking about it. Made a fortune during the war selling canvas to the army. I guess it's harder to be an explorer without family money. . . ."

One of the other teens laughed loudly. That was Buzzy Carmichael; his dad had died in the war. He picked up an unpleasant-looking rock and threw it into the pool, causing a large splash that wasn't enough to get anyone wet. His big life plans involved getting a motorcycle and a lifetime gig at the chop shop. Probably marry or date one of the girls around him at the swimming hole, or at the fry shack instead. Nice little life in a nice little town with just enough of a veneer of bad boy to make it interesting. That could very well be Ellie's future too. Exploring nothing.

"Hey, we'll figure it out," Carl said, sensing her mood change. He squeezed her arm. "Remember? I'll take you in my balloon."

His words were a break in the clouds, a hot ray of sunlight hitting her shaded face. She didn't *have* to figure it out all by herself. Carl was there to help, to stand by her, every step of the way.

"And you know, you don't have to do it all at once," he added. "Like, bam, go on your first trip and get lost in the mountains of South America. You could just go for a *visit* first. See if you like it! If you didn't, you could go visit someplace else and try that out. Africa, China, Australia . . ."

"I can't imagine anyplace being more spectacular than Paradise Falls," Ellie said with a smile. "And believe you me, I've imagined a *lot* of things. Those mountains, the tepuis, with their weird flat tops. The falls themselves! I wonder how hard it would be to just go visit, like you said."

"Aw, soon it'll be easier than visiting the Grand Canyon," Carl promised with a laugh. "Fred Harvey's company will make a train to the mountains with a teleferic up to the top. Or you'll go in a jeep chauffeured by one of the Harvey Girls. And they'll build a café that serves five kinds of pie, with a view of the falls."

"You think so? Gosh, that would be swell! Imagine eating a slice of huckleberry while gazing out at the sunset through a big picture window. Or maybe it would be banana, or mango, or something else tropical."

"You know, you could *be* a Harvey Girl, if you wanted. Like in that movie with Judy Garland? They hire all sorts of educated and classy women to tour and lecture for their patrons. They'll pay you to travel, to escort people around and plan things for their vacations."

"Just like a USO junior hostess," Ellie said, a little more wryly than she intended. "Nahhh. . . ."

She picked up a medium-sized rock and threw it into the water below, not even bothering to skip it. It plunked straight down into the depths, no splash at all.

"I don't want to just go around parroting stuff I've learned and dress pretty all the time. If I can't be the one who gets there *first* and writes what other people have to learn, I'd rather just . . . go it alone. You know? Visit places on my time with no dummies around who don't even know about Chihuahuan ravens or what kind of plane took them there. Yawn, what a bore!"

Carl grinned and patted her on the back. "Yeah, that definitely sounds more like Ellie McGill. But you sure would look great in one of those Harvey Girl uniforms. Put 'em all to shame."

Ellie also grinned; her front teeth stuck out a little in a way that she hated when she did this. Carl had such a nice smile. Perfect square white teeth that filled his wide mouth, like someone in a toothpaste ad or a short Burt Lancaster. The sun literally glinted off them.

"And, Carl—" she began, trying to say what she needed

to before she stopped herself. "There's no Harvey *Boys*. We're supposed to go *together*, remember? I don't mind visiting the falls for a slice of pie, but I want to share it with you."

"Well, yeah. Of course. There'd be no point without you."

He added: "But . . . I'd want my own slice of pie."

Ellie grinned.

"Last one in's a dirty coward!"

She leapt up and launched herself into the air, grabbing her knees and cannonballing in.

When she hit the water it was like an explosion—like one of those newsreels about a bomb missing its mark and hitting the ocean nearby instead. A strange ring of water uplifted straight to the sky, then a secondary blast sent droplets in all directions—completely soaking everyone around the edge of the pool.

Ellie popped up out of the depths grinning, her red hair plastered to her skull, the icy water giving her a headache and curing it at the same time. If she didn't keep treading energetically she would turn into an ice cube.

"For Pete's sake, Ellie!" Buzzy's friend Fred stood up and tried to brush the drops off his shorts. The girl next to him squeaked as even more water hit her bare back. Ellie wondered if she had screamed when she had initially gotten wet; she seemed the type, but Ellie hadn't heard with the rush of water in her ears.

"Grow up, why doncha?" Buzzy snarled. "You're the same old annoying little nine-year-old you always were."

Ellie's joy faded. Jumping in the water was *fun*—and not only for nine-year-olds. Just because she didn't want to lie on a rock with her bikini top untied to entice the boys and avoid tan lines, well, that didn't make her ridiculous. If someone else had done it everyone would have laughed—

"You're just jealous she did it before you thought to," Carl said.

He took his glasses off and casually put them aside, as if he, too, were about to swim—or prepare himself for something else that might involve getting physical. "And you're too much of a milksop to do it anyway."

"The water's too damn cold," Buzzy growled, grabbing a magazine as if that were more interesting. "I don't want my bazingas turning into icicles."

"Charming talk, fellas," Mabel's boyfriend—or whatever—said sleepily. "There's actual ladies present. Can we keep it polite?"

Ellie thought about male lions, how powerful they

could look even when they were doing something entirely innocent and lazy—like bathing their tails, or stretching. That older young man, who had possibly seen combat, could kick the snot out of any of the little boy teens without a second thought. So he didn't think about it.

In fact, he had probably already forgotten the whole thing.

Carl, shorter than the other high schoolers, who would have to actually fight if it came to it, was no guaranteed winner. And yet he had no problem speaking up, as casually as lion-man. As if his words were enough to silence the discourse.

And they were.

Ellie didn't need anyone—any boy—speaking up for her. She had no intention of apologizing. But Buzzy's words had cut her to the quick, found her secret hurting spot and delivered a painful blow to the restless little girl whom people were always yelling at to sit still.

It was *nice* that someone like Carl was so quick to defend her. Before she could even think of a reply, much less a good one.

He smiled and gave her a little wave.

"You coming in?" she shouted.

"Not if you paid me. I like having ten working toes, thank you very much."

Getting immediately out of the water would have been giving in—to everyone, even Carl. So Ellie paddled around the edge for a bit, pretending to have fun and trying not to bang her feet on the sharp rocks below the surface. There were no fish here, or at least nothing but the teeny tiny ones everyone called minnows without ever really know what they were.

Which, she realized, made her as thoughtless as Leroy and his crew flying into someone else's backyard and grabbing animals without knowing their names. There was a whole tiny uninvestigated world of fragility and watchfulness down there.

She came back out of the water more thoughtful than when she went in, taking the towel that Carl handed her and forgetting to thank him as she rubbed it through her hair, remembering at the last minute not to shake like a dog to get the excess off.

"Maybe Margaret's right," Ellie said. Carl moved over on the quilt and handed her a piece of jerky. She took it, ripped off a piece, and chewed it contemplatively. "About Leroy and his friends and grabbing random animals out of the wild, I mean. It's not very . . . scientific."

"Yeah. And, Ellie . . ." Carl began, then paused and looked to the side, like he was trying to figure out how to say something. "Maybe the sort of people who do that . . .

can't be trusted in general. On nonscientific things. Maybe they're not good people to be around."

"Oh, Carl, you're such a worrywart," she said, squeezing his hand. "But I'm glad you worry about *me*."

Carl didn't say anything. Then again, in situations like this, he rarely did.

FIVE

Weeks passed without word from Leroy and his crew . . . and then suddenly one day William received a telegram that said they were *already on their way home.*

The permanent Head Keeper immediately began bearing down on all the projects they were supposed to be finishing up (but had barely begun, in some cases). He had the men who were building the new South America exhibit work overtime, conducted surprise uniform inspections, and counted and re-counted the empty enclosures waiting for all the new animals they were supposedly going to receive (there was no information in the telegram about any of them). Margaret set up emergency quarantine cages and went over and over lists of potential new residents with

Mr. Hua, making sure they had enough different types of feed for any eventuality.

(Radio contact eventually confirmed there was at least one capybara.)

Ellie found lots of little reasons to drop by the office and listen in on the expedition's progress back; it had to be done in stages and with a repurposed air carrier to hold the animals they had captured. While the P-51s could make it back in a day if they had to, the giant plane didn't have as large a tank-to-weight ratio and would have to refuel more often. The zoo caravan wound up requiring almost a full week to return, with overnight stops for "the comfort of the animals"—some of which seemed to include two days at a resort on the coast of Mexico.

Ellie reported back to Carl on their progress; he had a globe on which he marked their updated locations with little *X*s, dashed lines in between to indicate their probable flight paths. He also researched potential civilian radio stations along the way and tried to find out if there were ham operators anywhere nearby, but no one in the local club had ever contacted anyone as far away as Central America, and there was no international directory of operators. There wasn't even one for the United States!

At one point, something, possibly a pit viper, escaped from its cage in Lucy's plane.

When the first army-style truck finally pulled up to the zoo, *everyone* lined up to get a peep. Leroy was driving, of course, flashing an ivory grin with his jaw held tight, arm out the window and waving except when he had to switch gears. Dan was sitting next to him, also smiling but looking a little queasy. Both men were much redder than before they had left (though on Leroy it was turning into a nice tan). They were unshorn and covered in bites (or sores, or pox). Ellie almost swooned with jealousy. They had done such things!

"Wait until you see what we have!" Leroy cried, pulling himself dramatically through the window. Dan sort of fell out when his door was opened, then began puking as delicately as he could manage while still keeping an arm on the truck for balance.

"A touch of the Aztec two-step," Leroy muttered in explanation. "Or Inca two-step, rather. Instant strawberry milk requires *water*, I kept telling him. That needs to be *boiled*. Not the most experienced traveler. Anyway, to the animals!—Miss Klein, get me a drink, would you? I'm just dying of thirst!"

He went into the back of the truck, undid the hatch, and threw the door open. Margaret ignored his request and followed at a cautious distance, letting others jostle in eagerly before her.

"First and foremost, the incredibly dangerous, nearly impossible to capture . . . *Halloweener*! Help me with this, will you, William?"

The Head Keeper climbed up into the bed and began to push out what looked like a very large dog crate . . . then leapt back as the most terrifying scream came out of it. Ellie was reminded of the morality plays that Carl's minister put on at their church fairs; Satan himself couldn't have sounded more bestial and evil.

A face—hairy, screaming, with fatal-looking tusks—suddenly pounded itself against the front of the cage, slamming the whole thing forward.

Everyone in the crowd oohed and aahed . . . Everyone except Margaret, that is, whom Ellie saw had put a hand to her temple like she was getting a headache.

Leroy had said the animal was something that sounded like *Halloweener*, which would certainly make sense considering the horror-story sound and appearance. But what he probably meant was *javelina*, a peccary: a small, very wild, very upset piggy.

"If you think that's impressive," he said, working the crowd, "see *here*!—the other cage, William, no, my boy, further—yes, lift it up! A *kinkajou*! Look at its ferocious, maniacal eyes! Its incredibly long furry tail! Have you ever seen something so terrifying? Can you imagine it clinging to a bedpost above you? Ready to drop down onto your chest and suck out your very soul?"

The mostly nocturnal creature was blinking slowly in the corner of its cage farthest away from the opening. It looked like it desperately wanted to go back to sleep and wake up later, when this was all over and everything had just turned out to be a bad dream. It even scratched its side like an old man interrupted in his sleep. Ellie cooed.

There was a small crocodile; an agouti; no cats; a beautiful, brilliantly colored macaw; some other birds; a coati; and an absolutely giant iguana that Ellie, even with her limited knowledge, suspected was more likely someone's pet than a wild creature. The thing didn't even try to move when Leroy and William picked it up out of its cage. Someone snapped a photo.

Margaret now looked like she was not just *getting* a headache but in the middle of the worst migraine of her life.

"And here, my friends, is the biggest treasure of them all!" Leroy declared, holding up a delicate golden-wired birdcage with a fancy carry handle, like something a rich and kooky aunt might have. At first glance the bird inside was nothing special to look at. A tiny, *tiny* thing, with what looked like maybe an interesting, if slightly dishabille, crest. Then Leroy tilted the cage a little and sunlight hit it full on: The tiny, nondescript little bird suddenly glowed. No, it *beamed* a brilliant iridescent purple like nothing natural Ellie had ever seen before. Not a flower, not any other kind of bird, not even a fancy fish in a tank. It was more like the purple of a faceted, sparkling amethyst, of grape soda at a picnic when there's only a little left in the bottle and the sun shines through it. Utterly unreal.

Ellie immediately fell in love . . . but the rest of the crowd didn't seem as enthusiastic. There were a few scattered *oh*s.

"Well," Leroy said, a little desperately. "Just . . . just wait until you hear how I got him. This bird . . . this *as yet unnamed* new species of bird . . . was a *gift* . . . presented to me by his own hand . . . by Charles Muntz himself!"

Then the crowd gasped—Ellie loudest of all.

"That's right," Leroy continued. "I ran into the famous explorer on one of our hunting expeditions, and he invited me back to his camp for a drink. . . . After we swapped stories he presented me with this *very* special fellow. A bycatch caught in one of his traps for those giant terror birds he's always trying to find, in the mountains of Venezuela!"

Charles Muntz!

Not only was Leroy Reardon living every dream Ellie ever had—exploring, adventuring, flying planes, surrounded by friends who loved the same things—he had *also met her personal hero*! Just like she and Carl had joked about! What was it like, she wondered, with the two of them in the middle of the jungle, talking about their experiences? She wished she were a fly on the wall. Or a kinkajou in a tree.

Leroy turned to William and clapped him in the stomach for emphasis. "I see a special exhibit for this guy, with a plaque dedicated to the day I met Charles Muntz and he gifted our zoo with this fantastic find!"

Everyone cheered.

Margaret finally spoke up.

"You only have *one* of each animal, Leroy."

"What?" he asked, confused.

"You only have *one* of each animal. Including this one."

"I got two toucans . . ."

"*They're both males.* Come on, even *you* have read the Old Testament, haven't you? Noah? Two by two? What are you going to do when your . . . 'terrifying' kinkajou *dies*?"

"Well, I'll get another fabulous creature to replace it! Something even better!"

"That's not very cost-effective. Even ignoring the ecological consequences . . . what about the discomfort of the animals themselves? You brought them here with no friends, no family. . . ."

"They're animals," Diana said, rolling her eyes. "They don't have *families*. Or *friends*."

"Well, pigs are social creatures. Leroy, you must know something about that."

"Very funny, Miss Klein. All right, all hands on deck! We're going to need everyone pitching in to get these fellows settled into their new homes!"

A second truck pulled up then, driven by Chester. Lucy, who had been lounging in the passenger seat, leapt out almost before the truck stopped and proudly strode toward the crowd, showing off the baby spider monkey that she was wearing. It clasped its arms around her neck and looked out at the zoo staff with concern.

"What happened to the pit viper?" William asked. "You were in trouble!"

"There was no pit viper," Lucy said, confused. "Not in my plane, anyway. There was just this pretty fellow monkeying around in my controls. But I caught the little rascal!"

Everyone laughed.

Well, everyone but Margaret and the old zoo hands. They were already back to work, teaming up and taking the cages away, tending to the obviously unwell animals.

"Get some water for the pig," Margaret ordered. "I don't like the way he looks."

Agnes, the woman previously in charge of the reptile house, paused to look at her questioningly.

"I mean the peccary," the ex-Head Keeper clarified.

Ellie was allowed to carry the cage with the agouti, which she did proudly. It was a funny-looking thing, like a tailless squirrel on stilted legs. When it walked, timidly, to the front of the cage, it moved like a deer, but then it would pause on its haunches and hold its front feet up like a rabbit, like it was saying *oh my, oh no.* Its face was a little too similar to a rat's for comfort, but Ellie felt enormous empathy for the displaced, lonely fellow.

"What's it like in Venezuela, little guy?" Ellie whispered. "Is it hot and humid? Does it smell like fancy flowers? Does the sun look different?"

But the agouti didn't answer her in a language she could understand.

Unsure where he—she?—would end up, Ellie took the rodent to what seemed like the most sensible place: the kitchens. Maybe it was hungry after its long trip.

The dark building was empty; everyone who had heard about the return of Leroy had dashed off to see. The only one still there was Mr. Hua, reading the *Times.*

"I have an agouti here, Mr. Hua," Ellie said, putting the cage on the counter.

"File it under M, for *Rodenti maximi,*" he said without looking up.

Ellie stood there for a moment, unsure what to do.

"No, *get it?*" He threw the paper down and barked out laughter. "From the Latin? Means 'biggest'?"

If Ellie's dad had made a similar joke, she wouldn't

have encouraged him. But since this was a higher-ranked coworker she allowed a (small) smile.

Hua sighed. "No sense of humor. No fun at all. Everyone else went to go look at all the shiny new animals, including our so-called veterinarian. Poor old Hua stays behind, working. . . ."

"It looked like you were reading the paper."

"*Ochotona* like it when I read them the funnies. Sophie especially likes *Beetle Bailey*—it distracts her while she's nursing."

He came over to the cage and crouched down to look inside.

"Nice specimen of *D. leporina*. Where are the others?"

He looked around the room, then behind her, as if expecting there to be another bearer of rodents, like a procession.

"Um . . . I think Ms. Klein and Leroy are having a . . . disagreement about the lack of . . . multiples . . . right now," Ellie said as delicately as she could.

Hua groaned. "Even *one* agouti requires a large habitat . . . this is not the best place for her. The zoo in Washington or San Diego would be better. Or Canton . . . Did you know that back in there I was the head of the royal zoological department? With several degrees, and everything?"

"Yes, Mr. Hua. You've mentioned that several times. If you don't mind me asking, why bother coming here, then?"

"Well, the revolution in 1911 was—do you kids study that? No? Let's just say it was a warning sign. The sudden end of two thousand years of monarchy is a big—and mostly positive—step. But just the first of many. . . . I think things are going to be difficult in China for people like me for a while. Just like for the Jewish people in Germany and Eastern Europe."

Ellie didn't want to sound stupid but didn't understand. "You're . . . Jewish?"

Hua laughed again. "No, although I do like a nice piece of smoked salmon. I'm an *educated intellectual.* We are usually the first to go in situations like that. So like a coward or a survivor I picked up and left to explore the great new world. Just lucky I didn't wind up working on a railroad, I guess."

Ellie knew about Chinese railroad workers—they had built the lines the trains ran on that made the West run. She couldn't see Mr. Hua—Dr. Hua—with a pickax. Actually, if she thought of him at all, she could only see him here at the zoo, carefully chopping up animal food or reading the paper.

"Let me take a look at this poor fellow," he said, picking up a flashlight. "Maybe we can convert part of the playground to a little space for her. Poor Ms. Klein will have to lead the charge on that. . . . You should go back and help her if you can. She's probably losing her mind."

He made kissy noises at the creature, having immediately and entirely forgotten about Ellie. She didn't mind. She went back to the trucks.

Scattered around like petals in a particularly vicious game of "he loves me/not" were the rest of the cages, some with animals still in them. People were scurrying around trying to decide what to do with the rest. Leroy had William sitting at a crate, taking down a list he was dictating.

"We're not far enough along with the new attraction for 'Lost Worlds,' Willy my boy. The roof needs to be done by the end of next week. Also, we're going to have to design and print up new brochures, and heavens, a new *map*, yes, a new map of the zoo. . . ."

"Leroy, can you eighty-six your grand plans for just a moment?" Margaret interrupted, slamming her slightly dirty hands on his temporary desk, causing the two men to jump back. "We can go over that later. Right now we need to figure out what to do for the animals. It's chaos and they need care. Extra bedding in the mews for the javelina. The smaller animals we can put in a quarantine paddock. . . . We'll have to add some climbing material for the forest creatures . . . maybe we can get a raw tree or something from Bernie's Lumber. . . ."

"I beg your pardon, Miss Klein," Leroy said with a smile. "Please don't interrupt. There are important things that we are getting done here."

"What *we need to get done here* is to get these animals settled as best we can. I can supervise the birds, but—"

"Oh no, Miss Klein. You are no longer even an *interim* Head Keeper, much less a supervisor. You are not permitted to supervise . . . *anything*. You are an office manager. Right now I need you to type up an account of my adventures for those who helped fund the expedition, and the paparazzi. You can use my journal for now and I'll fill you in on the details—it needs to be a good story to sell."

"Mr. Reardon," Margaret said, slowly, obviously trying to figure out how to be polite, "I think that whatever my title is, my *experience* would make me far more useful helping with the animals."

"I hear you're an excellent typist. That's the experience I need now."

"I see," she said.

There was a long, icy pause.

"All right," she added.

Ellie's face began to prickle with sweat. William looked

nervous too, his eyes flicking back and forth between Margaret and Leroy like they were his parents.

Finally Margaret took a deep breath and settled her shoulders.

"All right. I will get right on typing up your story . . . just as soon as I've had my lunch."

"Don't take too long," Leroy said airily, already turning back to William. "I know how you ladies like to gab."

The only indication that anything was off was when, as she walked by, Margaret saw Ellie and rolled her eyes.

Her "lunch," Ellie realized, was going to be taking care of the animals that needed her help the most.

Ellie looked back at Leroy. Didn't he understand what a gold mine he had in Margaret? What an incredible resource he was wasting?

Well, he would just have to see it himself over the next few weeks, now that he was back. How terrible the "new recruits" were, and how invaluable Margaret still was in managing the zoo.

He just needed time. . . .

SIX

Early the next week when Ellie stopped by the mailbox on her way home, she found a *very* not-USPS-authorized missive in the otherwise empty box: a neat index card with carefully rubber-stamped words, almost like letterpress:

YOU ARE CORDIALLY INVITED

To Celebrate the END of the BAN
on Amateur Radio Operation!

Place: THE CLUBHOUSE.

Time: AFTER SCHOOL.

RSVP not required. Cake will be served.

At the bottom was "W0CDF," which Ellie knew was Carl's radio call sign. She didn't *understand* the whole thing, but it was the ID he used when he was radio . . . ing. With a whoop of glee she grabbed her bike from the shed and took off.

Wait, should *she* bring something, since he was bringing cake?

She skidded to a halt, spun the bike around, and ran inside to look for whatever she could grab. It wound up being a mostly full pint of cold buttermilk and two clean mason jars to drink from; cups were a resource always running low in the McGill household.

Ellie pedaled happily, sitting up straight as the mast of a ship, her hair blowing out behind her like a wild pirate's pennant. In no time at all she was pulling up to the house; Carl's bike was already parked neatly against the large beech in the yard. She dropped her own bike—gently—into the dirt and gazed up at her beautiful aerozeppelin/house. It had been over a month since she had last visited, with an apple for herself and some nuts for the squirrels that after all these years still refused to move out. She just didn't have time anymore, with high school and the zoo and Carl and everything. . . .

The unusual single gable seemed to wink at her, and she grinned, feeling forgiven.

"Hello!" she called out, throwing the door open. "Explorers ahoy!"

"Ahoy! *Explorers on deck!*" Carl called back, trotting out of the other room with a pair of napkins. He had set up a nice little party: a tablecloth he must have stolen from his mom was spread out on a crate, and he had obviously cleaned and fluffed the old blankets they used for forts, folding them into cushions. She half expected to also see his radio receiver and the "key," the tappy thing he generated Morse code with, but he obviously thought that it was too delicate to take on his bike. Instead, there was a newspaper propped up on the tablecloth, folded to display an article about the ban (it was not on the front page). Before all this was the promised cake: a pretty little vanilla frosted one he must have bought at La Vie Du Gâteau, the expensive bakery in town. Carl Fredricksen *loved* a good cake. This radio thing was only an excuse.

"I brought the drinks!" she said, taking out the buttermilk and slamming it down with the cups, the way she imagined bartenders did.

"Perfect! I forgot," Carl said, rubbing his hands together.

"So what's all this about, anyway?"

"As you know, *technically* amateur radio operators haven't been allowed to, well, operate, since the beginning of the war," Carl explained delightedly. "No transmitting, and no receiving in case you wind up listening to some sort of classified band. Hasn't stopped any of us, really—"

"I know, you're always tinkering with that thing. You'd spend all day with it if you could."

"Well, now I can go back to doing it legally—and talking to other people. Why, today already I made contact with a man all the way in Kansas City!"

"Really?" Ellie perked up. Not that Kansas City was interesting, but the possibilities were. If you could talk to a man there, why not Canada? Or Mexico? Or . . . Venezuela?

"Yes! I wrote it down in my logbook, but he's going to send me his QSL card. And I'm going to send him *mine*! See?" Out of his pocket he drew a card with his call sign on it in big letters, some acronyms she didn't understand, and a rather shaky border around the whole thing doodled in pen. "It says the day and time we made connection, and at what frequency, and what kind of equipment I was using."

"Ah, Carl, why don't you let me make these cue cards or whatever," she said as tactfully as she could, imagining some fussy forty-year-old receiving something that looked like a messy kid had drawn it. "You know I'm good at art and stuff like that."

"*Would* you?"

"Yeah, of course, Carl. Anything for you. You just gotta ask."

She smiled at him, and somehow the ends of her mouth climbed higher than she thought possible . . . because he was smiling, also widely, and a little stupidly, in wonder.

The moment dragged out.

"Speaking of art, I . . . should get my old adventure journal," Ellie suddenly decided. "I want to draw a picture of a new place I want to go in South America. Ischigualasto in Argentina! It's also called Moon Valley, because it's full of crazy rock formations and *thousands* of dinosaur fossils!"

She went over to the fireplace and picked up the loose stone where she hid her journal. Carl always thought it was funny, but having grown up in a house full of nosy nellies, she didn't let anything she wanted to keep secret and secure just lie out anywhere. Even in her private clubhouse.

She flipped through its pages fondly. Her first love had always been South America; all other adventure ideas in her book came second after the picture of her clubhouse at the top of Paradise Falls. It would make a very nice base for dropping in on Argentina, visiting the Moon Valley, trying to catch a glimpse of Eva Perón, and then maybe seeing the penguins of Patagonia, or São Paulo. . . .

All right, none of those were particularly close to Paradise Falls, but they were a lot closer to it than they were to Bloomington.

"Yeah . . . uh . . . that's another reason why I wanted to

have the celebration here and not at my place," Carl said as she finally came to a blank page and began sketching.

"Besides the fact that I'm not allowed in your room anymore?" she asked archly. It still stung, his parents making that ultimatum. The issue hadn't even come up at the McGills'—there was always a pair of prying eyes everywhere. No "boy" danger was possible in that house.

"You had better take your adventure journal with you this time, Ellie. Just in case. They're putting this place on the market."

She looked up at him.

"Um, what?"

"I guess the family of the people who owned it finally got around to figuring out they still had it or whatever . . . there was some sort of fight or issue over a will. My dad told me." He saw the look on her face. "It probably won't sell immediately! It's kind of a wreck, and this isn't exactly a popular street. . . ."

But Ellie had stopped paying attention.

She closed her journal and gazed around at what had been her world for so many years. The ropes and wires that controlled her aerozeppelin. The beam that had broken, causing Carl to break his arm. The radio control station—Carl's contribution—which had a headset made from an old pair of earmuffs, with a broken hotel desk bell for the Morse code generator.

"Oh . . . Carl . . ."

She grabbed his upper arm and squeezed, seeing the other version of her clubhouse inside her head, the one perched over Paradise Falls.

"Oh, Ellie, it's okay," he said, putting his other hand on hers. "Anyone who buys this place . . . well, it's because they will have fallen in love with it. It would have to be a really special kind of person to want it, right? To do all the work to fix it up? To really appreciate all its little quirks?"

She bit her lip, wondering what that person would say upon seeing all the strange contraptions and drawings and things they had added to it over the years. Who would it be? A pregnant young wife and her doting husband . . . a retired couple looking for a quiet place out of the city . . . refugees from the war . . . She watched a parade of imaginary faces with happy looks as they all found their forever home.

"You're right. It would have to be someone who loves it just as much as we do."

Ellie smiled up at him, only a little sadly. They'd had great times over the years here. Other people would too.

Carl looked down at her, opening his mouth to say something.

Nothing came out. His eyes were speaking, though. Like he was drowning and hoped someone noticed.

"Carl?" she asked softly.

This was it. It—whatever *it* was—was really happening this time.

His Adam's apple bobbed; he leaned forward. His lips parted—

"SQUEAAAAK!"

It took a moment for Ellie to realize the sound had not come from Carl.

"The cake!"

That *did* come from Carl's mouth, and his voice was filled with anguish.

Ellie spun around to look where he was looking.

The cake.

It was completely hidden by the three or four small squirrels that clambered all over it, gobbling up every morsel of frosting and crumb as fast as they could. It was like they hadn't eaten in weeks—or had never tasted anything so wonderful.

"Oh, Carl." Ellie tried not to laugh; he looked so genuinely upset. She squeezed his arm again and kissed him on the cheek.

"That was a cake from La Vie!"

But a smile was ghosting at the sides of his mouth. Really, it was too ridiculous and adorable.

"I'll get you another cake. For your radio ban being over or whatever. I promise."

"Explorer's Oath?" he asked gravely.

"Explorer's Oath," she said, crossing her heart.

The "Lost Worlds: South America" exhibit was finally finished and ready for its debut—only a few days late. There was another party, of course; Ellie was beginning to think that Leroy loved parties more than exploring. But this celebration was open to the (paying) public: There were food carts, a mariachi band—which Ellie was pretty sure had nothing to do with Venezuela—and a giant archway made entirely of helium-filled balloons, a real luxury since the war shortages.

In fact, Carl could not be dragged away from the gorgeous pastel rainbow that gently rolled and tipped in the breeze.

"One hundred seven!" he told Ellie breathlessly. "There are one hundred seven balloons in it! I counted twice! Do you know how many pounds that could lift?"

"One hundred?"

"Well, more like six or seven," he admitted, crestfallen.

"That's like a small cat. Um, nifty. Carl, I'm going to go visit my agouti and see how he's liking all the attention."

(Carl wound up spending most of the party talking to the balloon vendor: asking where the helium came from, the source of the rubber for the balloons, what the optimum pressure for the tank was, and many other things the poor man didn't have an answer for.

"I'm just a salesman, Jack," he said plaintively.)

Ellie's entire family came, and the professional photographer hired for the occasion took their portrait, the first one the McGills had of all of them with the baby. Ellie was fiercely proud of how properly the twins behaved and neatly they were dressed. Mrs. McGill loved the arepas a woman was selling so much that she asked for the recipe—though the two couldn't figure out between them what the English word was for masarepa. Ellie wasn't sure about her mother's eventual decision that "fine grits would do," but she loved that she was interested.

Leroy had on a Panama hat with a wide brim and no band, which apparently he had bought in Venezuela; he wore it throughout the day, shaking important hands and a maraca he kept with him the whole time. The instrument was brightly lacquered, had "Ole" written on it in yellow paint, and, Ellie was pretty sure, was also about as authentically South American as the mariachi band.

He made a speech, of course—Leroy loved speeches as much as he loved parties—standing on a little platform, talking about the dangerous and wild time he and his friends had acquiring the javelina and the spider monkey.

"But adventure is out there, people," he finished. This got a cheer from many—including Ellie and Carl. "And so it is with great pride and joy that I dedicate the entrance of Lost Worlds to Charles Muntz, the famous explorer and one of the greatest men alive, whom I personally met in the mountains of Venezuela. The resident of this enclosure was given to me *by Charles Muntz* himself, and it more than pleases me to put the beautiful little bird on display!

". . . Unfortunately, the poor thing hasn't quite recovered from his travels yet."

Ellie frowned. She hadn't heard anything about the purple bird being sick. In fact, she hadn't heard anything about him since that first day when Leroy had returned. Strange.

"Come back again in a week or two and see him in his beautiful new home! In the meantime, give a round of applause to *Charles Muntz*, whose gift to me and this zoo is priceless!"

Leroy pulled a string and a curtain fell, revealing a gorgeous bird enclosure. It was painted bright yellow and had mock shutters around the viewing window for the eventual bird; bits of mirrored glass that caught and scattered the sunlight were mosaicked around the outside. Below the window was a shiny new bronze plaque with what looked like the silhouettes of Leroy's and Muntz's heads on it.

"But it would be a crime to rest on the laurels of our latest acquisitions!" Leroy continued once the somewhat confused applause died down. "You lucky people are the first to know that next week I and my crew will be taking off again—this time to *Burma*!"

The crowd oohed its approval, once again heartily enthusiastic.

"What wonders will we find in *these* jungles? Poisonous snakes crawling through abandoned temples? Wild cats guarding their ancient abodes? Butterflies the size of your face? Whatever we discover, we'll bring it home to *your* zoo so you can be amazed, too!"

"Oh, that's interesting," Mr. McGill said approvingly. "I heard a news program about that part of the world, the jungles of Siam—I mean, Thailand—just the other night."

But William looked grim-faced at the news and Margaret was gripping her drink like it was the antidote to a poison she had just taken.

Ellie later caught up with the ex–Head Keeper, who was

admiring the new plaque with Dr. Hua. They were sharing a cone of popcorn.

"Hey, Ms. Klein, I'm going to take off soon with my family, and Carl."

(Carl had *seven* balloons, acquired who knew how, and was holding the bouquet of them as happily as if he had won at the Olympics. The McGill children looked on with wonder and envy.)

"Of course, Ellie. See you tomorrow," Margaret said. She chose a single piece of popcorn and put it into her mouth, chewing contemplatively while still staring at the plaque. "Say, Ellie—before you go. It says there that Charles Muntz and Leroy Reardon met at Jimmie Angel Pass in the jungles of Venezuela."

"And?"

"Is that what it's really called? 'Jimmie Angel Pass'?"

"Well, sure?" Ellie thought about it. "Maybe in Spanish, though? I don't know, what is it?"

"I don't know either; I was genuinely curious, since you know so much about South America. But I would bet my paycheck it's not that."

"We call the Great Wall of China *Changcheng*," Dr. Hua said with a shrug, digging for the buttery-est bits of popcorn. "It just means Long Wall."

"I'm not sure I understand what you're saying, Ms. Klein, Dr. Hua," Ellie said honestly, looking at each of them for a hint.

Margaret gave a wry smile. "It's just that . . . this is a plaque about two very self-congratulatory American explorers meeting at a place in another country we've given an English name to, and the poor bird it's all for is nowhere to be seen."

Well, when she put it that way, it *did* seem a little funny. Especially all the fuss over it and the curtain and all.

"Where *is* the bird?" Ellie asked curiously. "It's not in the aviary, and I haven't seen it since Leroy first showed everyone."

"It's 'in quarantine.' I haven't seen it myself either. If I didn't know better I'd say Leroy was keeping it from me. Either he's terrified someone is going to steal his precious gift from Muntz or it's already dead and he's vamping for time."

It took a moment before Margaret noticed the horrified look on Ellie's face.

"Never mind, forget what I said. I'm tired and cranky, and worried about *Burma* now."

"Oooh, maybe they'll have curry at the next party," Dr. Hua said brightly. For just a moment Ellie was reminded of Carl.

"See you on Saturday, Miss McGill," Margaret said. "I have a whole little lesson planned for you on daylight and ovulation cycles in domesticated and wild birds. Also a demonstration."

"Fun! Can I come?" Dr. Hua asked. Ellie genuinely couldn't tell if he was joking.

In the end it didn't matter, because Margaret never got the chance to lecture either one of them.

Saturday at lunchtime Ellie presented herself eagerly at the administrative office. Leroy and his friends were there, supposedly planning Burma, but Lucy looked like the only one doing any actual work, flipping through pages of an atlas and making notes. Leroy was chatting on the phone with someone official-sounding, chuckling and smiling and making small talk. Diana was sitting at William's desk, applying powder to her cheeks with the aid of a pretty little gold compact. Chester was missing, but Dan had collapsed in another chair and was going through a receipt book. He still looked vaguely ill. William, having been ousted from his spot, was hunched on a pile of boxes, one hand on Sasha's head, the other trying to scribble something out using the back of a book as a lap desk. Gus was standing in a corner playing with a yo-yo, waiting for someone to tell him what to do.

None of them even glanced up as Ellie came in; she

took the opportunity to sneak Sasha a cheese-crusted bit of potato from her breakfast.

Then the door burst open and Margaret stomped in, something lumpy and ungainly in her arms.

Unceremoniously, she dumped a limp snake onto the center of Leroy's desk.

He leapt back with a yelp. Diana let out a scream—then went over to look.

"Oh, it's dead," she said in relief.

"Get it off my desk!" Leroy cried. "Is that the pit viper we lost? It's poisonous!"

"No, it's *venomous*. *Was* venomous. *Was* potentially dangerous. *Was* alive. *WAS* alive and happy in its wherever it was a week ago before *some*one caught it and brought it halfway around the world without knowing how to take care of it properly."

"You should get it stuffed," Lucy suggested. "Mount it for display."

"Oh no you don't," Diana cried. "Look at that skin! Those pretty spots and stripes . . . I want it for a pair of shoes. Can I, Leroy? I have just the Italian shoemaker in mind."

Dan lifted his head and said weakly, "As long as she mentions where the shoes came from, loudly and anytime she's asked, to reporters. Might as well get free publicity."

"GENTLEMEN," Margaret shouted. "And—'ladies.' This creature was a living being not a few hours ago. Show it some respect. Leroy, I *told* you this would happen. Your . . . your pigheadedness in grabbing animals willy-nilly without thought or concern for their welfare has gone too far. This is an outrageous waste, and a disgraceful treatment of a living organism."

"You know what, Miss Klein?" Leroy spoke casually—*too* casually. "I've been very patient during this . . . transitional period. I know it must be hard for you to give up the little pretend-time you had running the zoo during the war. But now you've gone too far, and I think I've had just about all the insults from a subordinate anyone could ever be expected to take.

"Your services are no longer required here. Please take your things and leave."

Ellie gasped. What was he *saying*?

Dan looked up from where he lay and started to speak—but saw the look on Leroy's face and slumped back down. That was all the movement in the room for at least a thousand seconds (by Ellie's reckoning). Time, dust, everything froze.

"Are you serious," Margaret finally asked, and there was no tone at all in her voice: it sounded like she was just curious about the matter, and not even very much. She delicately crossed her arms and rested her fingers against her elbows, tapping them there like she was a supervillain waiting for a lackey to realize that he had made a very deadly mistake.

"As serious as I've ever been about anything," Leroy said, leaning over his desk and crossing his own arms. "You've been a pain in my side ever since I got back from *serving my country*."

"You were serving . . . in the *Alps*, Leroy. And the only reason this zoo still exists in any capacity is because of what I and everyone else did to take care of it. I'm only a pain in your side because I'm the only one who will stand up to your ludicrous whimsies."

"I will not sit here and take this nonsense. And from a . . . *woman*, no less!"

"Oh, come on, Leroy," William said, moving to try to stand—well, if not between them, because there was a desk there, then to the side, with his arms out as if to stop physical blows. "You don't mean it. You can't fire her—she's the only one who really knows how to run this place. You know that. She knows all the addresses and what the animals need and where the secrets are buried and whatnot."

"Please. She's not irreplaceable. *Any*one could do her job. Any man. Why, there's an idea! Say, Gus—"

The young man looked up, instantly getting his yo-yo tangled.

"Congratulations. You've been promoted from errand boy to office manager. Go take a seat."

Gus dropped his yo-yo immediately, saluted, ran over to Margaret's desk, and sat down.

"This isn't a good idea, Leroy," William said, shaking his head.

"All right, then," Margaret said, grinding her teeth together exactly once. "I'll come back and collect my things later."

"You're never to set foot in this zoo again!" Leroy declared.

It was possibly the most ridiculous set of words ever said by a man who could, in some light, look like a movie star.

This wasn't that light, however. Ellie noticed for the first time the dull, animal stubbornness in his eyes, the sulky pout of his lips, the childishly defiant pushing out of his not-quite-cleft chin. His moustache looked like it had been actually oiled, as well as his hair. She blinked, wondering what had happened in that split second that caused him to change so.

Everything was confusing, like in an old Russian fairy tale: a magical, beautiful snake had been captured and died; a princess was driven from her kingdom; a villain learned no lessons. None of it made any sense. And whose side was William on, anyway? Was he Leroy's lackey, or not? Did he actually love the animals, and want to take care of them properly?

"This zoo is partially funded by the town and is considered a public resource," Margaret said, turning around and walking out. "You can no more forbid me coming here than you can me walking up and down the sidewalk in front of your house."

They weren't the most memorable or dramatic parting words ever spoken: it was more a calm statement of fact than dramatic farewell. But the silence they left behind was powerful. All the more so because Margaret wasn't crying, or furious, or slamming her heels into the ground, or screaming; she just didn't seem to care.

The door swung shut behind her.

Nobody moved.

Sasha whined, not liking the mood.

"Aw, criminy," William finally said, sitting back down on his pile of boxes and putting his hand to his head like he was getting a headache. Very much like Margaret, actually. Maybe it came with the job.

Leroy still stood, arms crossed, as if she were still there. Everyone looked elsewhere out of embarrassment. He shifted his weight back onto his heels. He twitched his upper lip, making his moustache dance weirdly.

"Gus, take a memo!" he finally said.

"Right away, Mr. Reardon sir!" Gus grabbed a random piece of paper, an envelope it looked like, and the stub of a pencil.

"To whom it may concern . . ."

"W-H-O-M," Lucy spelled out before the boy could even ask.

"The snake, Leroy?" Diana prodded. "Before it rots or whatever?"

"Oh, yes, erm, William, can you have that wrapped up for the lady here?"

"Is that an 'um' or 'erm,' Mr. Reardon?" Gus dutifully asked, writing it all down.

Ellie decided then was as good as time as any to leave.

Nobody noticed her, as she didn't quite *sneak* out; she walked as normally as she could, the way an animal might when it doesn't want to attract attention but needs to leave in a hurry, in a manner that wouldn't attract the eyes of a predator.

But the moment she was out the door she ran after Margaret.

"Ms. Klein! Ms. Klein!" she called—and she would always remember that moment: the elegant, sharp-nosed Margaret Klein, all in blue, her dark hair in its usual intricate bun, turning on her elegant heels under the golden zoo sign above the gate.

But as Ellie grew closer she saw the scene wasn't quite perfect, or at least not the shining example of undaunted female power it seemed at first: Margaret's eyes were red—yet she looked less angry than *exhausted*. Her skirt was twisted a little, and there was a dryness to her face that wasn't a testament to tears but to something else: the harsh, burning glare of reality, maybe.

Whatever declarations Ellie was about to make—"I'm going with you!" "I quit too!" "Please don't go!"—died on her tongue.

"Hey," she said aloud, wondering what her next words would be. "You . . . look like you could use ice cream. Can I—can I take you out for a soda? To the counter at Woolworth's?"

Something about the other woman shifted; her lips formed the ghost of a smile. She looked *relieved*: Someone else was going to take care of something for once, and that thing was her.

"I can't think of anything I'd like better."

SEVEN

The walk downtown was slow; Margaret moved as if she were looking around at the outside world for the first time, like a child or a tourist, *noticing* it instead of being caught up in work or her own thoughts like she usually was. A man half out of uniform whistled at her on the corner of Elm and Main and she rolled her eyes.

"Does that cheer you up or make it all worse somehow?" Ellie asked curiously.

"Neither. It's just another thing to endure."

The Woolworth's building looked like it had been there forever. It took up the length of a whole block and, with its equally long and narrow gold-and-green sign, gave the impression of an elegant sleeping crocodile. Just inside the grand doors was a display of everything you might need for spending a delightful summer on your own porch: drinking glasses with little daisies painted on them, red-check tablecloths, lemon- and bayberry-scented candles to keep the bugs away. Ellie noted the glasses for later; her mother would love them (and the McGills were *always* short on glasses).

A metal counter ran along the back wall of the main floor with a neat row of red leatherette stools mounted before it like mushrooms. Two soda jerks managed the chrome milkshake machines, the coffee station, the canisters of CO_2 for seltzer, and all the flavors of syrup you could imagine. Raspberry, strawberry, chocolate, ginger, peach, maple, butternut, coffee . . . The smell in the air was like all of them combined, spicy and fruity with a strong hint of cherry. It didn't make Ellie's mouth water quite as much as it had when she was smaller, but it still flipped her brain into a spin as she tried to figure out what flavor combination she wanted before the counter guy came over.

Margaret sat herself heavily down on a stool like an old, cynical cop in a movie, ready for his late-night pie and coffee; a young man with curly red hair springing out below his paper hat immediately ran over to serve her. Ellie wondered if she would ever attract that kind of attention. She *did* take a long time to order—everyone who worked there knew that—but sometimes she felt this boy in particular just plain ignored her.

"I'll have a ginger-mint soda, heavy on the mint—no, scratch that!" Margaret hit the counter with her hand. "Gimme a black and white—that's chocolate syrup and soda and milk with a scoop of vanilla ice cream. I want it all: whipped cream, peanuts, and a cherry on top. Boy, do I need it. You're paying, right?"

"Absolutely. Yes." Ellie was worried the whole way over that Margaret wouldn't let her. She had felt so mature asking—it would have been unsurprising but still embarrassing if the older woman had still gently insisted after all that.

"I'll have the same," Ellie said.

Then she thought about it.

"Um, actually, no peanuts, please. And make it strawberry syrup. No milk. With a strawberry on top, if you have it. And a scoop of chocolate pieces instead."

Redheaded counter boy gave her a look and didn't bother to write either of their orders down. Ellie wondered if the finished creations would be right, and if not, as the one paying, whether she should complain.

"I cannot believe it. I just cannot *believe* it," Margaret said, adding in a few words in a language that Ellie did not understand. They were probably swears. "I made it through the *war*, for heaven's sake! I went through college and grad school and research positions . . . only to wind up being fired from a *secretarial* position by an utter clown! What a joke."

"Um, office manager?" Ellie said hopefully.

"Yeah, right. Don't kid yourself. Leroy only wanted me making coffee and typing letters. I'd take William over him any day."

"I'm going to quit," Ellie said, trying not to make it sound self-important. "In solidarity."

"Thanks, Ellie, but please don't." Margaret reached over and gave her hand a quick squeeze. "For one thing, this is my fight, not yours. As long as you don't spend any time with Leroy or attract his notice you should be fine—you don't even directly report to him. Your pay comes out of a city fund for kids as part of a kind of wartime kick-start program. William is now the contact for that."

Ellie mentally turned over what she had said, trying to figure out what exactly it meant. It sounded like her job was actually a little bit of a government charity something or other. She wasn't quite sure how that made her feel. Her family wasn't *poor* poor; her mom had never had to take in other people's wash . . . True, her brother had quit school to help support them all, but didn't a lot of people do that?

What had Margaret said? *You spend so much time at the zoo we might as well pay you for it.* Her being hired wasn't such a casual decision, it seemed. There must have been paperwork to fill out, and who knows what city officials thought when it was a girl who got the gig.

She decided not to think about it too much. She loved the zoo, and whatever it had taken to get her a job there was fine by her.

"Also, those animals are going to *need* you, Ellie. It's more than just facts and figures and technical knowledge that keep the animals alive and thriving—which knowledge you have, in spades, far more than anyone else Leroy's hired! Where's the Gobi Desert?"

"China," Ellie answered without thinking.

"And who lives there?"

"Well, the Gobi bear, of course. And . . . wild horses. The wild ass and that horse whose name I can't spell or pronounce."

Margaret laughed. *"Przewalski's!"*

The sodas were placed in front of them, a little harder than necessary with Ellie's. She gave the guy an equally hard look back and decided not to tip; some of the whipped cream had been dislodged onto the outside of the tall fluted soda glass. She was just wondering about the best way to deal with the mess when Margaret used the tip of her ring finger on her own drink to delicately push a precariously sliding mound of her own whipped cream back into place, then licked it off in a way that was neither salacious nor disgusting. Ellie immediately copied her.

"See? You have to stay," Margaret said, picking up the long silver spoon and working it down around the ice cream exactly like Mr. McGill did in the garden with a hoe, making a hole deep enough to dig her straw through. "For the animals. I appreciate the sentiment, though. I really do."

"What will you do now? Carl said I should be a Harvey Girl. Maybe you could?"

"I think I'm a little old for that. They cull you when you're thirty. While they don't want any fraternization, they also want you to *look* like you *could* be available."

"Sounds like the USO," Ellie said with a rueful smile. "But I don't think they ever culled anyone. They needed all the volunteers they could get, at least during the war. They'd keep me until I was old and grey if they could."

"The USO, huh? You volunteer with them a lot, don't you? That sounds interesting. Hey, let's stop talking about me for a bit. Thinking about this all right now is driving me crazy, especially since there's nothing I can do. Let's talk about *you*. That's far more fun. I haven't been a teenager in ages."

"Well, I don't know if anyone would call me the most

fun teenager," Ellie admitted. "I like dances and stuff, but I also really like hiking. And airplanes."

"Airplanes?"

"Oh, yes. I have this book I've practically memorized about how to fly one so I'm ready if I ever get a chance. . . . I've always loved them, ever since I was little. Me and Carl used to make models of them from leftover trash when we were collecting metal for the war. We also made my bike look like a plane. When we first met, it was when I was pretending to fly a zeppelin in an old abandoned house. Or maybe it was a balloon boat. But it was also kind of a house."

"Ellie McGill, you're amazing," Margaret said. "And . . . what about Carl?"

"What about him?"

"I mean . . . I've seen you together a lot at the zoo. I've seen the way you guys act around each other."

Ellie felt her ears getting red, and the tops of her cheeks.

"I mean, it's not like we're going steady or anything," she blurted out before she could stop herself. Boy, that sounded stupid. Like a line from one of those films they showed in health class.

"You don't say," Margaret said, a touch ironically.

Ellie tried again. "We've always been friends. He's never . . . you know . . . asked me out. On a real date. Although we sort of go on things that are *like* dates. . . .

I think he's not really a date person. We prefer walks and exploring and nature. We went to the river last weekend." *Good clean fun.* She didn't remember ever saying so many stupid things in a row. She said they didn't date, and then she used "we" to talk about what they liked, as if they had one brain.

"Do you *want* to go steady with him?"

Ellie froze.

Did . . . she . . . want . . . to . . . go . . . .steady? With Carl?

"Eat some ice cream," Margaret suggested, pointing at her glass with her spoon. "While you're thinking. It's like in *Alice Through the Looking-Glass*; curtsy while you figure out what to say—but eating ice cream is better."

Ellie did as she was told—it wasn't hard to obey such an order. Once three big spoonfuls were in her belly things began to calm down and make sense.

"I kind of want to?" she admitted. "Sometimes, when it's just the two of us . . . It's funny . . . I don't tell anyone this stuff. Not my school friends, not even my mother."

Such a betrayal! The hardworking housewife and best mom of all to a flock of unruly kids, she who kept their clothes mended and clean, their stomachs well fed on what they could afford . . . and here Ellie was spilling her guts to this sophisticated, educated single lady who probably didn't give the best hugs. A tiny piece of Ellie's brain told her she was being maudlin and oversimplifying things, but listening to that wasn't as satisfying as feeling the drama of the moment.

Margaret gave her a smile around a mouthful of whipped cream, which suddenly struck Ellie as very young, and something she would do herself. "I'm honored. And I should make it as easy as possible if you ever do need to tell someone—me—anything really important about 'this stuff,' in the future."

She put her spoon down and clicked open her purse, not even needing to fish around in it any before she immediately pulled up what she wanted: a calling card, debossed and printed with her name and address: *Margaret R. Klein, 234 Oak Street No. 1.* Below that was her personal telephone number, *BLoomington 9-0648.* "Now you have no reason *not* to call on me. So please feel free to spill the beans."

Ellie took the elegant card with a little trepidation—there was whipped cream still sticky on her fingers, despite her attempts at neatness. She put it into her pocket immediately and vowed to admire it later.

"Thanks! It's just that I haven't really—*thought* thought about me and Carl before," she said, seeing the truth of her words solidifying as she said them. "Everything's fine, I guess? Or—smooth? Or . . . I don't want anything to change? Or maybe I do. . . . We don't talk about anything like dating, or the future. . . ."

Didn't they, though?

The very first time they met, didn't she tell Carl he would take them to Paradise Falls in his balloon someday?

And wasn't she *always* adding new places in her adventure journal for them to travel to, also someday? *Together?*

"I don't know, Ms. Klein," she said, a little unhappily. "Maybe we on purpose don't talk about anything like dating. Maybe it's always there, but also *not* there?"

"Here's what I think," Margaret said, scraping the inside of her now mostly empty ice cream glass. "I think Carl seems like a nice kid. I think maybe you guys are getting a little old for the 'best friends forever' situation—unless that's what you are. It happens! But more likely, one of three *other* things is likely to happen next.

"One, he tries something with you . . .

"Two, you try something with him . . .

"Or three, neither one of you does anything, ever, and then someone else looks in and says, gosh, what a swell guy that Carl is, or jiminy, what a fantastic gal that Ellie is, and sweeps one of you away. Which could be great—or it could leave one or both of you wondering what would have happened if only one of you had said or done something."

Well.

There it was.

Despite the succinct harshness of the words—or maybe because of them—Ellie immediately understood their truth. Those really were all the possible outcomes; the future's hazy swirl inside her head clarified. Which was a first, because Ellie never had any clear thoughts about the future, nor was she good at planning. The future was something that just happened. She joined clubs and causes because they seemed like fun and the right thing to do, and stuck with them if they were meaningful (and fun). She worked at the zoo because she spent all her time there and loved it. Other girls were doing silly things like planning out their perfect weddings—or what house they would have, or, sometimes, what college they would attend—but at least they were sketching out ideas of what they wanted. All she had was a drawing of a house plonked down on Paradise Falls.

What a strange idea: *Figuring out what you wanted* and *figuring out the future* were, in fact, the same thing. Or could be. But in between the two, between the wanting and the future occurring, was . . . something. Work. Decision. Action. Going to Paradise Falls was a dream to her, a folly to her parents, an inscrutable idea to the rest of the world . . . but nothing at all if she didn't somehow steer the Ellie-craft toward it.

And where did Carl actually fit into it all?

What if everything got ruined somehow?

What if she planned a thing, did a thing, *chose a path*—and it was the wrong one?

"I'm not afraid of anything," she murmured. "Not lightning, not crashing my bike, not fire, not muggers, not the Germans invading . . . Mom and Dad always called me Ellie the Brave or Ellie the Fearless. But thinking about *this*—it's got my stomach all tied up in knots and jittery!"

"Sorry," Margaret said with a wan smile. "I guess taking my mind off *my* troubles only made you more aware of your own."

"I think I need to think more about this. I think— I need more ice cream."

"I'll get this next round," Margaret volunteered. "But just a club soda for me this time. Unfortunately, too much thinking on ice cream ruins my digestion. Otherwise I'd drink an ocean of milkshakes this week."

EIGHT

After they said their goodbyes Ellie realized she had left her bicycle at the zoo and had to walk all the way back there before going home. It was now closed; Old Ned was on patrol and merely rolled his eyes when she pointed desperately at the bike rack through the bars of the gate, but then he took out his giant ring of keys and let her in.

Empty of people, long shadows obscuring detail, the zoo just looked like a fancy collection of buildings in an otherwise normal neighborhood: a college, maybe, landscaped with very normal oak trees and Callery pears, yews and privet, neatly mown grass between the paths with a boulder or two for aesthetics. All was silent except for the crickets and buzz of june bugs.

Then an exotic call cut through the stillness of the evening: the growly, distinct cry of the Australian owlet-nightjar.

The scene immediately transformed into the magical and unique place it really was. The bird was reminding the world that special things happened here; it wasn't just a cluster of administrative buildings. The zoo held tiny pieces of other worlds. Ellie felt her heart nearly explode with the wonder of it all.

"What's the holdup, McGill?" Ned prompted.

"Sorry!"

Ellie hadn't even realized she had paused. But even after she hopped onto her bike and sped into the night and the gate clanged shut behind her with a solid finality, the power of the moment still held sway; she pedaled extra hard, almost overcome with the feeling of the great and wonderful unknown that could be found anywhere, if you just paid attention.

And then she remembered Margaret, whose time at the zoo was over.

She faltered, the bike making an ugly, jangly sound as she mis-pedaled backward and the chain, always precarious to begin with, clanked with unhappiness at this maneuver. Ellie recovered herself and turned the wheel, pushing just as hard into this new direction. She turned down Ash Street and made for Carl's house.

It was summer, so the sky wasn't dark yet. Ellie had forgotten to check the town clock as she left Woolworth's, and she didn't have a watch, but she estimated it to be around five, deep into Fredricksen Late Afternoon Routine Time (Weekend Edition). Mr. and Mrs. would have the radio on while she prepared supper and he balanced the checkbook and paid bills.

(The show was always H. V. Kaltenborn with the news, turned down far lower than the radio at the McGill household, which had to be audible above the sounds of too many children.)

Carl would be quietly puttering in his room upstairs, either tinkering with his radio set or doing homework.

"Carl!" Ellie whispered as loud as she dared, stopping her bike on the lawn under his window. When he didn't respond immediately she picked up a small pebble and expertly chucked it at the the glass; it hit with a faint *tink*.

After a moment she saw movement, and the window slid quietly open. Yup: Carl still had his headset on; he must have been trying to "make contact" with someone on his radio or whatever.

"Ellie, it's early—both my parents are home and right downstairs!" he whispered back, looking alarmed.

"I know! I had to talk to you. A terrible thing happened today—oh, hang on."

It was ridiculous trying to "shout" an entire conversation as complicated as this one in low voices up to the second story. With the smooth, unthinking movements of years of practice, Ellie dropped her bike into the dirt and skittered up the trellis on the side of the porch, as agile and silent as a cat. She hauled herself up onto the roof and tiptoed over the stone shingles to his window, leaning into the slant so she wouldn't fall. Carl watched her while also glancing anxiously at the floor as if he could see through the boards to what was happening downstairs. But his look of anxiety was replaced every other moment with a rosy grin, like a record skipping. His face must have ached from switching so quickly between such conflicting expressions.

Ellie perched herself comfortably on the ledge of his window. For anyone else, it might have looked awkward.

"Leroy *fired Margaret* at the zoo today!"

She was still upset with the news, of course, but didn't mind feeling dramatic imparting it to him. It *was* dramatic. She wasn't doing Margaret a disservice in the retelling.

"What!" Carl whispered in horror.

"The snake that got lost—the pit viper? Remember? They found it—it was all sick already when they landed, sad and severely dehydrated, and it *died* today. Margaret had words with Leroy about how thoughtless his collecting of animals was and how it didn't serve the zoo or science, and how it betrayed the animals . . . and then he fired her on the spot! And *gave her job to Gus*."

"No, the . . . errand guy?"

She nodded. "Yeah, Leroy did it to embarrass her. And then she left, cool as a cucumber. Carl, boy, you should have seen her . . . cream wouldn't set in her mouth."

Carl shook his head, trying to understand it all. "Leroy fired her because she was concerned about the safety of the animals? And then he replaced her with an inexperienced dolt? That's not just cruel . . . that seems like a really stupid idea for the zoo. But also cruel."

Ellie watched the thoughts and feelings emerge across the skin of his face like dew appearing on a midnight field: mysterious, magical, dependable.

"Poor Ms. Klein," he said. "I can't imagine what she's going through right now. Fired *and* worried about all of her animals. With no way to protect them."

For reasons she didn't fully understand, these unromantic and sympathetic words made her want to lean over and . . . touch his cheeks? Grab him?

Kiss him?

Instead she said:

"I think she was holding it all together—barely—until

she got to the gates. She looked back and—Carl, it was awful. So sad. She's done so much for that place. I took her out for an ice cream."

"You *did*?"

"She's taken such good care of me, and told me so much about the zoo . . . and birds . . . and *life*. I just wanted to do *something* for her. So I asked if she wanted me to take her out for an ice cream at Woolworth's. She said yes. And we went."

Carl's smile was wide, pleased, and a little surprised: like he never in a million years could have guessed that would happen next, or that Ellie would do such a thing. He had discovered something new and previously secret about her when they thought they had known everything about each other entirely. There were still unplumbed depths.

Ellie felt herself glow under that smile.

"That was really, really nice of you, Ellie. Well done." He patted her knee as best as he could given how she sat. His eyes darted back as he suddenly became re-aware of their positions, maybe listening for a break in the radio's drone downstairs.

"She had an ice cream soda and a seltzer. I had two sodas," Ellie admitted. Carl laughed, covering his mouth at the last moment. "She's upset, but she's got savings. . . . And

I know it's selfish for me to even think about this right now but . . .

"I think—thought?—Leroy was *amazing,* Carl! Brave and adventurous and determined and all that. But I don't think he likes women, or maybe smart women. To the point of making decisions that don't even make sense. Maybe he just doesn't realize the terrible mistake he's made. Maybe if someone told him . . . I don't know. . . .

"Margaret made the zoo wonderful, and I think she created my job for me and kept it safe. What am I going to do now without her there to tell me about the birds? What if I need someone in the offices to fight for me?"

"Keep a low profile until you see which way the wind is blowing," Carl suggested. "Do your job, listen to what everyone is talking about, keep out of the way."

"I was going to quit too—"

"No! Ellie!"

"No, I really was. But she told me to stay. The animals are going to need all the help they can get, she said."

"Of course they are. And if Leroy doesn't like smart girls, your quitting isn't going to mean much to him. What else did she say?"

"We talked about—" She suddenly thought of the rest of the conversation, about her and Carl, and what they meant to each other. And here they were, perched on either side of an open window. Her position was precarious; he had both feet safely on the floor. It was a beautiful summer evening, with long shadows and sweet smells, and suddenly she recalled the cry of the owlet-nightjar. ". . . other things. I think she didn't want to think about herself right then. I think she was too shook up."

"It's so strange to think of someone, someone *else*, I mean, not your dad or your uncle, just someone you know, getting fired from his job. Her job. For no good reason. At least she doesn't have anyone depending on her."

"Nope, just a bunch of animals who might die," Ellie said sadly.

They were both quiet for a moment. A chair shifted downstairs; the control on the radio was adjusted. His dad's voice could be heard, authoritative and deep, and the murmuring voice of his mom in return.

Then the deep voice again, but louder:

"Carl?"

"Hang on, Ellie," Carl said, taking off his headset and handing it to her distractedly. "Be right back! *COMING!*"

Ellie used the noise of his thumping downstairs to pull herself all the way into his room. Might as well make herself more comfortable while she waited for him to return. She went over to his radio, a boxy science-fiction-looking contraption with dials and a thin whisper of static coming from the speaker. She plugged the headset back in to stop it. Like his bike and everything else he loved, he had personalized it, of course, with a decal on the side of his initials and some acronym she assumed was a radio club or something. She smiled and was about to head back to her window "seat" when she noticed his usually locked top desk drawer was open; some electronic bits and pieces were sparkling temptingly from it like jewels. This was where he hid his treasure. He used to keep candy in it when he was younger. Now it had some expensive hobby supplies, a silver half-dollar, his grandfather's cuff links, and . . .

Ellie's eyes grew wide as she gently picked up an old, slightly rusted bottle cap.

From a bottle of grape soda.

The safety pin was long gone, but the holes she had made for it were still there, a testament to its original use.

He had kept it? That piece of junk? For all these years?

Carl Fredricksen was born a neatnik. He had no trouble parting ways with old toys, worn-out tools, clothing that didn't fit, books that no longer interested him. His room from childhood through teenhood changed like everyone's—except that instead of accumulating the usual bits and bobs picked up along life's early journey (pretty rocks, terrible toddler drawings, broken pencils) it remained free of such impedimenta.

But he kept this . . .

She jumped as Carl's footsteps rang out on the stairs. She quickly shoved the pin back into the drawer and ran back to the window, unsure why she felt the need to pretend.

He kept the pin that she gave him on the day they first met!

"Whew," Carl breathed, closing the door behind him. "That was close. He wanted to know if I was exercising and suggested I do it in the basement instead. You're not as quiet as you think you are.

"Look, Ellie, I'm so glad you came over tonight, and I'm awfully sorry about Margaret. But . . . if my dad finds out you're here, practically in my room, he's going to—well, at the very least he's going to tell your parents. You know what will happen then."

"But I'm not actually *in* your room this time!"

Well, not anymore.

"Yeah . . . but we're not twelve. My parents are really, really strict. Things are different now." He didn't add that they might also not have exactly liked her. He didn't need to; it was obvious. They *tolerated* her as an old friend from the neighborhood but were still as formal as when they had all first met years ago.

Things are different now. It was so strange coming right

on the tail of what she and Margaret had been talking about. Or was Carl also feeling the whole outside world conspiring in hushed tones about this? Was he feeling something invisible from his parents, his friends, the radio, the magazines, the movies?

He had kept her pin.

Things were different . . . but his feelings for her had never changed.

If only he weren't so scared of his parents or whatever was going on in those moments where it seemed like something was going to happen . . .

If only *she* weren't scared . . .

If they were just left alone, if they had time, maybe they could figure things out for themselves.

"Yeah," she said woodenly. "I just wanted to tell you. I guess I should get going." She stood up, as easily as if she were on the ground, balancing carelessly on the edge of the roof.

"Ellie, wait, I—" Carl reached out to grab her, or stop her, but wound up just tapping her calf. "I'm *really* glad you came. It's the highlight of my day. I couldn't expect a better surprise if I had forgotten it was my birthday or won a lottery or something. I don't want anything to stop us from seeing each other. *Like my parents.* Who would."

She brightened. *Highlight of my day.*

"Bah, if we had a phone like normal people it wouldn't be a problem. I could just call you," she said gruffly.

STUPID. Why didn't she say the other things in her head?

"So get a ham radio! That would be just swell! We could Morse code each other all night," Carl said with a sigh, resting his head on his crossed arms on the window frame.

"That's *your* thing, Carl. If I had that kind of money I'd get a pet parrot."

"Yeah, I know. See you later, Ellie."

"Don't break an arm, Carl." It was their usual, secret goodbye. And without even looking, she leapt to the porch railing below, a single hand just touching the support column to guide her fall.

"What was that?" Mr. Fredricksen demanded, hearing the *thunk* of her landing. But by the time he got outside to look around she was long gone, pushing hard on her bike, breathing in nighttime air that tasted of grape soda.

NINE

The atmosphere around the zoo was dark and subdued. Of course there were a few of the new recruits—Gus, for example—who were loudly pleased with Margaret's dismissal, and also those who made inappropriate comments like "I was just getting somewhere with her" or "Well, maybe now that crazy dame'll settle down and get married!"

But *some* new recruits muttered quietly about how working for her was the first time they got their paychecks on time, and doubted the wisdom of Gus taking over payroll.

The old guard stayed stiff-lipped and grim; if it had been any other sort of workplace—a factory, say, or a department store—there probably would have been a slowdown or mass sick leave or other show of protest, but of course nobody worked at the zoo who didn't fiercely love animals. They needed care and love twenty-four hours a day, seven days a week, no matter what was going on with the domesticated house apes who were in charge. These employees, who broke into smiles and baby talk with the animals, offered only stony silence or enraged whispers to their fellow humans.

Nothing solidified the rift between the two factions more than the tearing down of the elephant paddock. Ellie only found out about the whole thing when she heard the noise of the giant steam shovel starting; she ran over to see what was going on and beheld to her shock that Mrs. Jumbo, the baby, and Fanny were in a temporary—and tiny—enclosure, watching the loud machine rip through the dirt while workmen pulled up the fences.

"What's going on?" Ellie asked Harry, who was digging a post hole. He was one of the old guard—not the best worker, honestly, but he had been there forever and generally preferred animals to people. His cap was pulled down over his brow and he had a thick piece of straw hanging out of his mouth like a cartoon of a hayseed.

"Told us it's for the next expedition. To Burma," he said, taking the distraction as a chance to stop and lean on his (traditional) shovel. "They're going to park the airplanes there. Make a real show of it for the crowds—they're going to take off into the air right after the speeches and all and fly away to the jungle."

"From the elephant paddock . . ." Ellie shook her head. "I wonder if they'll also land in an elephant paddock on the other side?"

Asian elephants were smaller than African ones, of course, so maybe not.

After such thoughtless treatment of the zoo's most beloved animals, the barbed silence between the two sets of employees became permanent and epic. One day when Ellie was in the animal commissary washing dishes she realized that it had been literal hours since she had seen anyone talk to anyone else (besides visitors). People who came in for the feed said nothing; they just pointed or took the appropriate dish and stomped out.

Dr. Hua must have also been depressed by the uneasy stillness of the zoo.

"That's it," he declared, leaping up with a *crack* from the bench where he was portioning out grain for the birds. "I think it's time."

Ellie watched curiously as he went over to a large carpet bag tucked behind sacks of Flamingo Feed™ and carefully took out what looked like a portable typewriter case. Which would have made some sort of sense; no one from the old guard wanted to go to the administrative offices for any reason anymore. Gus had cleared out Margaret's desk, slid pictures of pin-up girls under the glass blotter, and arranged the toys he was always playing with in the drawers (along with a stash of candy and soda bottles, all of which were already infested with ants). Dr. Hua getting his own typewriter so he could write up his own requisitions and memos seemed absolutely reasonable.

But he fussed with whatever it was for a while, so that couldn't have been it. Ellie stood on her tiptoes trying to see, impatient for the denouement. Finally he moved his body, and what a surprise! He was carefully dropping a needle onto a record already rotating on a platter. A gramophone . . . ? There was no cord for it to plug in; the player had a hand crank just like the old Victrola her parents owned. Tinny music began to come out of the speaker.

"Things were becoming a little too quiet around here." A rare grin showed all of Dr. Hua's perfect white teeth, and his years seemed to drop away. Why, he must have been no older than Margaret, really. "I think all of us—animals *and* people—could use a little music."

"I thought radios aren't allowed, zoo rules—"

"Well, good thing this isn't a radio," he said smugly. "It's a Capitol Model U-24: for travel and camping."

"You *camp* with that?"

"No, but I also don't play my *good* records on it," he said with a tone she couldn't interpret. Maybe it meant something to other people who owned record players.

A guitar riff played out, and then a drum with a rhythm that didn't make sense at first. Then a saxophone and a trumpet began playing, but not a tune, not exactly.

"Hey!" Ellie exclaimed excitedly. "It sounds like Dizzy Gillespie."

"You know jazz?" Dr. Hua asked in surprise. "This isn't the stuff you dance to. . . ."

"No, but Carl hates dancing. I think he likes this kind of jazz *because* you can't really dance to it."

"This is the Carl I always see you running around with?"

"Yes. Carl Fredricksen. And I don't know if I would call it 'running around,' Dr. Hua. . . ."

He held up a hand. "I meant literally. You never *stop* running, Ellie McGill. I'm just amazed he can keep up with you. You're always running or biking or leaping or climbing. But he likes jazz, huh? Good taste. Maybe he should come by sometime. Enjoy the swinging tunes of the Commissary Jazz Club."

With the music on Ellie definitely found herself perking up. She and Dr. Hua still didn't speak much, but he swayed to the music and occasionally pretended the different metal dishes were a drum and cymbal set, tapping on them in time with the mad drummer who went off on his own with a percussive tune from somewhere inside his head.

Some people who stopped by to pick up their animals' feed or to drop off dirty dishes just shook their heads at the music . . . but some smiled and nodded along, and a few even stayed longer than strictly necessary to listen. Old Ned tried to soft-shoe a little around the room, and Agnes, who insisted it was devil's music, wouldn't leave until the piece had ended. There was a strict no-eating policy in the commissary for fear of cross contamination—for the animals, not the humans—but in less than a week people started showing up at the end of the day with a bottle of soda or cup of coffee to just hang out. Sometimes someone would bring a bottle of grape Nehi for Ellie.

So there were five people in the crowded commissary late one afternoon when William sent for Ellie—specifically and formally, via a folded note delivered by an adult man now apparently on a lower tier than Gus. All eyes were on her as she read; gossip was an even hotter commodity now that there was less actual talk.

Ellie McGill, Please come see me at once. We need to speak. —Hodgson

Ellie hurried off, worried; she hadn't been inside the administrative offices since Margaret left. When she opened the door—cautiously—Sasha looked up from his corner and thumped his tail happily against the ground. Otherwise it was quiet; Leroy wasn't there, nor any of the Burma expedition crew. Gus was trying to sharpen a pencil with a pen knife, his tongue sticking out of his mouth over his blunt teeth in concentration. Ellie flinched without thinking, expecting blood. William was at his desk, frowning at paperwork.

"Ah, McGill," he said upon seeing her.

Then he paused; the moniker didn't sound right to either one of them.

"Miss McGill," he tried again.

Despite Margaret's name and absence not being mentioned anywhere, the "Ms." of "Ms. Klein" hung in the air like a persistent ghost.

"Ellie, take a walk with me?" he finally asked, getting up.

She was confused; if he wanted to fire her or ask about the record playing, there was only Gus to overhear a dressing down. And since William only carried out Leroy's orders, what else could he possibly say to her in secret? But as he strode to the door and opened it for her to go through first, his bearing seemed a little more military, more boss-like, and less hunched than normal. Between that and his fishing for the right title with her it was all a little strange.

Ellie followed him into the polar zone's main building and into its back offices. On a heavy metal table in an exam room was a large cage . . . and in it was the fancy Charles

Muntz purple bird! It looked too small for its oversized enclosure; it stuck to the perch, all tiny and droopy. Now it and William were a perfect match; the Head Keeper was back to his usual agitated self, hunched over with hands shoved deep into his pockets.

"What's going on, Mr. Hodgson?" Ellie asked cautiously.

"I don't know what's wrong with him," William said with a sigh. "No one does, honestly, but no one else has really tried to figure it out because *I'm* the Head Keeper, and by default now also the head ornithologist. But I'm not, not really. I worked with pigeons in the army. And that's because I used to raise them and race them, back on the Lower East Side with the Italian kids. I can patch a wing and incubate eggs and apply fungicidal powder, but that's about it. I don't know anything about any other birds! Especially foreign ones."

Ellie decided then was not the time to point out that pigeons were not native to his homeland, New York; they were from Europe, and terribly invasive, like English sparrows and starlings—and Norwegian rats and German cockroaches.

And humans, after all.

"But what about the other . . . more . . . bird people, who used to work with Margaret?" she ventured instead. "Elspeth used to help out Margaret, and Helen . . ."

"Oh, Leroy's got everyone so scared and jumpy after firing her that no one will say anything that might get them in trouble," William said with a groan. "Or they are *not* helping me, hoping I fail, but I don't think that's the case. Everyone here obviously loves the animals.

"And . . . all right . . . The truth is, I need to keep this hush-hush. Leroy's still got this cockamamie plan that this bird here is going to be the star attraction of the new Lost Worlds: South America exhibit. Which has already opened. So *of course* Leroy wants to do a second celebration, an official 'dedication' of the already-built Charles Muntz Pavilion. . . . Don't get me started. . . .

"So anyway, right now, as someone Ms. Klein mentored, you are the closest thing to a *helpful* certifiable ornithologist here, one who won't gossip with the others. I need you to do whatever you need to make this bird be happy and live."

Ellie approached and gave the cage a closer look. It was spotlessly clean and the bottom was covered in fresh shavings. A food bar had been set up with three carefully separated types: tiny black thistle seeds, a mixture of hulled sunflower and corn and grain, and mealworms. There was a sparkling dish of water and a bulb of sticky sweet hummingbird syrup, as well as a vase with several hibiscus blossoms. Without any idea of what actual type of bird it was—but since it looked a little like a hummingbird it might have a craving for bugs and syrup—all possibilities had been spread before it.

None of the food had been touched.

Up close, the bird itself was a thing of almost ridiculous, comical beauty: a deep purple all over with a little iridescent patch on the chest that would have been greenish on an actual hummingbird. The purple was saturated and luscious, like Ellie's favorite drink, grape soda pop. Its grey feet and long beak were clean, its eyes also clean but dull. The wings looked crumpled; she would have to hold the bird in her hands to figure out the problem but suspected it was just a botched clipping job. There was no indication of sickness or distress beyond one of the broken crest feathers on its head.

"But I'm not *really* an ornithologist, Mr. Hodgson. I don't know how to cure him or take care of him properly." Though more than anything she ached to run her fingers through its feathers and figure out what was wrong and ask the bird about its home. "I haven't even graduated high school! I'm just an intern. If something happens to him . . ."

Suddenly, Ellie saw where all this was heading. The intrinsic logic of assigning the care of a rare, one-of-a-kind (in North America) gift from Charles Muntz to a high school student.

"If something happens to him, it will be *my* fault," she realized aloud.

"Well, no one could blame you for trying," William said with a fake grin. "Not if you did your best."

"Leroy would fire *me*, not you. You'd be safe." She crossed her arms angrily.

"Aw, kid, cut me some slack, will ya?" he begged. "This is just . . . a weekend job for you. I'm an adult! I have responsibilities! I got a mom back home I send money to, and a little brother whose left foot don't work right."

"I give half my pay to my *family*," Ellie shot back. "My six younger brothers and sisters and my big brother, who came back from the war with a plate in his head. Everybody's got troubles, Mr. Hodgson!"

The permanent Head Keeper deflated. He ran a hand through his hair. "You're right. You're right. I know that. But look, you're a whip-smart kid and a smart-looking girl and you got more energy than a dynamo. You'll have no problems ever getting a job like this again—probably a way better one. Me? Guys like me don't *get* jobs like this. The only reason I'm the head of the zoo is 'cause Leroy took a liking to me . . . that and I didn't make a big deal about his cushy position during the war. I don't have a college degree, I got no work experience beyond pigeons and the war. If I get fired, it's welfare and maybe factory work if I'm lucky. This is . . . the gift of a lifetime. C'mon, Ellie. You know how it is: How many kids who dream of running the zoo actually get to?"

William's hazel eyes pierced her heart, and not in a romantic way. He had hit a nerve: He *was* living the dream. Just as she was, getting paid to work at a zoo. And, all right, he *was* an adult and needed the money for himself to live as well as support his family. But far more importantly than that, he admitted he didn't know what to do with the purple bird, and even if it was a secret, it showed that he was someone who cared at least a little about its welfare and not just his job. Someone else might have just washed their hands of it—claimed a fox or a cat got the bird, lied about the whole thing.

"Oh, all right, Mr. Hodgson," she groaned. "I'll take care of . . . Soda-Pop here."

She wasn't sure just when she had named it—him? Usually the most iridescent birds were boys. "But not just for you. It's for his own sake."

"Thank you, Ellie McGill," William said with a long let-out sigh of relief. "You have no idea how much this means to me."

She wasn't normally someone who kept a constant tally of the value of everything—it wasn't the way she was raised.

But growing up without much money *had* given her a sixth sense for detecting opportunity. And here was a doozy.

"AND ALSO," she added with great dignity, "I'm going to want a little something in return."

She didn't feel right about it, entirely. It was somehow betraying Soda-Pop and cheapening their new relationship.

William tensed. "What?"

"Next Saturday I want off—*with* pay. It's my birthday month and Carl has something special planned for me, I think.

"*And* Carl and I get to feed the sea lions from *inside* the enclosure. Three times. The first time, on my birthday. Promise me."

"You got it, Ellie."

She felt insulted by how quickly he answered and the sparkle of humor in his eyes.

Maybe she should have asked for something more.

TEN

The first thing Ellie decided to do with Soda-Pop was to get him out of the back room of the infirmary and into fresh air. She had no certainty this was a good idea and was well aware that some of the urge to do so came from mother mythology: *get outside in the sunlight, it'll do you good.* But she also knew that as clean as all the rooms and enclosures were kept, nothing was completely antiseptic in an underfunded postwar zoo—possibly any zoo (and the new recruits didn't wipe things down with bleach and disinfectants as often as they should have). Some animals that came into the clinic to be treated had bacterial, viral, and fungal infections; some of those bacteria, viruses, and fungi remained on surfaces and in the air.

After she discussed it with William they decided to put

Soda-Pop in an undistinguished-looking outside enclosure that was worked into the brick arch of the aviary; people barely looked at it in their haste to get to the More Interesting Birds. In the past it had housed red-tailed hawk rescues, crows, and "common" passerines in need of rehabilitating. Nothing exciting like a peacock or a hornbill or a toucan. Hidden there, no one would notice Soda-Pop until the big reveal at the official rededication of the Charles Muntz Pavilion.

She let the bird adjust to his new surroundings for a day and made her first attempt to pick him up for an exam the next morning. She wasn't wearing gloves—and instantly regretted it. The bird nipped at her, *hard*. Despite his long and almost hummingbird-like beak, he drew blood.

Ellie went to the first aid station immediately. She washed and swabbed the cut with betadine and wrapped it up in a bandage the way they learned to in the Outdoor Guides First Aid for Frontierswomen course . . . and then went back to try again. This time, wearing rubber gloves.

Soda-Pop was nearly weightless under all his shiny feathers; while larger than a typical hummingbird, he was still lighter than a normal songbird. Ellie didn't get the sensory experience of running her bare fingers through his luscious coverts—the feathers that covered the tops of his primary and secondary wing feathers—but she was still able to examine him enough to determine that she was right about some of the bird's problems. His wings had indeed been clipped very, very poorly, by someone who obviously didn't know much about birds or what they were doing. "Wing clipping" didn't mean literally and permanently injuring the wings of a bird; it meant cutting only a couple of the longest flight feathers, and not excessively. When done correctly a bird would still be able to glide; he just wouldn't be able fly *up*, gaining height.

But poor Soda-Pop had *all* his primaries and even some of his secondaries chopped off bluntly like it had been done all at once with a pair of kids' scissors. It would take a complete molt before they grew back, and without knowing what kind of bird he was, Ellie could only guess how long that would be. Weeks? Months? A year?

In the meantime, the poor thing couldn't even flutter to the ground. He sort of clumsily fell when necessary, flailing his useless wings as hard as he could to soften the crash. Once on the ground he hopped around unhappily.

"All right, you're definitely not a ground bird like a dove. You don't want to be there," Ellie said sympathetically. "I understand. I want to fly, and I wasn't even born—or hatched—being able to. I've just always dreamed about it. Oh, don't be sad! Someday I will; I'll get to fly a plane or ride in a balloon with Carl.

"I guess I mean I *assume* with Carl? He likes planes almost as much as I do. I can't imagine going without him." She thought about this for a moment as she stroked Soda-Pop. He bit her. She ignored it. "I was talking with Margaret—I can't imagine being in a plane or balloon or anything *without* Carl. What does that mean? I mean, I know what it means . . . I just don't *know* know. You know?"

She might have imagined it, but it seemed like Soda-Pop gave her a look.

"Anyway, I love biking because it's like flying. Too bad I can't give you a tiny bike to race around on, like those parrots at the circus do."

But that gave Ellie an idea. Macaws rarely flew if they didn't have to, choosing to walk on branches and use their beaks as gripping hands instead, crossing vines like bridges in between trees. Maybe she could set up the inside of the enclosure like a jungle with everything connected so Soda-Pop could at least hike or hop everywhere he needed or wanted to go.

She spent a full day weaving an intricate series of branches and ropes around the inside of his cage, creating paths that led to the feeders, to the ground, to a little platform, to the perch he seemed to favor. When she was done she looked at her construction with smug satisfaction, and left the zoo that night confident that she had solved all of the little bird's problems.

But the next morning she saw that Soda-Pop was in the exact same place where she had left him. He didn't hop anywhere.

He *could* have. He just didn't.

He still sat miserably on his perch and tried to bite her whenever she put her hands in.

Ellie felt the littlest bit miffed about this. She handled him very gently, spoke to him quietly, and was doing her best to make him feel better. Couldn't he tell that? Just a little?

In the best of all possible worlds Soda-Pop would have taken to her immediately, perched on her shoulder like a falcon, and tried to preen her hair with his long beak. She would be friends with a glamorous, celebrity avian from the other side of the world.

Failing that, couldn't he at least stop trying to attack her?

"What's the matter with you, buddy?" she pleaded. "I'm trying to *help* you. I know you're probably homesick, and maybe sick-sick, and we don't know what you eat, and you don't like being locked up . . . okay, actually, I'm surprised that more animals from Leroy's expedition aren't acting like you—but the agouti is doing just fine, actually. You probably wish you were home, where it's warm and full of plants, huh? Trees and vines? And it smells like perfume? A jungle paradise?"

She might have been imagining it, but it almost looked like he was listening to her, turning his head very slightly to pay attention.

When she reached out to gently stroke him he still bit her. But it was lighter this time. Almost half-hearted.

Wondering if he was nocturnal, Ellie lingered as late as she could at the zoo and came back in the morning as early as she could to watch him. Once she even tried staying at the zoo overnight. She had a whole plan in her head about telling her parents a version of the truth the next day—she got locked in, the guard had to leave because of some family emergency—but someone must have seen her hanging around a little too long and ratted her out to Old Ned. He didn't say anything, just walked behind her with a glare and furrowed eyebrows, pointedly slamming the gate shut behind her. She wondered if she could steal a copy of his keys.

But she gave up that idea and tried instead observing Soda-Pop from afar, hidden in a bush across the way, using binoculars. This was a technique the other keepers used when they needed to track a new behavior or watch an animal without interfering.

But what she observed was just him sitting there,

scratching or picking at his chest feathers with his beak occasionally, cocking his head to follow a free cousin—sparrow or chickadee—passing overhead, chirping and cutting deftly through the air. Okay, that was a little heart-breaking. No wonder he was so crabby.

Then, after several (boring) hours, Ellie caught him eyeing something interestedly at the bottom of his cage, turning his head back and forth to get a better look. He hopped down—finally using her system of fake vines!—and grabbed something off the floor of his cage, snapping it up in his beak. Movement! Hunting behavior! Success!

She couldn't see what the thing was, however; he swallowed it too quickly. Maybe a corpse beetle or isopod or some other bug that was slow enough to be caught by the disabled bird.

Excited, Ellie hurried to the commissary.

Dr. Hua jumped when she came in without knocking. He awkwardly stood in front of the record player with his arms out, blocking a view of it from any potential hostiles.

"It's just me, Dr. Hua! Oh, and Mr. Hodgson doesn't know or care about the music, I guess. It's all about Soda-Pop!"

"I keep telling people not to bring in their drinks. . . ."

"No," she laughed. "The new bird. Soda-Pop!"

She told him the story about William putting her in

charge of the special bird's care, and Dr. Hua looked more and more intrigued.

"Hm. Hodgson isn't as dumb as he looks. Or maybe he's not smart; just cunning, like a fisher cat. I'd suggest some overripe peach or other soft fruit—no, grapes, I think we're out of peach . . ." He opened the icebox and began poking in it.

"No, Dr. Hua. I said it was a *bug* he was eating. Do you have any fruit flies or something?"

He laughed. "Do I look like someone who can afford to order fresh bugs from some supply house? What is this, the Bronx Zoo? You put the fruit out in his cage and it *attracts* the fruit flies, Ellie. But you have to be careful and clear it out before it gets too rotten; that invites disease and worse things."

"Got it, Dr. Hua! That's so smart!" She took the proffered fruit—which already looked half rotten and disgusting—with a big grin.

The flies indeed came, but Soda-Pop didn't care.

He did *watch* them, at least, keeping one bird-eye in their direction when the cloud of insects became noticeably large and annoying, but that was all.

Outside the zoo Ellie did all the research she could on hummingbirds, especially the crowned wood nymph, which Soda-Pop most resembled. But her school and town libraries only had the most basic bird books. With much wheedling she managed to get an inter-library loan of *Birds of the Southern Hemisphere*—which was exciting! She had never borrowed a book from another town before. When she went in to get it, the thick volume was behind the reference librarian's desk on a shelf and had a special slip of paper wrapped around its spine with her name on it.

Sadly, there was only a brief paragraph about the wood nymph, and no references to any other bird like it.

Ellie met Carl at the fry shack after work, despondent.

"It just looks so hopeless. *He* looks hopeless. I don't want him to die, Carl—and it's not just about losing my job."

"I know, Ellie. I don't think anyone would think that about you," he said with a smile.

Ellie shoved five fries into her mouth. That was the optimum number for crunch and mouthfeel. "I feel like I'm just beginning to get through to him. We're just beginning to bond. He *listens* to me, Carl—it looks like he's really paying attention now. I wish he was better and we had more time. . . ."

"Hey, why don't you talk to Margaret? If anyone can help a bird, she can. And you've been saying how much you miss her . . . this is a *perfect* opportunity to call."

Ellie brightened like a cornflower opening its petals for sunny weather. Why hadn't *she* thought of that? "Carl, you've got a good egg inside that noggin of yours. No bird pun intended."

He nodded modestly. *Preening*, but Ellie decided not to use that pun either.

"Don't forget about next Saturday—you have to ask for the day off so we can do my surprise."

"Already done," Ellie said proudly. And she was getting paid for the day off, too. "Are we going to try to find the Haunted Rocks, over in Willington?"

"I'm not saying. Because, see, it's a *surprise*. Remember?"

"The Haunted Rocks would be incredible; that's all *I'm* saying."

They chewed in happy silence.

"So, uh, what do you talk to a bird about?" Carl eventually asked, maybe curious, maybe trying to distract her while stealing one of her fries.

"Oh, things, you know . . . life, you . . ."

"Me?"

"Sometimes. It's not like I have any girlfriends to gossip with."

"What do you tell him about me?"

"Geez, Carl, don't get a swelled head or I'll tell him about that too."

She stole back *two* fries, and dipped them in the ketchup

with mock annoyance—along with three of her own, of course.

As soon as they finished their shakes and burgers, Ellie went to the payphone at the gas station and dialed the number on Margaret's card: *BLoomington 9-0648*.

"Hello?" The voice sounded so demure—or maybe it was the electric signals warping everything weirdly—that Ellie was thrown for a moment. This was Margaret?

"Hello? Ma—uh, Ms. Klein? This is Ellie McGill."

"Ellie! How nice to hear from you!"

"I'm having trouble with a bird," she said immediately. Then she closed her eyes in frustration with herself. "I'm sorry, Ms. Klein. *How are you?*"

Margaret laughed, a very *not* demure cross between a snort and a bark. "I am absolutely fine, Ellie, and you never need to apologize for asking me about a bird. What's the issue? Who is it?"

"It's . . . the new one. From the tepuis in Venezuela. Soda-Pop. The purple one that looks like a crowned wood nymph that's going to be in the special Muntz exhibit, the one with the plaque. He's doing poorly and sort of wasting away. William's having me take care of him. . . ."

"William's making you do it? He's smarter than he looks," she muttered, echoing Dr. Hua's sentiments.

Ellie told her all the things she had tried: the food, the fresh air, the impromptu climbing gym, the fresh bugs. When she was done she waited while Margaret put the phone down and looked through her specialty journals and academic reports about South American birds. Ellie listened to the homey noises, the clips and clops of walking—*heels?* inside?—objects being picked up and put down and papers being shuffled. She wondered what her house looked like. Or *apartment*, she decided, looking at the card. *234 Oak Street No. 1.*

"Nothing leaps out at me immediately, Ellie," Margaret finally said, picking the phone back up. "You've tried all the obvious things—maybe you could try other different types of sweet liquid, like tree sap or honey. Where you'll get tree sap, I don't know—tap a birch tree, maybe? Probably not a pine. Try honey . . . and try bees, if you can. Some hummingbirds snap 'em up like candy. Otherwise it sounds like you're doing your best, Ellie. Either the bird came in ailing with a disease, or it's suffering from what we call 'failure to thrive.' Taken out of its environment, its social milieu, thrown into an alien world . . . some animals can't take the transition. This can apply to single individuals, you know, not a whole species. Soda-Pop might just miss his home."

Ellie's shoulder slumped and she leaned back against the back of the telephone booth in dejection. She wasn't *really* expecting a fantastic immediate answer that would fix everything, was she?

The image of a young Ellie appeared in her mind, looking somewhat chagrined and guilty. Yes, Mind-Ellie admitted. She absolutely was.

"It's not your fault," Margaret said as if she could sense what was going on over the telephone wires. "You are trying your hardest in a situation that would be difficult even with all the support in the world. It's good that the poor bird is isolated, anyway, in case he's carrying something communicable to the other birds. The best, *correct*, thing to do would be to return him to the wild and let nature take its course . . . But obviously that's not an option. Poor dear, I wish I could see him myself. And I wish I could see *you* myself, Ellie! Feel free to call me or drop by anytime, with a zoo problem or any problem at all, or just to chat. I'm mostly at home in the evenings, or you can call ahead. I miss our little lunches—and sodas."

"That would be swell, Ms. Klein," Ellie said, trying to sound grateful.

Her next day at the zoo was actually the paid Saturday off that she had bargained for with William, her birthday month treat with Carl. But she couldn't wait to try out Margaret's suggestions if they might help Soda-Pop. So she went into the zoo at 5:30 a.m. as if it were a normal Saturday, but with all her gear packed on her bike to meet Carl at nine in front of the clubhouse. She was still convinced that they were going to bike all the way to the Haunted Rocks—old stories said it took so long for the winter ice to melt under the rocks that even in early summer you could feel ghostly wisps of cold air when clambering over them and maybe even see mist issuing up mysteriously from beneath.

Dr. Hua gave her a sleepy raised eyebrow when she came in dressed for adventure and not in her zoo scrubs.

"Didn't the boy in charge give you the day off? Paid, I'm told?"

"Yes, I'm just here to beg for some honey, and birch sap, if you have it. I called Margaret—uh, Ms. Klein—yesterday and she suggested to try that with Soda-Pop. Well, she really thinks he should be set free at home, in Venezuela, but that seems unlikely."

"You talked to Ms. Klein, huh?" he said casually, opening up a cabinet and pulling out some jars. "How, um, how is she doing?"

"I don't know, I didn't really ask, I was being selfish and worried about Soda-Pop. But we're going to get together sometime for a real sit-down, she said."

"That's nice that you keep up with her. No birch sap—and no Russian markets around here where you could buy any. You'll have to tap your own. But here's some honey. Let me just put it in a petri dish for you."

"Thanks, Dr. Hua!" She took the dish from him carefully, trying not to spill a single amber drop.

"You know," he said, wiping his fingers with a rag, "you're like a real keeper now. Coming in on your day off to help an animal. Very admirable in a sixteen-year-old."

"Thanks, Dr. Hua!" It was the highest compliment she had ever received. Maybe not actually—maybe teachers or her parents had made more grandiose statements—but this meant more to Ellie than the goldest star on a five-page essay.

Soda-Pop was half asleep on his perch, beak tucked into his breast. Ellie opened the cage and delicately—but quickly—set the dish of honey in, just barely avoiding getting bitten.

"Here you go, buddy. I'm not going to be back today, so you have to promise me you'll try it and I'll just have to trust you."

He lifted his head, regarded her, and yawned.

"You can go back to sleep as soon as I go. It's my birthday adventure . . . I'm sure Carl has something great planned. He's really good at that kind of surprise. I should do something nice for him sometime. Ohhh, maybe I'll get him a cake because of the one the squirrels ate! That's a good idea, Soda! Only not today, because it's really *my* birthday month, and my birthday treat, and that would be weird."

The bird gave her what she was pretty sure was another *look*.

"No, I'm not being selfish. It *would* be weird. All right, I'll see you tomorrow, okay? Try to eat something!"

ELEVEN

Even after she left, all of Ellie's thoughts were devoted to Soda-Pop, hoping he was on a brand-new, healthier path. Which didn't keep her from noticing Carl's lack of backpack when she saw him.

"Hey, Carl, what's the deal? You forget your lunch? I thought we were picnicking at the Haunted Rocks today." He *always* brought a bag even if there was no picnic, for holding a magazine or book or little gift to delay her when he needed a break (he thought he was being sneaky about it; silly boy). And he did love his snacks. . . .

"We're *not* going to the Haunted Rocks today," he said, a little smugly.

Ellie frowned.

"Carl, it's been a very hard week. This was going to be our special treat. *My* special treat."

"Well, I have something else planned for us."

"What is it?"

"Guess you'll just have to wait and see."

She was going to argue, try to drag it out of him, but something about the look on his face made her decide to play along. No bag meant no hiking, and no prepacked lunch meant . . . maybe he was going to take her someplace fancy as an early birthday gift. He had definitely noted her and Margaret's little lunches. Maybe there would be steak.

So she followed behind him on her bike, which was unusual—unless they were racing, she always led. Bored with his pace, she began doing lazy tricks: over-wobbling from side to side as if she were about to fall and then *just* catching herself. Pedaling with no hands. Then, on a good stretch of coasting, *standing up* on the middle bar with her hands out, balancing like a wing walker on an airplane. She even managed to wave at some passing little kids who gawked at her with terrible envy.

Carl looked back at her and rolled his eyes (but smiled).

They headed away from downtown—no steak; disappointing!—and Ellie let herself imagine a picnic he had set up in a romantic field somewhere. There would be a basket and fancy cheese, and bottles of grape soda, and he would finally admit to her all his feelings.

And then they would kiss, finally?

But the landscape became barren, ugly, and faded—dried meadows and fields left fallow for some reason. There was nothing out this way except for the other factory, the one her dad *didn't* work at, the one that made things out of rubber and stank so bad it had to be outside town limits, and also the tiny aerodrome. . . .

"Jiminy! Did you get us a tour of the planes? A *ride* in one?" She didn't even want to think about anything so exciting.

"No, and stop trying to guess."

The airport soon came into view: it was really just a couple of hangars and a building for the U.S. Army Air Forces. Parked out in front was a line of planes currently in use; she could see Lucy's and Leroy's on one side, sparkling clean like new toys. There were several actual military planes, one with a painting of a buxom blonde sitting a little lasciviously near the nose cone. That one had dents and pings in its metal from artillery. There was a brightly painted Republic P-47 Thunderbolt, as perfect as a model kit, a dark Vought F4U Corsair, and one with a distinctive double tail—definitely a Northrop Black Widow. There was even one biplane, a Curtiss Goshawk, which showed a lot of wear but very little tear. Maybe that was Lucy's, too.

"Wow, this is better than a museum," Ellie said. "Gosh, we should have come out here *ages* ago."

Carl said nothing but smiled mysteriously and beckoned her into the first hangar.

Inside were, disappointingly, *not* that many more planes, and those few were being fixed or taken apart. The rest of the yawning space had an area set up with seats and desks like a classroom, a metal stand supporting a slide machine and a projector, a lectern with U.S. ARMY AIR FORCES painted on it, and what looked like an eye doctor's office in miniature, complete with light machines and lenses and a poster of big and smaller letters. All of it looked a little dusty already.

"Guess they don't get many recruits since Armistice," Ellie ventured.

"Yup, that's right, little lady," said a mechanic, coming over from the plane he was working on. He had grease smudges on his dark cheeks and hands. A fishing cap was cocked rakishly to one side on his short hair. "Far less call for pilots now, except commercial and shipping. That's why it's so slow around here. Used to get dozens of young men from all over the county training to fly. You must be Carl and Ellie."

"Yes, sir," Carl said.

"Pleased t'meet you. I'm Jesse Smith. Now let me introduce you to the reason y'all are here . . . Meet Aunty Blue, a gen-u-ine AN-T-18 Basic Instrument Trainer."

He proudly gestured to a thing Ellie had barely registered in the corner. It sort of looked like a rich kid's play plane, fat and short, painted dark blue with a yellow tail and fat yellow wings. Next to it was a table with a large piece of glass covering its surface and a strange mechanical arm hung over it.

"You got it, and me, for one hour, kids," he said with a grin.

"You?" Carl asked uncertainly.

"You got a problem with *me*, son?" Jesse was still grinning—but his eyes looked strained.

"No, sir!" Carl yelped, chagrined. "I just thought you'd be wearing a captain's hat, or a jacket, or pins. Something official." His hand hovered restlessly at his side, where he held his little camera.

Jesse laughed, obviously relieved. "We don't stand around on formality anymore here, Carl. I'll put on something, my cap and goggles, for a birthday picture if you want. But a hat won't save your rear end in a high wind, you take my meaning."

"Birthday . . . ?" Ellie asked, finally getting it. "This is my birthday present? A training session?"

"Happy early birthday, Ellie," Carl said proudly. "Now you can take all your reading and put it to the test on the Link Trainer—it's supposed to perfectly simulate flying."

Ellie squealed and threw her arms around Carl. "You're the *best*, Carl Fredricksen!"

He blushed, but not too much.

Jesse helped her climb into the "cockpit." Before her, in person, were all the dials and switches from her book and imagination. The manifold pressure gauge, the air-fuel ratio, the RPMs . . . the throttle, the ignition switch, the brakes, the pitch controller, the toggle to retract the landing gear . . .

"Now normally you'd start with a tire and external check," Jesse said. "Of course, old Aunty here doesn't really have none of that. So . . ."

"Unlock the surface controls, make sure the parking brakes are set, check the fuel reserve," Ellie said, immediately doing all those things.

"You know your stuff, Ellie."

Carl might have smiled proudly, but Ellie didn't see him. She was too overcome with the need to touch and click and flip things that she had only read about and imagined for so long.

But while Ellie "knew her stuff" she had never actually

done any of it, and flying a plane, even a simulator, was very different from her imagination.

She did everything exactly like she had memorized from the textbook and practiced in her head, and managed to take off successfully . . .

On the sixth try.

And she wasn't ready for the actual pitch and roll of the simulator. Along with the violent knocks and tilts, it huffed and squealed and bellowed—did a real plane sound like this? louder? quieter?—and she forgot what she was doing, confused by the very un-bicycle-like movements.

"Ease up on the throttle, Ellie, you're gonna stall—or hit the moon," Jesse instructed.

She did so immediately, too quickly, and it did indeed stall. If this had been real life, she would have been in a terrifying freefall.

Jessie made the long whistling sound of something plummeting through the air, then clapped his hands together to mimic a *crash*.

"Didn't quite make it, Ellie, but you also didn't panic. That's *great*," Jesse said. "Let's try it again."

By the fourth attempt she finally made it up, flew for a minute, and landed back down successfully.

"Hot dog!" Carl called out.

But it was only after she had done that several times that Jesse let her "fly" a real course: as if she were taking a trip down to the city of Springfield. While she directed her imaginary plane he sat at the desk with the glass top and called out instructions or directions as if he were on her radio. The mechanically controlled pen on the metal arm drew her path above a map of the country; he described what features of the landscape she would be seeing if it were all real.

"If you look down now you'd see the sparkling Deerkill River, and you would use that to head south for a while . . ."

Ellie had no problem with *that* part—imagining mountains and towns below. And Carl helped the feeling of immersion by pushing over a giant three-wing fan to blow in her face as if she really were in an open cockpit, the wind in her hair. Very quickly she realized that most of the time piloting an airplane was *not* panicking and fighting gravity and reacting to things happening; during peacetime, at least, once you were up, flying was mostly calm with occasional adjustments. Relaxing. Dreamy.

The trip ended far too soon. When she landed, Ellie almost saw a cloud of dust blowing up around her. She jumped out of the simulator with a whoop and threw her arms around Carl again.

"That was *amazing*! Here I am, in Springfield already! It takes *hours* for us to get there by bus. But flying it only took—"

A quick look at the real-world clock, giant and plain and hanging on the far wall, showed that quite a bit more than an hour had passed.

"Aww, thank you, Mr. Smith," she said, blushing. "For not stopping it early. Carl, you don't have to pay more, do you?"

"It was my pleasure, Ellie." Jesse stuck out his hand and Ellie shook it enthusiastically. "You know, I've never actually had a trainee, not a single man, make it through a full course on his first try."

"I practice every night," she told him. "In my head."

He laughed. "Well, maybe someday they'll have an all-woman air squadron too. The Amazons! Let me just go get my uniform and we'll get a real birthday picture for you.

"You don't know what you got in that girl of yours, there," he told Carl sotto voce as he walked by—but not sotto enough for Ellie not to hear. "She's a crackerjack."

"She's not my girl," Carl said, "exactly. Yet. But yes, sir, I know exactly what I—*she* has there."

Jesse laughed quietly. "Good enough."

Ellie smiled, not unpleased with the exchange. Except . . . "yet." What was he waiting for?

She thought she saw him tip Jesse, or pay him, in a smooth handshake with a little bit of green sticking out. She wondered where he learned to do that, or if it was just part of the magic of Carl; knowing how the world worked and choosing how he stepped out into it. He saw a thing that needed to be done and instinctively approached it the right way. He didn't lash out on a whim and then pay for it later . . . which *might* have been standard operating procedure for Ellie.

She almost skipped like a schoolchild as they left the hangar; she almost grabbed his hand and swung it. She wondered what was next. It really felt like this was going to be the day when *something* happened.

"Carl, this is the most amazing birthday gift ever conceived of in the history of man."

He laughed. "Well, that's a bit much, but I'm glad you enjoyed it. I've been keeping it as a surprise for months."

"What's the plan for lunch, then?"

"Well, I thought you would get it, since I got you this," he said airily.

"Absolutely! I'll get lunch! Wow, I've been getting a lot of lunches lately . . ."

"I was kidding and you know it. I thought we'd go to the diner and have a proper sit-down meal, not one of our usual picnics."

She hadn't even realized she had his arm; they were walking like a real couple. It was early enough in the day that the sky was still bright with promise, not the sly, metallic darkening that indicated the afternoon was on its way out, a stern reminder of all the things you had yet to get done by the end of the day. Right now the world was their oyster, their bikes nearby.

There was a bench facing the parked planes, perfectly placed for watching takeoffs and landings. Ellie pulled Carl over to it, unwilling to leave the moment and its feelings just yet. In a strange reversal it felt like she was flying, and getting on their bikes and pedaling away would be like landing, plummeting to earth. Carl sat down with her at the same time, and it was like it was planned, their knees touching as they sank down onto it.

Nothing much was happening on the runway—people were walking around, someone was shaking metal filings off of a tool. Carl wasn't watching any of that, though; he was focused entirely on her.

"Carl, this really was the best birthday ever," Ellie whispered. "You know me so well—so much better than *anyone*. I can't believe you did all this for me."

"It wasn't anything," Carl said. "Thinking about you and how you smile, what *makes* you smile . . . it's easy. It makes the whole world brighter for me. Making you happy is more a gift to me than you. I want to see you smile and laugh every day."

"Every *day*?" she asked, finally turning from the runway to look at him. His eyes looked deeply into hers; they were the color of the skies she had imagined flying through. Airplanes zoomed in her head.

"Every hour. Every minute."

"Carl . . ." she breathed. "What are you saying?"

"I don't know, Ellie. I just want—I'm saying—I don't know what I'm saying. . . ."

"Okay, let's stop saying anything, then." She closed her eyes and leaned forward.

She could feel his breath on her lips; it smelled of peppermint . . .

"Hey, you all almost forgot your souvenir picture!"

Ellie and Carl jumped apart. She could have sworn she had felt his lips on hers for the briefest moment, like a moth landing and immediately leaving, not finding any nectar at that blossom.

Jesse approached them in full uniform, a spotless cap smartly on his head, gold-buttoned jacket fitting neatly over a shirt and tie, decorated all over with pins and badges. He grinned at them, unaware of the moment he had just interrupted.

Carl jumped up, flushing. Ellie's face didn't seem any

hotter than it had been since she had "landed" the simulator; her emotions remained high, her cheeks and spirit unconcerned whether it was triumph and adrenaline, joy, or shocking embarrassment. She laughed.

"Why, we nearly did forget!"

She smoothed down her outfit and fixed her hair. Carl adjusted his camera, made little stammering noises about the light and shutter speed and how Jesse and Ellie should stand facing the sun. After several photos the airman offered to take a picture of the two of them; Carl gave unneeded careful instructions—it was barely more than a Brownie camera, after all, not a P-51 Mustang!—and then posed, and Ellie felt his arm around her waist like she always wished she would dancing. It stayed, warm, until it was really time to go. They shook hands again and laughed and Jesse winked and then their day at the aerodrome was really all over . . . but somehow things had not returned to the point where they were just before.

Ellie still felt silver planes arcing across the sky in her head. A real one was now coming in for landing; another took off, leaving for a new destination or its own real home . . . What a funny thought, a plane going back to its original habitat . . .

Margaret's words came back to her: that the best thing

to do would be to return Soda-Pop to the wild and let nature take its course . . .

Ellie's gaze drew back to the ground, where Leroy's and Lucy's planes were parked.

"Carl," she said, the idea breaking over her like an egg cracked over her head, coating her view of the entire world with its sticky intent. "I know what to do about Soda-Pop."

"Oh? Suddenly? Like, you figured it out just now?"

If she hadn't been so caught up her in revelation, she might have noticed the slightly worried tone in Carl's voice. He might have, once or twice—or dozens of times—witnessed one of her revelatory ideas, most of which had a habit of not turning out *exactly* the way she was sure they would.

"I'm going to tell Leroy he has to take Soda-Pop back to Muntz. To let him go in the wild. I don't know if he'll live or die, but either way he'll be back home where he belongs."

Carl was quiet for a moment, not telling her how brilliant she was.

"I see," he finally said.

"First of all, he might actually say yes. I mean, why not? Leroy can make another expedition out of it and maybe pick up another animal. Something hardier. And he'll get to meet Muntz again. Maybe *he'll* give him another animal.

And it'll be a whole new fabulous story! He can make himself another plaque and another exhibit. . . . *Brilliant,* don't you think?"

Carl took a deep breath.

"So your idea is to tell *Leroy Reardon* to take the bird he was going to have a giant exhibit about, *has* built a giant exhibit about, with a special cage and everything, and return it where it came from—actually, to return it to *Muntz*: 'Hello, this bird's defective, can I have a new one please?' "

"Yes," Ellie answered, not liking Carl's tone. Or Carl's answer.

"Ellie . . . that's not going to go over well. Think about it. Leroy has a bit of an ego and obviously doesn't know what he's doing with the zoo. It's a bad combination. Do you really think that *he'll* think it's the right thing to do? William told you specifically *not to talk to anyone about Soda-Pop* or how sick he is. I assume that also includes his boss!"

"But this isn't just some gossip I'm not supposed to repeat. Soda-Pop is going to die if he stays here! He's . . . fading away, Carl!"

"Yeah, and *if* Soda-Pop dies Leroy will probably just have him stuffed and put in a fake cage with a plaque underneath it, thanking Muntz for the gift of the unusual specimen."

Ellie was shut down for a moment by this idea. He wasn't wrong.

"Well, I don't know what else I can do," she finally said. "So I'm still going to ask him, because returning Soda-Pop to Muntz and his home is the right—the *only* thing to do. And if Leroy doesn't see something as obvious as that, well, at least I will have tried."

"I understand, Ellie, and I know how much Soda-Pop means to you, but Leroy is not going to like being told what to do by a junior employee—*by a girl*. He fired Margaret, he'll fire you for speaking up. Heck, he may fire you just so no one else hears your idea and it starts a mini revolution at the zoo."

"So what if I get fired? Maybe it's a thing worth getting fired over. For Soda-Pop. And the zoo. *And* me. And everyone!"

The energy of the airplane simulator and almost-kiss was taking a strange turn in Ellie; it had to get out somewhere, and this was its new path. She was keyed up and excited, or angry, and although a tiny piece of her acknowledged she wasn't even behaving entirely like normal Ellie, she couldn't stop.

"Come on, Ellie," Carl said, his voice rising. "You love the zoo and all the other animals too, not just Soda-Pop. You love that job! You even love some of the people who work—worked—there. And yet just a week ago you were saying 'Margaret was fired, so I'm quitting,' and *now* you're effectively saying you're going to do something and get yourself fired . . . it seems like all you've been doing recently is trying to find reasons to get out! Can't you figure out some other plan?"

"*'Reasons to get out'?"* Ellie demanded. "I don't want to leave the zoo ever, Carl, but the reasons I might have to quit have been good! I didn't just . . . randomly come up with them, or go looking for them!"

"All right, but can't you think of any other response to the problem with Soda-Pop besides quitting?"

"Are you accusing me of being *too stupid* to figure out something else? Of being dumb and reactionary?"

"Well, I'm confused why a smart girl like you always resorts to extremes. You don't ever try to find a compromise, come up with alternative plans, have a calm conversation . . ."

"And *you* don't have any idea what it's like to be committed to something!" Ellie shot back. "You're never all in! You never speak up about what you believe in or act on your feelings. Or you just don't have any."

"Being cautious doesn't mean I don't have feelings, Ellie."

"So then what does it mean? You can't ever make up your mind? You're too shy to say anything ever—or *you're just a coward*?"

The entire world silenced; maybe even a cloud swept over the sun.

Carl stared at her.

"I'm . . . I'm sorry, Carl, that was out of line." She said it quickly so she wouldn't start to cry.

"Cautiousness isn't the same thing as cowardice," he said coldly. "Sometimes thinking and planning keeps you from doing—and saying—terrible things you regret."

"And sometimes there are specifically *not* terrible things you need to say but never do!"

"Like *what*?" Carl shouted. "All I'm saying is you should try *thinking* about what you're doing before you throw away everything you've ever wanted!"

"How do you even know *everything I've ever wanted*!" Ellie shouted back, not even sure what she meant. He was ruining the best birthday ever. Which had airplanes and him. "You don't even seem to know what *you* want!"

"I thought I did, but maybe I don't!"

"You *don't*, Carl Fredricksen. You don't care about anyone or anything enough to stand up for it, stand by it! You can take your balloon to South America and just *stuff it*!"

And, turning before he could see the tears starting to tumble in an ugly parade out of her eyes, she grabbed her bicycle and rode off, pitching and yawing like an airplane out of control, unable to see the road when she began to sob.

TWELVE

Perhaps if she had just turned around—at any point—everything would have been fine.

The more she pedaled the more Ellie cried. The more she cried the more she felt how absolutely over the top she was being. Had been from the start. From somehow almost kissing Carl to picking a *brutal* fight with him, then refusing to listen or stand down, and finally continuing it to the end, when she biked off like some sort of silly movie character.

Her first instinct was to go home, crawl into bed or a good tree, and hide and weep. But there was no privacy on the weekends at the McGill house; she would be surrounded by the curious or empathetic and did not want to be surrounded by either, by *anyone*, right then. She wanted to wail and pick apart what she felt and replay exactly what she and Carl had said to each other, uninterrupted, in perfect solipsistic anguish.

Also she wanted comfort, not questions.

She wasn't surprised at all when the bike appeared to turn of its own accord down a different route: to the zoo.

"At least I can check on Soda-Pop," she murmured, licking the tears out of her mouth. "At least I can be *some* use to the world."

No one noticed the red-eyed teenager as she parked the bike in its usual place and headed for the aviary. Ellie hunched over when a zoo employee came too close, not wanting to be seen by or talk with anyone. She made it all the way to the sick bird's enclosure without being approached, which somehow only made her feel worse.

"Hey, buddy," she said, putting her hands up around the cage bars and leaning against them—despite *hating* it when zoo-goers did that. It made the animals nervous and was very unhygienic for the humans.

Soda-Pop actually pulled his head out of his feathery chest to look over at her in mild interest. Maybe he was wondering what the kooky human was going to try next to cure him or cheer him up. As if things couldn't get any worse, Ellie saw that another one of the lollipop-like crest feathers on his head had broken, the pretty purple polka dot swinging at the end of its crumpled shaft.

An earthquake-sized shudder shook through Ellie, starting at her head and ending at her feet, taking what little energy she had left with it.

"I can't do anything right, can I, Soda-Pop?" she murmured. She put her hand in to stroke him and Soda-Pop half-heartedly tried to nip her. "I really, *really* mucked things up with Carl. I don't even know exactly how it happened. Just wait until you hear about it, Soda."

Of course the bird didn't say anything. He sort of nuzzled his head back toward his chest, but not all the way, keeping one eye on the unpredictable girl.

She told the whole story of the day, beginning with the moment she left the zoo the first time (including a lengthy and possibly irrelevant explanation of what a Link Trainer was, because obviously Soda-Pop wouldn't know). She actively felt and thought about each of her words as she said them, trying to recall every specific detail, and retold it when she didn't get something right.

At some point Soda-Pop's eye drifted shut, though it popped open when Ellie sighed loudly at the end.

"So I suppose I picked a stupid fight with Carl because I was feeling—I don't know, high on my own success with the flight simulator or something like that. *After* he bought me such a wonderful birthday present. I ruined the day, and I think I ruined things between us, too.

"Oh, Soda-Pop, what am I going to do? Things were already a little . . . strange between me and Carl. But not bad. He was really going to kiss me, I know it! I keep thinking I know what he feels. I think I feel it too? But maybe he doesn't. . . . And now I've gone and made it all worse and more confusing."

Soda-Pop gazed steadily at her with his golden eye.

"I know, I know," Ellie said glumly. "I'm not ten anymore. This isn't a stupid playground fight where I run home to mom. Everything else aside, he's my best friend, and I said something mean and was completely ungrateful. I need to own up to it. But I don't think just apologizing could possibly make up for calling him a coward and spoiling his present."

Soda-Pop noticed a stray feather on his chest and seemed to debate whether he cared enough to fix it. He poked it once, tiredly.

"Hey, I didn't even ask about *your* day," she said with a rueful smile. "I'm being all selfish all over again. How'd it go with the honey?"

She stood on her tiptoes to see the dish of sticky amber liquid she had set out before. There was a yellow jacket feeding on it . . . and what might have been a yellow jacket's leg stuck by itself to the rim.

"Hey, did you eat that?" Ellie asked delightedly. "Did you actually grab a wasp and eat it?"

Soda-Pop coyly refused to answer. She stuck her face through the bars as far as she could to examine his face for signs of insectivorism, but there was neither a smear of honey nor a stray antenna stuck someplace strange. If the bird was eating bugs, he was doing it neatly.

"So you didn't like the fruit flies the fruit brought, but it looks like you ate a bug the honey brought. Which is funny, because the honey was supposed to be for *you*. Well, you're not exactly a hummingbird; maybe you don't like sweet things. Carl's actually more of a hummingbird than you are. He *loves* sweet things. Boy, was he upset when the squirrels ate that cake . . . hey, that's it!" Her eyes widened to saucer size.

Soda-Pop shifted nervously on his perch at her sudden change of mood.

"I said I'd make him another cake to make up for it . . . and I will! *Right now!* I'll find some extra sugar rations and get my mom to share her secret recipe for brown butter cake with caramel icing. And then I'll give it to Carl, and apologize, and . . . well, all *right,* Soda-Pop, I know it won't fix everything," she added, imagining a chastising look in the bird's eye. "But a cake can't *hurt*, can it?!"

Soda-Pop took a breath as if he were going to say something . . .

But of course he didn't.

Those extra sugar rations turned out to be harder to scrape up than the right food for an ailing mystery bird; there were plenty of weddings that season, and picnics and teas and socials. None of the McGills' friends or neighbors had any coupons to spare. Ellie began to grow desperate, convinced the cake was the *only* way to fix things between her and Carl.

Her last attempt was the grade school teacher, Mrs. Collins. She was a widow with grandkids far away and didn't have any real reason to bake sweets for anyone. But it turned out that she had already given all her rations that month to the children's hospital for a bake sale; wasn't that just like the old do-gooder! Walking back from her house, Ellie picked up a stick like a little kid and began beating it against things as she walked: fences, lampposts, garbage bins. She didn't even think about where she was until she crossed Oak Street.

She stopped and thought for a moment. Then she ran back and found number 234 and banged the knocker before she could think herself out of it.

Margaret's house was from the earlier part of the previous century and had a slate roof like the clubhouse. But *this* building was in perfect condition: painted historically accurate shades of blue, as neat and contained as a fancy lady's purse—one with iron spikes on the fence around it. Very much like Margaret. A small mailbox had three slots, for Numbers One, Two, and Three. Pressing her nose against the door's glass Ellie could see a long hallway going back to a sunny, large-windowed room and, closer by, a set of stairs going up. But unlike a normal boardinghouse, it had an expensive rug and a tiny sideboard with a vase of fresh flowers in the hall.

Margaret herself came to the door, and her face lit up when she saw Ellie.

"Well, I didn't expect you to take me up on my offer to visit *quite* so fast!"

"Um, I was just wondering . . . do you have any sugar rations you could spare?"

Margaret's left eyebrow rose. She crossed her arms. "Ellie McGill, did you come all the way across town to ask to borrow a cup of sugar?"

"Yes. No. Sort of. Yes."

"Fascinating. Well, come on in, let me get you a cuppa, and you can tell me what I'm sure is one heck of a story. Also catch me up with gossip from the zoo—*if* you have the time."

This was not the way Ellie imagined seeing Margaret again; she thought it would be a planned-for date, for tea, very ladylike. But here they were, and she craned her head around to try to see everything at once in case this was her only opportunity: the paintings on the walls; the photographs; the owlish-looking old lady who stared at them from a table in the kitchen, leaning sideways to track their movements with eyes magnified tenfold by thick round glasses.

Margaret hurried Ellie into a room—"I'll be right back with the tea"—and closed the door firmly against prying eyes. This was her sanctum sanctorum, Ellie saw immediately. A dark place absolutely overflowing with books, bound journals, botanical prints, cases of eggs neatly arranged from smallest to largest—white to blue to pink ones. Feathers, too, and diagrams of birds with Latin names in flowing script. There was a desk, an enormous one, not feminine or stylish at all, like something a banker on Wall Street would have in a movie. On top was a typewriter, her telephone, notebooks and note cards, and stacks of pages clipped together.

Margaret returned a few minutes later, derriere first, pushing the door open with her hindside. She carried a tray with two cups, two teabags—not loose leaf, like Ellie thought a fancy lady would have—a kettle of hot water, and a sugar dish with strange lumps of brownish sugar in it.

"Ah, that's from my cousin back East," she explained,

seeing Ellie's confused look. "The sugar is from Europe, for the way my grandparents took their tea. Instead of putting the sugar in your cup and pouring the hot tea over it, you would hold the sugar in your teeth and drink the tea *through* it. I think she still feels guilty for getting the samovar, but she was married first, what can you do . . . anyway, it's good news for you, because I don't wind up using my coupons—"

She held them up, the precious sugar rations . . . then whisked them out of Ellie's fingers as she reached for them. "Nuh-uh. Story first, gossip first. Actually, *bird* first. How's the little purple fella doing?"

"Well . . . the cake sort of has to do with Soda-Pop and how he's doing . . . or not doing. . . ."

Ellie wished the other woman were ten—fifteen?—years younger, the girlfriend she never had. And while she couldn't imagine the other woman in the clubhouse (even as a teenager!), with or without heels, she must have *hiked* without them in Australia . . . right?

Once again Ellie told the story about the perfect then horrible birthday. It should have been easier, because this time it was to a hominid who could understand the nuances of the tale, unlike an avian. But she had trouble explaining how the fight actually happened, and the look on Margaret's face when she told her about the cake made her wonder if she wasn't explaining *that* correctly either.

The older woman sipped her tea contemplatively. She did not make any slurping noises.

"Let's take this in order. Backward," she finally said. "A cake *does* seem like a good option. If Carl likes cake."

"He *loves* cake."

"All right then. But it's meaningless without a heartfelt apology and explanation. You know that, right? You can't just show up with a cake and expect him to dig in and forget everything."

Honestly, that was sort of what Ellie was hoping despite her suspicions that it wasn't the way things worked.

"That idea is . . . vaguely supernatural. Sort of poison adjacent. Feminine in the worst possible way. Cake inducing forgiveness. No, no, no. But as a token of how sorry you are, sure. Now, item number two . . ." She took a deep breath. "Carl is *not* wrong about Leroy and what he would do to you if you told him to take his pretty purple bird and shove it."

Ellie wanted to deny it; she wanted to cry in agreement and despair.

"He wouldn't think twice about tossing out a young girl who told him the right way to do things. And to return a gift from his beloved Muntz? *Fuhgeddaboudit,* as my cousin back East would say. He would fire anyone, even William, who made such an obscene suggestion."

"But it's the right thing to do," Ellie persisted. "You said . . ."

"No, I said returning the bird to the wild was the *best* thing to do. There's usually more than one *right* thing to do in any given situation involving humans. Don't be so generous in throwing opportunities away, not when you're so young. Not until you've exhausted every other possibility. Now tell me—point number three—is Soda-Pop really failing to thrive?"

"I think he ate a wasp, maybe, but even if he did, it didn't give him any extra oomph or energy. He still barely moves. I haven't found anything else wrong with him." Ellie took a big sip of tea. "I've tried everything. If it's an internal parasite, it's nothing we can check for—and I haven't found anything in his poop. Mainly because he hasn't had any. Dr. Hua had this great idea about getting him bugs and I have been trying all sorts of different things and . . ."

"Dr. Hua?" Margaret interrupted. "He's working with you? That's wonderful. How is he doing?" She took a small sip of her tea and didn't meet Ellie's eyes.

"Oh, he's doing all right. Everyone's keeping their heads down with Leroy on a tear. But then he brought in this record player . . ."

"A gramophone? Into the commissary?" Margaret spluttered.

"Yeah!" Ellie said eagerly. "It's been great! Really cheered up everyone. I love washing the dishes when it's playing. It's all jazz, not really what I love, but it's nice."

"Huh," Margaret said neutrally. Ellie tried to dissect the look on the other woman's face, but she was as unreadable as a South American horned frog.

"Anyway, if it's a disease Soda-Pop's got, the only symptom is not eating or drinking or—caring. His eyes are fine, his feathers and skin undamaged except for the bad clipping job. He's just not happy."

Margaret stirred her tea thoughtfully.

But Ellie didn't do well with long silences.

"So . . . what have you . . . been up to? Since . . . um . . . ?"

"Since I was *fired*?" Margaret asked archly. Then she indicated the pile of papers on her desk. "Actually, I've been quite busy writing to zoos and zoological institutions. Job inquiries. Also various animal rescue funds and charities. There may not be a ton of women *employed* in zoology, either academically or in the field, but there are many on the nonprofit side. Boy, wouldn't being rich be helpful? Think if I had Leroy's money . . . if my family could set up a zoo for *me* . . ."

She shook her head. "Do you know I'm actually contacting the daughters and wives of heads of state? King

George's eldest, Elizabeth, is quite an animal aficionado. She loves dogs, is a keen fisher, and supports endangered animal protections. And in Argentina, Eva Perón loves dogs too, or at least her little poodle . . . Oh, it's all ridiculous. But don't worry about me, I'm fine. It may take a while, but I'll figure out something."

"You can still afford those European yogurts you like?" Ellie asked teasingly.

"Funny, my stomach isn't as upset anymore now that I no longer work for Leroy. *Hey*." Margaret snapped her fingers. "That's it! *You* can't say anything about Soda-Pop to Leroy, but *I've* already been fired. There's nothing he can do to me anymore. We'll do it cleverly, strategically. I'll go during the big goodbye ceremony press party for the Burma expedition and tell him to give Soda-Pop back to Muntz. There will be reporters and politicians listening and recording, and he daren't lose his temper . . . And I have a friend at the *Eagle* I can get to follow up on any questions I ask."

"Wow, you would do that in front of all those people? I think I would just about die."

"I very much doubt that, Ellie McGill, if the fate of an animal depended on it. Which it does.

"All right. So we have a plan. You keep Soda-Pop alive and apologize to Carl. I'll talk to Leroy."

Margaret took a very satisfied sip of tea.

Ellie knew there was a lot of work behind each one of those declarations, but she too felt satisfied, as if they were already halfway done.

The cake was less a chore than a lovely mother-daughter afternoon that was rare in a household of ten, and highly appreciated by both women. When it was done they sat in companionable exhaustion, watching the plain but scrumptious-smelling cake cool in its pan.

"It will be better tomorrow after it sits a bit," Mrs. McGill said. "When you give it to him."

But Ellie had other plans.

She bought a bright yellow balloon at the zoo—Martin only charged her half, "employee's discount"—and as soon as the sun had set she biked over to Carl's house. It was a little tricky climbing up the porch with a cake in one hand and a balloon in the other, but she managed without making *too* much noise. She settled herself against his window, which was wide open for any summer breezes that might lighten the air inside, and gently guided the balloon in.

Almost immediately scrabbling noises came from the room; Ellie imagined a surprised Carl stopping whatever he was doing—tinkering with his radio, probably—and boggling at the floating yellow harbinger. He didn't scream, which was good (and always a distinct possibility).

He came over to the window and looked out, trying to figure where it had come from. In his hands was his ham radio logbook. She grinned: Just like she had guessed. He *had* been on his radio.

"SURPRISE!" Ellie whisper-yelled, shoving the cake in front of his face. "I'm sorry!"

The expression on Carl's face was so complicated she couldn't figure it out at first.

Definite surprise! A moment of joy. Then weariness, obviously remembering how they had left things. And . . . could it be . . . *annoyance*? And then resignation. But there had been a moment of definite joy, so she decided to go with that.

"Ellie," he whispered. "My parents are going to *kill* me . . ."

"But I made you a *cake*!" she mouthed, waving it—carefully—up and down.

Ah, and just one more look: a little bit of greed. The heat and humidity of the evening released all the confection's wonderful smells: fat, milk, sweet, baked, yum.

"I am *really sorry*," she added, remembering what Margaret had said about the apology needing to be genuine and heartfelt. "Carl, I don't know what got into me. I can't explain it. It's like . . . sometimes I'm like a little kid, you know? That flight trainer simulator whosiewhatsit was the best birthday present I ever got . . . anyone ever *thought* of for me. . . . It was like I was really flying. Somehow it made me feel amazing, like a hero, unstoppable. And . . . full of myself. I really am sorry I acted like such a jerk, Carl.

"I'm worried about Soda-Pop. But I know that's my problem, not yours, and it doesn't make what I said any better. I just . . . wanted you to know.

"And if you don't like the cake, that's fine, or if you're still mad at me, I get it. Just tell me whatever it is you want me to do so you forgive me and I'll do it."

"Ellie . . ." He sounded tired, conflicted, old. "Come on in, I guess."

She practically jumped off the roof in excitement and clambered in.

"Do you forgive me?" she begged. "Please, tell me, or what I have to do!"

"Yes, of course I do, Ellie. . . . You don't have to *do* anything. That's not how it works. Although . . . that cake looks pretty great. Let's cut into it."

She could have kissed him, but something told her not to: some tiny part of her brain that she was used to ignoring. It was bad enough to sneak into a boy's room at night—with a cake—but there was something more, about playing with emotions right now . . . everything was a little too keyed up, too tense and strange.

So she grinned and just said, "Thanks, Carl!" instead, and put the cake down ceremoniously in the middle of his floor. Carl went over to his desk, found a sharp knife from his modeling tool set, and wiped off the blade with a clean handkerchief. They sat down across from each other and he carefully sliced two pieces out as best as he could with the tiny knife. To her relief, the crumb was moist and tight enough that it held together and didn't fall into a thousand tiny pieces.

"Ellie, this is amazing," he said through his first mouthful. "You should open a bakery, or an automat. Quit the zoo."

"I had my mom's help. And it took—" she started to tell him about how it took extra sugar rations but then realized it would sound like she was begging for forgiveness or compliments or pity. "All afternoon," she finished. "And anyway, it's great, but I'd rather spend my days skinning herring and making bird chow with Dr. Hua."

Carl laughed, keeping his mouth closed so he wouldn't spray crumbs everywhere.

"Are we jake?" she asked shyly. "Really?"

"Yes, Ellie, really," he said with a smile. "I'm just worried about you. You have this wonderful job, and Leroy seems like he could be a really dangerous person if you got on his wrong side or insulted him or whatnot."

"Yeah . . . Margaret agreed with you, actually," she said,

a little reluctantly. "She said she wouldn't say anything if she were in my shoes . . . but she said she'll say something herself."

"Smart lady."

They were both quiet for a moment, chewing. Ellie took a deep breath.

"Carl . . . what I said to you, about you, was mean. But sometimes it's hard with you. I *want* to know what you're thinking. Or feeling. You don't . . . ever talk about it."

He didn't react, just licked his thumb and thought. Finally he said: "Neither do you."

"What?" Ellie demanded, shocked.

"You *do* things based on what you're feeling or thinking," he said. "You act on them. Immediately. But you never talk about what's going on inside."

"I do! I . . ." Talk to little purple birds about things. And zoologists who aren't directly involved in the situation. And . . .

"What are you feeling right now?" Carl asked, a twinkle in his eye.

"Accused. Put-upon."

"Hmmm."

". . . Maybe justifiably, but still."

"All right, well, maybe we both could use some practice

talking," Carl said. "But not twelve feet above my parents, after hours."

This was perfectly reasonable. No serious discussion could be had while they were both on edge, listening for movement and warning noises from downstairs.

On the other hand, this was not the sort of passionate declaration she would expect from a boy who maybe actually liked her.

On the third hand, *she* wasn't saying anything either. . . .

"Sure," she finally said. "We should make a date," she added, *almost* challengingly.

He nodded . . . then began to clean up their (minimal) mess. She helped. The tension was broken, the anger was over, but there was definitely something unfinished in the air.

He managed to fit what was left of the cake into his treasure drawer.

Ellie stood and adjusted her clothes, getting ready to go. Carl gave her an opaque look.

"You know I could never stay mad at you, Ellie. I . . ."

"Carl!" The voice, like a ghostly bell tolling, carried up the stairway from the living room. *"That show you like is coming on . . ."*

"Bye, Carl!" Ellie whispered. She turned to duck out to the roof.

"Ellie . . ." He grabbed her hand, stopping her. "This weekend, coming up. Let's have a birthday redo. Not with the Link Trainer, I mean. Like an old-fashioned explorers' hike? And we can . . . maybe . . . talk."

"It's a date!" she said with a mischievous grin. Then she *did* kiss him—on the cheek—and bobbed through the window and onto the roof like a pixie. She felt light as air despite the giant piece of cake that was now resting comfortably inside her belly. She stuck her head back in again at the last second. "Thanks. I really am sorry."

Then Carl's bedroom door opened and she disappeared, feeling like her bike was a broomstick and she was above the clouds all the way home.

THIRTEEN

Young-Ellie, a frequent visitor in Ellie's mind, secretly hoped that the nearly angelic energy that had enveloped her at the end of Apology Night would somehow also sweep up poor little Soda-Pop in its golden glow, and that she would come in and see him all perky and singing. But of course life didn't work that way. If anything, his feathers looked even duller as the days passed, and he barely tried nipping her anymore when she reached in to check on him. He didn't even protest when she put him in her coveralls' front pocket while she did her morning chores (she thought the walk would do him good, and it certainly didn't seem to hurt him).

So when the big day came for the expedition to leave for Burma, Ellie was understandably nervous while she kept an eye out for Margaret, waiting for the moment when the ex-keeper would confront Leroy. A stage had been set up behind the administrative offices, where the elephant paddocks used to be, which was now parking for four P-51 Mustangs. Well, three P-51s and one TP-51C converted Mustang with a passenger seat for Diana.

Hundreds of people had shown up for the airplanes and spectacle. Carl was arriving late because of a penny auction at the church that his mother was running—Ellie hoped he made it before Margaret's big moment. She wasn't sure she could stand to watch it all by herself.

At least Soda-Pop was with her—ostensibly it was in case he needed to be shown as exhibit A. But really it was for comfort. Mostly hers. She felt calmer with his soft, red-hot little form pressed up against her chest.

Dr. Hua came out of the commissary and stood at the back of the crowd. Even a recluse like him couldn't resist the allure of what was basically an air show.

Finally, right as the crowd noises changed and the reporters began aiming and adjusting their cameras, Ellie caught a glimpse of Margaret slipping into the middle of them like a jewel-toned thief. Purple! She had worn her purple suit for Soda-Pop! They locked eyes for a moment and Margaret gave her a knowing smile. Ellie felt relief loosen her entire body; she hadn't even realized how stiff her neck and shoulders were.

"It's going to be okay, Soda-Pop," she murmured, petting him. He tried to rip out her fingernail. "Okay, it might not be okay. But this is the last best thing we can do, and at least we will have tried."

Leroy stepped up to the podium and began bloviating. Ellie tried to listen but found herself losing interest immediately. It was the same old stuff he always said, only it sounded a little more hollow than usual. His friends stood behind him in a semicircle, Lucy in her usual pants and shirt, Diana in a skintight pair of jodhpurs and matching jacket, Dan in a slightly sporty version of his usual suit, and Chester in a comfortable but expensive-looking set of khakis.

Behind them all, mechanics were doing last-minute checks on the planes. Ellie tried to follow along and guess what they were doing: tire check, flaps, fuel, something in the engine . . . the P-51 Mustang was a much more complicated plane than the ones she had read about in her book and trained on with the Link Trainer, but of course physics stayed the same.

One of the men looked familiar. . . . It was Jesse from the aerodrome!

But of course it was; Leroy and Lucy would have only the best men working on their planes. Ellie wanted to wave, but he was (rightly) intent on his job and not looking her way. Another mechanic climbed up into the Mustang's cockpit and began to do something on the instrument panel; Jesse gave him a thumbs-up after watching the propeller carefully. She wished she could have been back there, asking questions.

". . . and especially hope to find a rainbow snake, but whatever we bring back, believe me, it will be spectacular, unlike anything this town—this state—this *country*—has ever seen before!"

Leroy waved as he concluded his speech, pre-assuming the crowd would be cheering. They did, maybe a beat later than he expected.

"Does anyone have any questions before we take off—literally?" he added, his smile a little strained.

Margaret put her hand up.

Leroy ignored her.

"Yes, you, in the hat," he said to a reporter.

"Harold Muldrow, *Sunday News Times*. Say, Leroy, what about something bigger than some sort of 'rainbow snake'? You have those African elephants, but what about some Asian elephants while you're over there? Or a tiger?"

"Not sure I can fit a whole pack of pachyderms in my airplane." The crowd dutifully laughed. "But we *could* ship 'em back by cargo boat. We'll see what we can do! Next?"

Margaret raised her hand again.

He ignored her again.

This performance kept repeating itself until *all* other questions had been answered; the reporters were starting to get bored, pack up, compare their cameras, natter and gossip about other things. The crowd began to shuffle, also sensing it was over.

Before anyone could actually leave, however, Margaret's voice rang out like a clarion call from the Old Testament.

"Mr. Reardon—what about the allegations that the zoo can't even take care of the latest animals you acquired? How is this 'conservation'? Why are you going out to get new ones?"

Leroy tried to ignore her, gripping the podium and looking out over the crowd as if still waiting for other questions.

"Is this true, Leroy?" asked the one reporter who hadn't turned to look at Margaret. "Fred Datlow, *Daily Eagle*. There *has* been talk of the health of some of the animals . . . where is the fancy bird Charles Muntz gave you? That's supposed to be in its own special exhibit? Is it sick? Did it die?"

Ellie felt her heart squeeze. This was it!

William, standing off to one side of the stage, turned white.

"Absolutely not," Leroy assured him with the calmest voice imaginable. "We are keeping the . . . *Leroymuntzus* quarantined while acclimating him to this new . . . um . . . climate. And safe from the other birds. He'll be all ready for our big debut next month!"

"He's not acclimating, he's sick!" Margaret shouted. "Why not just return him home so he gets better? I'm sure Charles Muntz would appreciate you not killing one of his finds!"

"Margaret Klein, everyone," Leroy introduced her serenely. "Recently fired from the zoo for . . . maladjustment. Her fiery attitude in defense of animals is a boon for them, her fiery attitude toward us, not so much. I suppose she has a grudge against me and the zoo now. If only I had one of her beloved birds up here with me, maybe she would be kinder."

A few people in the crowd chuckled. But otherwise his attempt to denigrate her seemed to backfire; the reporters immediately homed in on the conflict like yellow jackets discovering a petri dish of honey. They turned toward her with bulbs flashing and cameras snapping. She didn't appear to notice. Leroy did, and he frowned.

"Well, but why don't you just take him back to his home?" she pressed.

"And this, ladies and gentlemen, is the other reason we had to send Margaret to seek zoological opportunities elsewhere." He took a deep, sad-sounding breath, and gripped the sides of the podium. "Women . . . just aren't cut out for discovery, exploration, and scientific advancement. We love them, of course we do! We all have mothers, some of us daughters and sisters and nieces, and our world would be much bleaker without them. But they are, by their very nature, *conservative*. That's what it really means when Miss Klein speaks about *conservation*. All she wants is for the zoo to preserve and conserve what it has. She has no desire to expand our collection, to increase our exhibits and share new wonders of our natural world with our visitors."

"What about the animals that died from your last attempt to 'expand the collection'?" Datlow pressed. "Like the snake that got turned into shoes? What *about* returning the sick ones to the wild, where they belong?"

"You can't make an omelet without breaking a few eggs," Leroy said sharply. "An ornithological specialist like Margaret should know that. Obviously, we would love it if every animal came back in pristine condition, but the realities of transportation and our world at large just don't always allow for that. Does that mean we shouldn't *try*? Absolutely not!

"Good heavens, isn't this just what Philip Wylie was trying to warn us about? Mothers have taken all the spirit of adventure out of their sons! The war is over, the sky is opening up, and all they want to do is huddle down and keep things the way they were forever, haggling over ration cards. . . ."

Ellie frowned. He was twisting words and making it sound like Margaret was a sourpuss and spoilsport. Not someone who wanted to save animals. She put her hand to her breast pocket; Soda-Pop tried to bite her. The poor bird was getting lost in this strange battle of words and wills.

"Grabbing animals out of their habitats and flinging them into cages isn't science!" Margaret yelled, echoing Ellie's thoughts, but putting them more coherently. "You don't even bring along a professional illustrator, naturalist, scientist, or *anything* on your expeditions!"

Leroy looked around impatiently until he found William. Then he made a rotating motion with his hand and jerked a thumb at the planes. The other man nodded and ran over to the mechanics. After he had a word with them, they did things faster and more pointedly. The wonderful clucking and buzz of an engine start-up came from the first of the P-51s.

"Those are the angry words of a disgruntled ex-employee," Leroy finally responded. "A woman who feels jilted, come to ruin a great day for the zoo."

Ellie looked down at the little bird in her pocket and

he looked feebly back up at her, his golden eye meeting her hazel one. She felt like puking. Leroy was going to leave soon, and none of this would be resolved. Soda-Pop would just get sicker and probably die.

She was the bird's only hope, his only chance at survival.

Well. If you want something done right, do it yourself, Mrs. McGill always said.

The moment the mechanic slid back the canopy and hopped out of the cockpit, Ellie slipped out of the crowd.

"But do you have an official response to your alleged poor treatment of the animals?" a reporter asked.

"I have a lot to say about the treatment of myself at the hands of this screaming harridan!"

A few people in the crowd laughed. A very few.

Everyone was so caught up in the drama that no one noticed Ellie as she made for the plane. Well, no one except for Mrs. Jumbo, who raised her trunk in greeting or warning, and threatened to trumpet.

"Shhh!" Ellie begged, ducking down. With one hand against Soda-Pop to protect him from too much bouncing, she ran around to the other side of the plane, keeping its body between her and the crowd. She couldn't hear Margaret and Leroy over the roar of the propeller—which was an immense comfort. Except for a nasty blow to her head when she misjudged the height of the wing, it was much easier scuttling up into the cockpit than climbing up a porch with a cake and a balloon. She eagerly settled into the seat.

But then she saw the instrument panel.

It was *terrifying.*

There were *dozens* more dials and switches than in her little single-engine manual and the flight simulator.

On the bright side, the engine had already been started.

"Okay, Ellie, process of elimination," she said aloud.

Anything related to guns—this was a repurposed bomber/scout, after all—could be ignored. That took out a whole lot of dials, but most of these already had neat lines of narrow black tape over them. Someone had done the work for her.

"Right. There's the compass . . . and—another compass? And a clock, and airspeed indicator and . . . a fuel *selector*?"

Ellie thought hard. She knew the Mustang could go on some of the longest flights because of the drop tanks; they were the pupa-looking things tucked under its wings that could have been mistaken for bombs. When they were empty, they were even released like bombs. Between those and the fuselage tank and the two wing tanks she could go almost anywhere in the Americas as long as she fed from them properly. Which probably explained the fuel selector.

The throttle was the same as on any plane, a lever that you pushed forward and back, and the propeller was a knob just under it. This engine had a supercharger, which she wasn't familiar with, but it had a setting of "Auto," as did a few other knobs, which was just fine as far as she was concerned. The mixture control, which regulated the ratio of fuel to air, was clearly labeled and currently in "Idle Cutoff."

She needed more time to figure it all out, but of course, real life didn't work that way. The other mechanic was walking back to the plane with a stepstool—probably to make it easier for Leroy to get into the cockpit.

Then he looked up and saw her inside.

He shouted, probably something like *Hey, get out of there*, which Ellie could reasonably be assumed to not hear because of the noise of the propeller. She pointed to her ears and shrugged. Then she slammed the canopy shut.

"What do I need? What do I need? *Flap control!*" She found the lever on the side and set it to what she hoped was 20 percent. "Aileron, elevator, rudder, landing gear . . . eventually . . ."

"Hey, get out of there!" the man shouted, audibly this time, knocking on the plane's body. "Quit playing around!"

She couldn't help looking out at the crowd; Leroy had turned around to see what the commotion was—along with everyone else. The look on his face was one she would happily remember for the rest of her life; it was like a question mark just before it gets angry. She moved the mixture lever to "run." The mechanic kept screaming, more desperately now, and she increased the throttle until she couldn't hear him anymore.

"Okay, Soda-Pop, here we go." She took a deep breath and turned the propeller to "full."

The plane slowly began to roll down the elephant enclosure—er, runway.

People were beginning to run toward it now: Leroy, his friends, men from the crowd. One person just stood by and watched as she passed him: Jesse. She waved at him. When he saw who was in the seat of the cockpit his face broke out into an enormous smile and he waved back.

Then the plane really began to pick up speed, and she left everyone in the dust—literally. *Her* dust. When the engine reached a certain high pitch and she was going way too fast to be mucking about on the ground she checked the speed: just about ninety miles per hour.

She took a deep breath, grabbed the stick, and flew *up*.

PART II

Up

FOURTEEN

Ellie was brave, strong, loyal to her friends, and occasionally prone to doing rash things by the seat of her pants—like encouraging a nine-year-old to walk across the rotting beam of an old house.

Or stealing a plane to fly to South America.

The one thing she definitely was *not*: stupid.

When the altimeter hit ten thousand feet she banked until the compass said she was heading south-southeast. She set the plane to cruise at about 280 miles per hour and confirmed that all the indicators indicated that things were mostly okay for the moment.

Then she began to be scared.

She was sixteen, all alone, miles off the ground, speeding

like a bullet in a plane she didn't fully know how to operate, toward a country she had never visited.

She had never been outside her state before, actually.

Soda-Pop popped his head out of her pocket and looked around with interest.

"I've really done it this time," she murmured, the magnitude of her actions finally catching up with her. She could die. If something happened she would plummet to earth like a rock, like a fleshy meteor.

This terror gripped her heart and body completely. She forced her hands to move, checked and rechecked the gauges, and sweated like she was in a sauna, not a chilly two miles up.

But slowly . . . eventually . . . her heartbeat calmed: She wasn't crashing right *then*.

She was flying.

It was hard to stay terrified for very long when she was among the clouds and high as an angel. For the first time in her life there was blue sky ahead of her instead of only above; the green world spread out below like a living atlas.

"There's the Deerkill River!" she said excitedly, pointing it out to Soda-Pop. "Look, you can see Somerset Reservoir! And that's the town of Kenebex, I think!"

She had seen all these things before, of course . . . but

differently. In two dimensions, everything carefully inked on a map; she would run her finger over the lines that took her from the McGill house to her destination, filled with wonder that anyone thought her town important enough to record. And of course in three dimensions while actually traveling through or around the landmarks themselves (sometimes even *in*, like swimming in the Deerkill).

This was like those two views combined, like someone had somehow made a tiny sculpture of the world she lived in, down to its tiny trees. Small but beautiful.

After a few minutes reality settled around her shoulders again, but this time with less panic.

"All right. We can do this, Soda-Pop. I got us up here, I can bring us down. In the water if I have to." She had no parachute; ejection, were it even possible in the Mustang, was not possible for *her*. "Next stop, the tepuis!"

A sound that had been masked by the roar of the engine and the beating of her own heart finally resolved itself out of the background, demanding to be noticed: static and slightly more organized blips coming from the radio. She peered at the receiver helplessly. There were only four frequencies available as far as she could tell, and none of them played talk shows or music. One was probably set for the airport that had been the plane's original destination in

Burma, or, more likely, some layover along the way. One was the departure airport back home. One was for other planes in her squadron. . . .

"*ELLIE O'SHAUGNESSY YOU BRING MY PLANE BACK IMMEDIATELY!*"

Leroy's voice sounded scratchy over the airwaves, but his fury was transmitted loud and clear.

Sure, he was angry; she had taken his plane. But she was certain that he would at least begin to understand if she explained *why* she had stolen it.

She fumbled around the panel, looking for the push-to-talk button—until she remembered that it would be on the throttle so the pilot didn't need to take their hands away from controlling the plane (or firing the machine guns).

"It's McGill, sir. Mr. Reardon, sir—"

"*I AM BEING* HUMILIATED*! HOW DARE YOU! YOU DON'T EVEN KNOW—*"

Maybe he wasn't ready to listen to reason yet.

Ellie switched the radio off.

She looked around the cramped cockpit for anything she had missed, anything that might be helpful—apparently annoying Soda-Pop with her twisting and squirming. He nipped her through her coveralls and then, apparently fed up with the whole thing, *hopped out of her pocket* and onto the instrument panel.

"Hey! What's going on, little buddy?"

The bird seemed brighter-eyed somehow. He preened a few disheveled feathers back into place and then jumped interestedly around the front of the cockpit, picking and pecking at the shinier dials and knobs. Ellie watched him with amazement. It was like he was a whole new Soda-Pop. Had this little adventure somehow perked him up? Or . . .

"Air pressure?" she wondered aloud. "Did Muntz get you in the mountains? They're over eight thousand feet tall! More than a mile and a half . . . Soda-Pop, has that been the trouble? Was it too much oxygen for you down there with us? Did your little ears hurt all the time at the zoo? Or is it your tummy?"

In that moment any doubts she had about her (extreme) course of action vanished for good. Soda-Pop's new liveliness filled her with a serenity she had rarely experienced: like a weight on her back had been lifted, a question answered, a problem forever solved. No matter what happened, this had been the right decision.

Soda-Pop had no such revelatory, philosophical moments. He poked around the instrument panel happily and then became *very* interested in something behind Ellie. She loosened her strap and turned to look: He had found an expensive leather bag crammed up against the fuselage fuel gauge (probably a big no-no for actual fighter pilots). *LKR III* was monogrammed in gold on its cordovan flap.

"Brother," Ellie said, pulling it out to get a better look. "If I ever get wealthy, remind me to stay grounded, Soda-Pop."

But inside she found a treasure trove of prizes. There was a compass, a pocketknife, a flask of water, a flask of . . . something else, a compass, some carefully wrapped strips of pemmican and dried rations, a bag of pretzels, a couple candy bars, a radio book, a small bound atlas, a P-51 Mustang pilot's training manual, and *Leroy's personal logbook.*

(Also an unbelievably soft—cashmere? musk ox? vicuña?—tan muffler and matching socks, all three of which were embroidered with the letters *LKR III* in gold thread. The socks also had an *L* on one and an *R* on the other, which confused her for a moment before she realized that it might have nothing to do with his name.)

"All right Soda-Pop, if a guy who needs his feet labeled can fly this plane, there's no doubt at all that I can, too."

Ellie started to rip open a candy bar in celebration but then stopped. Maybe she should figure out where she was going and how long it would take first.

The atlas confirmed what she remembered: that it was around two thousand miles to the Canaima area of

Venezuela, where the tepuis were. She rechecked all the fuel gauges: full. Math promised she might just make it. Barely. Which was all right by Ellie; despite her newfound bravado she had no desire to try to land and take off *twice* if she didn't have to. . . . Also she had no idea how to find a friendly refueling place along the way. She didn't speak Spanish and, aside from the animals and major exports, didn't know a whole lot about Mexico. Or Panama—beyond the canal. Also she didn't have any money. What would happen if a young American girl landed in a foreign country and begged for gas to get a tiny bird home? The movie theater in her mind played two very different possible endings, one of which was happy, the other of which involved prison.

"Okay, Soda-Pop, work this out with me. Two thousand miles, two hundred and fifty to three hundred miles per hour . . . I guess we'll get there in seven or eight hours." She looked at the rations and did more math. "I'll have three meals of half a candy bar, two half bags of pretzels, and a piece of jerky, which should leave me some left over for emergencies once I'm on the ground. And for the water . . ." She looked at the "pilot's relief" stowed discreetly below the seat, essentially just a funnel attached to a tube that led . . . outside . . . and was certainly not made for a woman's shape. "Maybe I'll just save it until after I land."

Nor was she worried about potable water once on the ground; she had memorized dozens of articles about how to get clean drinking water in the wild.

And if the world below her continued to be as recognizable as it had been so far, navigation wouldn't be *too* much of an issue.

Well, as long as there weren't any clouds between her and the real-world map.

Keeping a hand on the stick and an uneasy eye on the trim, the altimeter, and the speed, Ellie opened Leroy's journal. The first few pages were dedicated to how much he loved his new plane and the initial jaunts he took in it—apparently there was a tiny airport near Los Angeles with a restaurant where pilots and aviation fanatics could eat deep-fried scorpion.

Then there were pages and pages devoted to the expedition to Venezuela. Sometimes he would write in overly ornate language (with occasional misspelled words), going on and on about the colorful local women and flowers in his drinks, switching from one to another so confusingly that Ellie had to go back and reread a page several times to figure out which was which.

"Pig," she decided. "And not even a cute javelina."

Ellie found herself filled with reluctant envy as she looked through ink sketches of landscapes and city streets and animals and birds. They looked effortless. She could see him sitting at a café—or whatever Venezuela had—having local coffee and recording his adventures with a light hand. It took forceful remembering of *Jane Eyre* to remind her that such skills could be taught, and rich people received better schooling than poor ones. Maybe he even had a governess or a tutor. He was born close enough to the previous century that it wasn't outrageous for her to imagine him getting shooting, painting, and diplomacy lessons as part of his education.

(And she herself could perhaps amount to something more artistically if she sat down and practiced the way the Beatrix Potter girls at school did every day. But who wanted to sit down and draw bunnies and mushrooms and trees when you could be *among* them, looking at them, climbing them, leaping over them? Ellie had no regrets!)

There was a nice picture of Leroy and his friends, sort of a redux of their photo at the zoo right before they left for Venezuela, but this time with crates of animals at their feet. They looked like a superhero team: Diana could have been *Princess* Diana, Wonder Woman, and Lucy another Amazon, and . . .

A sudden *whump* caused all the dials to spin and Ellie's heart to flop up into her mouth.

She grabbed the throttle tightly with both hands and

frantically checked all the gauges. After a terrifying second she realized it was just a pocket of air, the high-up equivalent of a bump on the road—but not righting the plane could result in a crash. She pulled back hard, overcorrecting, just like she had in the Link Trainer.

The engine began sputtering ominously. Visions of it cutting out entirely and the plane plummeting to the earth blasted through Ellie's mind.

But she reached over and adjusted the fuel mixture—just like she had practiced.

The noises quickly smoothed out; soon it was back to the healthy buzz of a happy P-51 Mustang operating correctly.

Her heartbeats steadied.

But even after the plane was level and quiet, Ellie decided to keep her entire concentration on just flying for a while.

Eventually, after an impatient flutter from Soda-Pop—and after the sweat collecting uncomfortably between her breasts had begun to dry, also uncomfortably—Ellie decided it was safe enough to take another peek at the journal. But she would check the instrument panel regularly from now on!

She came to a sketch of Muntz's fantastic zeppelin nosing through the tabletop mountains, more like a flying saucer from a science-fiction serial than anything you would actually see in a jungle. How terrifying it must have been to the animals, and the local people! They must have thought it was the end of the world.

There was an extra-long entry that she didn't feel comfortable pulling her eyes from the skies to seriously read, accompanied by a strangely formal portrait of Charles Muntz: his hands were clasped and his eyes sparkled like he was posing. Across from it was a simple map of the area with a circle indicating (she assumed) where they met.

She checked it against the atlas.

"The Orinoco and the Caroní rivers eventually meet, and the mountains are just beyond," she said aloud to set the information in her memory, eyes flicking back and forth between the atlas and the panel. "If I can keep this picture in my head, of how they look, I can just follow them inland from the ocean. Piece of cake."

She said that last bit to bolster her confidence, knowing full well that if Carl were there he would have told her not to jinx the moment.

Carl . . . she wondered if he ever showed up at the zoo, if he had seen what happened. Or if he only came once she was gone. What would he say when someone told him? What would he feel? Would he hit the air with his fist and let out a whoop, that she had "slipped the surly bonds of Earth" all by herself, for a good cause?

Would he be terrified? Call the Air Force, the Coast Guard, the State Department . . . ?

(For that matter, would her parents?)

Would he be at least a *little* bit happy that she was going on an adventure to save her bird friend?

Or would he just be angry, like when they fought? Would he think she was being rash and stupid?

If she knew as much about radios as he did, maybe she could have figured out a way to get in touch. A ham radio could reach a plane, right? Boy, that would be useful. She could tell everyone she and Soda-Pop were all right and what the plan was.

Ah, well. It would all just be a big mystery to everyone back home until she reappeared, triumphant.

Come to think of it, it was all a big mystery to *her* as well. One thing about making it up as you go along: You didn't spoil the ending.

With that cheery, explorer-y thought, she put the journal and atlas away and concentrated on flying. She eased the speed up to 300 mph without too much trouble and watched the ground below roll by with little change. And that itself was amazing: a difference of twenty-five miles per hour on the ground would have been dramatic. That was as fast as she could go downhill on a bike.

She found the Mississippi River with no problem and

followed as it bent and bowed. When they studied the great waterway in school, Ellie had always pictured the river long and flat like a well-engineered highway dividing the country, with barges and Huck Finn and steamboats and dreams all up and down it. But from the air the river looked like a beautiful mess, something organic and alive, looping, playing with the land instead of just draining and fleeing it.

"The Mississippi seems kinda *friendly*," she said to Soda-Pop. "You know, I kind of always thought of our mountains and fields, some of them, as being friendly. Maybe everything is, if we treat them right. How do you show *that* on a map?"

Ellie watched, entranced, as the giant bands of silver, green, and steel that marked out fields and forests and rocky hills surged and receded, and she lost track of the time. When she found herself getting sleepy or a little hypnotized by the view or the purity of the light she adjusted the air in the cockpit to make it cooler. At three-hour intervals she had a big bite of chocolate bar. Soda-Pop pecked at it curiously, though he didn't actually eat anything. She tried giving him a bit of pretzel—he just snapped off and nibbled a tiny scrap of the brown exterior. She was pretty sure he swallowed it.

"No bugs at ten thousand feet, not halfway to the stars, anyway. Sorry, buddy."

The Mississippi was now coming to an end: a sprawling, silent blue steadily filled her view.

"Oh my gosh, Soda-Pop! The sea! The Gulf of Mexico!" she shouted. The great river sort of got tangled up in human construction that was spread out along the edge of the gulf: Lake Pontchartrain and New Orleans.

She adjusted her trim and banked a little to the southwest, hoping she would be able to tell the difference between the slice of water between Florida and Cuba, and the one between Cuba and Mexico. But Cuba's northern shore curved recognizably and sharply, like it was just finished throwing a ball for the Yucatán part of Mexico to reach out and catch.

"Soda-Pop, I'm going to get one of these planes for myself one day," she declared. "This is a *way* more exciting way to see the world than biking. Even if it's a little cramped."

South of Cuba she slowly followed the chain of islands that continued with Haiti and Puerto Rico, Saint Lucia, the Grenadines, and finally Trinidad and Tobago.

She checked her fuel gauges—it wasn't pretty. Both drop tanks were empty, as was the fuselage. She switched back and forth between the left and right wing tanks, but the needles barely moved.

Worrying about this she almost missed the Orinoco.

There was so much water flowing below the trees or bushes or marshes or whatever that the entire ground sparkled brilliantly. She turned the plane to head west and managed to finally pick out the river itself, untangling it from its environs. There were fewer identifiable cities or towns along it than there were along the Mississippi; for a little while she saw absolutely no sign of human life. Not that this meant there was none; just that there were no giant shiny silver metal and glass and cement constructions to glint in the sunlight.

"I might be flying over places no one—or at least no North American—has been before!" she said in awe, wishing she could land the plane immediately. This was prime explorer country, green and full of mysteries.

Then her engine began sputtering again. And this time she knew it wasn't the mixture; she was running out of fuel.

"Come on!" She twisted the fuel selector left and right. "Just a few more miles! Please!"

Soda-Pop pecked at her fingers as if it were a game.

Below them a city grew into view, perched on the edge of a wide, dark body of water.

"That must be Guayana, and the Caroní river," Ellie said with more hope than confidence. "We just follow that down and we should see the tepuis in no time! And lucky for us, Soda-Pop, Paradise Falls is on one of the first table-top mountains. We can just . . . *coast* there. Maybe . . ."

But the plane didn't seem like it was willing to cooperate.

Something smelled like it was burning, and Ellie suddenly understood what *running on fumes* really meant. There was so little left in the tanks that all the impurities and detritus that sloshed around at the bottom of it were now being consumed, and stinkily. She eased back on the throttle, figuring that they should begin to slow down to a landing speed anyway. Which was probably what, a hundred miles an hour? Which meant she needed a landing strip the length of . . . well, she hoped the tepuis were very *long* mesas.

She had to also keep an eye on the altimeter; the mountains were, as she had said to Soda-Pop, probably about a mile and a half high: if she let the plane dip down too far she would never get it back up.

The land below her was at least flat now; plains or scrub spread out on either side of the Caroní for miles in all directions, becoming dark and green and jungly to the south.

Then she saw them.

Jutting out of the ground like a god had pushed unimaginably large rocks up from underneath: the tabletop mountains. Stark and stony, looking like they didn't belong in the lush world around them. Or any world, really.

"There they are, Soda-Pop!" Ellie cried over the

engine's splutter and cough. "Let's just . . . aim and hope for the best?"

On the bright side, the mountains' flat tops were mostly vegetation free. No trees to crash into!

Not that she had a choice; her plane was done. There was a *chunk* chunk-a-chunk as the plane consumed the last bit of its fuel.

Ellie adjusted her flaps for landing and grabbed Soda-Pop, shoving him back into her pocket.

A terrible sound of wind whistled and screamed around the cockpit.

The mountain rushed at them fast, faster than anything she had ever seen, even in the movies.

"This is gonna be bumpy! Hang on—"

She was going to close her eyes, duck, and cover . . . but as they hurtled downward she glimpsed something that made her stop and stare: the light off a glittering rainbow arc of water, cascading out over the side of the mountain like there was a crack in a sidewalk hydrant.

Paradise Falls!

Just as she realized what it was the plane smashed into the ground with such force that it knocked Ellie's brains around inside her head. She grabbed the brakes but that didn't seem to help; the bumping and pounding continued as they barreled past rocks and grass. How could the plane continue to roll after crashing?

It hit a large bump and her body was flung as far from the belt as its webbing would allow, lacerating her skin. Now there was nothing to see outside the window: dirt dust rock ground and air all flickered by in meaningless splashes.

Then the world turned upside down.

The bumps stopped; the plane didn't. It kept skidding on its side, on one crushed wing.

Blood filled Ellie's left eye and pooled into her mouth. Dizzy and sick, she hit the belt release button as hard as she could manage and pulled back the canopy—extra difficult because her brain couldn't remember how to close her fingers.

When it was open the slimmest amount she pushed herself through and dropped to the ground.

The plane was still sliding to a halt; she was dragged painfully along before part of her coveralls tore away from the metal where they stuck.

Somewhere, far away, there was an explosion.

And Ellie went to sleep.

FIFTEEN

She dreamed she was flying.

She knew it was a dream because she was in a plane but her arms were stretched out on either side of her for wings and she could feel the wind through her fingers. She closed her eyes and was amazed that someone had let her, a sixteen-year-old girl, fly a plane. She wished Carl were there.

Then her fingers got stuck in a wing flap as she tried to bank. It bit hard through her skin, the metal tugging at her insistently. . . .

The solid world grew slowly around her, replacing the sky and the wind. Hard stones beneath her head cut into her flesh. More pain, all over her body: lumpy and spread out over her back and legs, sharp and throbbing over her left eye. The air was softer than in her dream . . . and the *smell*!

Dry and alien and delightful . . . she imagined a thousand different things at once since she couldn't describe it.

The pain in her finger continued, renewing itself constantly.

Ellie's eyes cracked open—a difficult feat for her left one, sealed with caked blood. She saw a bright purple bird nipping her hand as if it were a sweet treat it couldn't quite bite into.

"Soda-Pop!" she cried, then coughed.

She sat up, far too quickly.

The world spun again and for a tense moment she was afraid she would vomit up bile and candy bar. When it all settled down she saw that things around her were still not making sense; there was empty blue directly ahead of her, like in her dream, and flat rock beside her, gleaming in the strangely colored sunlight.

She sat quietly, trying to let her pain go, and eventually it all made a little sense.

She was at the very edge of a rocky promontory on top of the tepui. The ground, which she could see by leaning over, was far below. A little *too* far. Pebbles stirred up by her movements and driven by the wind tumbled down, disappearing on their endless descent. When she had fallen out of the plane she had been very close to rolling off the cliff—wide-open air was less than a foot away. Ellie slowly scooted back until she was stopped by a sharp, thick-leafed shrub. Soda-Pop hopped along, eyeing her suspiciously, like he was just waiting for her to pass out again. His beak was ready.

"We made it," she said slowly. A smile grew across her face like a cloud leaving the sun. "Soda-Pop, we actually made it! We're in South America! On a mountaintop! I'll bet that was Paradise Falls I saw right before I . . ."

She put a hand to her head, suddenly fearful. But pressing around her skull she didn't feel any soft spots or punctures or breaks; there was a small, painful egg that might, according to her Outdoor Guide Safety in the Wilderness pamphlet, *might* have indicated she had been hit hard enough for a concussion. But since Soda-Pop had managed to wake her up and her vision seemed fine she wasn't going to worry about it right then. There was a deep gash above her left eye and itchy, drying blood all around it. She wouldn't waste water on cleaning the wound until she was sure she had another source of wat—

Panicked, she patted herself down and looked around wildly. The satchel! With the map and the candy bars and the water!

"We have to find it, Soda-Pop! I thought for sure I put it around my shoulder before I tried landing . . ."

She intended to leap up, possibly dramatically, but her body didn't cooperate. Her back only let itself be used by unfurling slowly, several vertebrae at a time, the way she imagined it worked for old people. Her legs finally got themselves into order with some unwelcome flashes of pain.

She saw the plane across a scrape of bare rock, and it was a sad, denuded-looking thing. One wing was entirely missing—she didn't remember that—and the propeller was broken off in pieces like an old tomcat's whiskers. Its metal body still glittered in the sun here and there as the wind drove quick clouds across the bleak mountaintop, and Ellie felt something stir in her heart.

"You got me here safely, Mustang," she said, saluting. "That was more than I could ever hope for. Okay, Soda-Pop. Let's you and me—"

And then the plane exploded.

Ellie instinctively ducked down, curling her body around the bird. Shrapnel screamed through the air and tiny bits of glass or metal pocked themselves into her exposed flesh like a thousand tiny ant bites.

Moments later, there was a strangely comforting sound: a domestic *whoosh* as the heat pulled harsh currents from the air and a "normal" fire started burning. Probably devouring the upholstery on the seat, the leather, the pretty dials and knobs . . . Ellie cautiously looked up and saw that where her injured but recognizable plane had been a moment before was now a nearly unrecognizable sea urchin of blackened metal. What little fuel was left must have aerosolized and caused the tanks to detonate like bombs.

(*And the drop tanks are made out of papier-mâché, would you believe it!* Mind-Carl reminded her. Lovely burnable material, better than tinder or kindling.)

A thick, ugly column of black smoke rose into the sky. Ellie shuddered. For hundreds of miles around it was the only sign of "civilization": a stain on the seemingly pristine world of stone and woods and sky.

On the bright side, the satchel lay undamaged about fifty feet away from the plane, caught up in another one of the spade-leafed, painful-looking plants.

"Hooray," Ellie said, a little weakly. She crept up to it, afraid of something else exploding. Still wincing she carefully untangled the bag from the plant and put it on, smoothing the strap down.

"Things are looking jake, Soda-Pop. We landed . . . um, safely . . . and didn't explode. We have provisions, water, and a map. It could be so much worse, you know?"

She took a deep breath and considered saluting the plane again. She wished she had a camera—boy, what a newspaper or journal illustration this scene would make! The ruined plane on a bare and lonely mountaintop . . .

Three more planes buzzing in from the distance . . .

Surely it wasn't a coincidence. There had been three

planes at the zoo when she took off in Leroy's—Lucy's, Chester and Diane's, and Dan's. The smoke from her own plane was like a giant beacon telling everyone where she had "landed."

"We'd better get out of here, fast," she said, picking up Soda-Pop and popping him back into her pocket. "Leroy sounded *real* mad. We'll find Muntz and explain everything, and then maybe it will be all right."

The sides of the tepui were sheer. She looked over the precipice that she had nearly rolled off and saw it had nothing to step on or grab hold of until a green "shoulder" twenty or thirty feet down, a slant of rock and scree at a kind enough angle to support vegetation. There was no way to get to it, and no rope even if she could figure out how to rappel.

She ran along the edge of the mountaintop, checking now and then to see if there was a crack or a set of natural steps she could use to descend. What a stupid end to her great adventure! Trapped on a high prison where only "enemy" planes could land and take off . . .

Then she saw a slight dip in the otherwise flat top, a crusty fold in the Precambrian rocks. She followed its crease, and sure enough, the erosion was less stark and more gradual down the back side of the plateau. While it wouldn't be a walk in the (flat, Bloomington) park, the jumbled-up boulders and ledges that eased down to the plains below looked at least manageable.

As the three planes circled loudly overhead, looking for an approach, Ellie lowered herself over the grey stone side and began scrambling as fast as she could.

Soda-Pop squeaked with indignation when she had to hug a wall to stay upright—but at least he was speaking! It was more than she had ever heard from him at the zoo.

The farther down they went the thicker the plants grew, making for easier handholds. It smelled great, too. Ellie knew from the articles she had read in *Muntz's Monthly* that she was descending millions of years geologically, and also through distinct environments; this was what had drawn Muntz to explore Venezuela to begin with. There were creatures and plants that had evolved on these mountain "islands" that remained separate from the rest of the world and existed nowhere else. Maybe there really were still dinosaurs somewhere that had survived whatever extinction event that had killed them all, like in Sir Arthur Conan Doyle's *The Lost World*.

It grew warmer as she got farther down, which was a big relief.

Moister too, which was not.

She wished she could focus on the plants and insects around her, or look for dinosaur scat, but the noise of an airplane engine suddenly roared behind her. Ellie ducked down under a thinly leafed, vaguely desert-y shrubby thing (Soda-Pop peeped in annoyance). She didn't have to guess whose plane was flying so close to the side of the tepui. It was Lucy, of course; she streaked by closely enough that Ellie could see the woman through the glass, a grim smile on her face as she craned her head around, hunting.

But where were the other planes? Maybe they had already landed and everyone else was heading out on foot. She was being chased by air *and* land . . .

But as Ellie lowered herself into the trees, she had no fear of being tracked. The green sea swallowed her in the best, most comforting way. Its smells and noises and shadows slipped around her like a warm towel after a bath. In moments she was on the jungle floor, completely hidden from the sky and the planes and pursuers by the friendly trees.

"Beep," Soda-Pop said very pointedly.

"I'm here, I'm *in the Amazon rainforest*!" Ellie cried, not sure if that was exactly 100 percent true. Maybe it actually began a little south of where she was. Still, it was a forest. Closer to the Amazon than to Bloomington. "It's like a dream! I'm finally *exploring*!"

Except that in her dreams, the jungle was a lot more . . . jungly. Vegetation so thick you had to cut through it with a machete to get anywhere. Here (it was slightly relieving to see) the brown ground was quite visible, and walking between the trees wouldn't be that hard. Most of the plants in the understory were large-leafed to gather in as much of the little filtered sunlight as they could. The canopy trees that managed to capture most of the rays for themselves were spindlier than she would have imagined, spreading out gracefully at their tops into lovely light fronds that had looked like an unbroken shag rug from above.

She thought back to her revelation at the swimming hole, about not knowing what the fish really were, or names for all the weeds. Maybe these elegant, unusual-to-her plants were weeds that went unnoticed by the locals here the same way . . .

She opened up her satchel and pulled out the compass.

"The Caroní river was to the west of us when we landed. We climbed down the north-ish side of the mountain. Paradise Falls I think was to the southwest of us, but I figure we'll just head to the river first. There's usually settlements by rivers, and maybe there will be boats or someone who can take us to find Muntz."

Soda-Pop peeped.

"Oh, I'm not worried about money the way I was about refueling." Ellie answered the question she decided the bird had asked. "Once they find out that I'm going to find

Charles Muntz, the famous explorer, and return you to him, everyone will assume there will be a reward or money or something for helping me. Also, if I pretend I know him a little, maybe anyone with . . . *evil inclinations* will be dissuaded from hurting me. Muntz is famous and powerful. I'll bet he's pretty dangerous if you cross him or anyone he knows. So all we need to do is make it to the river. We can drink rainwater from these big cup-like leaves along the way, or cut bark for sap. Tree sap is never poisonous!"

But she wasn't 100 percent sure of that, either.

After the first hour or two of constant delight at everything she saw, Ellie began to notice other things—like her thirst. It was strange being in what she was *pretty* sure was some kind of tropical forest and not actually seeing or hearing any water. Maybe it was the dry season. For a few hopeful minutes the sky darkened and what she little she could see of the sky looked like heavy grey clouds. But after an hour or so they dissipated and everything went back to just being hot and moist without any relief.

She used the knife to slice into a harmless-looking tree trunk. A thick, decidedly unpalatable, milky-white sap oozed out of the wound.

"Maybe I can use it to repair rips to my clothing, or my

shoes," she said uncertainly. Soda-Pop didn't even bother to peep.

The next tree took a moment to react to the cut she made, but soon enough delightful, fresh-looking beads of bright clear liquid began to appear along the cut. Ellie stuck the tip of her knife into one, and it was barely sticky. She brought the droplet close to her mouth. . . .

"Ellie!"

Carl's voice came from the depths of her mind so strongly she could hear him.

"Do you know what that tree is? Really? Do you really want to gamble with your life this way? At least wait until you're *really* dehydrated. . . ."

She sighed and moved on, knowing that cautious Mind-Carl was right. She would only try the survivalist's trick after she showed real symptoms: headache, dry mouth, fever.

Horrible insects, mosquitoes and gnats not actually that different from the black flies back home, buzzed invisibly out of the darkness and crawled all over her sweaty, itchy skin looking for a good place to bite down. She slapped at them ceaselessly (she also slapped away Mind-Carl, who was reasonably concerned about diseases they might carry). Ironically, the fairylike clouds of delicate winged things that congregated in the few shafts of sunlight that made their way to the forest mid-layer did *not* bite—despite their annoying interest in her hair and face when she moved through them.

She wondered if land leeches preyed on mammals. And how fast they were. And if they jumped.

When evening fell the woods grew loud with the chirps of birds or insects or frogs or all three. Ellie could have stood listening to it all night, enthralled by the foreign symphony, but the thought of javelinas and jaguars made her look for a safe place to sleep. The trees weren't branched in the same way oaks and maples were, and she soon found out that it was impossible to climb some of the smooth-barked trunks. As the jungle darkened and she grew more desperate, Ellie finally found some thick vines hanging down ropily between two trees. Praying they weren't cousin to poison ivy, she managed to tie enough of them together to make a very primitive hammock. A real Outdoor Guide would have taken time to weave sticks or vines at right angles as a weft to make it stronger and more comfortable . . . but at the first mammalian-sounding growl from the darkness she leapt into it and curled up as best as she could. Sleep came surprisingly quickly but did not stay for long stretches, interrupted by the sounds and even smells of the jungle night.

The snake that Ellie found the next morning wrapped

delicately around her ankle was probably just attracted to her warmth, she decided.

It was muddy colored with muddier spots, an ugly short head but beautiful sparkling slit eyes: a perfect (tiny) specimen of a green anaconda. Juvenile, because adults were up to fifteen feet long. This one was barely two.

"Shoo," Ellie told it. "Get!"

Soda-Pop stayed hunkered down in her pocket. The snake might be harmless to a human until it got much bigger, but the tiny purple bird would make an easy appetizer. The anaconda uncoiled itself lazily and slowly slithered off, as if to say it wasn't afraid of her. This was its home, its forest; she was the fragile guest.

"That wasn't so bad, our first night in the jungle, was it, Soda-Pop?" Ellie asked, patting his little hidden head. "We survived just fine. We'll get to the river in no time—just you see!"

But twenty-four hours later she was exhausted and out of snacks and had drunk the last of her flask of water. The gash above her eye still stung horribly whenever she washed it out with the alcohol in the other flask, which meant it wasn't completely scabbed over, and maybe wasn't healing properly. If it became infected . . . she had no idea what to do. She was reminded of all the movies and books about Amazonian jungles: How was it that no indigenous people had found her? She would have stood up to a little questioning if it meant she could have a sip of water.

She sat, slumped, at the bottom of a tree, not even bothering to react to the *absolutely giant* shiny black beetle that seemed a little territorial in the mostly plant-free flat patch of ground. She pulled Soda-Pop out of her pocket and let him perch on her finger, holding the little bird up to her face.

"Well, this is a pickle, huh, little guy? I'm sorry. I promised to take you home, and I can't even find it. Yet. Well, I guess technically all of this is home. Kinda like 'Alaska' would be home for me.

"Gee, I wonder if I'm ever going to see *my* home again. I didn't really think this through. . . ."

She would not cry. She would *not*. She was already beginning to become dehydrated and couldn't afford to lose any more bodily fluids. And what kind of explorer cried, anyhow? Not Muntz. Not Leroy. She bet Margaret never cried. Even if no one was around to witness it, Ellie would not give in and break down.

"I know we don't even know where Muntz is—but surely word about a giant silver zeppelin would get around, don't you think? We just . . . we just need to find people. It will be all right."

She wiped her cheeks hard with the palm of her hand, practically bruising her skin.

"Oh, what are we going to do, Soda-Pop?"

Suddenly the bird froze, completely and entirely, like a movie had broken down and the projector was stuck on one still frame. He didn't even blink. It was classic bird-senses-a-predator behavior: Animals weren't as good with pattern recognition as humans, so by staying still, Soda-Pop had a very good chance of remaining undetected by the hunter after him.

Ellie also froze. What had Soda-Pop sensed that she couldn't? A jaguar?

The vast silence of the forest stretched out. It was a long, aching moment before she could finally hear something: the fast, random crashing through the woods of something that didn't care who heard it or what it stepped on.

Classic apex predator behavior.

And it was coming directly at them. Zigzagging just a little, narrowing in on their location as it caught their scent or heard Ellie's breathing.

What should she do? There was no tree to easily climb, no rock to leap up on top of.

She shoved Soda-Pop into her pocket, pulled out the knife, forced herself to stand up. She would defend both of them as best she could until the end. Stab whatever it was in the mouth, or the eye, right?

A bush got bent aside; a blindingly white furry and fanged creature burst into view.

The golden retriever puppy leapt, aiming directly at her exposed belly.

SIXTEEN

Of course, it was just a puppy, so it missed her stomach by several feet. Instead, it sort of launched itself into her knees and then fell back onto the ground, where it delightedly shook itself off and then got down to the serious business of sniffing around Ellie's shoes.

Ellie watched all of this in a bit of a daze.

She hadn't actually wound up drinking any of that sap, right?

Was there some other sort of plant with psychotropic properties that gave you hallucinations if you just touched it? She had touched a *lot* of plants in the last forty-eight hours, most inadvertently.

Or maybe she was coming down with some sort of

tropical fever. She felt her forehead, but it was dry and not too hot. Maybe this was a symptom of dehydration. Or . . .

Soda-Pop cautiously emerged from Ellie's pocket and tilted his head to get a good look at the puppy with his left eye. He peeped disapprovingly.

"At least you see him too."

Suddenly the puppy froze, but not as thoroughly as Soda-Pop had earlier: the tip of its tail wagged as though nothing the little dog could do could contain its joy. Then it bounded away in the direction it had come from, disappearing into the underbrush.

"After that puppy!" Ellie declared. Surely nothing so adorable, fearless, and . . . *purebred* . . . could just be wandering randomly and wild in the jungle. There must be a human companion nearby.

She set off after it, fear of losing the puppy pushing hard against the inability to make her body move very fast. It turned out she needn't have worried; besides the exuberant (and unnecessary) crashing noises it made Ellie could soon hear shouting. Human shouting. It was indecipherable at first, but as she got closer she could make out words—and realized they were in English.

"See, I told you to leave the dogs!"

"They're my babies!"

"They do not belong in the jungle!"

Ellie broke straight through some shrubbery rather than going around, hands above her face to protect it from vines and bugs. Once out into the open she was greeted by the sight and smell of a beautiful green river pulling away from the jungle, its banks low and grass-covered and inviting.

It was the Caroní river! She had been right! She just needed to keep going a little longer . . .

There were also two women arguing, seeming not to have noticed Ellie at all.

"Are you joking? They're *dogs*! They'll be *fine*! They're wolves!"

The person shouting this was a Black woman in her forties who wore a jumpsuit similar to the zoo coveralls but in indigo denim. Her hair was pulled back in sort of a French bun, revealing a clear forehead with flawless skin that made freckly, itchy sixteen-year-old Ellie immediately envious. *Two* golden retriever puppies romped at her feet. Her accent was unmistakably American.

"Those aren't wolves, those are inbred, pampered poodle-chinchillas!"

The other woman was older, fifties maybe, with darkly tanned skin. Her pronunciation of English made Ellie think she might be local, Venezuelan. She wore wide pants and a white smock top and had thick wavy salt-and-pepper hair that right now sprang around her head like it was emphasizing her anger.

"Oh, don't you say that about my pups," the first woman said, picking one up protectively. "They're *fierce* little hunter wolves."

"I know," the other woman said tiredly. "Another reason I don't want them in the jungle. They don't belong here. They *shouldn't* be hunting *anything* here. It's like . . . taking a tiger and dropping it into your Central Park."

"Not a bad idea. Get rid of the muggers. *And* the tourists."

"Um, excuse me," Ellie interrupted, feeling a little ridiculous.

Both of the women jumped.

"Excuse me?" Ellie apologized immediately. "I'm Ellie McGill, and my plane just crashed?"

"That explosion before? And all—that?" the first woman said in awe, waving her hand at the smoke still rising up in ugly spurts. "You *walked out of* that?"

"Are you all right?" the other woman asked, coming over and taking Ellie's hands, narrowing her eyes, and examining her face, head, wounds, clothes, all quickly: she was either a doctor, a mother, or both. "Everything looks all right except for that nasty bump on your head. You'll live, thanks to God you survived that. I'm Ana."

"I'm Louise Jefferson." The other woman put out her hand and gave a solid shake, with only the slightest pause when she saw how filthy—and slightly bloody—Ellie's own hand was. "And these here are my babies, Mutt and Jeff. Jeff's a girl, though, for your information. Pleased to meet a fellow American woman in the jungle!"

"Why didn't you and the other survivors just wait for the other planes? We saw them—obviously looking for you," Ana said.

"It's just me," Ellie said. "There were no other survivors." Then she saw the horrified looks on the other women's faces and quickly corrected herself. "I mean, I was the only one on the plane. I was the pilot. And the passenger. And the cargo, I guess."

"You were . . . flying . . . solo?" Louise asked slowly. "From where?"

"Does your family own one of the diamond companies? Did you come from Caracas?" Ana demanded.

"No, and no, and I flew from the States."

Both women just stared at her.

Then they exchanged looks, and Ellie had the distinct

feeling it was the first time the two of them had ever shared a similar feeling or agreed on anything.

"Querida," Ana said, a little more softly than she had spoken before, "maybe you should tell us your whole story, from the beginning."

"One which ends with running away from a crash and also away from help, and right into the middle of a Venezuelan jungle," Louise added, a twang inflecting her voice with light chastisement.

"Sure," Ellie said hesitantly. "Can I please have some water first, though?"

An hour later Ellie was comfortably sat in a camp chair, full of water and chocolate and nearly empty of words. The two women had set up their base camp at the edge of the river with every comfort an explorer could want: a tent for sleeping, a cookstove, a prep table, a camp desk, and two trunks full of supplies and extra clothing—all of which was protected by a tarp. It was like a scaled-down version of what Leroy and his friends used. The wood and canvas smelled like spices—or no, like incense, like something slightly fruity and smoky, somehow both comforting and inspirational.

At the point in the story where she mentioned the whole reason for her adventure—Soda-Pop—Ellie took the little bird out of her pocket, where he had been silently hiding.

Both women gasped at the bright purple thing with the crumpled crown feathers. He took in his new surroundings (and companions) with bright, interested eyes.

But now he was back in her pocket and Ellie held a cup of hot chocolate, which was a strange thing to have in the jungle but which Ana also insisted on making—almost exactly the same way Mesoamericans had for thousands of years. Possibly since the Olmecs! It was unlike anything Ellie had tasted in the States . . . thick, complex, spicy, with some of the same scent of the jungle and the smoke from the fire that had boiled the water. She felt completely renewed after telling her tale, and decided that maybe it was a magic drink.

Ana sat on a mat on the ground, having given up her seat to the injured and (previously) exhausted Ellie. She drew in the dirt with a stick while listening to the story, knees bent and legs splayed in a position that looked more comfortable for a child—or at least someone much younger than a woman with wide streaks of grey in her hair. Ellie's mother would have been shocked at the unladylike position, especially from an adult.

"Well, that is the most outrageous story I have ever heard," Louise said finally, shaking her head. She had both puppies in her lap, where they snoozed. "And I'm a cartographer. I've heard things from explorers. But a teenaged girl from a small town stealing a plane and flying to South America to repatriate a stolen bird to its native habitat? That's . . . something else."

"Soda-Pop wasn't stolen," Ellie objected. "Charles Muntz gave him to Leroy. That much is true."

"Let's say that is true," Ana said with a wry smile. "Where do you think Herr Muntz found this little purple friend?"

"All right, he was taken from his environment and family," Ellie said reluctantly. "And I'm returning him."

"You are an incredibly brave little woman," Ana said. "Also maybe insane. I think I like you."

"You're a piece of work," Louise agreed, but somehow didn't make it sound like an insult. "Don't you have family who are worried about you? A mama who's going out of her mind?"

Ellie swallowed, her mouth suddenly gone dry. Her stomach flopped. "Yes. And . . . *other* people too. But . . . if I had to stop and think about what other people think or feel, then I don't know if I'd have done it, ever. And Soda-Pop would probably die."

"Spoken like a true revolutionary!" Ana said with a grin.

"I don't know about that," Louise said, a little disapprovingly. "But if I worried about what people thought of me or what I did, I wouldn't be a Black woman employed as an illustrator and mapmaker."

"So the jungle and plains are soon going to be crawling with crazy rich North Americans looking for you . . ." Ana said thoughtfully. "I'm still a little confused as to why they care about one tiny bird and one girl, but eh, who can understand you people. You want to find Herr Muntz and return little Soda-Pop here? Fine. That man is back here all the time looking for his terror birds." Ellie noticed that when she said *Herr Muntz* her accent completely changed; it sounded German. "I can take you there while I guide Louise here; it is not as far as all that and everyone knows where the big balloon ship is. But there is something I think you should see first. Tudo bem? All right?"

"That's great! Thank you so much!" Ellie squealed.

"Well this trip suddenly got a lot more interesting," Louise remarked.

After treating Ellie's wounds—they had a complete medical kit, with iodine and gauze—the two women quickly and professionally loaded up their rucksacks with enough supplies for a two- or three-day hike and improvised one out of a duffel for Ellie.

"What about a tent?" she asked.

"Too heavy. It should only rain in the afternoons. We'll sleep in hammocks, under a tarp, if necessary," Ana said. She held up a tightly wrapped, tan-colored bundle of knotted rope. Intriguing! Like the time Ellie had tried to tie a blanket to two trees in their back yard to spend the night in when she was nine. It fell down unexpectedly sometime after midnight and she bruised her elbow. She doubted Ana's would slip.

"I'll bet a tent made out of parachute would be light enough to carry," Ellie said thoughtfully. "I made a picnic blanket out of old scraps of them to take on my bike, and it's light as a feather."

"Huh," Louise said. "That's pretty clever. You could sell that."

They also brought mosquito netting to lay across their bodies as they slept, but everything else remained behind.

"You're just going to leave the camp set up here?" Ellie asked as, fully loaded up, the three (six) started heading into the jungle.

"My friends will look after it. And anything they take—like the medicine—well, they probably need more than I do," Ana said with a shrug.

What friends? Ellie wondered, but that wasn't even in the top ten questions she was bursting to ask them as soon as they set off.

"I can't believe you make maps *for a living*," she began, to Louise. "What an amazing life! So you get to explore wherever you want, and write it all down? Like, make notes of landmarks and where the interesting stuff is?"

"Sometimes," the woman answered with a smile. "We don't have much information about these forests, and very little on Venezuela's portion of it besides the mountains. So I booked myself a working vacation to come down here and see it for myself. But maps aren't just about landmarks and 'interesting stuff,' Ellie. My maps especially.

"I focus on the people who live *in* the landscape drawn on a map, and show their relationships to other peoples, what they do, and where they went if they had to leave. I created one recently about uprooted people of the United States: folks who had to move because of the war, because of the dust bowl, because of reservations, because of Japanese internment camps. Everyone who is forced to move on, with the *why* hopefully clearly illustrated."

"That's a strange idea," Ellie said thoughtfully. Then she realized how that sounded. "Oh, I'm sorry! I didn't mean to be rude. I'm just used to the other kind of map. Of things that stay still, like mountains and beef agriculture and factory centers. I'm trying to imagine a map of movement . . . the map stays still, but the people don't."

Louise laughed. "Imagine a drawing of a crowd of

Mexican folk walking north to California, with a sign directing them, and another drawing, farther up, of people picking apples out of a tree, with another sign that says 'Pickers Wanted.' Connect the dots. That's what my work is all about, connecting the dots. Between real people and their work, and real people and their land, and real people and their migration across new lands. Despite what you might have learned about Columbus and Amerigo Vespucci and all that, maps aren't *just* for European kings and queens to label countries, mountains, rivers, and states with their last names."

"That's fascinating," Ellie said thoughtfully. Then she turned to Ana. "And you're a professional adventurer and guide?"

"Oh, yes, apparently I guide weird North Americans into the jungle for fun but very little pay."

"Hey!" Louise piped up indignantly. "I'm paying you *above* the agreed amount!"

"Have you discovered anything really amazing on any of your trips? A cave full of crystals? Or have you named a stream no one has crossed before?"

Ana laughed. "I cannot say with any certainty that I have stepped anywhere anyone else hasn't stepped in all the wilds of Venezuela. Never found a crystal cave. As for streams, what I call it down here someone may call something else upstream."

"But you're an adventurer!" Ellie protested. "You must have, I don't know, found a really interesting rock formation at least that no one else has seen?"

"Ellie, I hate to disappoint you, but my explorations are . . . small and green. I am a naturalist. Or 'a botanist unfettered by a degree,' as my husband would say. I spend my time in the forest, yes, exploring—but also documenting and doing site surveys. My interest isn't finding a hill or a bug and sticking my name on it. It is understanding the forest, and writing it up before it all changes."

Ellie was silent for a while after this, her further questions quieted by new thoughts: These two women were—sort of—explorers and adventurers.

And they were *nothing at all* like Leroy Reardon and Charles Muntz.

They didn't have stories about their exploits published in international magazines; they weren't interviewed on the radio. Neither one of them had mentioned a word about "collecting" anything beyond information and data. They didn't dress the part, and she was willing to bet a week's pay that neither owned a silver Jaguar or her own plane.

They were a bit more like Margaret, but also more solo,

without the trappings and support of academia around them. They were mostly alone in their interests and careers.

Neither was interested in fame, it seemed. Even Amelia Earhart had posed for publicity shots and given interviews.

Strange. And something to think about.

As they walked, Ana occasionally picked fruit and gave them to the others to try. One was the size of a small apple and had a creamy white interior whose taste was indescribable. Literally: Ellie had no words for it. Maybe custardy with a mellow but unusual spice. They nibbled on juicy dark ruby-red marbles that were neither berries nor whole fruit, exactly, and tasted like flowers. Ana also pointed out things in the trees that Ellie would have completely missed, probably *had* missed when she was by herself: tiny bats hanging under leaves while they slept to stay dry, normal-looking plants with thick green leaves that turned out to be the expensive—in the States, at least—cattleya orchid, which here could bloom at any moment now in the rainy season.

She also showed them little marks on tree bark, scrapes on stones, and other nearly invisible signs of other humans passing. "It's all on purpose. Someone made these. Helps to keep you from getting lost," she explained, pointing out where a thin branch had (apparently) been purposefully twisted and broken off.

Louise kept a constant eye on her puppies, occasionally carrying them when they got tired. One on each shoulder, slung like market bags.

If hiking behind two amazing women on the far side of the world in a magical rainforest with beasts that were poisonous to the touch (possibly) was the most extraordinary, exhilarating thing Ellie had ever done, well . . .

. . . sometimes, unbelievably, it could get a little boring. Even frustrating.

"I have no idea what this is!" Ana would declare, and then they all would stop, take their packs off, and wait while she patiently sketched the flora. Sometimes the botanist took out a tiny jeweler's loupe and spent what to Ellie seemed like far too many aggravating minutes silently poring over leafy surface detail. She always invited Louise and Ellie to also take a peek, and to be fair, what was revealed at 20X was magical and unexpected: geometrically crisscrossing veins that looked like train tracks, bracts that (even magnified) had nearly invisible hairs at their tips and required words like *tomentose* and *hispid* to describe them.

But still, they were plants; they didn't move. How could they be more interesting than a bright purple bird?

Ellie had to keep reminding herself: Before her rescue, these women were here for their own reasons.

"We have to stop for some extra provisions," Ana

declared at one point. "Since we're taking a little side trip with an extra person. And Louise, I think you will like this."

Ellie noticed the path they were now on was well-trodden by *human* feet, not animals. Farther along there was a clearing that had been made artificially; old burn marks blackened the trunks of large trees. They marked the edges of a char-strewn area in which a dozen healthy, bright-leafed shrubs grew.

"Plantains," Ana said, pulling down a stalk to show them: green, sort of like bananas, dozens of them bunched tightly against one another.

"Slash-and-burn agriculture," Ellie said, remembering her world history.

"A gift from the missionaries," Ana said dryly.

Somehow when they were taught it, Ellie had imagined neat rows of tomatoes or cabbages. Not bananas. "Where are the farmers?"

"The Pemón people are cautious with outsiders. They won't show themselves while we are here. We'll leave them some things in trade—chocolate, iodine—in return for the things we take and eat. Plantains make up most of their—and my—diet. Porridge, fried, everything. Like potatoes for other people."

"*This* is what I'm talking about," Louise said

delightedly, finding a log to sit on. "You're dead right, Ana. I *love* this."

Ellie nearly groaned when she pulled out her sketchbook. "Can I have a banana?" she asked as Ana cut them off their stalk with a deadly-looking knife.

"They're not bananas, and they're not as good raw. They aren't sweet and soft, like the Cavendish ones you're used to," Ana said. "But you can have one if you want."

She tossed a brownish one to Ellie, who went to catch it—only to have it swiped out of the air right before it touched her fingers. Mutt looked back at her with glee as he kept running, prize clamped tightly in his teeth.

Ana rolled her eyes and started to toss another one—and then saw that Jeff had paused, watching her sharply, ready to run and intercept a second plantain. She tossed it *high* so it curved up in a sharp arc and came straight down over Ellie, who caught it deftly above her head.

Jeff danced and yipped back and forth between her and Ana, wanting the game to continue.

"Hush, Jeff, I'm working," Louise murmured.

Despite managing to keep the plantain this time, Ellie then had trouble peeling it. It held strangely in her hand. Ana was right: The flavor was mild, starchy, not very sweet. But it filled her stomach nicely. She was still several meals behind, and her teenage body was crying out for more.

She broke off a tiny piece and held it out to Soda-Pop, who nibbled it gratefully. Bugs *and* bananas, Ellie thought. Omnivorous? Opportunist? She should be writing this down, like Ana.

Jeff whined, put her paws on Ellie's feet, looked up with hopeful eyes: *Why are you feeding that prey-bird instead of me? Am I not friend?*

Ellie dropped a big chunk down for the retriever puppy, who was *definitely* a scavenger/opportunist and gobbled it up immediately.

"Whatchoo 'ooing?" she asked Louise in between her own bites. The cartographer was making quick sketches of the bananas, of the chunks taken out of trees with machetes, of char marks. *Pemón* was written in big and beautiful letters. She pulled out a map—a much larger, more detailed one than the sad atlas Ellie had in her satchel—and consulted it, drawing an approximation of the landmarks they were near.

"This whole area of Venezuela is bound for . . . change. There's talk of turning the grasslands and the tepuis into a national park, which would be fantastic, because it would help preserve the plants and animals and environment, which is like nowhere else in the world. But what about the people who live here too? Will they be removed, or put on display like just another native species?"

"The people here aren't all 'native,' either," Ana added, packing plantains into her bag. "Besides immigrants and colonizers, enslaved people were brought in to work the chocolate plantations . . . some escaped, some were freed.

"The government also wants to put in a giant hydroelectric dam across the Caroní. It will generate power for cities . . . and submerge acres and acres of forest. How will it affect those who live on the rivers?"

"See? This is what I was talking about before, Ellie," Louise said eagerly. "I don't just map *places*. I map people . . . people who move, people who are forced to move. Geography is identity."

Ellie thought about her words. It was all true . . . and it didn't just pertain to people. She looked down at Soda-Pop, quiet for now in her pocket, and considered the massive distances the poor little guy had already immigrated in his life. Four thousand miles.

"Almost there, Soda-Pop, I promise," she murmured. Then she turned to the two women. "You can't bring Soda-Pop to the Arctic; he would die. But *people* can live there. Animals have even fewer choices than people."

"Who? Oh, the bird. He does sort of look like grape soda, I suppose. I understand your point exactly—you are correct. They have fewer choices and do not do as well as humans do everywhere.

"But sometimes animals and plants move to places where they thrive even better than before . . . better than they should. Your dandelion wasn't a native to the Americas. It walked with the colonists along with their enslavement and smallpox and gunpowder. Maybe you should do a map of the movements of plants, Louise."

The other woman chuckled. "That would make for a very pretty map. But plants can't be enslaved or freed, Ana. They just are."

"Tell me that the next time you see a sugar plantation. Stalks forced into unnatural rows, then cut down like murder with giant scythes. And what about the plants that come with disenfranchised populations? Sorghum is from Africa. . . ."

"Now *there* you have a point, my friend. That could be interesting. . . ."

The two women bantered and sparred gently as they packed up. Whatever Muntz and Leroy had talked about in their own Venezuelan adventure meeting, Ellie would bet it was nothing like this. The most amazing animal they had found and brought home, certainly. Dinosaur bones they had assembled, maybe. Number of countries they had toured, oh, without question. Certainly not anything about sorghum and enslaved people.

After some time the land began climbing and they followed a sandy path that led up quickly. Its left side was a wall of stone; vines clung to the few scattered sunlit patches the forest afforded, then ranged out over the whole escarpment when only scrub and brush remained. On the right side it was open air, the woods soon far below.

"Are we climbing another tepui?" Ellie asked.

"Oh, yes," Ana said.

"Is it the—" Louise began.

"Shh! Don't spoil the surprise, map lady!"

It was fascinating for Ellie to be slowly rising up through the jungle instead of descending quickly into it, fleeing. Now she had time to appreciate the canopy layer of the trees, filled with bugs and butterflies and tiny flitting birds.

The air got cooler as they climbed higher, though somehow the sun burned Ellie's pale arms.

Soda-Pop got agitated and began to peep.

"Everything okay, little guy?" Ellie asked him, concerned. "Or are you just happy we're climbing up again? Not a jungle bird, are you?"

After another hour of working steadily uphill around the mountain, her legs were burning. She couldn't understand how the older women managed. But Soda-Pop was getting more and more excited, to the point where he clawed at her skin through the cloth with his tiny sharp feet and flutter-hopped until he was on her shoulder. Once there he beeped and fluffed his wings and bobbed his head like he was directing her, a giant ship with a tiny captain.

Ana looked back and smiled.

A sound that had been quietly filling the background grew louder: Ellie didn't notice anything unusual until it reached a certain volume. Then the whisper became a rushing became a roaring, and the air turned moist and delicious.

"A waterfall!" she cried in delight as they rounded a corner and finally saw it.

And what a waterfall!

So much pressure from such a height caused the ribbon of water to leap out from the top of the mountain in a way that was visually pleasing but somehow didn't make sense from a physics standpoint. As they fell, droplets spread out like a white mare's tail, becoming blurrier and wider, turning to clouds of water vapor before they finally hit the ground below. There were rainbows everywhere, every angle that Ellie turned her head: the sunlight scattering gloriously as water hit stones on the path before them, was redirected by a sudden breeze, or shifted due to some change in pressure or temperature she couldn't see.

"Not just any falls . . . *Paradise Falls*! Soda-Pop! We're here! I can't believe we're here!"

The etching from her adventure journal, with the badly drawn, brightly colored house perched on top of it, faded—but not in a bad way: its black-and-white form bloomed to accept the majesty of the reality before her. When she looked at the picture next time, she would see *this* in her head.

But, of course, Carl wouldn't share that vision. Because he wasn't here with her, the way he was always supposed to be.

Ellie felt a pang. She was having the adventure of a lifetime *without* him.

Soda-Pop hopped up and down excitedly on her shoulder and nipped the side of her cheek, interrupting her spiraling thoughts.

"Ow! I know this is all really about you, not me, Soda," Ellie said ruefully, rubbing her face. "But geez, give me a second. This is *Paradise Falls*."

"Kerepakupai Merú," Ana corrected. "That's what local people call it in their language. But yes, it is like paradise, isn't it?"

"It's even more breathtaking than I expected," Louise said, leaning back on her heels and shading her eyes to look at the top. Mutt and Jeff ran forward to play in the spray. A shallow pool of water had collected on the ridge where they stood; it constantly overflowed and joined the rest of the water in its majestic journey down—and made a perfect pool for hot and tired dogs.

Ana pointed up: There was another path, almost vertical, that led to the ridge above them, alongside the waterfall. She began climbing.

Louise followed and Ellie and the puppies came next, reluctantly leaving the little pool. The teen's knees popped as she stretched to make each foot- and handhold. By the time she pulled herself all the way up to the ridge she was far behind the other women and couldn't see them. Or hear them; the waterfall was much louder now, a brute force, a hurricane, a reminder of the violence it was capable of. Ellie now stood on a narrow path with death below and beside her.

The puppies at her feet—who took a little longer to leap their way up—didn't like any of it; they whined, shook their heads, backed up, and growled.

And then Soda-Pop suddenly leapt off Ellie's shoulder and fluttered straight into the waterfall.

"Soda-Pop! No!"

She lunged forward to grab him before the poor thing was caught in an updraft and got smashed against the rocky wall—but he had disappeared.

She stood at the very edge of the fall, getting soaked, trying to figure out where he went.

And then a hand reached out from the water and pulled her . . . *inside.*

Ellie stumbled her way into a dark, cool space: There was a cave behind the waterfall, completely hidden by it! When she managed to shake water out of her hair and eyes she gasped.

There were Louise and Ana, and Soda-Pop . . .

. . . and hundreds of other little flitting purple birds.

SEVENTEEN

Ellie's eyes were still adjusting to the dim light, so at first she questioned what she saw: tiny bursts of purple that looked exactly like the strange stars of color she saw behind her eyelids when they were closed or she was in a perfectly dark auditorium (waiting for a school concert to begin, for instance). They *moved* like shooting stars as well: suddenly gliding down to the floor or zipping up to a nook in the rocky wall, or flitting directly across the open space of the cave, in no readily categorizable pattern—not quite as fast and humming as hummingbirds, but close enough to warrant a solid second glance. Sometimes one would buzz through the waterfall from the outside to join them, cutting straight through a stream of water like it wasn't even there, like bees at the entrance of a hive: no hesitation, no slowing down. They either somehow didn't get wet by virtue of whatever spot they chose to enter or they didn't care. A few gave alarm calls probably directed at the humans—and the dogs—but otherwise they seemed to be just carrying on with normal purple-birdie life.

The cave wasn't some dead stony hole like in the movies or the shallow ones in Bloomington that were just overgrown ledges. It was a whole living environment: The fall provided lots of mist and let in just enough light for an Eden of bright green flora to grow. Soft mounds of moss puffed out of shallow niches, sometimes spilling down to the floor and carpeting several feet of it in bright chartreuse. Places where enough minerals had broken down to make "dirt" exploded with leafy plants. Some vegetation with exposed roots, like orchids, clung to the walls. There was even a small bush at the entrance of the cave, leaning toward the water and light like a supplicant. It seemed healthy enough, though, and had what looked like twists of frayed, brightly colored cloth tied to several of its branches.

Clashing starkly with all this green were the purple birds.

A quick and educated look around, honed by her experience at the zoo and time with Margaret, revealed to Ellie no nesting adults, no young, and no paired-up couples. There were a few old nests made of grass and mud that were stuck to the sides of the cave walls. Whatever their schedule, this was not breeding season (if it had been, she would have felt terrible about intruding).

Soda-Pop hopped back and forth, not quite looking at his flock. He whistled a complicated call that Ellie had definitely not heard before. Someone responded, from far in the back. Was it a remembrance of territory? Finding his mom or his siblings? She would never know unless she devoted years to studying them—like Margaret.

She waited tensely for more of a reaction from the crowd, but nothing happened. No one came forward to attack Soda-Pop; no one approached him at all. Maybe their response song was the avian equivalent of "Oh, you're back. Whatever. We were just talking about lunch." Soda-Pop repeated *his* song again and hopped back and forth a few more times. Then he hopped farther into the crowd and joined them properly.

Ellie hadn't really prepared for this moment. If she had thought about it at all she assumed she would be feeling *more*: that she would cry, or laugh and cry, or enjoy a comforting blanket of adult satisfaction settling over her for a job well done, an afghan knit with sadness that this was the end of their friendship. Soda-Pop would live, happily ever after, in the right place, with the right crowd.

But she wasn't feeling anything just yet. Not even

sadness. There was still too much excitement; she was behind *Paradise Falls*! And in a cave that absolutely begged to be explored. The plants—and lightly glowing fungi, which she had missed before—were probably unique to Venezuela, maybe even to this single mountain. Ana was already sitting cross-legged on the floor, writing and sketching. But not hurriedly; it was obvious she had been here before.

(Louise had taken Mutt and Jeff outside to splash in the waterfall. Ellie silently thanked her; the birds would be much calmer without them there.)

She cautiously moved deeper into the cave. The other Soda-Pops were nervous but not extremely alarmed around her; they stayed out of reach and didn't scream.

The stone walls and ceiling all angled toward each other as Ellie progressed until all that was left was a sharp, tight tunnel, far too small even for her. Fresh air gusted out that wasn't moist; the other side must have let out some distance from the waterfall. There was so much of the faintly glowing, map-like fungus on the walls back there that everything was lit a ghoulish green.

Which was how Ellie saw the orange peel on the ground.

It was so weirdly normal that she almost didn't notice it for a moment, her mind automatically ignoring it like any street garbage. Then she realized she hadn't seen or heard about any oranges in her (admittedly) short time in Venezuela. Plantains, mangoes, and the jungle fruit Ana had fed them or warned them away from . . . but not citrus, and she hadn't seen a single citrus tree in the jungle. There was something about how the peel sat there, discarded and bright orange and bright white, *not* the colors of the forest, that irritated her.

She bent down to pick it up and saw boot prints around it, driven deep into the fine dirt of the cave floor. Large, treaded, men's boot tracks.

Keeping her volume low and not looking at the birds—they and prey animals scared more easily if you caught their eye—Ellie directed her voice as best she could to the front of the cave, to Ana.

"Do people come to this cave a lot?"

Ana shook her head definitively once, not looking up from her journal. "The local people treat this as . . . not a sacred spot, exactly, but one that's special. I mean, obviously, it *is* special. Only recently have European types discovered it."

That made sense; the sort of people who for whatever reason tied souvenirs or offerings carefully to the living branches of a cave bush didn't seem like the type to stomp around and drop garbage. It had probably been Charles Muntz, when he first acquired the bird.

She hoped desperately it hadn't been Muntz.

It didn't fit with her image of him at all.

This was what she imagined instead: Charles Muntz was standing there and saw an assistant, a dumb lackey, mindlessly munching on a snack while the great explorer was setting up traps for his monster birds. He then called the boy out in extremely articulate and angry language.

"This is not the sort of expedition Charles Muntz leads, young man! I pilot a zeppelin, not a garbage scow!"

Ellie grinned, putting one foot inside the giant boot prints, thinking about how she was literally following in her hero's footsteps. Soon she would catch up to the man himself, and . . .

She stopped for a moment in confusion. Wait . . .

Muntz told Leroy . . . or, rather, Leroy told everyone . . . that Soda-Pop had been accidentally caught in a trap set for one of Muntz's monster birds, the creature he was currently pursuing in South America. There was no evidence of a monster bird *or* a trap for it in this cave. There were just hundreds of the little purple birds.

That was odd. . . . Maybe the trap was outside somewhere nearby? Maybe Muntz came in and explored this cave while he was hunting his monster bird elsewhere? That *seemed* like an adventurer, explorer-y thing to do.

Still, strange coincidence . . .

Maybe the orange peel wasn't evidence of Muntz's being there at all. Maybe it was some other "European type," as Ana said.

But this all distracted from another, more obvious point: in her excitement over the cave and the other Soda-Pops Ellie had forgotten about that part of her journey that was supposed to involve Muntz. How was she going to return Soda-Pop to the man herself and get to meet him now? How would they become friends? Of course she wanted to save her bird's life, but meeting Muntz was a huge bonus to fleeing south. The thought was that maybe he would even help figure out—pay for, arrange, take Ellie himself!—a way home for her.

Now there wasn't really any point in insisting that Ana take her to him.

And that was only fair, Ellie told herself. It was amazing luck she had run into her and Louise at all, and they were already being incredibly generous in taking her on and taking Soda-Pop home. She couldn't ask for more.

Still, she was *so close* to Muntz . . . in his natural habitat . . . *exploring* . . .

She wouldn't be disappointed. She *wouldn't*. Soda-Pop was home. That was the most important thing of all.

As she was thinking about this, scuffing the boot tracks into oblivion, her shoe hit something that wasn't rock and wasn't dirt (and wasn't an orange). It was soft, but crumpled in such a way that it looked like it *could* have been a rock, and it was camouflaged in a fine layer of cave dust.

Ellie reached down and picked the thing up before she remembered she wasn't home anymore and that the object could have been alive, poisonous, or some sort of disgusting scat. But as it deformed in her hands it turned out to be none of those things, thank goodness—just an old rag or cloth. She shook it out, carefully pulling the corners apart until it made a square, wrinkled and covered in what looked like drops of black blood or oil. *Handkerchief,* she realized. Irish linen, with the neatest rolled hem and the tiny square windows in the trim that her mother found so fancy. There was a black monogram in one corner, no embellishments or flowers around it, not even a daisy.

LKR III

Ellie's mind fit the puzzle piece in and realized everything immediately.

Her heart, who only wished the best for everyone, took a little longer to reach the correct conclusion.

Why would Muntz have Leroy's handkerchief?

"Maybe Leroy loaned it to him when they met," Ellie murmured to herself. Yes, Muntz had a cut, maybe from shaving or something, and he forgot to give it back, and used it to . . .

No, wait. They didn't meet until the night that Muntz gave him Soda-Pop. Muntz wouldn't have had the handkerchief when he was trying to capture the monster bird; that was *before* he met Leroy. And littering the floor with orange peels and boot tracks . . .

. . . like some sort of careless, second-rate would-be explorer . . .

Mind-Carl insisted on voicing his (her) thoughts about the matter.

"Do we have any proof, besides his own word, *that Muntz actually gave Soda-Pop to Leroy as a present*?"

Ellie thought hard. None of the other expedition crew had mentioned anything about it. None of them had talked about meeting Muntz. Or told reporters, or tipsily regaled onlookers with stories of meeting the legendary man. In fact, they had all looked kind of weird when Leroy announced it. She remembered noticing their expressions at the time—only Diana had looked undisturbed.

"But Leroy's having a whole plaque and exhibit designed around it!" Ellie argued back. "That would be . . . insane! To make up all that!"

"Maybe he thought just having a spectacularly beautiful, exotic little bird wasn't good enough. Wasn't *big* enough," Mind-Carl said patiently. "He's not like you, Ellie. He doesn't actually work with any of the animals . . .

or zookeepers. He doesn't think about the animals. Only himself."

Ellie walked slowly back to where Ana was, still holding the offending handkerchief in front of her.

"Querida," Ana said, "you look like a mad prophet. Joan when she just heard from God. Saint Teresa maybe. I should have my husband paint you there with that rag and all the little birds flying around you like angels."

Ellie looked up, drawn out of her thoughts, at the Soda-Pops so close to her. Soda-Pop himself was perched on the top of a formation that wasn't quite a stalagmite.

"I don't think Charles Muntz came here and . . . *accidentally* trapped Soda-Pop," she said, sinking down to the cave floor next to Ana and showing her the dirty handkerchief.

"Mm," Ana said noncommittally.

A strange sort of depression came over Ellie suddenly, like all her energy had been drained out her feet—and not in a good way, like from honest work, like trudging through a jungle. The realization was too much for her to deal with.

But she had to say it. She had to complete her thought.

"I think the head of the zoo—Leroy Reardon, my boss—lied about Charles Muntz giving Soda-Pop to him as a gift for the zoo. I think Leroy came here and just grabbed him."

"I don't know about all that, but I can tell you: Charles Muntz was never here," Ana said matter-of-factly. "He *was* nearby, several mountains over in his giant silver blimp, chasing after that giant bird monster he thinks hides in the forests. But I didn't think you would believe me if I told you—why would you? And anyway the most important thing, it seemed, was to get your bird home. And then you home. And part one is now done."

"Yeah," Ellie agreed. "It *is*. And I'm glad I did it. But . . . Ana . . . I know you don't know anyone involved, but . . . Leroy . . . my boss . . . I can't believe he lied about something so huge . . . so huge that I don't even know what is true anymore!"

"You're upset about the big people who lied to you? Your boss? That he controlled information for his own benefit? Ah, poor young North American. You somehow saw less of the great war than we did. If you had Nazis immigrating to your country to escape punishment alongside the Jewish people and Communists and artists they were trying to eradicate—and saw how your government dealt with it all—you would perhaps be a little less surprised."

Ellie nodded, getting her general point.

But . . . *Leroy Reardon* . . . with his sure, booming voice, bright blue eyes, and private plane . . .

Louise stuck her head back in the cave.

"How we all doing back here?" she asked.

"I think we're done, for now," Ana said, gauging Ellie critically. "Let's go make camp . . . there's a place not too far from here with an overhang and great view. A good place to spend the night."

Ellie nodded absently, too caught up in the thoughts rushing around her head to do more than shoulder her bag and watch blankly while the older woman packed up her journal and strode jauntily through the curtain of water.

"Bye, Soda-Pop," she murmured at the little bird, who was preening himself in the middle of the chaos of his family. If it hadn't been for his broken crest feathers, Ellie wasn't sure she would even recognize him among all the others. "I'm glad we got you home. I hope you have a safe, wonderful life. And lots of babies, and your line stays strong, and you live happily ever after."

She turned, closed her eyes, and walked through the waterfall, but the water was barely mist, neither soaking her nor washing her clean of all the sad thoughts.

Ana had already begun descending back the way they came; Louise held one puppy, and the other waited patiently—tiredly—at her feet for his turn.

"BEEP!"

Ellie turned around.

Soda-Pop was hopping through the waterfall after them.

"Aw, Soda. You can't come with us. You gotta stay with your folks."

She scooped him up and gently tossed him back through the waterfall. Then she turned to hurry down the path—but Louise was taking her time, picking her way carefully with the puppies.

So of course Ellie was only halfway down when Soda-Pop came hopping back out again.

"BEEP!" he said, and almost sounded annoyed.

"Go. Go away," Ellie said as harshly as she could. She was going to start crying. "You need to stay here. This is where you belong. You didn't even *eat* at the zoo. Stay here."

Refusing to meet the bird's eyes, she hurried after the others. Louise was finally down on the main path with both puppies. Ellie put on her duffel/sack and tried not to sniffle.

Soda-Pop popped his head over the side of the ledge.

"BEEP!"

"Dang it, Soda-Pop!"

"Persistent little fella," Louise observed.

"He's with his family. He's too old to have imprinted on humans. He's back in the right habitat. Why is he following us?"

"Maybe he's still waiting for his wings to heal," Ana suggested. "You're his safety and meal ticket until then. Just because he's home doesn't mean other birds will take care of him. They're not like people; they won't care for a sick creature that's not one of their young. Wild animals don't act the way they do in a zoo."

"He knows you'll protect him," Louise added. "Did you ever have a pet finch or canary? Pretty little birds. They sing and hop and dance around and you can never tell if they're sick until one day they just drop down dead. This little mister here is smart."

"But I can't take him back home," Ellie moaned. "That was the whole point of this."

"Let's deal with that later," Ana suggested soothingly, like she was talking to a young child—or someone on the brink of having a complete breakdown. Ellie pretended very hard to not see *another* look that the two women exchanged over her head. "Soda-Pop knows where he lives. Birds have excellent navigation skills, as you well know. He can fly back home whenever he can fly again. If he wants. Let's set up camp, have a good dinner and a good night's sleep, and see what the morning brings us."

"Listen to the naturalist. She knows her stuff. Including how to cook plantains," Louise said. "Which I am very eager to try tonight."

Ellie nodded and hung back so the women wouldn't be looking at her. She knelt and Soda-Pop was hopping toward her hand before she even put it out, nimbly fluttering up and settling himself—not onto her shoulder, as she expected, but directly into the safety of her pocket.

"I guess it's been a long, exciting day for you, huh," she said. "Me too, Soda-Pop. Me too."

Ellie kept herself busy doing whatever needed to be done to get ready for the evening. Although she wasn't familiar with the specific equipment or techniques Ana used—and Louise was learning—her general knowledge of outdoor-related things, like tying knots and how tight to make canvas so it would hold against wind and water, was very useful. She helped hang the hammocks from sturdy little trees, and Ana was impressed with her ability to strike a spark on the first try for the camp stove. But Ellie remained empty and silent, stirring the pot of chocolate without a word, only nodding when Louise mentioned (too many times) how delightfully smooth it was.

In truth, Ellie had never felt this weary. Not even when she was falling apart at the end of her jungle trudge from the plane crash. Her brain couldn't fit in all the implications of the last couple hours.

Muntz didn't give Soda-Pop to Leroy.

The plaque? The special exhibit? It was all a fantasy, an intricate construction involving so many people and things—and all based on a lie. Getting everyone excited about the myth of Soda-Pop's origins.

Origins, ha! Leroy had gone to the cave of the purple birds and grabbed one.

Actually, she didn't even know that, Ellie realized with horror—she knew he had taken *at least one*. Maybe he had taken more, and the others had died along the way. That was a terrible thing to contemplate, but not an impossible thing. A likely thing, even, considering the dead viper.

Leroy came to Venezuela, dropped his garbage all over the place, snatched a bird (or two), and then lied about it.

("Remember the giant iguana, Ellie?" Mind-Carl reminded her. "You *knew* it was someone's pet. This isn't the first animal he's lied about.")

Ellie had once thought Leroy was a handsome, heroic, not-really-war-hero with a few personality flaws (that were almost offset by his enthusiasm for the zoo). Now she saw him for who he really was: a dirty rotten lying liar.

(A *libelous* lying liar. What if Muntz found out about everything? Would he take legal action, having seen his name used in vain?)

Ellie remained silent throughout dinner, working up just enough energy to compliment Ana on the porridge or soup or whatever it was she made from the plantains. It was good, in a strangely bland way; salt helped. She could see it being a beloved comfort food and staple, but equally as hated as cream of wheat served too many winter mornings in a row.

"Needs something crunchy," Louise said thoughtfully. "I want something on top, like fried scallions or broken-up toast points, or bacon."

When they were done Ellie volunteered to do all the washing.

"I should take a teenager on all my trips. Such service!" she heard Louise saying sotto voce to Ana.

"Mmm, this one is different. Usually they are more trouble than they are worth, I've found."

The puppies were sleepy but restless; they played tug-of-war with what looked very much like a sock—but Ellie was still wearing the same ones she had crashed in, and the older women said it wasn't theirs. Strange. Where in the jungle had they found it? Maybe Leroy had dropped it?

It began to rain, softly and straight down, and there wasn't any wind, so they were perfectly comfortable and dry under the ledge.

That was something. Back home, there would have been gales with a storm. The rain would have been driven in several different directions over the course of its falling, and definitely into the shelter. She thought about the boulder with the overhang where she and Carl had seen the petroglyphs, and how the ancient drawings were protected by being on the ceiling.

"Ellie, why are you *so* surprised?" Mind-Carl asked. "Margaret and I both suggested that Leroy wasn't a great human being . . . and I know you had your doubts. But you wouldn't listen, because you built your whole world around wanting to be someone like him. A famous, adventurous explorer with planes and endless stories and no fear of anything."

"Maybe," Ellie answered reluctantly.

"So what? There's other people in the world you can model yourself after. Other explorers, like Ana and Louise. And what about Margaret?"

But she wasn't done being disappointed in Leroy yet.

When she was finished cleaning the pots, Ellie sat down on a mat and pulled Leroy's log out of her satchel to read it again. Soda-Pop, still feeling needy but a little braver now, roosted in a half-dead bush behind her, letting her know he was close with little whistly noises.

On closer scrutiny, Ellie now saw that the pages in his expedition devoted to Muntz looked *very* different from the others. They were thinner and scratched up, like they had been written in once and then thoroughly erased. She held the book up to the firelight but couldn't make out any of the previous words, only that they were there, light engravings like an ancient tombstone that had lost its language to time and lichen. The phrasing in the "final version" was more formal, too. "Came around a bend . . . and there was Dr. Muntz's incredible airship, a silver zeppelin of exemplary design, a beacon of humanity in an otherwise heart of darkness."

Ellie was pretty sure she had heard that last phrase somewhere before. A book, maybe.

Double underlined was a seemingly casual note: "Recounted a story about a cave I should check out on a return trip someday." With coordinates, latitude and longitude. Ellie didn't bother looking it up, because she knew what it would be: Soda-Pop's cave. It was like a secret note Leroy wrote to himself for later reference, a little bit of the truth in case he needed to go back there again.

"This is all fake," she said disgustedly. "Everything he wrote about meeting Muntz. It was all carefully written in afterward."

"What a strange thing to do," Ana said.

"It's *terrible*!" Ellie said. "From a scientific standpoint—okay, grabbing animals willy-nilly from their natural habitats is questionable, but geez, at least document it. I don't know if we can trust anything he's ever said about any of the animals he's brought back. No wonder we can't take care of them.

"And if Soda-Pop dies or disappears . . . he can just grab another one. He's already back here looking for me—you saw the other planes. He can grab as many pretty purple birds as he wants and keep telling everyone lies about how he got them."

In a fit of rage and resolution, she ripped the pages out of the journal and tossed them into the fire.

Mutt and Jeff looked up interestedly, thinking it might be the beginning of a new game, but flames quickly caught the black-and-white leaves and turned them into ash. Mutt whined sadly.

"Hey, you know what I can do?" Louise said, comforting Mutt by rubbing his head. "I can contact the U.S. Geological Survey and update their maps of the area. I can say there must have been a rockslide or something in the last year that buried the cave."

"That's a good idea," Ana said. "And look, I can speak with the locals. Tell them to be a little more . . . *wary* about letting tourists get to the waterfall and the cave. So far they have had a live and let live philosophy about it, but I think at the very least the presence of garbage in their special spot will make them likely to guard it more carefully."

"Thanks," Ellie said with a sigh, watching more black smoke rise up into the air, just a little bit this time, but just as ugly as the plume from the plane. What a mess North Americans were making of this place.

"It's going to be all right," Louise said, leaning over and gently touching Ellie's knee. "It may seem like the end of the world . . . but it's just one man, and one bird. Even if it's an incredibly stylish bird like Soda-Pop."

Almost as if he recognized his name, Soda-Pop suddenly looked up from his preening and said "BEEP."

Then he hopped from the bush where he was roosting to the one next to it, investigating its bark interestedly.

Then he hopped to a farther tree.

"Okay, Soda-Pop, come back," Ellie said.

As soon as she said the words aloud, she realized how strange they were. Why, just a few hours ago she had been trying to get him to *stay* with his bird family, and not follow her! Now she was reluctant to let him go. Maybe it was because of the horrible revelation about Leroy. She was sad and down and didn't want her little friend to leave. Maybe it was because of the encroaching night.

Sure, that was it. Ellie decided the still-flightless bird wouldn't be safe yet in the world outside his safe little cave. The rain had stopped but the world had gone very dark over the last few minutes; details of the landscape more than twenty feet away were beginning to be obscured by shadow. Anything could have been hiding out there.

"BEEP," the bird said, to no one, fixing a chest feather and obviously ignoring her. Then he moved on to a farther tree.

"Soda-Pop, come back here right now!" Ellie stood up and ordered, as if he were one of her sisters, like Bobby or Darlene. He hopped away again.

"Dang it . . ."

She began to trot after him.

"Don't go too far," Louise said, scooping both her puppies close. "No bird is worth your life."

"Don't fall off a ledge," Ana added.

"I won't. Come on! Soda-Pop, get back here!"

She reached for him but he evaded her grasp, more serious about running away now that he was being actively pursued. He hopped and fluttered determinedly through the rocky gloam. Ellie had to run to catch him.

Seeing he was outmaneuvered on the ground, Soda-Pop awkwardly beat his wings and managed to clamber up to the top of a spiky bush at the very edge of the path, overlooking the forest below.

His tail hung out over open space.

"Soda-Pop, no!"

Ellie lunged to grab him.

And then, in the confusing twilight, what she thought was a solid rock tipped—and slid her down off the side of the mountain.

EIGHTEEN

It wasn't a straight plummet, at least.

On the mountain where she had crashed the plane the walls were sheer and there was nothing to stop or slow a fall. *This* mountain had a much milder descent, and they hadn't even climbed that far up, camping right above the broad bottom that supported greenery. Which, with its clumps of grasslike plants, spiky bushes, and thorny trunks, helped slow Ellie's descent—albeit in painful, skin-ripping ways.

She also skidded for dozens of feet at a time on slick fragments of broken-up, platelike rock. It felt like she was an evil stepsister in one of the Grimms' fairy stories, punished by being driven around town inside a barrel studded with nails. Like them she screamed the whole way, her shouts punctuated by gasps as the breath was knocked out of her.

Somehow she managed to curl her arms over her head and avoid being knocked unconscious.

Ellie finally came to a stop at the base of a tree that her mind, playing tricks on her, suggested was a coconut palm, like in the cartoons, with Bugs Bunny about to drop coconuts on her head. She narrowed her eyes, trying to resolve the tree into something more likely, but the coconuts kept spinning. Or they were monkeys. Or maybe birds? Or . . .

She decided to close her eyes and try again.

She didn't think she had them closed for that long, but when she reopened them, night had fully fallen. She couldn't make out the coconut tree—or whatever it was—at all. She tried to reach up under her hair to once again probe for concussion—this was getting ridiculous—but her arm hurt too much to bend that way.

She closed her eyes again, trying to summon the strength to sit up.

When she opened them again there was a man looking down at her.

Ellie jumped—as much as she could; it was more of a wiggle of shock. She forced herself up onto one elbow, hissed at the pain.

There were *three* men standing silently over her; silently they had come out of the forest. Two were shirtless, while one wore a slightly worn men's cotton shirt. Two wore shorts, or pants that were cut into shorts; one wore what looked like a skirt (Ellie was sure there was a more appropriate term for whatever it was). They had thick, straight dark hair of various lengths and dark brown eyes; one carried a machete, one had a stick balanced back over his shoulder, and the other had a small knife.

They spoke among themselves, not quietly, obviously aware she had no idea what they were saying.

"I'm an American!" she said as loudly as she could manage. "American!"

Red, white, and blue, fought the Nazis, saved the world! Her government would (probably) protect her!

The one with the stick said something that sounded like an order.

She looked at him and shrugged helplessly.

He repeated himself and twirled the stick over and down, prodding her leg with it like a child might do with a sick bird.

When she woozily didn't do anything, he barked the order, prodded harder.

She forced herself to sit up all the way.

He poked her *again*, this time in the side.

One of the other men said something, and it sounded more polite, like a request.

"All right, all right, I'm trying."

Shakily, she rose to her feet. Everything went swimming for a moment; the world spiraled in front of her eyes like a Catherine wheel. She could almost see the sparks. When she inevitably began to fall Ellie grabbed at one of the men, who caught her—it was shirt guy—neither roughly nor tenderly; he just held her there, then pushed her so she was literally standing back on her own two feet.

Stick man said something, and he and machete man left. It took her a moment to realize she was supposed to follow, the man behind her making sure she didn't lag too far behind.

At least he didn't have a stick.

Well, here she was, exploring the other side of the world, and she had already been captured by the local indigenous people!

That was pretty fast work, if Ellie did say so herself. She had already checked off a bunch of "lifetime achievement goals" from an imaginary game of Famous Explorer Bingo. Flew a plane, crashed a plane into the wilderness, was taken prisoner by people who didn't speak English, protected a rare find (Soda-Pop) . . . No, wait, maybe it was Humphrey Bogart Movie Bingo. Soda-Pop was the MacGuffin, the Maltese falcon; everyone wanted it for no darn good reason. . . .

Wait, where was Soda-Pop? Had he followed her? Or had he headed back to camp, safe?

They stopped at a small clearing. Without waiting for permission she sank down at the base of a tree, among its somewhat comfy-looking roots or knees or weird stumpy bits, hoping to pass out. But before she was allowed to, knife man prodded her with the hilt of his knife (Ellie suddenly had the somewhat insulting revelation that the poking of her with objects was less about keeping her in line and more about not wanting to touch her). He offered her a leather flask. She immediately wrapped her lips around its mouth and chugged—but it was not water. She just barely managed not to spit out the slightly sweet drink; it alleviated her thirst, anyway. Shirt man lit a torch.

She tried to go to sleep, but machete man crouched down before her and began talking reasonably, like if he just spoke to her calmly enough, she would understand what he wanted. Shirt man quietly disappeared.

"I'm sorry, I have no idea what you're saying."

He tried something else. Spanish, maybe. Portuguese?

"I'm sorry. I don't have anything worth anything on me. Are you asking about a ransom? Money?"

His eyes shone in the torchlight but didn't show any comprehension.

There was a strange whistle, loud and piercing, that

cut through the shadows in the forest like a bullet. It didn't sound animal in origin.

She had been all upset that Leroy was a fake before? What a stupid thing to waste time and energy on! Her current situation was something actually *worth* being terrified about.

She wasn't allowed to lie down; she sat like they did, arms resting on bent knees, and quietly panicked.

At some point during the long, changeless night, the piercing whistle sounded out again. Machete man jumped up; knife man paused for a moment from endlessly sharpening his knife.

Moments later, manifesting out of the shadows like a dream, was shirt man . . . and someone new.

If Ellie had invented or imagined a savior to come to her rescue in an adventure movie, he couldn't have looked any more exactly like this guy.

He was younger than the others—maybe her age, maybe a couple years older. He wore khaki pants and a shining white cotton shirt that didn't look pressed but didn't look dirty either. It was tucked into his pants and cinched with a nice-looking brown leather belt whose simple buckle wasn't silver but still somehow quietly elegant. On his feet were strange shoes that were part leather, part canvas, and laced like tennis shoes—but with square toes. His dark hair was curly and short and recently cut. His eyes were a light brown, like agate.

And as soon as he saw her, they sparkled dramatically.

The newcomer spoke with the men in their same uninflected tones. Ellie thought she heard a little Spanish, but mostly it was in a language utterly unknown to her. The fluency with which the boy switched back and forth was incredible.

He finally turned to her.

"I'm Jean. What's your name?" His English was accented like Ana's but his pronunciation somewhat better. "How did you come to fall off the ledge and—" Machete man interrupted him, and he switched gears. "What do you have to do with all the awful planes in the last few days?"

"I'm Ellie McGill, I'm an American," she said, unsure how much detail they wanted. "I flew here in a plane that crashed on the tepui. You probably saw the smoke. I'm sorry about that." The boy translated everything she said. "I'm trying to return a bird that was stolen from a cave in the waterfall. He's purple. He . . . wandered off somewhere. The other planes were people trying to stop me." She decided not to add that it was one of their planes that she had stolen.

Knife man muttered something, the tone of which was easily understood even if the content was not.

Ellie looked at Jean questioningly.

"Roughly, 'the doings of northern people are weird,'" he explained. "But if you're telling the truth, they are thankful you were restoring the bird to her nest."

"It's a boy."

"It's a rough translation. How did you wind up down here, then?"

She explained being found by Ana and Louise, and at this everyone in the tiny torchlit circle reacted; the indigenous men immediately relaxed. Or grew bored. Like they knew Ana, and Ellie was safe, and it was all over.

Jean, on the other hand, looked wary.

No one had seemed particularly surprised or interested that she had tumbled down off the ledge into the black forest. It seemed almost expected of such a ridiculous girl.

Finally shirt man said something, picked up his torch, and blew it out. Giant white moths disappeared up into the sky, their bright star gone. Machete man was already heading into the forest. Knife man went to follow—but he paused before entering the shadows and said one final thing before disappearing.

"All right, I think it's best we spend the rest of the night here," Jean suggested before she could ask what the man had said. "It's no fun wandering around the woods or climbing a mountain in the dark. At first light we'll find Ana and Louise and let them know you are safe."

"How are you going to find them?"

"You said you camped below the cave with the purple torong—everyone knows where that is. Literally everyone now, if northerners are flying by and just grabbing birds and returning them there."

"That's not what I . . ."

He laughed, and a dimple appeared left of his mouth, above his chin. It distracted her entirely from whatever she was going to say.

"The women won't go looking for you at night, it's too dangerous. *Trust* me," he added quickly, seeing the look on her face. "We'll go at first light. It won't be too long."

Ellie squirmed around the tree base that seemed like it was going to serve as her chaise longue for the duration. It wasn't too bad, once she wiggled around enough to make sure one knobby bit didn't dig into her lower back. And actually, being forced to sit up a little made her bruised shoulders and spine feel better.

"The . . . local people were—very polite," she said, unsure what to say, prepared by years of lurid movies and books that had her half expecting to be tied up and tortured.

Jean sighed; she couldn't see his face. "Could you say

that a *little* more patronizingly, perhaps? Ellie, they are just people. You crashed your plane into their neighborhood. They didn't want to hurt you, they wanted to help you on your way. You might excuse their shortness because it's the middle of the night."

Ellie felt a mild sting of chagrin and decided it was completely justified. She had assumed things, and, as the saying went, it had made an ass out of her. "You're absotively right. I'm sorry. How did they find you?"

"They knew I was in the area," Jean said, shrugging. He opened his rucksack and pulled out a sleeping roll, which he unfurled with a dramatic shake. There was a blanket top, which he chivalrously gave to her—it wasn't really cold enough to warrant it, but the pressure and weight were comforting. Almost like she was sick sitting up in bed at home with a rug on her feet, deliriously listening to the radio, her mom coming in occasionally to check on her. "Friends of friends fetched me. I wasn't too far. No one else around here speaks English well."

"Well, thank you for helping me."

"Saving beautiful young ladies in distress is a task I all too rarely get called to perform," Jean said with a tragic pout. "Translation services usually involve people clear-cutting ancestral land, or dummies hunting where they shouldn't, or negotiating a trade."

"What would they have done to me if they hadn't found you?"

"Oh, made a nice hunter's stew with your gizzard," he said sleepily, turning over in his roll, looking for a comfortable position. "Or sold your scalp for weaving supplies."

She wasn't certain how to respond.

"I'm kidding, Ellie."

"I know!"

"They would have taken you to a village and left you there for those people to deal with. Eventually you would have been handed off to someone who knew what they were doing. No one wants to hurt a girl who is lost and alone, silly. What would your own parents do?"

Ellie tried to imagine a South American version of herself falling from the sky into her backyard. What would her mother and father do? Contact the authorities, and stuff her with food. She smiled at that but fell asleep thinking of Jean's agate eyes, and his sudden appearance, and the way he had swooped in and handled the situation.

Now *he* was an adventurer and explorer. Not like Leroy at all.

And much, much cuter.

Somehow Ellie managed to sleep, and even deeply for the first hour or two. But sometime after the crest of the night had passed all the strange noises of the woods began in anticipation of dawn. She would suddenly wake and find herself in that strange position of half sitting up, like she was snoozing in her father's favorite chair or against the wall of her tree house. Little pains all over kept her from going back to sleep. When there was enough light, she looked over at Jean, who slept like a statue—if a statue had its lips parted slightly and made little wheezy not-quite-snores. She wanted to pull a curl off his brow, out of his eyes.

She very much wanted to brush those lips with her fingertips.

(She must have fallen asleep again at some point after that.)

"Come on, lazy *North* Americana, time to get up! This little guy has been worried sick about you!"

Ellie didn't think Jean was that little; he was taller than Carl, and Ana and Louise. Then she opened her reluctant eyes and saw whom he really meant.

"Soda-Pop!"

The bird was perched on a root next to her, burbling as if he were having a long conversation that she had just joined. When he was finished, and only then, did he hop over to her and onto her shoulder, and nuzzle into her hair.

"I assume this is the fellow you flew across the world

for?" Jean asked. "He is pretty impressive, I must say, even for his species."

The boy packed away his sleeping mat and put his hand out for the blanket he had loaned her. Feeling somehow stupider and slower than when she had awoken earlier in the night, Ellie stumbled to her feet and tried to give him the blanket without its touching the ground and wound up smashing into him.

"Easy there! Too much rum last night?" he asked, laughing, steadying her back on her feet.

"I've been through a lot the last few days," she protested.

"If even half of what you said is true, you have my admiration forever. Did you really fly a plane all by yourself?"

"Yep. Never actually flown one before." She tried not to sound too smug. Her mother would have scolded her.

"I have *been* in ones . . . crop dusters and the emergency one the doc uses to pick up sick people," he said. "Nothing fancy."

"Oh, this was fancy. A P-51 Mustang." She ignored Mind-Mom yelling at her.

"A *war* plane?" Jean asked, entirely shocked out of all flirtatious behavior. "That's . . . insane."

"It's all I could grab."

Jean muttered something she couldn't understand in one or a combination of a number of languages she didn't know.

Imagine being able to switch back and forth so quickly . . . to be able to *think* in another language! Ellie was awed . . . and also slightly ashamed. She could fly a plane but could barely recite any French from her three years of taking it.

"All right, back to the mountain! Ladies first," he said with a bow, holding a leafy branch aside and sweeping his arm in invitation. She gave a little curtsy and was surprised to see that the path was fairly obvious. What had seemed like a meandering, meaningless march during the night had kept to a strict route. She was just too banged up and tired to notice.

"You know, if you're so good at planes, I think I might have an answer to get you home," Jean said thoughtfully. "I have a friend on the other side of the Gran Sabana who . . . collects planes. I bet in return for your P-51 Mustang he might loan you something to get home in."

Get home in. It sounded like Jean maybe didn't know enough about planes to understand refueling needs—or maybe he just assumed she knew what she was doing.

"A loan of a copilot might be nice, too," she said carefully. "One who speaks Spanish."

Jean barked laughter. "I'm sure than can be arranged."

She decided not to mention the shape her plane was in. Details like that could be discussed later.

Trying to keep up with her new friend, she doubled her pace and unsuccessfully tried to dart around a fat little tree with thick thorns around its base. One point caught her flesh and pulled: Ellie choked; pain shot up and down her leg like an electric fire. Terrified it was some sort of poisonous tree, she ripped up her pant leg to see—and only then realized that there was very little "leg" left to that part of her coveralls, or the hem of her skirt underneath. The material had been split from ankle to knee, and under the flaps of cloth was a large stretch of ugly, raw skin that oozed blood and lymph from where she had skidded down rocks. She must have been too exhausted (or in shock?) the night before to really notice it.

"Ouch," Jean said with feeling when he saw why she had stopped. "Usually the thorns of the pochote don't hurt that much, but I can see you're in bad shape. Let's deal with that quickly now and get it wrapped up properly when we find the others."

He looked around for a moment, and then his face lit up: he went over to a scrubby, scraggly tree with two sets of alternating oval leaves on each branchlet that Ellie would have taken for a sumac if she hadn't known better. He ripped off a bunch of the bright green leaves and mangled them in his hands, tearing and crushing them efficiently.

"Here," he said, handing the slimy green mash over to her. "I'll let you do it—I'm not very gentle. This works as an antiseptic and should lessen the pain a little."

Ellie reluctantly dabbed the mess onto her leg—really, it wasn't that different from using a plantain weed's leaf for a bee sting—and was stunned at the sensation it immediately imparted. First came *more* pain, like a burn or a freeze, where the leaves touched her raw skin . . . and then everything faded away, like she was applying a cold pack or oil of cloves, or the menthol rub her grandmother used. The smell was more peppery than minty, but it stung her nose similarly.

"This is amazing," she said, smashing the plant on harder and all over.

"Cordoncillo," Jean explained. "Good for when you have ulcers in your mouth, too. Or numbing it if you have a toothache."

"Wow, I can't feel it at all now," Ellie said appreciatively. She could still bend her leg; just the surface was deadened, like her skin had fallen asleep. "Thanks!"

"The whole forest is a medicine cabinet, a doctor's black bag," Jean said, whirling his hand around to indicate the trees. "When they chop it down for diamonds and cattle grazing, they don't even know what they're destroying. A cure for cancer? Leprosy? The common cold? We may never know. I'll tell you this, before I ever go to the doctor, I go to the forest. It heals me better than some old white man who comes to the jungle for retirement."

Ellie had questions about the term "white man"; Jean's skin was much lighter than the other locals', lighter than Ana's. Darker than Ellie's only by more time tanning, maybe. She decided this wasn't the time or place to ask what he meant.

"Are you a guide?" she asked.

"Sometimes," he said carelessly, pursing his mouth. "There is always work to be found if you're clever and you want it . . . I don't always want it. I just want to live my life freely in the land where I grew up, at peace with the woods.

"But I do love adventure. There are springs in the mountains that make the clearest pools you've seen—cold as ice, utterly refreshing. And other ones that are like hot tubs. I've seen wild harpy eagles climbing the high winds, and jaguars hunting. I want to always be able to see them; I want to *be* like all of them. Wild, in my wild home."

Perfect, was all Ellie could think. Jean was a very different kind of explorer than Muntz—but he was also very different from Ana with her studies and Louise with her maps. He was someone thoroughly entrenched in the real, forest world, living what he believed in. And he knew so much about so many helpful things in the jungle! Useful, helpful, brave, enthusiastic—she couldn't imagine a better companion for adventures in the unknown. Why, the two of them together would be unstoppable. . . .

Mind-Margaret spoke up for the first time, albeit quietly.

"That's an awfully nice cotton shirt he's got on, and those shoes are something special. He shaves regularly. I've never met a shaving jaguar."

"Shut up, Mind-Margaret," Ellie murmured back. "He's pretty. Let me just look."

"Hey," she said aloud. "What did that man say last night—right before he left? When they all left?"

Jean cocked his head, thinking for a moment. Then he laughed.

"He said: 'Young miss, you say you're an American, but we are *all* Americans here. Or none of us are.'"

"But they're not from—"

"*The United States* of America, true. But they *are* from Venezuela, South America, which is part of the Americas. Latin America. Sometimes people here get . . . annoyed at how Yankees forget that."

"All right, that's fair—but what about 'or none of us are American'?"

"This place had its own name long before Amerigo Vespucci made a bad map of it. Abya Yala . . . 'land of palm trees' . . . or just 'the land.' We are people of the land of palm trees, not tiny Italian map people."

"Huh," Ellie said, thinking about it. Something to tell Louise. She bet the mapmaker would find that fascinating.

They heard the two women long before they saw them: calls of *Elllll* and *Elllllie* came floating down from the mountain like the feather of a long-gone dove. Ellie felt terrible. The day was just beginning to brighten—she couldn't have been gone more than twelve hours total, but she bet they worried about her for at least eleven of them.

Jean let out a whistle-cry, the same one she had heard in the forest before he showed up.

The shouts cut off immediately.

Soon enough Mutt and Jeff came leaping and rolling joyfully through the underbrush and bonked their heads against Ellie's shins, punishing her for her absence with furry nuzzles. They also ran around Jean's legs, sniffing and yipping and putting their paws up on his calves to try to better examine this new friend.

Jean's face lit up with utter delight—Ellie didn't think he could have gotten any more attractive. He danced around, making soccer-like moves, and the puppies went wild with thc gamc.

By the time they reached the campsite, the sun was

fully risen above the flatlands below and Ana and Louise were lit from behind with a stark white, angry-heavenly glow.

"I am so sorry—" Ellie began.

"Young lady!" Louise began. "Do you know what—Oh my dear lord, what happened to you?"

The two women's eyes snapped wide at the same time, tirades cut short by the bruises and wounds on Ellie's legs, arms, and face.

"Um, remember when you told me not to fall off a ledge?" she mumbled, not looking at Ana.

"Yes, I—"

"I fell off a ledge."

"We've been worried sick about you!" Louise cried, but half-heartedly, like she couldn't stop herself from the rant she had meant to deliver earlier. "Let me see your leg. Ana wouldn't let us look for you in the dark. I was sure you were lying somewhere bleeding to death . . . and here you are, *bleeding*!"

Ana's face had frozen, settling into an appraising glare. She crossed her arms. Ellie waited for the remonstrations to begin, but the woman wasn't looking at her—she was looking *past* her, at Jean.

"Good morning, ladies," he said brightly. "Look what I found on the forest floor!"

"Jean," Ana said evenly.

"Oh, you two know each other?" Ellie said in surprise.

"The woods are small, when you have friends and relatives," Jean said blithely, sounding like he was quoting something. "Lucky I was traveling this way! Oh, and these fellows helped out!"

He put his arms out and Jeff and Mutt jumped into them immediately, tails wagging. He hugged them to his neck and laughed while they licked his face.

"Let's get your leg cleaned and bandaged," Ana said to Ellie, ignoring him.

"Jean showed me how to put cordoncillo on it to make it stop hurting," Ellie said eagerly as the two women led her over to the campfire and helped her sit down.

"Did he," Ana said.

"Hey, have you made the chocolate yet?" Jean asked cheerfully, sniffing the air.

"We were too worried about Ellie for Ana to have time to make breakfast," Louise said archly.

"Oh, well, I can start it then, if I must," Jean volunteered, helping himself to supplies. He winked at Ellie. "I have a special ingredient that will make you flip your lid, as they say on the radio—a secret no one knows, not even Ana."

Ana didn't roll her eyes at this; her mouth just tightened

a little, like she couldn't even be bothered to react. Ellie wondered how the two knew each other. Ana must have been at least twenty or thirty years older than Jean . . . did they live in the same neighborhood? Was she a friend of the family? And what made her completely immune to his charms? Even Louise let her gaze linger on Jean slightly longer than necessary. She took her puppies and her journal and settled down next to him as he tinkered with the pots and ingredients, keeping a watchful but appreciative eye on him.

"Tell me about your friends, Jean," the cartographer said. "I want to hear all about life in the wilds of Venezuela."

"Are you an anthropologist? Ana often leads them through here," said Jean.

"No . . . a little bit. I'm a mapmaker and a professional busybody. . . ."

Their conversation drifted out of Ellie's consciousness despite her eagerness to hear every word he said, because the spirits with which Ana was efficiently—and, in her defense, gently—wiping down her wounds were also wiping out her ability to think. The pain was short but excruciating and went right to her head.

"You're lucky you didn't die in the fall," Ana murmured. "You're lucky they found you. I'm beginning to think you're a cat, Ellie, with all of those lives. Don't use them all up here. Save some for when you are older, maybe, and have cancer."

"Who *is* Jean, exactly?"

A smile came and went on Ana's face so quickly it was almost like Ellie imagined it.

"He is a young man. He sort of has a base at the camp they are trying to build up in Canaima . . . he has a good heart, but it is too light to be settled. He's always seizing on one project or another . . . supporting the indigenous people against the dam or trying to unionize the cocoa workers . . . and in between he guides people who want to hike to the top of Roraima. But he is like your little purple bird, flitting everywhere. But without a cave. No . . . place of permanence."

Somehow Ellie didn't think she was talking about a physical house.

Once she was all bandaged up Jean poured the chocolate and they sat around sipping it and basking in the heat of the sun, which, when allowed to sit quietly for a moment without the wind to push it away, felt expansive and healing.

The chocolate *was* better than Ana's. Ellie couldn't believe it was possible. Her eyes widened.

"See, I told you," Jean said, grinning. His lips, neither too dry nor too moist, pulled back from teeth that were as white as his shirt. "Amazing, isn't it?"

"A gentleman never brags about his talents," Louise said primly. "It's good, son. Leave it at that."

Ana reached into her supply bag and passed out what looked like little hand pies, pockets of thick pastry with a thick border where the edges were sealed. Ellie bit into hers and was surprised to find it was savory; corn and bits of something white. Maybe fish? It was delicious, but very strange.

Jean crowed. "Ha! It's like we're at the beach and the empanada ladies came around! I love these!"

Ana broke one in half and held the pieces up in the air, dramatically pretending to admire them. It achieved the intended effect: Mutt and Jeff ran around in crazed circles, jumping, too well behaved—or little—to leap up and grab them. Their whines were heartbreaking.

Finally Ana relented and tossed the bits into the air; like trained athletes, the two puppies leapt, perfectly synchronized, and snapped them up with wolfish efficiency.

Ellie thought about her discussion with Carl at the lake about visiting Paradise Falls for a vacation someday. Well, there was no restaurant on the top of the mountain (yet), as Carl said there would definitely be someday, and no Harvey Girls either—but there *was* pie. Not a fruit pie, but it still counted.

"So where are you off to," Ana asked Jean pointedly, "now that you have rescued our lady here?"

"Actually, I'm going to see her safely home," Jean said with a warm smile at Ellie. Her toes tingled. "Well, not all the way. You know Jesus? With the small airfield? I'm going to take her there and bargain for a trip home. A quick two-day journey and she will be on her way back to the States."

Louise spluttered into her chocolate. Ana slammed her drink down on the ground.

"Absolutely not—"

"Are you out of your mind?"

"Not even if Jesus—I mean the real one, Himself—"

Ellie felt embarrassment creep up the back of her neck and told herself she hadn't at all been imagining a sun-dappled journey through the spicy-smelling woods with a smiling Jean explaining everything to her along the way. Maybe taking her hand to lead her along. Maybe . . .

"What's the problem?" Jean asked, hurt.

"*Please.* It is *not* appropriate for you to escort a young lady alone by herself through the jungle for days on end," Louise said, shaking a finger at him.

"Jesus is a . . . what does Liev call him? A *shyster*? Absolutely untrustworthy. He acquires his planes from . . . all over the place. You have to be clever and bargain hard—and make sure the tank is actually full of fuel. Also, no, you can't take Ellie by herself," Ana added, almost as an afterthought. "We will *all* go."

Ellie quietly fumed. Ana might have been older and more experienced in the wilderness . . . and life . . . but that didn't make her the boss of Jean. Or her. Or the entire expedition. The tone she took and the way she was taking control of the entire situation! It wasn't fair. Jean was perfectly capable of handling himself, and Ellie had flown a plane all alone for thousands of miles! They didn't need to be coddled. . . .

Louise groaned. "Not that I don't love adventure and whatnot, but am I ever going to get to see those petroglyphs you promised?"

"Yes, of course," Ana said soothingly. "But I think you'll like this digression: We travel through some homesteads abandoned by the people who once lived there because they were promised jobs at the diamond mines."

"And they moved to the mining camps with their families to work?" Louise asked.

"No, they moved deeper into the jungle, to the south, to get as far away from the mining men as possible."

Ellie wondered: when she thought of mining, she thought of the Dwarfs from *Snow White*, or forty-niners looking for gold in the hills, or grizzled Appalachians pulling up coal. This sounded something like the latter, if it struck so much fear into the hearts of people that they fled a life of modern comforts that came with regular labor and a company store.

"All right," Jean said with a sigh. "We'll all go. But you older ladies had better keep up."

"You watch your mouth, young man," Ana snapped before Louise could form a similar sentiment; she followed it with a torrent of fast Spanish with what sounded like maybe some Portuguese thrown in. And was that German? Ellie was amazed by how the words mixed without pause. Jean paled a little; his body stiffened defiantly but he said nothing.

Only after she was done did he mutter something under his breath in a *fourth* language as he began to pack up.

Tensions were uncomfortable and high in the little group; despite her slight annoyance with Ana, Ellie wanted very much for the subject to change.

"How do you two know so many languages?" she asked Ana with real interest.

"I grew up near Santa Elena de Uairén, near Brazil. Everyone there speaks Portuguese and Spanish. Half my family is from Brazil. And I've needed to learn Pemón and other indigenous dialects for my work. And you have to speak English these days, for academia—and if you want to earn money with tourists. My husband is German, which isn't really so different from English. Easy once you know one."

"Wow," Ellie said. Fluent in five useful languages, and none of them was French. She wondered if she should double down on her French, try harder, or switch to something else.

And maybe the older women were right, Ellie eventually allowed as she helped pack up camp. She could hear her own mother agreeing with them, practically see her sitting next to them, drinking chocolate and nodding emphatically. Carl would too; she couldn't imagine him *not* looking at Jean distrustfully.

Which was ridiculous. Just because Jean was a handsome, brave, useful, skilled, charming, and upbeat adventure companion was no reason not to *trust* him.

Besides, he and Ellie barely knew each other. . . .

NINETEEN

Ellie and Jean walked in front, side by side when there was room. Louise and Ana brought up the rear. Jeff and Mutt ran back and forth between the two sets of humans like runners with messages from command to the front lines. But for the two young adults most of the time—except for the occasional, unexpected wet puppy kiss—it was like the dogs and older women weren't even there.

"Do you see that tree?" Jean pointed out a friendly-looking specimen sporting bright green compound leaves that looked a little like a paper birch, but its peeling bark was shiny red rather than white. He pulled off a leaf and crushed it under her nose; it smelled of bright chemicals, like turpentine. "It's a gumbo-limbo, and the bark is good for bug bites and rashes. We also call it the tourist tree. Can you guess why?"

"Because tourists are always getting bug bites and need the bark?"

"No, because of the bark itself: it's red and constantly peeling, like the tourists who come from Europe and the north and try to tan in our equatorial sun!"

Ellie laughed. "I burn pretty easy myself. I've always thought that someday all the freckles on my face and arms will merge and I will finally look like a bronzed movie star."

"Your freckles are adorable," Jean said, touching her nose gently. "More freckles would be more adorable."

Ellie felt a thrill of heat redden the cheeks behind those freckles. He was so audacious . . . Carl never said anything, *did* anything like that.

"This is a quinine tree—" Jean added a moment later, as if nothing had happened. "The cinchona. You get quinine from the bark."

"To treat malaria?"

"Yes! People here have been using it for thousands of years, since before Europeans and the Jesuits came. But it was especially useful for the colonists, who were prone to getting the disease. Then your—what shall we call them? second wave? third wave?—colonists from the United States came back here to harvest more of it during the war, after

China captured Indonesia and eliminated the West's only source of quinine, from the estates there."

"When *Japan* captured *Java*," Louise yelled up to them, not even pretending not to have been listening in on their conversations.

"Read a newspaper once in a while, querido," Ana suggested sweetly.

Jean might have flushed a little, but he shook his head as if the details were unimportant.

"Anyway, your country sent expeditions all over South America looking for new sources of quinine—and found it, in Ecuador and Colombia. You call it scientific cooperation, but it was just one more instance of tearing a vital resource from the grasp of indigenous peoples."

Ellie felt a little attacked by this, though there wasn't any real emotion in the way Jean said it.

"Well, on the bright side," she countered cheerfully, "I think scientists just figured out how to synthesize quinine in a lab. No more stealing trees for us!"

"Your reliance on science and inventions is going to fail you someday. You need to return to the earth's roots to thrive."

"You can't have it both ways! You're angry at us—rightfully—for stealing your resources, then condemning us for creating our own? Where's the logic in that? I think you're just mad that you've lost something to be mad at us *for.*"

His face darkened, but he didn't disagree.

"You know heaps about the plants here," Ellie added quickly. "More than local names and indigenous uses; also their place in the bigger political world—er, when you get your facts straight. Are you a botanist too? You sound just like Ana."

Jean rolled his eyes. "We share some of the same interests," he said carefully.

The day crept on in shades of green and the changeable sunlight, which was yellow in the sky and white shining off the glossier tropical plants. For lunch break Ana and Louise set up their mat a little distance from the two teens and ate their dried sausage and porridge quietly while Jean and Ellie talked and talked, barely slowing for an after-meal rest. His stories were wild and captivating; there were no crystal caves, but there were quick escapes and crocodiles.

After an hour they started up again and soon came to the abandoned village Ana had told them about. The jungle had grown drier and thinner; the landscape transitioned from forest to flat grassland. Tepuis loomed in the distance, their details faded to a dark blue. The air was crisp and there were fewer insects. A river flowed silently almost at land level, the banks wide and sandy. Set back from it were several decaying cylindrical structures with once-conical roofs made of thatch; they looked too big for the houses and sat atop like gnomes' hats. Ellie at first thought their sides were made up of oversized bricks stacked in precarious vertical columns, but on a closer look saw the walls were made of solid mud kept together by crossed and woven poles. Holes had formed where water and time and rodents found their way in once the place was abandoned.

Picking their way through the empty village was a trio of tiny deer with short legs and curved backs like a cat arched in a permanent stretch. Visions of *Through the Looking-Glass* came to an enraptured Ellie—but before she could approach them, Mutt and Jeff decided that this was the hunt they had been born and bred for. Yipping like foxes they dashed madly at the deer, leaping over each other in their eagerness to bring down the giant prey.

Two of the deer took off, perhaps not quite as gracefully as their longer-legged whitetail cousins; they bounded purposefully, muscles working hard under their short-furred flanks.

Jeff bayed once in triumph.

But the third deer planted its front legs solidly in the soft dirt and lowered its head in challenge. Though the adorable, slim antlers pointed the wrong way for defense—backward—they somehow still looked shiny and menacing in the sunlight.

The two puppies immediately changed their minds about the attack.

Their puppy brains worked faster than their limbs could obey, however: Mutt flailed his paws in all directions, trying to stop his forward momentum. Jeff tumbled over him, rolling through the dust and whining.

Louise cracked up. "My babies!"

Ana shook her head in disgust. "Invasive carnivores. Barely domesticated. Good thing those weren't opossums, or bush-tailed rats."

"Why? Because they're poisonous?" Ellie asked curiously. Some shrews were.

"No! Because then the dogs would *kill them*!"

"They're just playing . . ."

"Tell that to all the native species in Australia the cats and dogs have wiped out!"

The antlered deer seemed to understand some of what they were saying, or the existential danger that would eventually come for its kind, and slowly turned and ran after its companions. Jean laughed.

Louise took out her sketchbook and stuck her head

into a building and looked around. "Mud, wood—ooh, and palm leaves coating the interior. One family lived in each home?"

"Mm-hm. Down south there is a similar kind of building, but larger, with an open center, that multiple families live in. But here they are more private."

The two puppies, now recovered from their encounter, scampered off to explore, nosing into and out of the empty houses like they owned the place. It felt disrespectful, but neither Jean nor Ana seemed perturbed, so Ellie decided not to be as well.

"I can't believe they just . . . left . . ." Ellie murmured, imagining her own neighborhood with all of the houses abandoned the same way. As if everyone just picked up and fled one day, taking their food and radios. She sat down on a threshold, and the wind whined sadly around the bits that stuck out. Soda-Pop hopped off her shoulder and onto one of the support poles, poking his beak into the dried mud curiously, looking for bugs.

"Legal mining is dangerous and terrifying, illegal mining twice so," Jean said. "The Pemón are not always willing laborers. It was their best option."

"What are they mining, again?"

"Diamonds, of course," Jean said with a smile. He took

her hand and stretched out her ring finger. "For your pretty engagement ring."

"Remind me not to get one, then, when the time comes," she said with a shudder. "Anyway, I don't even know if anyone I marry will have that kind of money."

Jean laughed. "A pretty girl like you? When you're done with finishing school you'll have the pick of the crop."

He thought she was pretty!

Carl would never call her pretty . . . or if he did, it would be the point of what he said, and he would say it simply, and mean it. If he meant it. If he *thought* she was pretty.

She was pretty sure he thought she was pretty.

Did Jean mean it? Or was it all meaningless? If he meant it . . .

"*Finishing* school? I go to public school. I have seven brothers and sisters and everyone wears hand-me-downs, even me, from my cousins. This whole adventure I'm having is originally because of my job at the zoo that I have on the weekends—and some of the money I earn goes to support my family."

Jean looked surprised for once. "I just thought . . . how could you travel so far unless you were rich, running away, or something?"

"I stole the plane," she said, a little smugly.

Jean threw his head back, guffawing. "Ellie, you are

something else. But it still seems like a rich girl thing—trying to save a single tiny purple bird you fell in love with?" He gestured with his chin at Soda-Pop, who seemed to be watching the two puppies with either disdain or interest.

"I don't know what rich has to do with it," Ellie said. "I was saving the life of an innocent animal—and making a point to a man who has turned out to be . . . not the man I thought he was."

"Some say only the rich have the luxury of morality and scruples."

"That's one of the dumbest things I've ever heard. If you have nothing else, not even the clothes on your back, you have your beliefs. Look at martyrs and religious hermits and monks and Jesus."

"I'd rather look at you," Jean said frankly.

Ellie blushed and turned to find something interesting—hopefully—to look at behind her. Finding nothing, she decided she had a bad mosquito bite instead, which was true, and scratched it vigorously.

Jean rose and Soda-Pop gracefully fluttered onto his shoulder. Was he leaving because he sensed her discomfort? Or because he felt he had "struck out" and was embarrassed? Or was he just leaving? He was so changeable and hard to read! And fascinating . . .

"Come give me a hand with this, here?" Louise called, and he went, Ellie's question unanswered.

And *why* should she be nervous? Carl had never formally asked her out. They didn't have an "understanding." The one time she really thought they were going to kiss . . . they didn't. As she had said to Margaret, Ellie didn't exactly understand what they had at all. That was the whole trouble. If nothing was declared, certainly it wouldn't be cheating on him to kiss another boy, right?

Well, no.

It would.

She could *feel* it was wrong. But why?

What would Margaret say?

Mind-Margaret wasn't as fully formed as Mind-Carl; she could just as easily see the woman saying "Life is short! Go for it! Adventure is out there!" as "Perhaps there's a *reason* you feel like it's a bad idea."

Ellie looked over at Louise and Ana, who, with Jean's help, were carefully moving aside a decaying piece of wall to gain access to one of the larger structures. It was obvious what those two women thought: Boys were bad and couldn't be trusted, and girls couldn't be trusted to make their own decisions about them. Typical. Ellie couldn't look for advice or a friendly ear there.

Soda-Pop perched on the edge of the roof of the building

where they were working, beeping occasionally, as if he were managing them. Ellie smiled. She wished she were as good an artist as Louise—or even Leroy—and could quickly sketch the funny scene. How would she describe it to Carl when she got back?

How would she tell any of this to Carl when she got back?

(And how much? About Jean, especially?)

Suddenly Ana and Jean froze—in the middle of another fight, it seemed—and cocked their heads like Soda-Pop.

"A plane," Ana said.

"Probably one of Jesus's," Jean said.

"Might not be, though. Might be a scout looking for our plane thief here," Ana said. "Let's maybe get back to the jungle, out of sight."

Ellie stood up and scanned the sky: she finally saw a silver plane with a painted nose cone. Definitely a Mustang.

Upset by the bird of prey–like thing, Soda-Pop fluttered off the roof to land on her shoulder—managing to flap and fly for most of the twenty feet!

"Nice job, Soda!" Ellie said, stroking him on the head.

"Perhaps we could move a little faster?" Ana said, grabbing Louise's bag in one hand and a puppy in the other. Jeff, Ellie thought. "We stick out against the landscape like targets. We should get under the trees!"

Ellie thought that perhaps this was not the first time Ana or Jean had hidden from overhead threats. Jean jogged in front of them into the closest clump of trees, holding a bush aside courteously for Ellie as if it were a curtain at a restaurant. She stumbled through and found herself once again sinking gratefully into the green mansion of the forest, the bright harsh light of the plains cut into a thousand chunks of shadow and dappled light that were easier on the eyes.

The little group waited with a hush for the plane to pass overhead, breathing silently as the sound of its motor slowly trailed off to the south and disappeared, as if they could be discovered by a whisper.

"Do you think they saw us? They didn't, right?" Ellie asked anxiously. "They would have kept circling if they did."

"Sure," Ana said. "Why not."

"Explain to me again why a rich zookeeper cares so much about one bird, and its thief," Jean demanded, quite understandably. "This seems a little ridiculous. Like wartime Nazi hunting."

"I don't think he's entirely right in the head," Louise said. "If I understand everything Ellie has told us about him."

Ellie hadn't even considered that. She would now.

"I really didn't understand why he was chasing me at first either," she admitted. "Just to get his plane back? Or his bird? Yeah, it seems a little bananas. Extreme lengths to go to. But now it all makes more sense: If it gets out that he lied about getting the bird from Charles Muntz—and it *will* if I get back—once I get back—Leroy will be exposed as a liar and an idiot. And there's a very good chance Muntz will sue him for libel or slander or whatever—he has his magazines, movies, and journals to think about.

"At the very least, no one will take Leroy seriously again, or fund his expeditions, or put up with any of his ridiculousness, or maybe even support the zoo. His name will be mud. He'll be a laughingstock."

"Oh, his *reputation* will be ruined," Jean mused. "I think I understand."

"You need to have a good reputation for it to be ruined," Ana said pointedly.

"I'm not worried about my name."

"You should be," Ana muttered.

"Let's keep it moving, shall we?" Louise suggested tactfully. "My pups could use some water, and they missed playtime at the river. Speaking of, where did the Pemón go after they left this area? I want to put it on my map."

"South, toward Brazil. But it's not their traditional home. Here, I'll show you. . . ."

Ellie followed the group, a little distractedly, still thinking about Leroy. Really: What sort of person *did* all this? Put so much effort into personal glorification, lying and obsessing to the point of chasing a teenaged girl all over the globe? That wasn't what normal people did. Sure, all adventurers had their quirks; you had to have a strong belief in yourself to set out into the unknown (or maybe a death wish). But this was more than that. Was Leroy a movie-style antagonist or something else a little more complicated?

In the matinee serials the smarter bad guys cut their losses at some point, like the Shadowy Grifter, or gave up entirely, or even wound up joining the hero, like the Spy Smasher did with Codename Felix.

Why wouldn't Leroy just wait and see if Ellie ever even made it back? If she didn't, his problem solved itself. And even if she did, couldn't he spin it all differently somehow? With his money he could probably buy off anyone he wanted—newspapers, journalists—or even pretend he supported her all along. Have a press release about it. Turn it into a win for the zoo.

A movie villain was predictable. Leroy Reardon was . . . not.

An unpredictable nemesis in a foreign country who had planes and probably guns? That was a formidable enemy indeed. Something to be actually scared of.

"You're very quiet, Ellie," Jean said when they stopped for a breather and some water from their canteens (Ana made disgusted noises when Louise let Mutt and Jeff drink directly from hers). Clouds had gathered overhead for their afternoon release, and a light rain began to fall—almost none of it making it through the treetops.

Ellie leaned back against a tree, flexing her shoulders against its rigidity where they ached from carrying the ad-hoc pack Ana and Louise rigged for her. But it must have looked like she meant something else, like in one of those movies they saw in health class when a girl leans back provocatively against the bleachers or something stupid like that. Because Jean came closer to her, close enough that he could look down into her face.

She didn't hate it: He smelled of fresh sweat and jungle greenery, and it was really something to be the only subject of his gaze.

He reached his hand up to her face, to the side of her head, and brushed back her hair.

Ellie tried not to look away or tremble, but it took all of her effort. She was sure he could see her heart beating rapidly in her chest, pushing its way through her bones.

He pulled his hand back and showed her the ant he had taken out of her locks.

"Love these, but not on the skin. Very itchy." He popped

it in his mouth and bit down. "Tastes like lemons or limes. You should try it!"

Ellie laughed, pretended she wasn't disappointed.

"All right," she said bravely, trying to cover up anything else she might have felt. "Give me one."

He gently pulled her away from the tree that was covered with them, daintily picked up an ant, and dropped it into her open mouth. She bit down like he had, and it wasn't that disgusting: it exploded in a burst of sour like a candy.

"Wowee," she said, impressed. "Not bad at all!"

"Let's go, children," Ana said. "I want to get to Jesus's by tomorrow at the latest."

Children.

Ellie felt her face flush, but she hadn't done anything. And Jean hadn't either. Her mouth still tasted of sour; she wished she had a few more ants.

"Carl will never believe this, that I ate a bug."

"Carl? Who's that?" Jean asked.

"He's a . . . friend of mine. Back home," she said, perfectly honestly.

"A *friend*. I see," he said, perfectly innocently.

Ellie wanted to argue but she wasn't sure what she would be arguing about.

"I'm sure you have *many* friends back home, like Carl,"

he added impishly. "I'll bet you have to beat them off with a stick."

"No, I don't, Jean. I'm considered a little bit of a . . . well, an outsider, back home. A tomboy who's not interested in sports. I'm smart enough to do all right in school, but it's hard for me to stay interested enough in anything to get straight As. I have a job at the zoo, not at a dress shop or makeup counter or office or even the plant. And my hair is *just red enough* for people to call me names. I don't really belong in any group, except with my older friends at the USO."

"I couldn't stay interested in school either. But that was because I was too smart for the teachers. I'd get bored and ask them questions they didn't like. The best day was when I left. Besides, my father says school only teaches you to be narrow-minded and to swallow the propaganda of the middle class."

"And what does your father do?" Ellie asked. She couldn't help wondering if he was like some of the other fathers she knew back home who made fun of education. They either worked at the plant, or . . . didn't work.

"He's an artist," Jean said proudly. "He doesn't adhere to the norms of the petit bourgeoisie."

Ellie sighed. Jean was so very capable, from negotiating

the situation with the Pemón to eating ants and brewing camp chocolate; he was the perfect adventurer's companion. She could see a magazine cover with his beautiful eyes and genuine smile, pointing at something in the distance. Heartthrob material in a way Charles Muntz could never be.

If only he didn't talk *quite* so much about himself. . . .

Didn't his school show the same health movies as hers, that taught how a girl liked being asked about *her*self?

And speaking of girls being asked about themselves . . . Margaret was the head of a zoo. Ana was a naturalist. Louise was a cartographer and illustrator. So . . .

"What does your mother do?" Ellie asked sweetly. "Is she an artist as well?"

She could tell from the very slight pause in his movements that she had hit a nerve. She wondered what look his face was making.

"No, she isn't," he answered shortly.

"What kind of artist is your father?" Louise poked in with interest. "That's my main line of work, when I'm not producing my maps. I even wrote and illustrated my own book. Does he paint, or do any of that?"

"He is not a *commercial artist*," Jean said haughtily. "He makes sculptures and installations that speak to the political struggles our nation is going through."

"My book was banned in the state of Georgia because it

showed Black children and white children playing together," Louise said flatly. "I think I know something about art in *political struggles*, young man."

"My apologies," Jean said, seeming honestly chagrined. He turned around and bowed to her, and Ellie couldn't tell if it was completely sincere, making fun of her, or making fun of himself. He was a myriad of different possibilities at once, each unclear and subject to different potential interpretations.

"Did you think I was sketching the abandoned houses before for *aesthetics*?" Louise pressed.

"Honestly, why not?" Jean admitted. "Tourists love etchings of ruins."

"Excellent point, but my main job is illustrating pamphlets and brochures for the NAACP, not making comfortable art for the masses to consume. My maps trace the movements of displaced people. And speaking of maps, where exactly is this airstrip we're looking for? In relation to where we have been? I'd like to know where we're going for once."

She held out her sketchbook and turned to a page with a rough map of her trip: from Caracas through several villages, up to Canaima, then a little tent drawn in where Ellie had found her and Ana by the river. Ellie was amazed how so few hastily drawn lines could tell an entire journey.

"Well, don't publish *this*. Jesus likes keeping off the radar," Jean said, taking the pencil offered to him and sketching landmarks, arrows, and finally the airfield. Not as beautiful as Louise's drawings, but sure and precise. You could tell that art ran in his family. "Lizard Rock, the Orinoco tributary over here, the ford is here . . . and the jungle thins out into two arms. They go around the old field he uses as his strip. Happy?"

"Very happy," Louise said smugly, taking her sketchbook back. "Thank you."

They stopped early to set up camp because the next day, though short, would be rough. Lizard Rock, Ana explained, was more of a mesa than a rock, and it needed to be skirted and scrabbled around rather than gone over, and the place they were supposed to cross the river wasn't always easy going in the rainy season.

Everything made Ana grumpy that evening; she even tsked at the *very nice* fire Jean made.

"It's too big. It's still light out. It's not cold at all. We don't need it. Waste of resources," she muttered.

"What else are the logs going to do? Sit there and rot?" he countered.

"Yes, and provide homes for termites and hiding places for small mammals. I don't think you understand just how delicate the balance is between the woodland fungus and the surrounding . . ."

Louise gave Ellie a wan smile. But it *was* a nice fire, and cheery. Funny how despite the general heat of the woods, the warm lick of the flames comforted her, like at a family picnic or a USO social at the lake. She felt safe. She wished she had marshmallows. She watched Mutt and Jeff tiredly play tug-of-war with what looked like another sock. A *blue* one this time, the garter still attached. Not hers, obviously, and she hadn't seen them rooting around in anyone's bags. Strange. The wonderfully scented smoke drifted up through the branches of the trees, into the mostly clear sky. Maybe they would even see the stars that night. . . .

Jean pulled out a little wooden penny whistle and began to play. Ellie snuck a look at Ana, assuming she would show disdain at such an obvious move, but the woman had a slight, almost grateful smile on her face.

The melody he played wasn't one Ellie recognized; maybe it was Venezuelan. She was a little surprised that the instrument wasn't a panpipe or a more traditionally South American instrument, but then nothing about Jean was predictable.

"That was nice," Louise said when he was done. "I always like the kind of music you can take with you—a harmonica, or whatnot. I like guitars too, but they don't travel as well."

"Or a portable record player," Ellie said, thinking of Dr. Hua and the animals. She wondered if he would have enjoyed the trip. Margaret certainly would have. "Or a radio."

"I don't think I packed one this time," Jean said, pretending to feel his shirt's pockets. "But I listen to one all the time at home. If you name a song I could try to play it."

"Oh, do you know 'Personality' by Johnny Mercer?" Ellie asked eagerly.

"That's kind of a hard one to just do a solo of," Louise pointed out. "How about some Glenn Miller? Or the Ink Spots?"

"'String of Pearls' first,'" Jean declared. "Then 'When the Swallows Come Back.'"

He fumbled a bit on the descending notes of the opening for the first tune, then figured it out and played the rest all the way through perfectly. He performed over a dozen pieces, switching back and forth between the big bands, popular songs from movies, and orchestral pieces—all of which he had picked up just from hearing them played on the radio. Amazing! Carl's radio didn't even play music.

Jean broke off suddenly in the middle of "Moonlight Serenade" and turned his head to listen. Ellie followed suit.

It wasn't just one plane this time: multiple angry roars came from slightly different directions of the compass. One of them—Lucy's, Ellie would have put money on it—suddenly swept in low, just above the treetops, close enough that leaves and twigs snagged and ground up in the prop and were reduced to green rain by the snarling machine.

"The fire, put it out!" Ana yelled, already using her feet to kick the logs apart. Louise grabbed her puppies first, one on each shoulder, before she too began to dismantle the fire, stomping on the flames.

"They already know where we are—we should run!!" Jean cried.

Another plane swooped right over them, a noise so loud it was like the world was being ripped apart. Ellie screamed, partly in defiance, covering her ears.

"They're trying to flush us out," Ana yelled. "They *want* us to panic and run."

"I'll lead them off!" Jean declared, unbuttoning his shirt.

Ellie couldn't help gaping. Not just because of Jean's smooth, tanned and muscled torso that would have put any of the lakeside boys to shame . . . but also because, well—why was he doing it?

Then he began waving it over his head like a flag and she suddenly understood.

"Come and get me!" he cried out.

(Like they could hear him?)

"Jean, this is stupid!" Ana yelled as another plane came in low, harrying them just like in movies about the war.

"I'll find you once I've led them on a merry chase!" Jean shouted, grinning. He picked up a still-burning log like a torch and waved it aloft. "Good luck, mes amies!"

And then he ran off into the jungle.

TWENTY

The three women stood for a moment, as if planes weren't swooping overhead and the fire wasn't guttering out and flaring up at the same time, as if puppies weren't whining, as if the noise and smoke were all just an illusion.

"That stupid . . ." Ana began angrily.

And then the planes veered off.

Ellie listened, stunned, as their evil noise slowly faded.

Jean's idea actually worked . . . ? They were really following him?

She started to ask what they should do—and then one of the planes came back and made a final pass. They all ducked down again, covering their ears.

But then it too disappeared into the night.

"Well," Louise said eventually. "That was . . . dramatic."

A statement that didn't quite encompass the feelings that were welling up through Ellie. Jean's snap decision, his selflessness, his disappearance into the green unknown—it all spoke of something so great she wasn't sure whether to cheer or cry. It felt somehow like she would never see him again.

Although . . . wait. The number of planes . . . It sounded like three of them at first, all coming from different directions—but only two had flown away. Or had only one harried them, and then it circled back from farther off? Maybe Ellie had miscounted, or . . .

"All right," Ana said, hands on her hips. "Let's make sure the fire is well and truly out and then move deeper into the jungle."

"They already know we were here, and where we were," Louise said. "Why bother covering our tracks?"

"It's not to cover our tracks, it's to keep *the entire woods from burning down*!"

Exasperation thickened her accent. Ellie would have giggled at the single tendril of hair bouncing down over the older woman's forehead like a spring, but fear of repercussion stopped her. Instead she immediately found a long stick and carefully mixed the ashes into the dirt with it.

When it was done to Ana's satisfaction they put on their packs.

"I think we should still make for the airstrip," she said. "Let's see if we can get Ellie home. Jean will catch up to us when his . . . antics are done."

"I'm not leaving until Soda-Pop is safe," Ellie warned. He watched her from the branch where he had flown during the fright with the planes, but did not beep in acknowledgement of his name.

"None of us are safe with those zany zookeepers in planes after us," Louise said, but it sounded almost like she was reciting a line from a play. Like she was secretly excited by the whole adventure but didn't want to admit it. Ellie thought she saw a gleam in her eye. "Especially near an *airstrip*. Where else would they fuel up?"

"Mm, it's a good point," Ana allowed. "We should scout it out first—come at it a different way than anyone would expect and take a look."

"You know where 'Lizard Rock' is?" Louise showed her the rustic map in her sketchbook. "You studied the lizards there, I assume. . . ."

"I studied the *snakes*. The rock just *looks* like a lizard. The fer-de-lance makes a home there."

Leroy's dead snake was a pit viper—maybe it was from right here . . .

"The most dangerous snake in the world," Ellie murmured.

"It's only the most dangerous because it often lives close to humans, querida. Don't corner one and you're fine."

"Now *that* would make an interesting map," Louise said thoughtfully. "Human mortality by wild animal . . . and human population density nearby. Anyway, looks like we could skirt Lizard Rock—and not just because of the snakes, mind you—and head a little further north, coming at the airstrip from the west. If Jean was right about the jungle, it should cover us. The river is the only thing I question. I mean, if we can cross it."

Ana pursed her lips as she looked over the map, then shrugged. "I don't know if I trust his directions, but it's either that or a long trip back to Roraima or Caracas."

She pulled out a compass and checked the map one last time before letting Louise put it away. Then they all adjusted their bags, took a swig of water, and set off down the trail.

All except Soda-Pop.

He sat on the bottom-most rung of a thick vine and watched the three humans and two puppies pass by with a curious but strangely detached air.

"C'mon, Soda," Ellie said, turning and offering his preferred shoulder, her right one. "We have to hide from the bad guys."

Soda-Pop fluttered his wings and beeped. Then he preened his chest. Then he sat still.

"Aren't you coming?" Ellie asked, hating the way she sounded. She waited.

And waited.

Ana came back to stand next to her, a soft look on her face.

"Ellie, you should be happy. He feels independent now. Strong enough to stay on his own. That was the whole reason you came down here. And now you can go."

"But . . . his feathers," Ellie protested. "They're not entirely grown in yet. He can fly a little now, but—he would have been safer back with his family. Here he's all alone in the jungle, all by himself. . . ."

"Surely as someone who has worked with animals you know about a bird's loud calls. One is a way of saying *Here I am. This is my home. Where are you?* He is not really alone, you know that. He has a whole invisible forest full of friends. And he knows how to get back to his home."

Ellie looked up at the bird. His iridescence was muted in the twilight of the woods and he barely looked purple at all; even his rakish crown with the two still-broken crest feathers seemed drained of color as he faded into the background.

"And you have to get back to *your* home," Louise added. "That's the priority, now that your little guy knows what he wants. You have a mother and a father who have no idea where you are and are probably sick to death over your disappearance—I imagine that an entire small town in somewhere, USA, there's a big commotion over the nice girl who stole a plane."

"Yeah, I know it," Ellie said with a sigh. "I guess I just thought his leaving would be . . . on my terms? I would drop him off, say goodbye. He wouldn't . . . leave *me*."

Ana patted her on the back. "That's the part that's hard, isn't it? But come on, we really have to disappear now, like our little feathered guy."

"Right." Ellie took a deep breath and saluted Soda-Pop. "Goodbye, friend. Good luck. I hope you find a lady Soda-Pop and have *many* generations of pretty purple children, and no one ever bothers you again."

Soda-Pop beeped almost like he understood her.

Ellie turned and walked away, pretending it was sweat leaking down her cheeks.

But eventually—perhaps inevitably—Ellie's hollowness at Soda-Pop's absence was slowly filled with other emotions stirred up by the day, ones that were just waiting in the shadows like a jaguar to pounce on her heart and beat it around.

"That was pretty amazing of Jean," she finally said. She felt bubblingly, embarrassingly *full* of questions about him—but didn't want to seem too eager. "Giving himself up as bait."

Ana shrugged. "It was a strange choice. We could have simply moved deeper into the woods. Or split up. Or a dozen other things that wouldn't have him ripping off his shirt and running off like a matinee hero."

Louise guffawed at that.

"But—he led them away from us! That *is* heroic!" Ellie protested.

"But it wasn't necessary," Ana pointed out. "It was rash. A teenager's decision."

Teenager's decision! Boy, didn't that sound contemptuous. As if age always improved one's decision-making thought processes. One merely needed to look at Leroy to realize the myth of that truism. These ladies thought they were really superior to her and Jean, just because of their years.

"He didn't have to do it," she objected, trying not to stick out her lip in obvious objection. "He's not a coward."

"There's a difference between not being afraid and being an actual hero," Louise said. "I can tell you about many Black men and women who are terrified every time they try to vote or drink at a water fountain. They're heroes. Also, they don't need to take their shirts off to do it."

Ellie grumbled inwardly at this but couldn't find fault in her logic.

"He isn't a coward, and he isn't stupid," Ana said. "But *also* in the way of young men, he is not as smart as he thinks he is. And you should probably know . . . there are many broken hearts in the villages and towns Jean has passed through."

That stung a little. Ellie wasn't in love with him or anything.

Really.

"It sounds like you don't like him very much," she muttered, trying not to sound peevish. How could this woman not appreciate a young man who *tried*? Who showed *passion* for things? Who took the lead when he found it necessary?

Ellie saw Ana give Louise a long-suffering look—so infuriating!

"Quite the opposite," Ana finally said.

Oh . . . !

"Did he break your heart, too?"

Louise sniggered and then covered it up as best she could.

"In a manner of speaking," Ana said thoughtfully. "Let's just say I am disappointed by what he is doing with his potential. He should go to school. If he cares about people so much, he should go into policymaking, government. The occasional protest will change this country only so much."

"If you feel so strongly, why don't *you* do it?"

"People are not my specialty. My job is to keep track of the woods, to see how it changes, to record when a plant hasn't been seen in years. When there are no more of a certain kind of animal. This is the quiet side of revolution: gathering the facts and numbers to show how we are changing and destroying the world that gave us life. People are important, but they have voices. Animals and plants do not."

"Some of us draw maps and illustrate political pamphlets, and write books to educate children. All of these 'quiet' ways also work wonders," Louise pointed out. "'They also serve who only stand and wait.' That's John Milton."

They were smart words. There were other ways to do things that were just as effective as tackling a problem head-on, guns blazing. Wait, didn't Carl say something like that? Well, it didn't sound as good when he did. Or maybe she wasn't listening properly.

But . . .

Also . . .

"So did Jean grow up here in the forests, or in Caracas?" she couldn't help asking.

Ana made a noise like she was strangling.

***

When it was time to set up camp this time they did it without a fire, under the thickest-leaved trees they could find. As if to add to the mood, it rained again. No stars that night, Ellie thought glumly as she chewed on the dried meat and flat heavy bread that passed for dinner. There were delicious chocolate bars for dessert and juicy green fruits to quench her thirst, but without Jean or Soda-Pop everything felt dull.

The two puppies sensed her sadness and showed how much they wanted to take care of her by constantly getting tangled under her feet when she was trying to fix her bedroll and demanding to be played with when she wanted to be alone and nipping her heels where she was covered in bruises and scrapes (which seemed to be always and everywhere these days). She couldn't get mad at them, of course, not even when Mutt presented her with a very old sock, full of holes and dirt, that had probably been buried somewhere for a while. Since none of the indigenous people Ellie had seen wore socks—in fact, neither did Jean—she had no idea who could have lost it. Muntz, maybe? Some other European type? It didn't have anything embroidered on it. . . .

"Here," she said, reaching into her satchel. She took out Leroy's *cashmere* socks (feeling her mother's angry, thousand-mile stare hot on her neck) and held one out to each puppy. They wagged their tails madly and went wild with excitement, checking out the other's sock (maybe it was better?) then running around triumphantly with the socks flying out behind them like banners.

But all three still somehow managed to fall asleep immediately when it was time, out cold like the dregs of water at the bottom of a canteen.

The next day Ellie kept putting her hand up to pet Soda-Pop, or to make sure he was comfortable in her pocket—which of course he wasn't. Had he roosted somewhere high up during the night? Had he made it home already? Had his awkward fluttering allowed a snake or jaguar or even a monkey to grab and eat him? It wasn't fair the way she would never know. She had gone to all this trouble to do the right thing and now she would never get to see the real ending. Did Margaret feel like that when she was at the end of her scientific trips? A sense of loss at leaving her ducks or whatever to their fate?

. . . and what about Jean? Despite the alarming buzz of certain insects that caused her to look up in fright, there was no sign of any airplane. Thanks to him, they might very well be safe until the end of their journey. But what did Leroy plan on doing once he got "Ellie" (Jean, pretending to be her) out into the open? Was he going to land, get out, and scream at her (Jean)? Threaten her (him)? Or had he gone so berserk that he would just try to steer a plane into the person he thought was Ellie in order to kill her (him)?

If they managed to get Ellie safely onto a plane she would never know what happened to him, either.

Lizard Rock turned out to be a hill-sized stony oval pile with some scrub on its back like a gopher with a bad shampoo. Maybe the diminishing line of boulders and rocks trailing out from its back side looked vaguely like a lizard's tail, but to Ellie it more resembled the long string of a limp balloon that the depressed gopher was dragging along behind it. Carl would have seen it instantly.

Ellie felt a pang: She didn't have a camera so she could show him a picture of it later. She had made it to their dream destination—without him. And there was no way to share with him any of what she saw.

Wait—

Was she looking forward to telling him all about the trip more than she wished he were here? How did you measure something like that? What would she give—or give up—to have him right there, right then? He had promised to take her to Paradise Falls someday, he swore it. And now here she was, but without *him*. What did that mean?

Did he still owe her a trip, with the two of them together?

"Hey, Louise." She ran over to the woman, who was frowning at her map and the rock. "Can you do me a favor?"

"What do you need?"

"Can you draw me a quick picture of Lizard Rock? To keep? I want to show it to a friend back home."

She looked at Ellie appraisingly. "That's an . . . interesting request. Thoughtful, too." She took out her sketchbook, flipped to a blank page, and began immediately, her pencil flying even as she squinted at the formation, eyes away from the page. "You know, it doesn't even look like a lizard to me. Of course, we don't have lizards in New York. To me it looks like a giant rat with its nasty old tail."

"I know! To me it looks like a gopher with a balloon."

"Is this your . . . special friend *Carl* you were talking about before?" Louise asked fake-casually.

"Um. Yes, ma'am."

"You have anything else you'd like to tell me about him? Anything on your mind?"

"Oh, there's quite a bit on my mind . . . but it's all a little jumbled. He wouldn't be . . . as useful as Jean on a trip like this. But I still want him here, seeing it all with me. But he's not here. . . . But would things be different if he was?"

"That is a *big* set of thoughts there. You have a lot going on in that red head of yours."

"If art class is almost over. . ." Ana said pointedly, coming up behind them. "Maybe we could get to this guy's place before the sun sets? You know, put you on a plane home to the United States, happily ever after, and so on?"

"Almost done—there," Louise said, smudging a line deliberately with her thumb. Then she signed it and tore the picture out of her book and handed it to Ellie.

"Wow! That's like magic. . . . It looks exactly like it." With just a few lines and shapes, the cartographer had perfectly captured not just the image of the rock, but the feeling of the landscape where it was set.

Louise tried not to beam. "It's what I do, honey."

Ellie carefully pressed it between two pages in the logbook inside her pack, keeping it as flat as she could. Somehow her bag seemed a little lighter after that.

When they finally made it to the front of the gopher that was Lizard Rock, Ellie moved *very* slowly, taking a good look at every place she was about to put her foot down, making sure it was clear of snakes, twigs, debris, loose rocks, or anything that might hide a snake. Louise carefully cradled Mutt in her arms, high above any potential dangers. Ellie picked up Jeff—but tried to get her to perch on her shoulder the way Soda-Pop had. It was much more difficult to manage the larger, squirmy thing. Finally the puppy settled and snoozed there, pleasantly supported by Ellie's hand on her rump. Except for the slight discomfort and her arm falling asleep she could *almost* pretend she had her bird friend back.

But after an hour of walking, Jeff began scrambling uncomfortably, digging her claws into Ellie's flesh—excited, sockless, and maybe confused about where her brother and Louise were. Just when Ellie was about to stop and set her down, the puppy sprang free from her grasp and went bounding into the underbrush—away from everyone else. With a squeaky yowl that would someday be a resonant baying (maybe), Mutt ran after her.

"Oh no you don't. I'm not losing any more friends out here!" Ellie plunged forward into the bushes, arms held up to protect her eyes and trying to remember where the poisonous manchineel tree was supposed to grow—more like in marshy areas, right?

Which was how she entirely missed seeing the person just standing there, and slammed into him.

"STAY AWAY FROM ME!" Ellie immediately screamed, pulling her bag around to her front the way she had been taught to in the Outdoor Guides' Anti-Mugging Self-Defense Course for Ladies. Step one, screaming, was to set the attacker off guard and also to direct as much attention to

yourself as possible so anyone nearby would hear and come to your aid. Step two was making the purse or pack a shield against any violent or lascivious advances.

"But then I wouldn't be able to say goodbye," Jean said, holding up his hands in surrender. Mutt and Jeff jumped and rolled around his feet, delighted at finding him.

"Jean!"

He still wasn't wearing a shirt, Ellie noticed.

"In the flesh," he said ironically.

"You're back! And are all right!"

Without thinking, Ellie kissed him—on the cheek—rapidly and spontaneously and a little louder than she meant to. She obviously wasn't going to *hug* his naked torso.

He laughed and didn't blush.

Ana came running up—was that a *knife* in her hand?—followed by Louise, who had her fists balled up like a boxer.

"Whoa whoa whoa, it's all right, stand down, men," Jean said.

"Oh, for the love of suffering Mary," Ana swore. "Was the surprise really necessary?"

"It got me a kiss," he said with a shrug.

Ellie blushed furiously.

Sure, it didn't mean anything, but what kind of boy kissed and told? And so *quickly*?

"And what did you do with the planes?" Ana demanded. "Did you take them out all on your own? Make your own ack-ack out of . . . your shirt?"

"Actually, yes. I led them out to the Niño Verde, and I was terribly clever. I tied my shirt around a rotten log and sent it downstream, so it looked like me—I mean you, Ellie—on a canoe, or swimming, or something. They took the bait! They circled once and then followed—I saw them come in for a landing on the plains nearby."

"Waste of a good shirt," Ana muttered.

"Speaking of, put another shirt on, boy," Louise ordered. "If you don't have one, I'll loan you one of mine."

"Sheesh, some thanks for the conquering hero," Jean said with a bow that was somehow sarcastic. "I literally saved all of us any more trouble from those despicable men—"

"Two are women," Ellie found herself saying.

"—and this is how I'm thanked?"

"*Thank* you, noble savior," Ana said, crossing her arms. Where had her knife gone? Disappeared, like a magician's rose. "Good job finishing up the loose ends of a . . . questionable decision. Maybe for your next magnificent act you can take us to Jesus without any more drama?"

"It would be my pleasure, my lady," he said, digging through his bag. He did in fact have another shirt, an unbleached cotton one without buttons that was carefully balled up. Ellie wondered why he hadn't bothered putting it on before, on his way back.

"For you, Ellie." He carefully pulled the shirt apart, and inside was—

"Soda-Pop?" Ellie cried.

The little bird looked a little haggard from being stuffed in a sack and wrapped up in a shirt; another one of his little crest feathers had bent. But he immediately perked up when he saw her, and flapped his wings excitedly.

"Beep!"

She scooped him up and stroked his feathers; he leaned into it, enjoying every moment.

"I found him on a bush, on my way back to you," Jean explained.

"Jean, she let him *go*," Ana said in exasperation. "He *wanted* to leave. It was time. We left him behind on purpose."

"I didn't know that," Jean protested. "I saw him and figured he was lost!"

Ellie was torn. It was an honest mistake. She was overjoyed to see Soda-Pop again so soon. But she had begun to make peace with his absence, and now she would have to start all over again.

Just to see what would happen she tried putting him on the branch of a tree. All four humans watched as he trilled and burbled to himself, preened his chest feathers, and looked around, cocking his head left and right.

Jean took the moment to put his shirt on.

"All right, goodbye," Ellie said carefully, and turned around—

—and Soda-Pop immediately grew agitated, fluttered to her shoulder, and bit her ear. But not that hard.

Ana groaned.

"All right, all right, we'll figure it out, let's just get going," Louise suggested.

"My thoughts exactly," Jean said, gesturing for them to walk.

Ellie couldn't help bouncing a little: Soda-Pop back on her shoulder, Jean beside her, the group all together again. Maybe—if she stayed at the zoo, got promoted—she could be put in charge of a rescued bird, a small one, and it would ride around her shoulder like Soda-Pop the whole day while she did her work. She would smile at the little kids as they looked at her with awe, and bend down so they could get a better look, but she would warn them not to touch, or get too close . . .

Oh, but wait. Assuming she got back home, there was no chance Leroy would let her near the zoo ever again. Maybe not even as a visitor.

"What are you thinking about, Ellie?" Jean asked. "You

look so sad. Aren't you pleased that I'm back? And you have your little friend?"

"Oh, yes, of course, Jean. I was just thinking about Soda-Pop and my job. I knew I *liked* working at the zoo . . . but I've realized I *love* working at the zoo," she said. "I don't think I even knew how important it was—besides being able to work with all the animals, I mean. Saving wild places begins with education, with children. If I teach future voters and taxpayers and presidents how important and wonderful animals are, that's a big deal. Once you meet a bird like Soda-Pop, you can't help falling in love a little bit. And maybe you'll think about that in the future when you're all grown up."

"The hand that rocks the cradle?" Jean said knowingly.

"No—I'm not talking about being a mom, I'm talking about educating the public. Weren't you listening?"

"These are deep and serious thoughts," Jean said. "I can't think about them right now, I'm too triumphant! Wasn't it crazy, my fabulous plan with the planes? It actually worked!"

"It did. It was great. I'm sorry Ana wasn't more grateful, but she seems to be . . . gruff. It's just her way, maybe?"

"She wouldn't know how to properly compliment someone if she read a book on it," Jean growled.

"Not even after *years* of seeing what happens when you don't."

"Beg pardon?"

"Oh, look, forget it. I don't care about what she thinks. I want to hear it from *you*."

"It was amazing." She had *kissed* him, for heaven's sake. Some of that was just the thrill that he had appeared again, unscathed, but still . . .

"Kind of like in the movies," Jean said, swinging his hand out to grab a dry twig and snap it playfully.

"Do you get to see a lot of movies—out here?" She hoped she wasn't being rude. But in her defense, there hadn't been signs of a store, much less a cinema, since she had landed in the wilds of Venezuela.

"When I travel back to Caracas, or Maracaibo," he said with a shrug. "It's one of the few good things about being in the city."

"Which are otherwise home to capitalist imperialist colonists and their delusional middle-class supporters?"

"Now you got it!" Jean laughed.

"I wonder what speeches you would give to my dad and his 'working-class' friends at the plant," she said thoughtfully. "Which is where my dad works, by the way. Before the war it made bins for grain and farm equipment.

Then it switched over to containers for munitions and things. . . ."

Jean broke off another twig and then saw something on the ground. "Hey, look at this! I'll bet you don't have anything like this in the United States!"

He scooped up something large, shiny, and black and held it up to her face, possibly expecting her to flinch. Instead she squinted and drew closer. It was a fat armored beetle with a neck shield that extended into two dangerous-looking points and an equally martial-looking horn on its "nose." Almost like a tiny triceratops except for its coloring and its barbed, jointed legs, which it flailed pathetically trying to slip out of Jean's grasp.

"A titan beetle," he said proudly. "The largest beetle in the Americas."

"That's a rhinoceros beetle," Ellie corrected politely but immediately. "You can tell by the, uh, rhinoceros horn on its front."

"I think I know what I'm talking about. We used to play with these as kids, have them wrestle each other."

"*Titanus giganteus*, the real titan beetle, is nocturnal," Ana yelled from where she and Louise had strode ahead. "That's why despite being so large they are unstudied—barely anyone ever sees them. Remember in Valencia, that girl brought one in—"

"Yes, yes, I misremembered the English name," Jean said irritably. "Still, you have to admit, it's pretty impressive, isn't it?"

"You used to play with these as kids?" Louise asked, dropping back to look. She held Mutt, who took one look at the bug and began to growl. "That's . . . something else."

"We just had ants," Ellie said as Jean put the insect back down and they kept walking. "I'm afraid we were a little cruel to them—like, dropping water near their houses to see what they would do, put a rock in the middle of a line of them walking, or a piece of sugar out of the way . . ."

"We have leafcutter ants. You do *not* want to get in their way," Jean interrupted.

"Oh! Show me if you see them!" Ellie begged. "I would love to see them in the wild. At the zoo we have an exhibit. . . ."

"Leafcutter ants in a cage! What a joke. Here they walk for *miles*. Really. Miles!"

Ellie doubted that. She knew that ants were amazing and could do all sorts of fantastic things like carry objects many times their weight, but they were still tiny and couldn't fly—wings were the only reason why insects like butterflies and bees could travel for long ranges. She was as sure of these facts as she was her own name.

And she recognized a rhinoceros beetle when she saw

it despite never having seen a *live* one before—the museum in Springfield had an amazing, if somewhat morbid, collection of pinned invertebrates and even sold some in the gift shop.

But this was Jean's home—shouldn't he know more about its residents than she did?

Or couldn't he at least stop pretending that he knew more?

Maybe she couldn't recite the names of all the plants and animals at the swimming hole, but at least she didn't act like she could. And . . .

Ellie suddenly choked, remembering the ant she had eaten just a day before. It had been delicious, but what if it was the wrong kind of ant? What if Jean was wrong about them too?

"So—would your Carl have thought to lead the bad guys away like that?" he suddenly asked, giving her a sly look.

Ellie blushed.

Then she got angry for no reason she could immediately put her finger on.

Finally she thought about the question.

"No," she decided.

Jean grinned. "I thought not."

"He would have suggested just hunkering down in the jungle and letting them pass, like Ana said."

Jean made a scoffing noise. "Who knows if that would have even worked."

"I guess we'll never know," Ellie said neutrally. It could have been an admission or an indictment. Even she wasn't sure.

She focused on walking, now irritable and uncomfortable. Jean picked up Mutt when she picked up Jeff. Why was he being such an ass? Had his little adventure with the planes caused some sort of ego-inflating tropical fever to take over his brain? He was so nice and wonderful before . . .

Wasn't he?

She tried to replay all their interactions for the last few days, but it was hard: much like scenes in adventure movies, all she could remember were the action sequences. Jean appearing by torchlight to talk to the locals who had found her, the swooping planes, the crunchy ants, the hot chocolate . . .

When it was time for a break she excused herself and walked some distance away from the others. For the first time since being alone in the jungle after the crash Ellie *wanted* to be alone, really alone. She needed some breathing space and time to think without interruption. There had just been too many revelations about personalities in her life in the last few days.

Too bad Jean followed her.

"Can't I have a little privacy?" she pleaded.

"It's dangerous for someone like you to be by yourself in the forest," Jean said easily. "Also, I want to know what's going on with you."

"I'm just . . . thinking about things, all right? And—I have to powder my nose!"

She said it challengingly, into his face, hands on her hips. Jean looked like he didn't believe her at all and really, really wanted to object—but of course he couldn't.

So she spun around and began to stomp dramatically away—only to see a man standing there behind them, holding a gun.

"Apologies, Miss McGill, but I believe you have something of mine," Leroy Reardon said with a twitchy smile.

TWENTY-ONE

Ellie stared at the revolver for a moment in disbelief.

Then she pushed Jean out of the way, to face Leroy alone. "Oh, knock it off, it's *me* you're after."

(She kept her eyes on the man with the gun but could *feel* Jean gazing at her with something akin to love.)

The zoo owner wore his usual full safari-style outfit, complete with jacket, which must have made it feel like a sauna under the equatorial sun. He had only a straw hat, at least, not a pith helmet, but his high shiny boots completed the look perfectly. Except for the questionable glint in his eye he could have been mistaken for the hero, braving the jungles for whatever his quest was. His cheeks were covered in reddish splotches from his exertion in the woods and his moustache seemed even more oiled than usual. Or oily.

This was the man Ellie had idolized? *This* guy here, with a *gun* pointed at her?

"And are you really going to shoot me over Soda-Pop?"

She just barely stopped herself from pointing at her pocket for emphasis. So far the bird was keeping shtum, tucked down and unseen.

"Soda-Pop?" Leroy asked in confusion. "Oh, the bird."

"*Yes*, the bird. I've only been calling him that for weeks—and so has everyone else at the zoo. You didn't even notice."

"This is all serious," Jean said, with wonder. "You really did have a deadly maniac from the zoo after you because of that bird."

"Not a maniac, just someone who wants back what is rightfully his," Leroy said.

"How did you even find me?" Ellie asked. "Jean said he fooled you into following him away from us . . ."

"Oh, he did, clever fellow," Leroy said with a nasty smile. "He made it look very much like someone—maybe even you—was escaping south, down the river. But *we* had a trick up our sleeves too. I only sent two planes after the fake you—"

"I knew there was a plane missing!" Ellie cried.

"Yes, yes, clever girl. Lucy and I kept the third and landed it back near where we first discovered your campfire. Then we watched and waited. When this . . . shirtless . . .

boy appeared, I followed him, and he led me directly back to you."

Ellie glared at Jean.

He didn't hang his head in embarrassment—boy, Ellie would have—but stared straight ahead at nothing, admitting nothing, eyes flashing.

"Anyway, I radioed to my friends to come meet us, and here we all are," Leroy finished a little fliply. Then he leveled his gun at Ellie again. "Now where is it? Where is the bird?"

"*He* is being repatriated," Ellie said as coldly as she could, crossing her arms. "Because he wasn't doing well at all at the zoo. He was sick and only getting worse. Not eating, just wasting away. He was going to die if he stayed there. Ever since we got to Venezuela he has been improving. So here he'll stay."

"He was doing just fine at the zoo," Leroy said with a sniff. "William reported to me every day about him."

"Mr. Hodgson was lying to you. He was terrified of losing his job if Soda-Pop died and couldn't star in your special exhibit. He put me in charge of the bird because you had already fired Margaret. I was probably the only person who could have helped him at all." And been trusted to keep quiet, she didn't add.

Leroy looked uncertain. No less prone to violence, but less certain of this one fact.

"That is neither here nor there," he finally said, waving his gun back and forth. "The bird is coming back with me now. Where is he?"

Ellie had no idea what her next play was, so when Mutt and Jeff came bounding over to investigate this new friend to play with, it gave her a moment to think.

(And to Leroy's credit, although he re-aimed his gun at the loud and unexpected interlopers, he didn't fire.)

"Jean, Ellie, are you all right?" called Ana as she followed the dogs into the clearing. *"Oh, por dios!"*

"What in the name of . . ." Louise demanded, right behind her.

Mutt and Jeff raced around Leroy's ankles, nipping at them playfully. "Oh, you have backup," he said breezily. "Well, I do too. *Come out*, fellas. And ladies."

Melting out of the jungle a little less gracefully—more like the swaggering, devil-may-care citizens of the United States that they were—were Dan, Chester, Lucy, and Diana. Dan had a gun, and so did Diana, a pretty little pistol with mother-of-pearl inlay. Ellie doubted that either it, or its owner, could hit anything with any degree of accuracy. Maybe that was why Diana also carried a sharp-looking hunting knife in her other hand.

"Wait a second—how did you all get down here?" Ellie said, frowning. "I stole one of your four planes . . ."

"You stole *my* plane!" Leroy roared.

"We had to radio back to get another one," Lucy said, shaking her head. "Not the one I special ordered for Leroy. She's fine, but—"

"It's a whole army of bad guys," Louise interrupted in wonder. "You're *all* demented zookeepers after Ellie's little purple bird?"

"Not zookeepers," Chester said. "At least I'm not."

"It's not Ellie's purple bird, it's *mine*," Leroy growled.

"Property is theft," Jean suggested. "No one can own the means of production—"

Ana snapped at him in Spanish. Then she turned to Leroy: "Why don't you just go away and get another bird?"

Ellie listened to this in shock. Why would the *naturalist* suggest such a thing? Stealing another creature from her country and its natural environment?

Maybe, unlike Ellie, she had actually dealt with dangerous, gun-toting criminals before.

"I mean," Dan said with a prevaricating wag of his head that made him look exactly like an accountant tallying up numbers. His perfectly round black-rimmed glasses didn't help, although he held his own gun steadily. "It's been suggested . . ."

"I couldn't possibly," Leroy said with a sniff. "That rare and exotic bird was a personal gift from *Charles Muntz* himself. Besides the principle of the thing, I couldn't ask him for another. That would be rude."

"Oh, *come on*!" Ellie said in a strangled voice. "You're not really standing by that load of horse-hooey, are you?"

The moment the words came out of her mouth, Ellie realized she had screwed up.

Ana groaned something in Spanish. A bird called from somewhere far off, like out of a dream.

Leroy put his left hand on the gun to brace it, as if he were readying to shoot.

"Just what," he said with a false calmness, "are you implying? With that statement?"

"I just . . . I was just saying . . ." Ellie tried to think of a quick story or line, anything that would smooth over the situation. Of course he had to shut her up now. She knew the truth behind the one lie that tied together everything about Soda-Pop and his exhibit and Muntz and *everything*. What could she say to fix this?

Nothing came to mind.

What the heck; she would just keep going with it.

"THIS MAN," she announced primly, looking at each of his friends in turn, making sure they were paying attention, "*LIED* about where he got the purple bird, Soda-Pop. He *said* it was a personal gift from famed Charles Muntz, but in

actuality he stole it himself from a cave nearby. He doesn't know Muntz at all!!"

She crossed her arms like a prosecutor done arguing her case and tried to look as stern as possible.

"Well," Dan said, pursing his lips. "*I* knew that. And I don't really care. It's a good story. Good for him, good for the zoo, no harm done."

"No *harm*?" Ellie demanded.

"Really? Is this true?" Chester asked Leroy, intrigued.

"Oh, come on, Chet," Lucy said in disgust. "We were with Leroy almost the entire time on that trip. When did he meet with a guy in a giant silver zeppelin? I think you would remember that."

"*I* didn't know," Diana said, "and now I do, and I still don't care. You have his bird. Give it back."

"Muntz and I would have met eventually," Leroy said, drawing himself up and trying to muster some dignity. "We travel in the same circles. I'm sure, even if we didn't become the best of friends or bosom companions, we would have struck up a jocular, manly relationship built upon professional admiration and the sharing of mutual hobbies."

"Leroy, that's weird," Lucy said with a laugh. "Who cares where you got a pretty bird for your zoo?"

"It matters because people love Charles Muntz!" he roared. *"As they will someday love me!* The gift of this bird will bring them *flocking* to the zoo!"

"*Flocking*, nice," Chester said with a delighted smile.

"So I guess that means now we have *two* little problems to solve here, Leroy" Dan said, glaring at Chester. "You need to get the bird back . . ."

"And I need to make sure no one ever finds out about how Muntz was actually never involved. *Yet*," Leroy growled, gripping his gun more tightly.

"You're totally unhinged," Ellie whispered. "This is all—insane. Ana was right. Why do you need something like that, a big lie, dragging Muntz's name into it, for your perfectly happy, perfectly fine little zoo? It's doing just swell without all this!!"

"It is not 'just swell,'" Leroy—again—growled. *Growled.* Once again Ellie had to reconcile this version of the head of the zoo with the one in her mind. Had there been no warning signs? No tells? Had she really been so infatuated with his image she had somehow missed clues? She had a *lot* to talk to Carl and Margaret about when she got back (and probably apologize for).

"It's just a penny-ante, small-town, nothing little zoo—that my family saddled me with. When I should be out there doing great things—hero things. 'Here's your chance,' they said. 'Make something great of *this*,' they said. So I am. I am making it *great*."

"I don't think there is any reasoning with this man," Ana said quietly.

"Don't you dare suggest I am being *unreasonable*," Leroy said. Flecks of spit came out of his mouth. Dan and Chester exchanged looks. "First things first. Hand over the bird."

"And then what?" Ellie asked. "We promise to never tell anyone about how you really got him?"

"Sure. You can promise. After you hand over the bird."

"I think the bird's our only collateral," Louise said. "You're not really making this work for us."

"Enough talking!" Jean suddenly cried. "They can't get all four of us!"

And he rushed Leroy.

The puppies were right after him, unsure what the game was but desperate to join in.

Leroy looked genuinely surprised, as if he hadn't the slightest idea that the situation could turn this way. He was the hero, for heaven's sake, with a gun, holding the unwashed at bay, getting back what was rightfully his—and giving really good speeches at the same time. It took him a dangerous second to regroup himself.

Diana was faster. She raised her stupid little gun, with her finger on the trigger.

"No!"

Ana threw herself at the starlet.

Reacting far faster than Ellie would have given her credit for, Diana immediately pivoted and thrust her knife at the naturalist. Ana let out a guttural scream as the blade sank into her thigh.

"Ana!" Ellie cried.

Louise didn't waste any time; she took her pack and slammed it into the head of the person standing closest to her. It was Lucy; the smaller woman fell backward with a fleshy thud.

Chester immediately grabbed Louise, wrapping her body in his much larger arms. Locked in the wrestler's hold, she struggled in vain; her hands (and bag) straitjacketed against her sides.

Jean was taking way too long to get up off the ground, stunned by the sight of Ana's collapsed, bleeding body.

Soda-Pop took this moment to add to the chaos: Chirping and shrieking, he clawed his way out of Ellie's pocket.

"Beep!" he cried triumphantly, fluttering into the air.

"There it is!" Leroy cried. "Get it!"

"Run!" Ellie screamed at Soda-Pop. *"Fly!"*

The little bird did his best, bobbling desperately but imperfectly off into the jungle.

"I'm going after it—the rest of you, take care of the others!" Leroy shouted, running off after Soda-Pop.

Lucy staggered to her feet and gave Jean, who was just getting up, a solid kick in the chest. He gagged, coughed, and fell back to the ground.

Louise bit down hard on her attacker's arm. It didn't seem like it could do much through Chester's shirt and jacket, but he let out a scream and dropped her.

Diana, looking a little wild, raised her gun again.

"*Don't*, you asesina!" Ana hissed from the ground.

"Shut up, you," Dan said, shaking his gun at her. "Stay still and no one gets hurt. More, I mean. Diana, stop playing with your toy—you're going to get one of us killed. You there, McGill, come over here so we can tie you and the others up."

But Ellie turned and ran into the woods.

"Chester!!" Dan barked.

"On it!" Chester said, running after her.

She tried to move like something being chased by a predator—like a rabbit or a gazelle. Zigzags, random turns, giant leaps over rocks and brush . . . anything to avoid being captured. But she also had to keep Leroy in her sights. He had a good start but made *so much noise* crashing through the woods that it wasn't difficult to follow. *Go, Soda-Pop!* she thought. *Go!*

She could hear Chester catching up behind her and tried to increase her speed, but she was going all out, and his legs were much, much longer than hers. Did he have a gun? She couldn't remember. He wasn't ordering her to do anything, shouting anything. Just chasing her while she chased Leroy, who chased Soda-Pop . . .

Imagining the strange line of hunted and hunters they made in the woods might have distracted her concentration the tiniest bit; at that moment, Chester launched himself at her.

It felt like a thousand fleshy pounds smashed into the small of her back. His body's impact with hers and her own momentum caused Ellie to fall forward over her own legs and roll into a thicket. She sprawled to a stop in a bush, legs tangled in vines. She began to kick and struggle randomly, desperately, trying to fight her way out before he could hurt her.

"DON'T."

Chester rose up above her like a giant. He knelt and put a hand on her right shoulder to hold her down.

"Don't get up," he ordered. "Hide here, then run *away*."

She thought she saw something like concern or pity in his brown eyes, but it was hard to tell; the wound over her own eye had opened up again and blood was blurring her vision.

And it didn't matter.

"Soda-Pop, my friends—" she protested, and tried to roll out of his grasp.

Chester let out a huff and pulled some rope out of his pocket with his left hand. Working awkwardly but swiftly, he soon had her ankle tied to the tree. Even in her current state Ellie couldn't help admiring his ability. Maybe he was an Outdoor Scout . . .

"You won't listen to common sense, so this should hold you until it's safe. And believe you me, it's *not* safe for you to be around Leroy and his guns. Uh, and Diana and her gun. This is serious. He will not stop. Once he's got his mind set on something he's like an automaton. And he doesn't let anything get in his way. Not even a kid."

She opened her mouth to scream, to deliver a scathing insult, to retort—but he put a finger to his lips.

Then he left.

"Come back here, you!" he shouted into the woods. "Kid! Get back here!"

Ellie didn't bother waiting for him to be gone; as soon as his back was turned she immediately got herself into a more upright, crouched-over position and tested the rope. But it was tied with an arbor knot, which only cinched tighter the more pressure she put on it. Chester *definitely* must have been an Outdoor Guide.

She had dropped her pack—which had her knife, with her portion of the kitchen gear—in the clearing when she ran, but she still had Leroy's little satchel. Unfortunately, now all it had was the logbook (and Louise's picture), a dirty handkerchief, a cashmere muffler, and a flask. Nothing with a sharp edge.

A gunshot rang out somewhere deep in the forest.

And Ellie, alone and bleeding, frustrated and trapped, exhausted and aching, curled into a ball and wept.

She didn't cry for very long. Too many people depended on her.

She sobbed just until she felt the tranquility and release that sometimes only a good cry can bring on.

Then she took one deep gulp of air and another; when she was breathing steadily again, Ellie searched around as far as the rope would let her. There were no sharp stones or brittle bones (or broken bottles, or handily dropped razor blades, as there always were in the movies), but there *was* one of those pochote trees growing at the very edge of her reach, its trunk dotted with giant thorns like the one that had punctured her leg. It took some gymnastic maneuvering to get into the right position, but she finally managed to insert the tip of one thorn into the braiding of the rope. Then she pulled her foot back and forth, like a saw, moving the rope over and through the spine. One or two fibers broke every other pass.

It was long, boring, meticulous, tedious work. The rope often popped off the thorn's tip and then Ellie had to correctly reposition herself to get it back on, which always resulted in leg and foot cramps that needed to be waited out before she could start again. This was exactly the sort of thing she hated at school: pointless busywork, like sewing seams no one will ever see in home economics or writing down the multiplication tables a hundred times if you got them wrong once. Hateful.

But if she didn't . . .

Soda-Pop . . .

Ana . . . Louise . . . Jean . . .

She recited their names over and over as she sawed and repositioned and sawed again.

She screamed when some rope finally tore away *but not quite enough* to let her break it entirely.

Finally it snapped and Ellie went tumbling onto her backside.

She forced herself to stand up immediately (titan beetles, lemon ants, land leeches, etc.). Then continued to stand there for a moment to collect herself.

She was free. Now what?

Soda-Pop was gone; Leroy had disappeared into the brush after him. If she followed, there was a chance it wouldn't even matter, because Soda-Pop might have flown off, safe.

Also, Leroy had a gun. What Chester had said felt true: He was *not* a safe person to be around, with or without guns. She wasn't sure what she could do if she had to face him.

And on the other hand, Ana had seemed badly wounded, bleeding and unable to get up. Jean and Louise had still been fighting with the rest of Leroy's gang when Ellie had fled the scene to try to save Soda-Pop.

The only thing to do was go back and try to find them, free them if they were caught, and figure out what to do next once they were all together and safe.

She ran through the brush, following her own trail back almost without thinking about it. There was the rock she had darted around, there was the branch she had snapped, just like Ana had shown her the locals did to mark their way. Her feet, considered so petite back home, had made deep heel thrust marks in the ground where it was soft. She apologized to a leafcutter ant trail, the workers resolutely trying to reconnect ends of their path where someone else's much larger foot (probably Leroy's) had demolished it.

"Well, at least I got to see wild leafcutter ants," she muttered to herself.

When she finally arrived in the clearing where Leroy had confronted her, she was shocked. The place was a *mess*. Their packs and their contents were strewn around, trod on, ground underfoot. Ellie winced at the garbage humans seemed to make everywhere.

Something—or someone—let out a terrifying groan.

Lying against a fallen log was Ana, white-faced and sweating.

"Are you all right?" Ellie ran over to her. "Where are the others?"

"Eh, I may live. Three of those thugs took Louise and Jean—I guess they figured I couldn't do much harm here, bleeding."

The woman's wide pant leg was soaked in blood around her thigh; she had unsuccessfully tried to bandage it with a strip of cloth from her shirt, but her right hand was curled into a painful claw, obviously unusable.

"It's not as bad as it looks," Ana said, seeing Ellie's face. "The knife didn't hit anything vital—well, beyond an artery or something. I broke my thumb when I fell. So stupid, really."

"All right. I can fix *some* of this."

Ellie's Outdoor Guide training took over; here was something immediate and real she could deal with. And wasn't it fitting to use Leroy's fancy monogrammed cashmere scarf as a bandage? Ellie carefully cleaned the area around the wound with what little alcohol was left in the flask and then searched around the mess of their packs for another canteen. She found Louise's, a shiny new one obviously bought in anticipation of the trip. There was just enough water left to get most of the dirt and muck out of the wound; maybe it was clean enough to remain uninfected until they got to a doctor or another one of the forest's "magic" healing trees.

When it was as clean as it was going to get, Ellie tied the muffler as neatly and tightly as she could around Ana's leg. Then she looked around for an appropriately shaped stick and set to splinting her thumb.

"You're a real professional at this. A bush doctor," the other woman said with admiration. "You should consider that as a job if the zoo doesn't work out. I tried to convince Jean it would be a better path for him if he was so interested in helping people—there are plenty of people out in the woods who could use medicine."

"He doesn't like doctors," Ellie pointed out. "Hang on—this is going to hurt—"

She pulled Ana's thumb straight to align it with the stick she had found. Ana gasped and bit her lip.

"You know," Ellie kept talking, to distract her patient, "all you ever do is talk badly about Jean. Always with disappointment. So why on earth did you try to take a bullet for him? What made you do that?"

Ana looked at her in shock. "Ellie, he's my *son*. What mother *wouldn't*?"

Ellie stopped in the middle of winding the strip of fabric around the stick and Ana's thumb.

"Um, what?"

"You didn't know?"

"*HOW COULD I HAVE?* No one ever said anything!"

Suddenly everything from the last two days made a whole lot more sense. Of course she hadn't been able to work out the strange relationship between the older woman and the younger man! And he had said his father was an artist . . . Ana *also* said her husband was an artist. But that meant Jean's father was German . . . but he identified with the native people . . . but Jean didn't seem to like Ana . . . but . . .

"But neither one of you said anything," Ellie said again, frustrated. "You guys acted so strangely around each other but never said why."

Ana sighed. "Eh, it was stupid. We had a big falling-out a few months ago—as one does with teens who think they are fully adults. He thought I had embarrassed him, made him look like a child—*my* child—in front of some men he worked with.

"I promised that going forward in professional situations I wouldn't, *we* wouldn't . . . make a big deal of who we were to each other. The jungle is large, but also very small. Word gets around, you know."

"What did you do? What could be so bad?" Ellie couldn't help asking.

Ana rolled her eyes. "*Nothing.* I just pointed out he was wrong about something he was saying . . . I would have done that with anyone; it wasn't just because I was his mom. I don't know if you have noticed, but Jean gets *very* touchy when he's told he's wrong . . . there's no nice way to correct him."

"Well, that's very true."

"And then right after that maybe I licked my finger to get a piece of schmutz off his cheek."

Ellie blanched. Yup. That would utterly destroy anyone, including herself. She imagined her mom doing it to her in front of her older USO friends, or Dr. Hua and Margaret, or really *anyone* at the zoo.

"Yeah, um, it all makes a little more sense now. But I'm not a 'professional'? I just dropped into your life. You two could have told me."

"Sorry, I thought it was obvious, him and me," Ana said with a moue. "Or Louise would have told you. And you might not be 'professional,' but you definitely fall into the category of 'personal'—very personal—another place where mothers aren't always welcome."

"And yet you still warned me about him being a lady-killer."

"I'm a woman as well as a mother," Ana said with a smile. "And I was a girl once. I love Jean, but if I had a daughter I would warn her against boys like him. He's not a murderer or a thief—he's good, don't misunderstand me. Just don't go into anything with your eyes shut. He's young and not looking for love or a commitment, if you know what I mean."

"Um, thank you. I guess."

"Especially if you have complications back home," Ana added.

"All right," Ellie interrupted. "I'm done. I don't know much about thumbs—they're more complicated than fingers and toes—but that should hold it straight until you can get to a real doctor."

"Excellently done," Ana said. "All I need is an aspirin now and I'm good to go."

"But go where? We don't even . . ."

"Mom? Ana?"

Jean came wandering out of the woods, looking a bit like Soda-Pop on his worse days: If he had a crest, it would have had broken feathers and been slumping down over his eyes. His hair was too short and thick to do that, but his face was haggard and there were shadows under his eyes.

Ana pushed herself up with Ellie's help, launched herself at her son, and squeezed him tight. Jean looked anxiously over at Ellie—

"It's okay, she knows, boychick," Ana murmured.

—and he then slumped in relief, hugging his mother back.

"You escaped," Ellie said after the mother and son had detached.

"Escaped?" Jean looked confused for a moment, then shook his head. "No, they didn't want me. They made me close my eyes and count to thirty, at gunpoint, while they left. Then I followed them. Apparently they have no plans to do anything to Mom and me—we're locals. We're not going to go back to the States with wild tales of stolen birds and millionaire explorers or whatever. But Louise . . . They took her to their camp, where all the planes are parked, and tied her up. Then that big guy showed up again later. He said that he lost you in the woods—I was so relieved!"

"He didn't lose me in the woods—he tied me up and then pretended not to find me. Not the worst of the lot, I guess."

"And what about Louise?" Ana asked anxiously. "What are they going to do with her?"

"They were discussing that when I left. They're not sure what to do about her. But Ellie and Louise are . . . a problem. They said that at the very least they shouldn't be allowed to return home anytime soon. They'll make a final decision when Leroy returns."

All three were silent for a moment, processing this information.

"Well, Jean, these lunatics are only a problem," Ana eventually said, "because *you led them straight to us*!"

And then she let off a string of rapid-fire, furious Spanish.

Jean shouted back defensively, also in Spanish.

Ellie was also angry and had questions of her own—which Ana was probably asking/demanding as well, but who could tell. Soda-Pop might be in Leroy's hands, Ana was wounded, Louise had been kidnapped . . . and it was all because of Jean. How had he, such a self-proclaimed expert in the jungle, let a bunch of loud (and rich) North Americans *follow* him? All the way—and directly—to their location?

Carl wouldn't have done . . . any of it. He wouldn't have thought it necessary to lead the planes astray, or if he did, he wouldn't have gone off and done it without discussing the plan with the other people in the party first. He would have listened to Ana and Louise. He certainly would have stopped and made sure he wasn't being followed if he *had* drawn Leroy's attention away. That was like introductory lesson one for escaping the enemy from any war movie.

Jean just moved from one idea he decided was brilliant to the next idea he thought was brilliant without considering the ramifications, the alternatives, or the intelligence of his decisions.

"*GUYS*. This is really bad," Ellie said loudly, interrupting the shouting mother and son.

Jean stopped; Ana trailed off with one last invective.

"Jean, you really bungled things up—" Ellie continued.

"I didn't! I—"

"But we don't have time for that right now. We need to get Ana help, and we need to go rescue Soda-Pop and Louise."

"There's a group of people that still lives somewhere nearby, isn't there, Jean?" Ana asked. "That didn't go south?"

"Yeah, let me go get them, they would be more than happy to help the woman scientist—" Jean started to go.

"WAIT!" Ellie barked. "We are *not* done talking. You go, you tell them where Ana is, *and you come back here*—can you do that in two hours or less?"

"Sure. Even faster if they hear my whistle earlier."

"All right. After you talk to them you come. Straight.

Back. Then you and I will see about rescuing Louise and finding Leroy and Soda-Pop."

"You don't get to order me—"

"Yes, I do," Ellie interrupted. "You have botched up everything every time you go off on your own. Leading the planes away, leading the bad guys straight to us, randomly throwing yourself at them and getting your mother stabbed in the leg. Yeah, that was you too, Jean. Until things start looking up you will do exactly what I say—or what everyone together decides on. We clear?"

"Well, aye, aye, sir, captain, *sir*," Jean growled.

But then he twirled around and ran off down the trail as fast as he could.

Ellie carefully lowered herself and Ana down so they were both sitting up against the log. There was literally nothing to do for the next two hours, and for once in her life she didn't feel like talking or jumping up and fiddling with something or planning anything. Her mind was an exhausted blank.

Except . . . for one little, nagging thought.

"In the end, it's not *really* Jean's fault, though," she said slowly.

Ana rolled her eyes. "Please don't tell me you—"

"No, listen: I got you guys all involved in this in the first place," Ellie said, taking a deep breath. "If I hadn't decided to fly a plane into a mountain in Venezuela, you and Louise would still be fighting about the puppies, not bleeding and running around the jungle and . . ."

"That's true," Ana said with a shrug. "My life would have been so much easier just guiding a cartographer and her ridiculous pets around the forest. But you didn't bring the *guns,* Ellie. You didn't kidnap an innocent woman. You didn't decide it was worth it to chase a crazy teenager around the globe for a little purple bird and then threaten everyone with her. You chose a path and everyone else chose theirs, and theirs was violent and stupid."

She put a hand awkwardly on Ellie's shoulder, wincing from the pain. Ellie almost began to cry: here this woman was, bandaged and bleeding, comforting *her.*

"Thank you," Ellie mumbled. "I'm still sorry I got you into this."

"Thank you. But I forgive you," Ana said with a wry smile, and gave her shoulder another pat before settling back wearily against the log.

They were both silent for a while, listening to the sounds of the jungle.

"Is some sort of insect or fungus going to eat into our pants while we sit here?" Ellie eventually asked.

"No, querida. I mean, probably not. Land leeches—"

Ellie held up her hand and shook her head. *Forget it.*

And they both fell quiet again, waiting.

TWENTY-TWO

Just a few minutes shy of two hours later Jean reappeared, puffing hard, having apparently run at top speed both ways. A girl of indeterminate age was with him; she had thick black hair pulled back with a woven thong and wore a simple white shift.

"This is Cahpeah," Jean said. "She'll stay here until others come with a sledge to pull you on."

"I can walk," Ana protested.

"No, you can't," Ellie and Jean said at the same time.

They suddenly were back on the same page again; maybe everything would be all right.

"We'll see you back at their place after we have sorted this all out and gotten Soda-Pop and Louise back," Jean promised, taking his mother's hands in his.

And now suddenly Ellie was irritated again. Whose plan was it, anyway? Whose fault was it they were gone?

Cahpeah said something to Jean in a language that was neither Spanish nor English, and Jean thanked her, and then it was just him and Ellie walking through the woods.

"Do you have any water?" he asked after a bit.

"No, I used all mine up on cleaning your mother's wounds."

"Ah, too bad."

"You never mentioned she was your mother—"

"We had an agreement," he said shortly, and they fell silent again.

How did you restart a conversation that had begun in anger, with someone you were walking next to and whose help you had to rely on for an undertaking of serious potential danger? If Ellie kept walking without saying anything, she would explode.

"Well . . ." she finally began. "Aren't you going to apologize?"

Jean looked genuinely surprised. "For what?"

"For—" Ellie stopped walking, also surprised. "For . . . leading Leroy directly to us? And Soda-Pop?"

"I didn't know he was going to *follow* me," he said carelessly. "How could I have known something like that?"

"Are you serious? You didn't think it was a possibility?

You didn't imagine it *might* happen, and take precautions against it?"

"Ellie, how could I predict something like that?" he demanded, repeating himself. "I did what needed to be done. Things didn't turn out perfectly. That's life."

"You *didn't* do 'what had to be done.' Running around with your shirt off didn't 'have to be done.' You—*we*—*our*—only need was to avoid Leroy until Soda-Pop could take off on his own. And I could get home. The dramatics, the hero act, was not necessary."

He rolled his eyes. "Now you're just parroting Ana."

"You mean *your mother*? And no, I am not parroting her—although it turns out she was right about everything," she added, partly to herself. She replayed Old-Ellie calling him a hero and defending him to Ana, and mentally blushed. And Old-Ellie was only a day old! "You lack basic sense. You're like a . . . valor-seeking idiot."

"Do *not* talk to me like that!" Jean snapped. "You women were too afraid, too slow to figure out what to do. You weren't willing to take a risk. You never are. It took me to act or you would still be sniveling, hiding in the woods somewhere."

Ellie felt like she had just been slapped. He sounded like Leroy! Was this the way all men—boys—really were? Once you confronted them, once you made them face the ugly truth about themselves? Did they always turn it around and make it all about you, about how women were terrible?

No, not all boys, of course.

Not Carl.

She thought about all their fights, especially the one at the aerodrome, after her ride on the flight simulator: the way he argued *for* himself and not *against* her, how he didn't attack her.

What Jean was doing was not the way good and reasonable men acted. This was the way creeps, monsters, cowards, and idiots did.

"Horse-hooey," Ellie said flatly. "It was a rash and bad decision—"

"I cannot even *listen* to this . . ."

"—which you made on your own, and then carried out on your own, and it resulted in this, a far worse situation than we were in before."

"Worse? Who knows if—"

"Jean, shut up. No one had been *stabbed* or *kidnapped* before you made the decision to act for the group. If anything happens to Louise before we get to her, or your mom dies, it will be *your fault*. Your fault. Their lives. Your fault."

Jean said nothing. In fact, he stayed blessedly silent for the rest of their journey.

* * *

Eventually Jean put his finger to his lips and they slowed, walking carefully to not make any noise. He gently pulled aside a branch for her to look.

(Ellie hated herself for being relieved, but she *was* glad that however bad their fight was, it was forgotten or forgiven in the spirit of saving the day.)

All four planes were parked together now in a clearing that opened out into the grasslands. (One was pitted and dented—it had definitely seen combat, and better days. That must have been the backup Leroy had to take.) They were set in a sort of protective circle, the way wagons were pulled up for the night in the Old West. In the middle was a smoking firepit, supplies unpacked and spread out on tarps around it, little camp chairs in metal and canvas unfolded and assembled. Two tents were set up across from this—one for girls, one for boys, maybe?

And there was Louise, sitting on the ground, tied to a stump that had been a tree not that long ago. At least she had her puppies: they snuggled at her feet as if there were nothing wrong. The woman looked a little banged up and tired but otherwise none the worse for wear. Chester sat easily in a chair near her, reading the paper. Dan also sat, farther away, methodically and neatly cleaning his gun, using a soft rag to wipe out any grit. Lucy was crouched under her plane, tinkering with the landing gear.

Diana stuck her head out of one of the tents.

"Any of you have an extra nail file?" she asked.

"Yes, I packed it with my polish and manicure set," Chester answered, flipping a page.

"I have a metal file in my tool kit," Lucy called back from under the plane. "For, you know, metal."

"None of you are funny," Diana said with a pout, and pulled back into the tent.

"If I did have a nail file I certainly wouldn't file my nails *inside the tent*," Dan muttered, not looking up from his gun.

Ellie turned to Jean and whispered, enunciating very clearly: "Is Leroy back yet? Did you see him return? Is he in the other tent?"

Jean shook his head and shrugged. "No idea. But he's a *very* loud man—I think we would know if he was back, and did or didn't have Soda-Pop."

This was true. Ellie carefully let the branch go and they withdrew into the woods to talk.

"Okay, there's at least four of them, maybe five, and three of them have guns," she said, thinking.

"I'll distract them!" Jean said, looking determined. "I'll draw their fire while you release Louise!"

"No, Jean," Ellie said, slapping a hand to her forehead. "Do you even hear yourself? Is that all you do? Offer

yourself up as a distraction? You just rush in without thinking, one idea in your head that you think will fix everything—oh, wait, I see it now." She cocked her head at the sudden realization. "Exactly what Carl and Margaret were getting at with me. Rushing in without seriously considering alternatives. Yup, they were one hundred percent right.

"Anyway, Jean, that's . . . pure chaos. And the numbers aren't in our favor. We need to be clever about this, not just rush in and hope it all works out.

"Because often it doesn't!"

She hissed this last part, trying to keep from yelling.

Jean at least had the decency to look chagrined.

"We'll get rid of as many as we can before trying to untie Louise," she went on, a little more calmly. "Lure them away, bop them on the head, one at a time. Tie them up. I don't know—you're in charge of the bopping. And then the tying up with vines or whatever. You can do that, right, with vines?"

"Can I 'tie things up with vines' . . . ?"

"Great, that's you then. I'll bring 'em in here."

"And how, oh genius Ellie, do you plan on doing that?"

"By using my genius brain."

And a whole lot of luck, she added silently.

***

Chester had just finished the Arts & Entertainment section and the crossword *in pen* when he heard the cry.

"Ka-*kaw*! Ka-*kaw*!"

"Say, Dan," he said, sitting up in his chair, "did you hear that?"

"Another damn jungle animal. At least this one speaks clearly." His friend sighed happily, admiring his disassembled pistol. "You know, I never thought I'd get into the whole 'gun' thing. But I like the craftsmanship. They're like watches."

"Dan, please focus. I don't think that was an animal. That sounded exactly like the *here I am* or *danger* call from Outdoor Guides!"

"From a bird?" Dan asked in confusion.

"No, from a person, you ninny. It's a way to track another lost Outdoor Guide. It just *sounds* like a bird. Was Leroy an Outdoor Guide, do you know? I'll bet he was, when he was a kid."

"Haven't the faintest."

"Ka-*kaw* ka-*kaw*!"

"I'll bet that *is* him! Probably having trouble with that bird of his or finding his way back or something. Watch Louise, will you?"

"My revolver isn't reassembled!"

"I don't even have one. You don't need a gun to watch a tied-up captive."

Dan made a dismissive noise and waved his hands at Chester to go.

"Ka-*kaw*!" Chester shouted eagerly as he walked into the bush. He put his hands around his mouth to make it louder. "Ka-*kaw*!"

Thump.

Ellie helped Jean tie up Chester, to make sure he was doing it right. He might have been a local, but he *wasn't* an Outdoor Guide. She felt a little bad; Chester was definitely nicer than the others. Or at least he recognized the insanity of threatening teenagers with guns. Still, he had gone along with all of Leroy's crazy plans. She wondered if every rich person was like this; law-abiding in their own countries or where there were people and cameras watching them, and then acting like there were no laws anywhere else.

"Okay, we're down to just three—Diana, Lucy, Dan. Things are definitely more in our favor—as long as we keep an ear out for Leroy."

"Ka-kaw," Jean said, rolling his eyes.

Lucy finally got out from under her plane, face covered in grease, groaning as she stretched out her arms and legs.

"Getting too old for this," she muttered. "I need a squire, a young man, to do all the bending and grease work for me."

A monkey screamed from the jungle somewhere.

Another monkey answered.

Then the creepy jungle fell silent.

Lucy wiped her wrench off on her coveralls.

A rotten piece of fruit suddenly came flying out of the woods. It *splatted* all over her nice clean windshield. The flesh was puky orange brown and the smell was indescribable.

"What the green inferno?!" Lucy demanded.

A chorus of monkeys—or at least two (or at least two primates)—chattered and made imbecilic simian screams, laughing at her from their hiding places.

"Go away!" Lucy screamed back, showing her own teeth in a display of hominid rage. She waved her wrench at the invisible bullies. "I'll brain you!"

Another piece of fruit came arcing out of the darkness, once again landing *splat* on the windshield, coating it in sticky, stinky goo. It dripped and slid in an organically repulsive way down the glass.

"You bastards! I just cleaned that! It's like you *know*! Fine, you asked for it!"

Lucy ran into the woods, swinging her wrench, spitting furious.

Thump.

"Lucy? Something wrong? Did you say something?" Dan asked, looking up from his gun but not seriously concerned.

Lucy responded unintelligibly from the other side of her plane.

"I don't speak swear words," Dan said primly, "or mumbles."

"I think she said 'Why don't you let that poor tired Black lady go,'" Louise filled in helpfully. She shifted her feet, which disturbed the baby-selfish puppies. Mutt gave a tiny growl at her in annoyance.

"You have no idea how much I would absolutely love to. This whole thing is a horrid mess. I don't know how we're going to clean it up stateside. I suppose you have family who would miss you?"

"*And an employer.* You're going to have all of the NAACP after you for what you've done!"

"Ouch. Very messy," he said with a sigh, going back to polishing his pistol.

***

Of course it was Ellie making "muffled Lucy noises" to answer Dan. She had moved closer in, hiding behind Lucy's plane. But now she had two problems: Dan wasn't moving from his chair, and Diana wasn't leaving the tent.

"Can I get some water?" Louise asked, weirdly loudly.

"Not until Chester or Leroy comes back to relieve me."

"What about that *other girl*, in the *tent*?" Again, very weirdly loudly.

Suddenly Ellie got it. Clever Louise! It was like she knew something was going on! She wasn't sure what, but had picked up on something that Dan hadn't: the thumps, the highly unrealistic animal and bird noises. The slow disappearance of her captors.

Maybe it was just hope that she was getting rescued.

"Oh, believe me, you don't want that crazy dame with a gun guarding you. You're far safer with me."

"What about—"

"Why don't you just pipe down for a bit? You can have your water soon enough."

Soon enough Dan would begin to worry about Chester, though, and wonder where Lucy had gone off to. It was now or never.

Ellie found a giant, club-shaped piece of wood and slipped into the tent. Diana was kneeling on a mat on the ground, trying very carefully to use the hunting knife to pare her nails.

"Hey, Lucy, honey, will you hand me that . . ." Diana began—then saw who it was.

Ellie leapt at her, swinging the club high to bring it down on the other woman . . . but then Diana did something totally unexpected: she grabbed the gun that was on the mat next to her and aimed it at Ellie's stomach.

There was no way even that ridiculous little pistol could miss so close. Ellie had to admire Diana's reaction and speed; it was not at all what she would have expected from the pretty, vacuous-seeming dilettante.

"See? Never judge a person by their looks," Mind-Mom chastised.

"Later? Please?!" Ellie mentally begged.

"You're going to get indicted for kidnapping, at least," she said aloud, raising her hands up peacefully. "Maybe murder. Do you really want those headlines? That prison time?"

"This place is so far off the map it doesn't even matter what we do," the other woman said with a very unglamorous cackle. "And if we get caught down here, they're not going to extradite us. I mean, they could try, but we'd pay everyone off."

"Why are you even doing this?" Ellie asked, desperate

but also genuinely curious. "This is insane! And it has nothing to do with you!"

"The trips to other countries and getting zoo animals were fun," Diana said with a shrug. "This other stuff isn't what I signed up for . . . but it's kind of fun, too. Definitely not boring."

Ellie was about to try another tactic—begging seemed the most useful—when Diana shouted:

"Chester! *DAN!* We got an intruder here!"

Once again Ellie was surprised by the starlet's quick thinking. She wasn't going to give the girl a chance to find an opening or talk her down.

"But—the woman—the gun—" Dan spluttered, clearly piqued. There was a thump as he obviously jumped up from his chair, knocking it over, and went racing over to the tent. Then there was another, heavier thump as something knocked him over the head. Then a third, final thump as his body hit the ground.

Well! Jean finally did something right for once! And of his own accord.

And then he came into the tent, throwing the flap door wide open in triumph.

"Ellie, I got him! Now we only have . . ."

"The girl with the gun," Ellie said with a sigh. Jean was

nothing if not inevitably disappointing. "Who has you in her sights as well."

"Oooh, 'the Girl with the Gun,' I like that," Diana said, giggling. "That's a great name for a movie. I'll pitch it. Both of you, on your knees. Now."

"Don't worry," Jean whispered to Ellie. *"I've got this."*

"No. Nope. Not even. Don't you dare, Jean . . ."

"Querida," he cooed at Diana.

"Oh *no*," Ellie groaned.

His hand went to the collar of his shirt; maybe he had forgotten he was no longer wearing the one with buttons. He wound up just adjusting the material, pulling it down.

"Are you a movie star?" he asked, slinking forward.

"Well, yeah, sure," Diana said. "Sometimes."

"I knew it immediately. You are, without a doubt, the single most beautiful woman who has ever graced our jungle with her presence."

"Aw—you flatterer," she simpered—and might have actually blushed.

Jean drew closer to her slowly, like he was approaching a cornered wild animal.

Ellie immediately hated herself for thinking of that metaphor. It didn't do animals justice.

"What is such a pretty lady doing here among these thieves?" he purred. "I think you got tangled up in something very complicated."

"It's just a bit of fun." She tilted her head, made a sort of *aw-shucks* look. "Nothing serious."

"Let's talk, querida," he suggested, moving closer. "You and I—I'll bet we could find some common ground . . ."

"You're absolutely adorable," Diana said, raising her gun to point directly at his heart. "*You're* the one who should be in pictures. With that body and smile. Back up, please."

Ellie sighed as Jean stumbled back, hands raised in supplication. He seemed genuinely shocked that his plan hadn't worked.

"Oh, you guys are in *trou*-ble," Diana sang. "When Leroy gets back, he is going to be furious. I hope he has that dumb bird. Otherwise he's going to be *really* impossible. You shoulda seen him the first time we came to Venezuela."

That froze Ellie's brain for a moment. All this time she had been worried about Soda-Pop and herself . . . but had anything like this happened before? Had Leroy threatened—or actually hurt—other people? She remembered the giant iguana that was too happy and slow to be anything but a pet. How had Leroy acquired it?

Never mind that now. He would be back any second. It

was bad enough dealing with one trigger-happy kook with a gun—but two would be impossible.

Maybe—sadly—it was actually time for a classic Jean move.

"Now," Ellie said, almost casually.

"Now?" Jean asked, confused.

"Now *what*?" Diana demanded. "Don't you—"

A Jean *move*, but not one made by Jean: Ellie threw herself at the other woman. At her legs, specifically; hopefully below the path of any potential bullet.

Diana immediately fired.

Ellie connected with the woman's knees. It didn't bring her down but threw her off balance; the shot went through the roof of the tent, singeing the cotton.

That's one, Ellie thought. How many were in the revolver's chamber? This, in the movies, was where the hero (or villain) would count and keep track.

Because Diana was nothing if not persistent; she just kept firing.

Ellie's ears couldn't recover between each blast. Two . . . three . . . four . . .

Jean somehow avoided her wildly aimed shots and grabbed her around the torso.

She fired once again; the bullet went straight down into

the ground past Ellie. She could feel the heat as it burned by her face. *Five . . .*

"Cut it out, you lunatic!" Jean swore, sounding exactly like his mother. "Do you want to get *yourself* killed?"

"Let go of me!" Diana yelled. "Get off!"

Ellie pried the gun out of the woman's twitchy hand. When it hit the dirt she kicked it as far away as she could.

"I can't believe you're the hardest one to deal with," she muttered. She found a pale silk scarf lying across Diana's duffel bag like the instar of some exotic butterfly. The nicest thing about silk—besides its softness—was how strong it was. Protein fibers, like spider web and silkworm silk, were much superior to cotton and linen that way. Perfect for tying someone up. When Ellie was done, she and Jean pushed Diana out of the tent.

"Put her with the others," Ellie told him without thinking.

Then she thought about how that sounded.

"How do you like that?" she asked Diana. "Being treated like that? 'Put her with the others'? How does it feel being on the other side of power, without your stupid gun?"

"You'll never get away with this," Diana huffed, quoting any one of a thousand different movies.

"Really? I was told that what happens in the jungles of Venezuela stays there, and extradition is easily avoidable."

Ellie heard all sorts of voices in her head yelling at her for gloating, for feeling as gleeful as a bad guy. Even her so far quiet Mind-Dad shook his head in disapproval.

But couldn't she have a win, just this once?

"Hey!" Louise shouted. "That you, Ellie? Can you be a bit quicker with your comeuppance speech and get me untied?"

"Coming!" she shouted back. "Okay, Jean, I'll get Louise. You take Diana. I don't know how much time we have before Leroy returns—"

"*Chester? Dan?* I heard shots! What's going on?"

Leroy had to show up right then, of course.

Jean quickly dragged Diana into the woods. Ellie snuck behind a plane and crouched down.

"Where is everyone?" Leroy K. Reardon (the Third) barged into the clearing, stomping and shouting. He had *two* guns out, and a bulge over the left side of his chest as if there were a third hidden there.

"I think they went to go get a Coca-Cola," Louise said pertly. "I prefer grape Nehi myself, but I don't know if you can get it down here. They said they'd ask."

"Shut up, damn you. What did you see? Who fired shots?"

Mutt and Jeff did *not* like his tone. They pushed back up against Louise's feet for safety, giving tiny growls.

"I did not *see* anyone fire a gun," Louise said clearly—and truthfully. "I heard a couple shots ring out over there, behind that plane." She indicated, with her chin, the plane that was farthest from the tent.

"I'll bet Chester found that girl," Leroy muttered. "I bet that girl came back to try and rescue you or something. I bet they're struggling with her and her boyfriend—or their indigenous friends."

"Well, if it's all over, might as well let me go," Louise suggested.

"Actually, as long as no one is around, I may as well *tie up loose ends*," Leroy said, leveling the revolver in his right hand at her head. "With no one around, no one will 'see anyone fire a gun' *here*, either."

"No wait no wait no!"

Before she knew what she was doing, Ellie was running out and waving her hands. Who knew if Leroy was even being serious, if he actually possessed the capacity to murder anyone? But if there was even the slightest chance . . .

Leroy whirled around and trained both of his guns on her.

"You can't shoot Louise!" she growled—though she stopped where she was.

"Hurrah! That's right, you can't shoot Louise!" Louise crowed. Then she took a better look at the scene. "Um, is this . . . *it* for the rescue party?"

"Shut up," Leroy snapped, waving a gun vaguely back at her but not turning around. "Miss McGill, you have been a thorn in my side since the beginning."

He sounded put out—and *disappointed.*

Ellie couldn't help it: For just a second she saw her entire time at the zoo, past as well as future, disappearing, and felt disappointed, too.

But. There were more important things.

"Where's Soda-Pop?" she demanded.

"He's safe." It was strange the way he said it; a little defensively, pulling his chin back. "He's in my possession."

"He's not dead, is he?" Ellie howled, furious, moving closer and curling her fists in anger. Because, of course, she was angry.

But also: her screaming and over-the-top monkey-like behavior caused Leroy to react just like a primate would, mimicking his opponent. He came closer to *her* and loomed over her, looking as intimidating as possible.

So he was completely distracted from seeing Jean, who appeared in the background behind Louise like a shadow. Jean held up a knife, obviously showing it to Ellie, communicating his plan to stealthily free Louise.

Or so Ellie hoped. She *really* hoped he didn't intend to try to knife Leroy in the back.

"No, he is *not* dead," Leroy growled. "*He*—it—is in my

possession. He will come back to America and go on display with a golden plaque explaining how Charles Muntz himself gave him to me as a present, and there will be no Ellie McGill around to refute it."

"Just what exactly is your problem?" (She tried to ignore the "no Ellie McGill around" part of what he said.) "This is all *really* bananas. Nobody cares if Muntz gave you Soda-Pop or not. Not really. Why can't you just let him go?"

Jean silently made his way over to Louise—*really silently*, like he wasn't there at all. Everything else aside, the boy definitely had outside skills. He was almost given away by the puppies, who happily frolicked toward him, but the faint noises they made didn't distract Leroy at all.

"Of course they care." The zoo owner drew himself up frostily. "Everyone loves Muntz. Just like they'll love *me* someday."

"They might, and you might get a crowd when Soda-Pop is first displayed. But Leroy, people don't come to a zoo because someone did this or wrote that or donated a bird. . . . They come to see the *animals*. The animals they don't get to see at home every day. They come to see healthy, happy, exotic and regular animals, to watch them play, and be together in families . . . and to learn about them. Not about the people who donate them. If you actually spent any time in your own zoo, you would know that."

Jean very deliberately and firmly put his hand on Louise's shoulder and put a finger to his mouth; she jumped at the unexpected touch but immediately understood what was going on. She made herself as narrow and upright as possible to give the ropes as much slack as she could. Jean began cutting through them.

Leroy sneered. "Everything I have been doing is for *my own* zoo!"

"No, it's been for *you*. If you actually cared about doing things for your zoo you would build bigger, cleaner enclosures, improve the veterinary equipment and supplies, maybe not use the elephant paddock as your own personal airport . . ."

"I will not stand here and be lectured at by a girl. The bird is mine whether Muntz gave him to me or I found him myself. He's not yours. You can't just *take* him. You didn't spend thousands of dollars on planes and supplies and plan expeditions and find the right people and *you didn't get the bird*. I did. It's my bird."

Ellie almost took a step backward away from Leroy. How had she ever admired him? How had she never seen a *hint* of the person he really was, inside? He was arguing about Soda-Pop as if the bird was a ball and he was the rich kid on the playground claiming he would literally take his fancy ball and go home.

"My bird." He tapped his bulging left breast for emphasis.

The pocket there tapped back.

Or . . . *squiggled* back. Ellie stared at the bulge and realized that what had at first looked like one of Leroy's stupid monogrammed handkerchiefs balled up was actually one of Leroy's stupid handkerchiefs *carefully tied up* in a pouch containing something that was soft and alive.

Ellie glanced over at Louise and Jean, trying to keep the look as short as possible to not give them away. Louise was standing up, creakily—she probably ached terribly from being forced upright like that for hours—and the puppies were ecstatic as they all followed Jean back to the woods. A little too ecstatic.

"HE'S NOT YOUR BIRD," Ellie shrieked as loudly as she could.

Jean and Louise finally made it to the trees and disappeared into the shadows. Ellie continued shouting, just in case.

"He's his own bird! Let him go! And let me go! I won't tell anyone about your making up stuff about him and Muntz."

(Total lie. If she got out of this and back home she was telling everyone: her parents, reporters, everyone at the zoo, random people on the street.)

"You expect me to believe you?" Leroy scoffed (quite reasonably).

He patted down his pocket more; it was starting to be very agitated.

"Please just let me go," Ellie begged.

She had no idea what else to do. She was all out of angles, gimmicks, tricks. Louise was safe, Ana was safe, Jean was out of harm's way. That just left her and Soda-Pop and an absolutely unhinged man with two guns and little superego to control his id. "You can fire me, and I'll just go away, forever. . . ."

That was the wrong thing to say.

"Firing people does not make them go away forever. People like *MARGARET* do not go away forever," Leroy growled, using one hand to try to hold Soda-Pop quiet against his chest, keeping the gun in the other aimed at Ellie. "You and she were *always* scheming. You're like two sides of the same awful woman. Can't stand to see a real man doing things, making changes in the world. All you want is to take him down any way you can. You want to ruin me and make people laugh at me."

When he pulled the hammer back on his pistol the metallic *click* of it filled the clearing.

"No, you don't want to—" Ellie began.

But she had forgotten something important:

She was not alone.

Jean and Louise were not only safe, they were nearby and looking out for her.

An explosive *crack* echoed out like a bullet. A rock

smashed into one of the planes' windshields; birds flew up out of trees, terrified.

Leroy jumped around at the sound.

"What the—"

His twisting movement was the last straw for Soda-Pop.

"BEEP!"

The bird triumphantly exploded out of his pocket prison. Leroy slapped both hands (both still holding guns) to his now bird-free chest a second too late.

"Soda-Pop!" Ellie cried.

After tumbling to the ground, the purple bird shot straight up into the air, like a falcon's stoop in reverse.

"Get back here!" Leroy shouted.

"Soda! You're *flying*!" Ellie cried in delight. "You're really flying!"

Not perfectly, however, and not like a completely healthy, uninjured bird. Soda-Pop's victory flight ended as he fell back down, catching himself just a few feet above the ground. Trying desperately to recover, he flapped hard toward the woods, bobbling up and down as he relearned how to adjust his altitude with his newly growing in feathers.

Leroy growled and grabbed at the purple bird, but was clumsy with the two guns, just slapping at his tail feathers.

"Go, Soda!" Ellie yelled.

But apparently the bird was finally enraged by the big, clumsy predator trying to attack him.

He spun around and dove at Leroy's face.

And here was where his similarity to a real hummingbird came out: he lunged in, attacked, flew backward out of the way, and immediately swooped in again, making deadly jabs with his sharp beak at Leroy's cheeks. And eyes.

Leroy screamed, trying to cover his face with his hands. He dropped one of the guns.

It wasn't perfect, but the odds were suddenly doubled in Ellie's favor.

She ran over and gave Leroy as solid a kick in the kidneys as she could manage. *Thank you, Outdoor Guides' Defense Training for Young Ladies. Also, thank you, growing up among seven brothers and sisters and on playgrounds where there were no rich kids at all and fewer balls.*

Leroy doubled over in pain but didn't quite collapse. Soda-Pop didn't stop attacking, and neither did Ellie; she gave him another kick in exactly the same place.

This time Leroy *did* fall to the ground, curled up on his side. Ellie grabbed the remaining pistol out of his hand.

"It's over, Leroy," she said, enjoying the sound of the movie-clichéd words.

If only Diana were around to hear them too.

TWENTY-THREE

Louise and Jean came cautiously out of the woods, Mutt and Jeff bouncing around their feet like it was all part of a great game and they wanted to know what was next: More hiding? Seeking? Finding socks in the jungle? Ellie didn't want to take her eyes off Leroy—he was down, not out—but couldn't help grinning at the scene. Soda-Pop, satisfied that the nasty domesticated primate was no longer a threat, flew over to Ellie and landed on her shoulder, where he preened himself and made some self-satisfied burbling noises as if the entire happy ending were due to him.

"Ellie, taking charge of the situation!" Jean came over and picked up the other gun, pointing it at Leroy.

"Better get him tied up," Ellie suggested.

"*. . . with the others.* Yes, I know how this goes!" he said with a laugh.

"Make sure it's real tight," Louise suggested, rubbing her arms. "Maybe too tight."

"Did you see that rock I threw?" Jean mimed throwing the gun. "*Bam!* Look! So hard it broke the windshield."

"Yes, Jean, as always, you are amazing," Ellie said with a sigh—but also a smile.

"What now?" Louise asked.

"I think I'd better figure out how to get home before Leroy or any of the others do," Ellie said, a little reluctantly. "I was so worried about Soda-Pop that I didn't really realize how much serious danger I was in—how completely and utterly wrong about Leroy I was. I'll feel safer on American soil. Um, I mean United States soil."

"I don't know if any of these planes will take you that far with the fuel they have," Jean said doubtfully. "Especially the one whose windshield I hit."

"You don't have to make it all in one go," Louise pointed out. "You just need to make it out of Venezuela, where Leroy obviously knows the officials. Head north to Cuba or Puerto Rico."

Ellie looked doubtful. "I know Leroy's family has connections in Mexico and other places in Central America. . . ."

"Fine, then head west to Colombia—Cartagena, on the north coast. They just finished building a big international airport there. I'll bet someone hoping to get in good with the U.S. would take pity on a stranded citizen and ship you home."

"How did you know about Colombia's airport?" Jean asked curiously. "I mean, it's a big deal down here. But for someone in the United States to know?"

"I'm a *cartographer*, I make maps!" Louise said in exasperation. "About people *connecting* and traveling places! Haven't you been listening? *At all?*"

"He's not so good with that," Ellie said, handing him the other gun and pulling out her logbook to look at the atlas. "But he's really great at throwing rocks and making hot chocolate. Hmm . . . yeah, it looks like that will work, if there's enough fuel. All right."

She carefully lifted Soda-Pop off her shoulder and held him up, looking him straight in the eye.

"Soda-Pop, this is really it, this time. You can't come back with me. You belong here. You can stay with Jean and Ana if you want . . ."

"And *me*—until I get to see my petroglyphs, at least," Louise muttered.

". . . or return to your cave, which is what you *should* do, but no more plane flights for you, my birdie friend. Good luck. Finish healing."

And then she carefully set him on the branch of a tree.

He stayed there, beeping a little. Not sad, not angry, maybe not even happy; he was a bird, and this was just the way it was.

Ellie sighed.

And then Jean kissed her.

She jumped and just stopped herself from hitting *him* in the kidneys.

"What was *that* for?"

"Well, you kissed me when I came back, so I am kissing you goodbye," he said mischievously.

"You're a dope." She punched him—lightly—in the arm. "Say goodbye to your mom for me, will you?"

"I will. Bah—now I can't bring home any girl who doesn't measure up to the great Ellie."

"Darn straight. Goodbye, Louise!"

Louise handed her a piece of paper torn out of her sketchbook—it was a drawing of Ellie with Soda-Pop sitting on her shoulder. It also had Louise's address and telephone number. "Safe travels, Ellie. Look me up if you ever come to New York, would you?"

"Absolutely!" The drawing was minimal—just a few

lines—but precise; she had perfectly captured Ellie's smile and freckles and energy. She gave the cartographer a big hug. "I'd give you my phone number, but we don't have one."

"Oh. Child," Louise said in dismay.

"G'bye, Mutt! G'bye, Jeff!" She knelt down and snuggled the puppies to her chest. They obligingly covered her with drool and dirt.

Jean gave her a hand up into the cockpit of the best-looking single-seater plane. She didn't need the help but didn't feel like arguing about it. The instrument panel, which was still terrifying compared to a Cessna, was at the same time familiar, like an old, difficult friend.

"No fancy tricks," she whispered, as if it were a horse she were trying to gentle. "Just get me to the airport in Colombia, and then someone better than me, someone you deserve, can take you from there." Looking around revealed that there were no snacks in this plane, though there was a *very* nice camel hair coat folded very neatly. Dan's plane, of course. He was kind of short—maybe it would fit her. She wondered if he was the type of man who kept candy in his pockets. He seemed like a bag-of-licorice or butterscotch kind of guy.

She hadn't checked the tires or the brakes or any of the outside equipment; she was taking a gamble that the one

Lucy *hadn't* been working on was more functional. But everything seemed all right as she started the engine, and the fuel tanks were very nearly full. She wondered when they had refueled—it was probably at the airfield of the mythical Jesus; she almost felt bad about not having made it there. Well, maybe someday.

She made sure the mixture of air and fuel was set to "idle" and opened the throttle a little, pushed the propeller control forward, primed the engine. When it began to catch she quickly switched the mixture to "run."

It chugged and died. *Not* catching.

She took a deep breath and reset everything. Then she did it all again. On the third time, it caught.

Without breathing she adjusted the flaps, rudder, and elevator trim, and opened up the throttle further.

When it was going fast enough for her to begin to taxi, she slowly pulled out of the clearing, turning the plane around so Louise and Jean and the puppies (and Leroy) were behind her. Then she took a deep breath, pulled back on the stick, and took off into the deep blue sky.

The flight was glorious and smooth for the first half hour.

Ellie had just settled herself in for a good long—but not quite as long—haul, wondering how she would mark the time and not sleep, when the radio exploded into life.

"—Ellie—"

She jumped at hearing her name come whistling out of the tinny speaker, mechanical-sounding and full of distortion. But it was *not* Leroy this time.

"Hello?"

It was on a channel reserved for other aircraft: other members of a bombing run . . . or zoo expedition, in this case.

"Ellie—he's after you! We tried, sorry—he overpowered us—"

"Overpowered *Jean.*" That was Louise's voice, unmistakable despite the noise.

They must have been calling from one of the remaining planes. That was the only thing that made sense: Leroy somehow got free of Louise and Jean—or maybe some of his crew helped him; maybe they escaped from where they were tied up in the woods. Either way, an enraged Leroy must have grabbed a plane and taken off after Ellie . . . hadn't they told him she didn't have Soda-Pop? Maybe he didn't care. Maybe he hated being beaten by a sixteen-year-old-girl.

"What am I supposed to do about that?" Ellie demanded.

But there was only noise on the radio now. She tried

adjusting the dial, remembering something Carl had once said about multipath and phases and weak signals and what happened when a receiver changed position (which she was, very quickly). But Jean and Louise were gone.

"ELLIE MCGILL, I'M GOING TO GET YOU!"

It was like the scariest ghost story ever told: the voice of an *insanely* evil supposedly dead monster coming suddenly out of the radio like it was still alive and after her.

(Carl would love that.)

After Ellie's heart stopped trying to claw its way out of her chest, she laughed.

"How are you going to 'get' me?" she shouted back before remembering she had to click the push-to-talk button. "How are you going to *get* me?" she repeated. "You gonna shoot? All these planes have had their weapons removed."

Almost as if in answer, a terrible roar that wasn't from her own engine joined hers.

Leroy rose up in the last of the single-seaters behind her like an angry hornet.

"I'm on your six," he broadcast, rather unnecessarily. He really liked saying military-ish things.

"So? You got a gun?"

Leroy increased his throttle and came closer to her, rolling to the right.

Did he think that if he just swooped at her, like you might raise your arms at a stray cat, she was going to get scared and flee? That she would just give up and try to land?

Leroy rolled his plane hard to the left and almost brushed her wing as he slipped away. It was a terrifyingly close maneuver.

But nights of staying up late and practicing maneuvers on her pillow and imagining combat in class kept her mostly ready: she immediately adjusted her trim and eased back on the throttle.

After a moment everything had righted itself again.

"Are you trying to *ram* me?" she transmitted as soon as she felt emotionally and aerially stable enough to. "You're going to get us both killed, Leroy!"

"That's Mr. Reardon to you! And I'm just here as an escort . . . to make sure you land in Cartagena as you planned."

Ellie frowned. She almost asked Soda-Pop what the heck he thought was going on before she remembered he wasn't there. Escorting her? Why? That sounded—on the surface—like a nice thing. Like maybe he had rethought all his evil plans and had decided to do right by her and make sure she got home safely. Which, of course, wasn't like Leroy at all.

"The police there have already been notified of your theft of

a private American plane. As soon as you land, they will take you into custody. Ever been in a Colombian prison, Ellie?"

Oh. That was why he was escorting her.

Time to head north! Cuba it was. She banked to the right.

Leroy was back on her port side now, so there was nothing preventing her from just opening up the throttle as far as it would go and . . .

Like a nightmare, Lucy rose up from the clouds below, blocking her path with the double-seater. The windshield was still cracked, but the woman wore a mask and goggles. She waved.

Ellie felt prolific and stinging sweat break out all over her body. Lucy was an expert pilot, and of course Leroy had far more experience than Ellie did. What were the chances she could break free from *both* of them? This was what the Mustangs had literally been built for. Escorting bombers safely over hundreds of miles . . .

She pushed the control stick and dropped several hundred feet below them, then banked hard. The change in altitude caused her stomach to flop and her breath to stop. She tasted bile on her lips.

Lucy followed her maneuver precisely, with a smooth serenity Ellie couldn't help admiring. Leroy popped down on her other side a moment later like a bad shadow.

Ellie tried climbing *up*, steeply and quickly, with the vague thought of looping above and over her enemy combatants, down past their tails, but almost immediately her engine stalled. She didn't have any training for that kind of trick.

Next she tried letting them relax into thinking she was just giving up by doing nothing for a while. When she had waited what she thought was long enough, she suddenly banked to the left and pulled back hard on the stick, trying to escape just above her captors.

But no matter what she did, Lucy matched her move for move.

Nothing Ellie tried shook them.

She would be forced to put down in a foreign country where Leroy once again seemed to already have a relationship with law enforcement. She wondered if she really would be thrown in prison. She wondered about extradition laws in Colombia. She wondered if the women's prison was nicer. She wondered if her parents, if Carl, would ever find out what happened to her. Surely Ana and Louise would make her story known? Maybe when Louise got back to the States she would hear what had happened and do something?

As the port city of Cartagena came into view Ellie felt her heart sink. It was quite beautiful from the air, and the new airport was unmistakable with its gleaming tarmacs and runways and tower—which politely contacted her.

"Unidentified American P-51, you will land as indicated on the main runway. Do not try anything. Repeat, do not try anything. Escorts, stay locked."

Ellie felt sick. She decided to just focus on the not-super-easy task of landing the plane, and if she came out of that alive, she would then deal with whatever came next.

Slowly she dropped her altitude and speed, trying to remember the differences between a Mustang and a Cessna. She managed to keep the nose up at the angle of the picture in her book. The ground rose beneath her sickeningly fast.

WHOMP!

She hit the runway hard, cracking her neck back.

The plane bounced back into the air, then hit the ground again (with a *slightly* softer bump).

Third time was the charm: She landed—hard, again—but stayed down. The tires squealed and burned, the stench of melting rubber filled the cockpit.

It was difficult with the searing headache she now had, but Ellie still managed to brake and cut the propeller. When the plane was still she threw back the canopy and flopped sickly out, trying to look insouciant as she forced herself to stand up straight.

Leroy and Lucy had landed—much more neatly—beside her and hopped out much more gracefully.

There were a *lot* of other people on the runway. Soldiers in uniform with guns in neat formation. Armored cars and police cars. A bunch of somehow much scarier men in crisp suits with frowns and bodyguards. And one chic-looking blond lady with her hair back in a bun and a fabulous business *dress*, with her own bodyguards. Also a small poodle.

Leroy came striding over, so gleeful he almost steamed. Lucy followed.

"You're in for it now, Ellie McGill," he said with a grin. "End of the line!"

"This is the girl I was telling you about," the chic blond woman said to the man next to her. He looked a little less serious but older than those around him; his hair was slicked back on either side and his cheeks were round and rosy. His suit was much finer, too. "And the fellow pursuing her."

"Yes, this girl stole a valuable, rare bird from me, and *two* of my planes, one of which she destroyed!" Leroy said smugly. "I've brought her in for justice."

"Sí," the man in the suit said, then said something else to the men around him.

Ellie stood straight and tried not to close her eyes. This wouldn't be a firing line, at least.

Policemen—or soldiers, it was hard to tell—surrounded Lucy and Leroy.

"What is the meaning of this?" Leroy demanded, trying to shake his arm away when someone grabbed it. "I am the one wronged here—I am the one who is out of a plane, and a bird!"

"What a strange thing to say," the blond woman said. "We have heard . . . conflicting stories about this whole business. Anyway, my Colombian friends will hold you until we figure out what to do. Miss McGill, let's get you dressed in something that isn't terrible"—Ellie tried very hard not to blush, but her coveralls were bloody, muddy, and torn to shreds—"and then let's have a chat, shall we?"

"Thank you!" Ellie said as the woman turned to go. "Thank you so much for everything! Ms. . . . uh, Miss . . . ?"

The blond woman laughed. *"Perón."* Then she waved and walked off, her retinue marching behind her.

Ellie was taken to a large black car by one of the serious suited men and a woman wearing a uniform like a flight attendant's. She had time to give a little wave to Leroy before being driven off; his face was literally red with fury. If looks could have killed, the entire tarmac would have been up in flames.

They drove just to the far side of the airport, where

there was a very large, very fancy hotel. Beautiful palm trees were planted up the sidewalk like oaks or elms would have been back in Bloomington. Birds fluttered from top to top too quickly to follow, and the *lizards*—why, there was an iguana almost as large as the one Leroy had brought back, sitting atop a wall, its skin a stripy blue and black.

The woman took Ellie to what looked like a private suite at the hotel and led her to an absolutely gigantic bathroom.

"A bit of a wash-up, then?" This was said politely in flawless English with a slight English accent. The woman gestured to the washcloth, towels, and soap that had been neatly laid out.

Ellie wished she could take a bath in the gigantic claw-foot tub, but anything would do at this point. While she washed the woman disappeared and came back with a couple of different dresses, gauging her for size with calculating eyes. She chose a simple one with the same natural-colored cloth the girl Cahpeah had worn. Her shoes, sadly, did not match at all, and the only ones the nice woman could find were heels several sizes too big.

Ellie did a turn in the mirror, wondering what Carl would think. She had sprouted about forty more freckles in the last couple of days, but other than those and the gash healing above her left eye she looked like pretty much the same Ellie as ever.

Which was odd, when she thought about it: At this time last week Ellie had never been to another country, slept in a jungle, eaten a plantain, repatriated a bird, or had a crush on another boy—who crushed enthusiastically back.

When she was done, Ellie was taken to a *very* nice room with a fancy plush carpet, long velvet drapes like in a theater, and a tiny ornate table set for tea. As fancy and adorned as the bone china sat Eva Perón, her little dog at her feet.

"Do you know, I am going on a tour next year to Europe, and the queen has invited me to tea?" she said. "Well, that is nice, of course, but I expect to be entertained with a banquet, like all the other heads of state. Anyway, I shall practice. One lump or two, and tell me how a small-town girl from the United States winds up in the wilds of Venezuela?"

"Two, please!" Really three, but it wasn't offered and seemed impolite to ask. The unimaginably chic lady served Ellie herself, wrist twirling dramatically as she tipped the sugar in. No rations here—at least not for her.

Ellie tried to remember all the things her parents had told her: sit up, no elbows on the table, swallow before speaking . . . but the sparkling eyes of Perón didn't even seem to register any faults, so fascinated was she by the story Ellie told.

"So this Leroy Reardon pulled two guns on you to get a

bird," she said at the end. "He came down with other armed banditos and guns and threatened all of you."

"Yes, ma'am. I really think he was going to shoot Louise."

"This is better than a radio drama! If only it didn't happen in real life. The man stole animals from a sovereign country without permission—and who knows what else he did the first time he went? He desecrated an indigenous cave, brought *guns* into the country, landed a foreign plane in two countries' airspace—"

"Technically four planes, ma'am," Ellie said. "But, truthfully, so did I . . ."

"Shush, we are not talking about you. This man has done a *lot* of damage and is treating our fellow South Americans like they are no more than a United States–controlled banana republic. I will make sure Ospina and Rómulo hear all about this. No doubt Mr. Reardon will pull strings to get extradited back to your country, but at least it will be as a criminal."

"If you don't mind me asking, ma'am, how did you even hear about me, or any of this?" Ellie asked.

Perón laughed. "It's a funny story. This woman zoologist approached my government for a position in our animal rescue and conservation department—Margaret Klein?—weeks ago. I didn't know about it until recently, understand.

I have been very busy. But I do love a clever woman who works so hard to make her way up in a man's world! I have a nice letter from Clarice Lispector, you know, and a signed first edition of one of her books. Brilliant woman."

Only much later would Ellie remember the name Lispector and look for her books. Right then the first thing she thought was: *Margaret!!* She remembered her talking about applying for jobs all over the world, including Argentina with Eva Perón! And here Ellie was . . .

"Then a few days ago we received a *telephone call*—well, it was a little more complicated than that." The woman frowned. "I don't understand all the technology. It started with a radio, somehow. Or . . . maybe a radio engineer? Someone named Carl was worried about your disappearance and suggested Ms. Klein try contacting me directly for help. Very bold move—but then again, he was *very* worried about you, I think."

Her eyes twinkled even more. Ellie blushed—but also smiled.

"Your young fellow kept on it and my secretary talked to Ms. Klein and the whole thing sounded so crazy—this purple bird of yours must be the most beautiful bird in the world. And then someone from your government stepped in. . . . Anyway, so here I am. At this lovely new airport in Cartagena!"

"I'm ever so lucky and grateful, ma'am," Ellie said, still unsure about how to title "Perón."

"All right. Let's get you safely on a plane home. I think your parents—and your 'Carl'—must be out of their minds over you."

"Uh, I can't pay for a ticket right now, but I promise I'll—"

The other woman made a face and swept her hands at Ellie. "Bah, it will cost me less than this jacket I am wearing. Please, don't even speak of it. We'll get you home and my friends will deal with Leroy. But I must insist that someone send me a feather, or a photograph, of this fantastic bird at the end of it all."

"It's a promise!" Ellie said, holding out her hand. Laughing a little—but not unkindly—Eva Perón took it, and shook.

TWENTY-FOUR

Flying on a commercial plane was *not* like flying for your life in a plane you barely knew how to operate. Ellie was seated in first class—*thank you, Ms. Perón!* As guilty and grateful as she felt, it didn't stop her from oohing and aahing over the fresh flowers in tiny vases that came with every meal and snack, or the giant leather reclining chair that swallowed her up when she sat and unfolded into a perfectly flat bed for when she slept. Of course she didn't want to sleep at all; she wanted to look out the window, to ask the intimidatingly beautiful flight attendants questions about their altitude, to not miss a single fancy tidbit they served to mark the hours. No chocolate bars and pretzels here; there was a tiny lamb chop, a jellied fruit salad, cake, a tiny slice of beef Wellington . . . she was even offered a glass of champagne but politely turned it down. They did not have grape soda; they had Shirley Temples, which were new to Ellie. She had three.

She didn't *want* to sleep . . . but the moment she extended the chair to try it out she fell unconscious immediately. When she woke it was hours later and there was a vague memory of purple feathers fluttering to the ground. She wasn't sad, though; she looked out the dark window and thought happily about Soda-Pop being back at the tepui—where he belonged. Maybe he was even still with Ana and Louise for a little while. Her journey had been a success.

(And she was coming back in style!)

They gave her a little washing-up kit (to keep!), and once again the luxury of fresh soap and hot water was something Ellie reminded herself to never take for granted.

By the time they landed she was refreshed, no longer sleepy, and maybe a little too full. They transferred her onto a much smaller prop plane, a Cessna with room for four passengers behind—but Ellie chose to sit up front with the pilot and pepper him with questions the entire way. He was polite and kind despite having a moustache like Leroy. Word of her adventures had preceded her, and seeing her excitement at an instrument panel she actually understood all of, he let her touch a few non-imperative switches and read off gauges to him.

"Wish my daughter was as excited about flight as you," he said with a sigh. "She likes horses. I mean, she can put on a saddle and gear herself and list off all the possible infections they can get . . . but she has no interest at all in flying."

"Not yet, maybe," Ellie said with a smile. "She just doesn't understand what she's missing."

When they circled for landing above the aerodrome in Bloomington she saw a boisterous crowd below waiting for her arrival. At the front was her family: the six younger kids were holding up a banner that said *"WELCOME HOME ELLE!"*

(The "I" was scribbled in, tiny, at the top, with an arrow showing where it was supposed to go. Classic Bobbie, misspelling her sister's name. And classic Dorothy for trying to fix it.)

"That's my mom and dad, and sisters and brothers!" she said excitedly, pointing them out to the pilot.

"They're a lucky bunch," he said with a smile. "Go get 'em!"

She exited the plane and started to descend the little stepladder they had set up—but was immediately blinded by all the flashes from camera bulbs.

"Say, Ellie, what made you do such a cockamamie thing?" a reporter shouted out, pen poised over pad.

"What happened to the bird?"

"How did you ever learn to fly a plane?"

While Ellie stood there dizzily, a woman pushed her way through the crowd and past the reporters.

"Let's give her a chance to meet her family first—then she can answer all your questions," Margaret Klein said firmly. She put a protective arm around Ellie and led her through the crowd.

"Margaret! You saved me! You talked to Eva Perón and . . ."

"Well, I didn't speak to her directly. And it was actually Carl's idea. He came to me after your mad airplane heist, certain you were headed to Venezuela. The phone calls we made, and the radio . . . ! It's funny, after all of his bragging and blustering, Leroy wound up having less influence abroad than a zoologist and a teenager."

"What's going to happen to him?"

"It's not entirely clear. We already have lawyers ready here for when he comes back. The same lawyers, I might add, who are going to defend you for *stealing a plane*, Miss McGill."

Margaret's voice had a tone in it.

"I did the right thing," Ellie said a little sheepishly. "Soda-Pop is *home*, where he belongs."

"Oh, ketzeleh," Margaret sighed, giving her a squeeze

around the shoulders, "there are always multiple right things. You chose the . . . showiest one."

"Ellie!" Mrs. McGill came running over and enveloped her daughter in a gigantic hug, yelling like she was in the middle of a tirade that had begun long before the plane set down. "You! Going to a *foreign country*, stealing a plane, we thought you were dead, why would you do that, you are *grounded for the rest of your—*"

Margaret coughed.

Mrs. and Mr. McGill looked up and around and saw reporters listening closely, waiting to see what punishments parents would dispense to the girl being given a hero's welcome.

"You're in *so much trouble*," Dorothy sang wickedly.

The reporters—and everyone else—laughed.

"We'll discuss this later, Ell," her father said in a low voice.

William was there along with many others from the zoo, including Dr. Hua. The Head Keeper saluted her with a grin. "Well, that stunt of yours got the zoo some pretty good publicity. More than Leroy's 'expeditions.' "

"There's been a bit of a shakeup after the news about Leroy's . . . rather violent actions became public knowledge," Margaret said. "The city stepped in and made some changes. Mr. Hodgson here is now Chief Administrative Officer."

"And Ms. Klein is now *permanent* Head Keeper and President of the Collections!" Dr. Hua added.

"That's just what you deserve!" Ellie said proudly.

Margaret chuckled. "Boy, do I. Guess I won't be doing any research expeditions anytime soon."

"That's all right," Dr. Hua said mildly.

They were standing very near to each other. And smiling coyly.

Margaret and Ellie would *definitely* need to have a lunch so Margaret could tell her *everything*.

"Hope you're okay with all this change, Mr. Hodgson," she remembered to say politely.

"Fine with me," he said with a shrug. "After what Leroy did I'm lucky I still got a job, being so close to him and all. I don't get a pay cut and can spend less time on bookkeeping. Might even start a pigeon club for teens here—just like in my old neighborhood."

"And he's fine with me playing my jazz in the commissary!"

"We'll talk about that later, Dr. Hua," William said with a sigh.

Ellie finally spotted Carl: He stood with his own parents—who, for the first time, looked smaller than he did. Imposing, but a little . . . *less*. She had been afraid of those two? With their tight lips and quiet radio? Maybe it was being held at gunpoint that changed Ellie's perspective on what was scary or wasn't. Maybe her adventure had just hastened the process of figuring out the world and where she stood in it.

"Carl!" She ran forward and threw her arms around him, heedless of any parents watching.

"Ellie," Carl said, barely breathing.

At least he was smiling.

"Are you mad at me?"

"Am I *mad* at you? You *stole a plane* you barely knew how to fly and flew it *thousands of miles away* to a foreign country, crashed in the jungle—"

"On a tepui, actually—"

"And ran around getting shot at and kidnapped and who knows what else—all for Soda-Pop! And you didn't tell me you were going to do any of this!"

"I didn't know I was, until it happened."

Carl's tirade was cut short by this honest admission. He slapped a hand over his face. "No, I guess you didn't, did you. You just saw an opportunity and took it."

"Well, you told me not to tell Leroy to return Soda-Pop . . ."

"Don't you dare, Ellie McGill!"

They were silent, but Ellie wasn't worried. He was too glad to see her back—and though he might not be saying it aloud, too impressed with what she had done to stay angry with her.

"So you worked with Margaret to get in contact with all the bigwigs in South America, huh?" she asked.

"Yeah," he said with a grudging smile. "After you disappeared and then refused all radio contact in the plane, I realized I might be able to help. I mean, even with tropospheric ducting and skip there's no way any signal of *mine* could get all the way to Venezuela, but . . . Well, anyway, eventually the State Department got involved and sort of took it out of my hands. But up until then Ms. Klein and I kept working to try to reach anyone *she* knew down there. Which wound up being the head of Argentina! Eva Perón herself!"

"She's so glamorous. Meeting her was incredible," Ellie said with a sigh.

"I'll bet. So . . ." Carl paused nervously. "Paradise Falls. You got to see them?"

"I got to *go* in them, Carl!" She took his hand. "They are more spectacular than I could even have imagined. Someday we'll go together and I can show you the secret cave behind them that's not on any maps. Or won't be, soon."

"So you'd want to go back, with me?"

"Carl." Ellie took a deep breath. "I want to go down to

the candy store and look at all the kiddie comic books with you. I want to go to the movies with you. I want to go to the end of the block and talk about nothing with you.

"*Yes*, I want to go to Paradise Falls with you someday—you promised to take me there! And build our house there!! But I also want to go everywhere else with you. It was a big, exciting adventure down in Venezuela, Carl, and I learned a lot about the jungle, and people, and things . . . and myself.

"I learned that I never want to go on another adventure again *without* you."

She squeezed his hands and looked him in the eye, making sure he knew she was serious, that he understood what she was saying.

"We never had . . . that talk," Carl said, his eyes twinkling.

There were a lot of possible responses to this: "We're having it now" or "What do you mean *never*? We have the rest of our lives to talk and figure things out" or "Who needs to talk? We know how we feel."

Ellie leaned forward until her head was just touching his.

"So? *Talk*," she whispered, their lips so close she could feel his breath on hers—even though she was the one speaking.

"Ellie McGill . . ." His voice trailed off into silence.

"Mm-hm?" She turned her face ever so slightly, the tip of her nose brushing his.

Whatever he wanted to say was then lost—for several days, anyway—as he *finally* kissed her. Ellie put her hands around the back of his neck and pulled him in closer when he started a little too hesitantly. After that there was silence and the warmth of a green jungle flowing through her skin and limbs.

"GROSSSS!" Bobbie screamed.

Big brother Reggie gently pulled her back into line with the rest of the McGill children.

Ellie smiled. "We can have that talk later. Let's go get some of that punch I saw they had."

"You're on," Carl said with a grin.

And the two of them, and the McGills, and the Fredricksens, and William and Dr. Hua and Margaret, all celebrated the return home of Ellie McGill, zoo intern and USO junior hostess and pilot and general all-around swell girl.

In the little town of Bloomington, USA, their life was about as peachy keen as it could get.